THE ALL IN **BILLIONAIRES** SERIES

ALSO BY ELLE NICOLL

The Men series

Forget-Me-Nots and Fireworks (novella)

Meeting Mr. Anderson

Discovering Mr. X

Drawn to Mr. King

Captured by Mr. Wild

Pleasing Mr. Parker

Trapped with Mr. Walker

Time with Mr. Silver

Resisting Mr. Rich

Handling Mr. Harper

Playing with Mr. Grant

Beaufort Billionaires series

The Matchmaker

The Rule Breaker

The Love Hater

The Risk Taker

THE ALL IN BILLIONAIRES SERIES

ELLE NICOLL

Published by Montlake, Seattle

www.apub.com

EU Product Safety Contact:
Amazon Media EU S.à r.l.
38, avenue John F. Kennedy, L-1855 Luxembourg
amazonpublishing-gpsr@amazon.com

ISBN-13: 9781662541193
eISBN: 9781662541209

Cover design by Tom Sanderson
Cover photography by Michelle Lancaster PTY LTD
Cover Image ©HASSAN ALI 777 / Shutterstock

Printed in the United States of America

To Tee, thank you for everything

Prologue

Gold sequins cast a honeyed glow over smooth, bronzed skin as the spotlight illuminates her.

I lean back in my seat and reach up to loosen the knot of my tie. The muscles in my neck tense as she spins slowly, arching her back towards the silver pole in the centre of the stage.

Her eyes catch mine in the crowd and my breath stalls as light blue sparkles back through her heavy eye make-up.

'She's new.'

I keep my eyes locked on the dancer, the slow tip of my chin an acknowledgment to my companion, Dominic.

'She is.'

'Nice legs,' he comments as she wraps herself around the pole, using it as an anchor to seductively lower herself into the splits.

The sequins on her tiny dress glitter. It's like staring into a vault of pure gold bars. Millions of pounds' worth.

My fingers curl around the edges of my seat, nails digging into the leather, as sourness creeps over my tongue.

Two hundred and forty million, to be exact.

That's what he cost me. The man whose name I only ever speak with a curse as I drive my fist into something.

The song comes to an end and Dominic rises from his seat, squeezing my shoulder with a warm chuckle before he's led towards the private rooms at the rear of the club by a dancer.

But it's not her.

Not the one in the gold sequins.

She's mine.

Elegantly, she descends the stairs at the side of the stage and makes her way towards me, hips swaying with each step in sky-high Perspex heels.

She smooths a long curtain of blond hair over one shoulder as she stops in front of me. The move makes my eyes drop from her pretty face to the hint of hardened nipple pushing against the thin fabric.

I lick my lips as I lift my eyes to meet hers. She smiles, like she has me exactly where she wants me.

'I saw you watching me onstage. Would you like a private dance?'

Elbow resting on the arm of my chair, I run my index finger over my lower lip, not missing the way her eyes follow it in anticipation.

That's right, sweetheart. I'm the one in control here.

'I would,' I reply smoothly, standing and extracting from my pocket a money clip inlaid with diamonds and stuffed with crisp notes.

Her lips part as I slide a fifty free. 'I'm Luc—'

I arch a brow at her. 'Until I tell you otherwise, your name is Beauty. Understood?'

Her glossy lips twist into a coy smile. 'Of course, sir.'

'Hm. Good.' I slide another fifty out and hand both to her.

Following her across the darkened club, we pass occupied tables lit with small lamps that cast sinful shadows across the sensuous bodies that snake between them. Some dancers are sitting, chatting and drinking. Others are performing topless dances, rolling their bodies up and down the suited clientele of London's financial district.

I was preparing to write this place off. Nothing here held my interest any more . . . until tonight.

I drop my eyes to the blonde's curvaceous hips, the lower swell of her arse cheeks visible beneath the tiny scrap of sequined fabric.

I wet my lips.

She nods at the bouncer standing at the entrance to the bank of private rooms, and he unclips a deep ruby-red velvet rope, granting us entry.

Topless table dances in the main bar area are okay. But back here is the inner sanctuary. In each one of these private rooms someone is sitting, indulging in their fantasy of having a beautiful woman completely naked and grinding all over them.

It's an oasis where nothing is more important than the clients' complete satisfaction.

The blonde looks at me over her shoulder, giving me an appreciative sweep up and down as she stops in front of an open curtain.

She turns her body towards me, pulling her shoulders back so her nipples push against the fabric of her dress.

'Is this okay for you?'

She's asking if the booth meets my approval, but they're all the same. I've been inside each one multiple times, searching for that elusive release which still escapes me.

I lower my gaze to her breasts, not even attempting to be subtle about it.

Perhaps tonight that could all change . . . *finally.*

'Perfect,' I say, my blood heating as she tips her head, inviting me to enter first.

I slide past her, noting the way her breath hitches, and she looks at me from beneath thick lashes, her eyes tracing my face and jawline.

She's not the first stripper to look at me like this. Like they're actually going to enjoy dancing for me. Like I'm the answer to all their goddamn prayers.

I slide another fifty out of my money clip and hand it to her.

'You hate me.'

Her brow creases. 'S-sorry?'

I curl two fingers beneath her chin and tilt her face up. She blinks up at me like she can't look away, her eyes studying mine, softening as though she can see into my soul.

'You. Hate. Me,' I repeat gently, sliding my thumb along the dip beneath her lower lip. It's glossy and plump . . .

Just like hers.

'I want you to look at me like you despise me. Like you dream about my agonising and brutal death.'

Her brow creases again, her eyes losing their adoration as it's replaced by confusion.

'Better,' I muse. 'But not quite. Try again.'

She stares at me for a moment before a veil slides over her eyes and she falls into character, a look of distaste crossing her features.

'There,' I praise. 'Good girl.'

I slide my hand from her chin and pull out two more fifties, pressing them into her palm. If she's capable of what I want from her then there'll be plenty more of them heading her way.

She glares at me, before baring her teeth.

'Sit down,' she spits. 'I don't have all night.'

My heart pounds in my chest and blood rushes to my dick as I comply, settling into the centre of the leather seat.

She closes the curtain with force, like she's angry, sealing us off from the outside world.

Turning to me, she strides over with purpose and forces my knees apart with slender fingers, positioning herself between them.

I stare up at her, entranced as she sways, running her hands up and down her sides in time to the low, heady music pumping through the speakers. She lets her fingers trail over her ribs, dragging the gold sequin fabric with them, before she lets it drop, cutting off my view of her perfect, silky skin.

'You don't deserve to even look at me,' she hisses in disgust.

I draw in a deep breath, my eyes pinned on hers.

Light blue glitters back at me in contention.

This is exactly what I need.

'Now, Beauty. That's no way to talk to me. Not when you know what you did.'

Her eyes narrow in question and I reach down and readjust my rock-hard dick in my trousers.

'I want you to take that dress off,' I tell her, spreading my arms wide across the back of the seat. 'And I want you to beg for my forgiveness with your pretty little tits out.'

Her eyelids hood and for a second her façade slips as she gazes at me with lust-filled eyes.

'Now,' I instruct sharply.

She blinks, her mask slotting back into place seamlessly.

I inhale through my nose as she undoes a ribbon around her neck which sends her dress falling to the floor and pooling around her feet.

Pursing my lips, I admire the dusky pink of her nipples. I wonder if *hers* would be the same shade.

She hooks her fingers into the sides of her G-string, and seconds later it joins her dress on the floor.

My dick swells painfully in my suit trousers as she climbs on to the seat, placing her knees either side of my thighs.

I let out a rich groan as she brings her tits closer to my face and lowers her bare pussy into my lap.

'That's a good girl.'

She circles over my aching cock, and I flex my fingers against the back of the seat, tipping my head back and closing my eyes as euphoria floods my veins.

It's about fucking time.

I suck in a sharp breath as she grinds down on my dick like she's using it as a tool to chase her own release. Her breathy whimpers are like music to my damn ears.

I spread my thighs wider, forcing her to stretch around them.

'That's it, Beauty,' I hiss. 'Now beg me.'

She gasps as my solid cock pushes hard against her pussy.

'I'm sorry,' she pants. 'Forgive me.'

'Fuck. Again.' I clench my teeth, screwing my eyes shut as she places her hands on to my shoulders and uses them as leverage to ride my dick harder.

'I need you to forgive me. It wasn't my fault. I didn't know,' she cries.

I tense, a flash of anger spiking in my gut at the blatant lie. Of course *she* knew. How could she not?

I could give two hundred and forty bloody million reasons why.

The dancer mistakes my sudden rigidness for the torture of having to exercise physical restraint, rather than what it is . . . pure unfiltered rage.

I screw my eyes shut tighter, desperate to get back to where I was moments ago.

Blond hair. Gold sequins. Guilty blue eyes.

And perfect little tits that would fit inside my palms.

Warm lips brush my ear and a sweet voice purrs, 'You know, touching's against the rules. But I don't mind if you want to.'

'What?'

I wrench my eyes open and deep blue is waiting for me.

It's too dark. More like the sea during a storm. But *hers . . . hers* are a light aquamarine of the surface being hit by rays of sun on a bright summer's day.

My stomach caves like I've been gut-punched, and realisation dawns on me, bringing with it a wave of ice-cold nausea.

What the fuck am I doing?

The blonde realises her mistake, her eyes popping wide before she furiously backtracks.

'I'm sorry. I didn't mean that. I'll beg. See?'

She scrambles to the floor, kneels between my thighs, and peers up at me with pleading eyes.

But the sight of long blond hair there does nothing for me, and my dick deflates faster than a slashed tyre.

'Never mind,' I grumble, swallowing down a mix of disappointment laced with self-disgust.

I stand abruptly and she slumps back on her heels, looking up at me with a mix of disappointment and confusion.

I place two fingers beneath her chin and tilt her face up.

'You're a stunning woman.'

You're just not her.

She gazes at me in wonder, her eyes sparkling back to life, still so eager to please.

I get it. I've been told I have the face of a god, and the body of the devil. Women are usually more than happy to fall into bed with me with no expectations. Or they were, before I found I was only interested in them if they looked like *her*. And even then, none have quite been close enough for me to actually finish the job, as much as I bloody crave the release.

But I'm not looking for that here. Not tonight.

Sighing, I pull my money clip out once again and thumb four crisp fifties from it, then offer them to her.

'I'm not in the right headspace tonight. Busy week at work,' I say, the excuse rolling off my tongue easily.

Relief washes over her face as she takes the money.

'So you'll come back? Another night?'

'Maybe,' I reply, not wanting to dampen the surge of hope that lights her eyes.

She really is a beautiful woman when she smiles. I could almost believe she's *her*.

But almost isn't good enough.

Almost won't quell the anger in my veins urging me to take my dick in my hand and fist it hard until I release all over her face. Picturing pouty lips tasting me as aquamarine eyes burn into mine.

The back of my neck flashes with heat.

Jesus Christ, I need to get out of here.

'Make sure you ask for me . . . Lucinda,' she says.

I allow myself one last fleeting look at her perky little tits.

They're as close to perfect as I've found.

She's as close to perfect as I've found.

But it's not enough.

I won't be coming back.

'Of course,' I lie smoothly.

I walk out and leave her naked and staring after me.

Chapter 1

Aurora

Okay, so two p.m. I have to be at the Winslows', who are in Notting Hill. Then after, I'm taking Freddie to the groomers.

'So good.' Charlie grunts in time with his thrusts, his balls slapping against my skin.

I need to remember Freddie's pink collar. The blue one makes him itch after he's been groomed.

'Yeah, baby,' Charlie groans, speeding up.

I'll go to the shop and pick up some crisps on the way. Salt and vinegar. Ooh, or maybe barbecue.

I stare at the pendant light fitting above the bed as Charlie circles his dick, awakening a glimmer of hope inside me.

'Oh, oh, just there,' I encourage, eager not to let a rare opportunity pass. My eyelashes flutter as he circles again and anticipation blooms low inside my core. 'Yes . . . don't stop,' I plead.

He repeats the move a couple more blissful times and my toes tingle. Just a little more and . . .

He stops abruptly and I bite back a disappointed whine.

His dick stays rigid, buried inside me, and his abs tense between us.

'You okay?' I ask.

'Yeah, just . . .'

A loud fart rips through the air.

'That's better,' he groans.

He begins thrusting again with renewed vigour.

I wrinkle my nose as a waft hits me, projected through the air from the motion of his clenched butt cheeks.

He gives one final big thrust, accompanied by a throaty grunt like he's impressed himself.

I trace my fingers up and down his shoulder blade idly as he comes inside the condom, burying his face in the crook of my neck.

I should take Freddie's favourite toy too.

Charlie rolls off me and lies on his back. He pulls the condom off with a snap, before admiring the meagre dribble of liquid inside it with pride.

'Did you come?' he asks, looking at me expectantly.

'What? Oh, yeah,' I lie.

He smiles, then flings the condom across the room, punching his arms in the air when it successfully lands in the bin.

'Thought so. I can always tell when you do,' he says, climbing out of bed and pulling his boxer shorts on, then reaching for his shirt and trousers on the floor and swiping them up. 'I've got to go.'

'I know.' I give him a sad smile. But it's due to my lack of orgasm – again – not the fact he's returning to work after our lunchtime tryst.

'Don't be sad, babe. I don't get to choose my hours like you do.'

I open my mouth to argue, then clamp it shut instead. I'm wasting my breath going over this with him again. Charlie doesn't consider my jobs to be 'real' ones. Regardless of the fact I put in more hours than him most weeks. I don't wear a suit and swing my dick around with other men in suits every day, so what I do can't be a 'proper' job.

'See you tonight?' he asks, leaning down to kiss me.

'I can't tonight. I have dinner with Dove.'

'Okay. Tomorrow then.'

He kisses me again, then walks from the room, pulling his shirt on.

'Oh, and Rory?'

I look up from his bed as he cranes his head back around the doorframe. Hope lifts my chest as he smiles at me.

'Remember to lock yourself out and post the key through the letterbox, okay?'

My smile tightens. 'Sure.'

He winks. 'Good. Later, babe.'

I fall back against the pillow with a huff as his retreating footsteps pass over his polished hardwood floors and the sound of his front door opening and closing echoes up the hallway.

We've been dating for a few months, but he doesn't trust me to have a spare key. He's happy to have me over all the time, but when I've suggested it would be easier to have my own key, rather than waiting outside for him in the rain – and getting pitying looks from his elderly neighbour – he's quickly changed the subject.

I grab my phone and shuffle up the bed, resting my back against the padded headboard. I'll take a shower before I leave. Charlie's shower heats above 'freeze your tits off' level, and the water pressure doesn't resemble a gnat's pee like that last shower I took. *Bliss.*

I smile as I type out a text to Dove. Having dinner with my best friend is exactly what I need.

Me: Can't wait to see you later. Shall I meet you at your place first and we can travel together?

Her reply comes almost instantly, and my initial happiness is replaced by an ickiness as I read.

Dove: I'm so sorry. In a meeting that's likely to run over. Can you meet me here?

I swallow the acid that's threatening to rise up my windpipe.

Me: No problem. I'll meet you at the restaurant.

Dove: It's hard to find. Meet me at the office. Don't worry, and I promise it'll save time that way. Trust me.

I type back okay and a kiss, then throw my phone down on the duvet with a huff.

Dove doesn't need to concern herself with me being *worried.* Meeting her at her office will only result in one emotion *if* I have the misfortune of being in close proximity to her older brother, who she works with.

And that's indifference.

Complete and utter indifference.

I'm not worried about seeing Rafael Fairfax.

The man is positively vile. The fact he and Dove are related continues to astound me. She's kind and considerate. And she knows the truth when she hears it.

But Rafael?

That man wouldn't know truth if it came and rammed itself down his stupid thick neck. Although the sight would be welcome. Especially if the arsehole choked on it.

I smile as I slide out of bed and pad over Charlie's plush bedroom carpet to his en suite.

Rafael Fairfax being choked to death. Now there's a wonderful thought.

Twisting, I show the back of the Chanel suit I have on. It's a beautiful white tweed with fine gold thread as soft as angel's hair weaved through it.

'So gorgeous. And look at the shoes,' I say as I perform a cute little leg flick behind me to show off the patent Mary Janes I'm wearing.

I spin back around and grin, placing a hand on my hip. 'The perfect workday outfit.'

I allow a few seconds to pass before heading to my phone propped on top of the dressing area drawers and stopping it recording.

'Perfect,' I murmur, checking the video and trimming it before I write a quick caption and add my saved hashtags. I click 'post' and turn to survey the space.

Rails and rails of designer outfits all in my size line the oyster-coloured walls. And there's a whole display purely for designer bags and purses. One in every colour you can imagine. Then there are the shoes . . . oh my God, *the shoes*.

I step out of the Mary Janes, stroking them lovingly as I place them back on the shelf with the tenderness one would cradle a premature baby.

They're exquisite. Just like everything else in here.

I sigh, unable to muster my usual enthusiasm. It's not the same without him.

Nothing has been the same since my father went to prison three months ago.

His girlfriend managed a month.

One month of the press hounding us and waiting on our door-steps, harassing us for interviews. One month of seeing my father stripped of his freedom and dignity, locked up in that place. One month of living with the stigma of him being found guilty of theft from the investment company where he worked, before she packed a bag and left. She had the decency to say goodbye, at least, before suggesting I should move out of London and start fresh somewhere no one knows me. But that would have meant leaving my father to deal with this alone.

With a five-year sentence to serve.

But he's not a quitter. He can do it without a girlfriend who doesn't believe in him. *We* can do it without her. We've always done okay by ourselves anyway, me and him. I just wish I got to see him more than the measly one visit per week the prison allows.

The beautiful Chanel suit suddenly feels hot and tight against my skin. I pull it off quickly, grabbing my jeans and t-shirt, and sliding them back on.

My phone beeps and I check it, finding over one hundred notifications, most admiring my outfit choice and some asking me to film a dressing-room tour. I gnaw on my lip, checking my watch. It'll have to wait until another day.

I place the Chanel suit on its hanger and wink at Freddie, sprawled out on his belly in the corner, watching me with big, doleful brown eyes.

'Aww, come on, boy,' I coo. 'I know you hate the idea of the groomers. But you always feel better afterwards, don't you? And you'll get steak strips for dinner as a treat.'

Freddie's ears prick up at the word 'steak' and he tilts his head to one side. I walk over and his tail wags harder.

'It'll be worth it, I promise.'

He rolls over so I can scratch his belly.

'Sometimes we have to go to places we can barely stomach, because the outcome will be worth it,' I tell him, before I glance around the lavish dressing room.

It's filled with hundreds of thousands of pounds of the most coveted labels in the fashion industry. But since I lost my father, all I see are *things*. Things weighted with guilt. Tarnished with dishonesty and corruption.

I tear my eyes away as nausea threatens my stomach.

'Believe me,' I whisper, gazing into Freddie's eyes. 'It'll be worth it in the end.'

Chapter 2

Aurora

I snag the stray dog hair from my pencil skirt with my lint roller, then stuff it into my bag beside an empty tube of crisps seconds before the lift doors slide open.

Fairfax Guardian.

That's what the gold letters spell out above the long, sleek black reception desk. 'Devil's Lair' would be more accurate. Although, that's not entirely fair. Not everyone who works here is a total arsehole like their CEO.

I mean, Dove works here. My best friend, who I've known since one very random night a couple of years ago that involved a bar, one too many cocktails, and a guy with an orange fake tan named Leroy who didn't know when to quit.

We're complete opposites. Dove is a ball-busting career woman who heads her family insurance firm's contracts that – what were her words? Oh yeah – 'insure the hare-brained, crazily brilliant ideas from people and companies no one else in the industry will touch'. But she loves it. She says innovation never comes from sitting around and doing what's been done before. You have to be a trailblazer and be prepared to fail faster than your opponents, so that when you do win . . . well, then you make millions.

She's the only one of her siblings – and all of them help run the firm – who would want to do what she does. Insurance is all about negating risk. But Dove runs towards it. And her brothers let her because, more often than not, it pays off.

Her brothers. Only one brings a sourness to my mouth. Her other two, Gabriel and Angelo, seem okay the couple of times I've briefly met them. And the stories she tells me about them don't set alarm bells ringing.

But, of course, in every family there's that one person who you'd gladly wish didn't exist.

That blot.

That bane on society.

'Good afternoon. I'm here to meet Dove Fairfax,' I tell the receptionist sitting behind the immaculate desk.

He flashes me a megawatt smile. Maybe they pump out endorphins through the air filters. Surely no one can be that happy working under *him*.

'Who should I tell her is calling?'

'Aurora Thorne.'

'One moment, please.' He presses a button on his keyboard, before talking into his headset. 'Miss Fairfax, I have an Aurora Thorne here for you.' He pauses. 'Of course.'

He looks at me. 'She'll only be a few minutes. Please take a seat.'

'Thank you.'

I head to the waiting area, which is overpowered by a giant concrete table in the centre. I sink into one of the plush seats surrounding it and scan the meticulously displayed financial magazines and papers on the cold grey surface.

My eyes snag on a glossy insurance magazine. There are more copies of it than any of the other titles and I scoff as the reason why becomes apparent.

The object of my disgust is taking up the front cover, filling out his perfectly tailored designer suit and standing with one hand in his pocket like a self-entitled prick. His rich, amber-flecked eyes glow like he's thinking about a billion and one ways he can ruin you and come out on top.

Emblazoned on the cover beside his image is their company slogan.

Protecting the priceless. Providing you peace.

An exclusive interview with Fairfax Guardian's CEO, Rafael Fairfax.

I snort, earning myself a quizzical look from the receptionist as I pick up the magazine.

The only peace Rafael Fairfax knows are the lies he tells himself about him being a good man with integrity.

Arsehole.

'Hey, AJ,' a guy calls, passing the desk on his way out. 'Thanks for fixing those reports. See you in the morning.'

'No problem, Gabe.'

Dove's brother stops as he spots me. 'Hello, Aurora. Dove said you were dining together this evening.'

'We are.' I smile as I stand to greet him, but my attention's caught by the baby sling tied to his front.

'Benedict prefers to travel like this. It takes the weight off his hips,' Gabriel says easily.

I smile politely, schooling my surprise at the sight of not a baby but a ginger cat bundled inside the carrier. He surveys me with luminous green feline eyes that hold a surprising air of authority.

'Um, he looks very . . . comfortable.'

Gabriel smiles, his warm eyes crinkling behind his Clark Kent glasses. My cheeks heat a little. He's beautiful. Tall and broad. Short dark hair. Perfectly proportioned cheekbones and angular jaw. And he smells incredible. The Fairfax male genes in full force, leaving little hope for the rest of the male population.

He massages Benedict behind one ear and the cat's eyes narrow into drugged slits as he purrs loudly. 'He is. He'll be asleep before we leave the building, I guarantee it.'

He grins at the cat with the pride I'd expect on the face of a parent of a child prodigy, before he looks up at me. 'Nice to see you, Rory.'

'You too,' I say, listening to the cat's retreating purrs as they leave.

'They're so adorable together,' the receptionist comments.

'Oh, yeah,' I agree, taking my seat again and biting back my smile.

My father will love hearing about a cat in a baby carrier. I can almost hear his warm chuckle now. My smile falters. I haven't heard it in a while. Each time I've visited him over the past months I've grown more worried. I know he puts on a brave face for me, but I can see right through it. I *know* him.

My eyes drop to the magazine in my hand, and I stare at the man on the cover. *He*, however, doesn't know my father.

'I haven't forgotten what you said,' I spit under my breath, glaring at his face.

'She's the daughter of George Thorne, a criminal who defrauded the company he worked for, stealing millions, and almost causing the collapse of several firms as a result.'

'Oh my God,' the beautiful woman with him had gasped. 'What happened to him?'

'He's in prison, where he belongs, eating slop and panicking if he drops the soap,' Rafael grunted. 'Best bloody place for scum like him.'

His words are etched into my brain. I'd come to meet Dove after work, a few weeks after my father lost his trial and was sentenced. Rafael had greeted me as he exited the lift with his date on his arm, asking what I was doing there with more than a hint of suspicion in his tone. It was laughable really, because the first time we met, when Dove introduced us, he was nothing but polite – even friendly. Especially once he learnt that my father was an investment manager who worked for a prestigious London firm he was familiar with.

I know his type. He's a man who only knows how to behave with a modicum of class when he thinks there is something in it for him.

Bile rises up my throat and I tighten my grip on the magazine as I pull out a black marker from my bag. He probably thinks I didn't hear what he said to his date that day. Somehow I doubt he'd care even if he knew.

The thing that stings the most is the way my father's face had lit up when I'd told him who Dove's older brother was, and that Rafael had shown an interest in meeting my father one day. He'd glowed, like being on Rafael Fairfax's radar was an honour. He even proceeded to regale me with Rafael's business accomplishments and tell me how much he had achieved for such a young CEO in the insurance business. How he had won larger and larger clients, including a global diamond jewellery business, airline, and hotel chain.

My father spoke with respect and awe for someone he saw as a fellow businessperson. Whereas ever since the trial, Rafael Fairfax spat out words laced with disgust and superiority for someone he hadn't even met.

'Rory? I'm so sorry!'

Dove rushes past the reception desk towards me with a flushed face, pulling on her coat.

'It's fine, I've only been here a few minutes,' I reply, tucking my pen away and sliding the magazine underneath another one before rising to greet her.

She flings her arms around me, pulling me into a tight hug. Dove's immaculate in her power suits and tailored workwear. Grown men sweat when she walks into meeting rooms. But with her friends and family she's softer than the cosiest sweater straight out of the tumble dryer. However, in all the time I've known her, she's never so much as glanced in a man's direction. She's got all this love and affection but won't share it outside of her close circle of those she trusts.

'Did you see Gabe?' she asks. 'I wanted to catch him, but he left already.'

'I did. And Benedict.'

Dove unwinds a beautiful silk scarf from around her neck, tucking it inside her bag. 'Was he in the baby sling?'

I giggle. 'Yeah.'

She rolls her eyes with a smile. 'My brothers aren't insane, I promise you. Just . . . protective over those they care about. And Gabe is . . .' She tilts her head, her eyes twinkling. '. . . *resourceful*. He claims the sling is for Benedict's benefit, but I swear he loves carrying him around in it just as much as Benedict likes to be pandered to, if not more.'

'When did he get him—?'

My cat curiosity is cut off as a striding force of dark blue suit topped with wavy chestnut hair exits the lift, making a beeline for the reception desk.

The man sitting behind it straightens. 'Mr Fairfax,' he greets.

'AJ, did you send Miss Jones the red roses I requested?'

'Two dozen, as instructed,' AJ replies.

'Hm, good,' the broad, suited arsehole replies, before his attention is ripped away by movement outside the window.

'The window cleaners came late today,' AJ comments, his eyes ping-ponging between the two cheery-looking men outside washing down the windows in their special crane, and the stiffened form staring at them, colour draining from his cheeks.

Rafael clears his throat, tearing his eyes from the window. 'Ridiculous way to clean the goddamn windows.'

'Are you okay, sir?' AJ asks.

'I'm bloody well fine,' he snaps.

'You don't look so good,' AJ continues. 'Is it your h—?'

'I don't pay you to play doctor, AJ. I pay you to do your damn job! So stop asking ridiculous questions.'

I bite back my scoff.

This man is so shamefully rude, it's a joke.

As if he can feel the force of my glare, he turns, looking straight at me and Dove before he scans me up and down ruthlessly. His upper lip curls into a grimace.

I square my shoulders, refusing to be intimidated.

'Rafael? You remember Rory?' Dove calls to him. 'We're heading for dinner. You can join us if you like?'

I do a better job of hiding the vomit that's just flown up into my mouth than Rafael does. He physically recoils like Dove had suggested we go out on to the street and look for small puppies to skin alive.

'I have dinner plans,' he barks back.

Dove, unperturbed by his brashness, shrugs. 'Okay. See you in the morning.'

She steers me towards the bank of lifts and is drawn into a conversation with someone as they exit. I can't help but glance back as I wait for her, like a rubbernecker at the scene of a grisly crash.

Rafael Fairfax is standing where we left him, glaring after us.

I hold his eyes in challenge.

I know what you think of my father, arsehole.

The harder I stare back, the darker his gaze gets, until it's boring into me like I'm looking down the barrel of a gun.

Men like him think they know everything. They think they're better than everyone. That the world is theirs for the taking. I can't help myself; my mouth is calling out to him before I can engage my brain.

'Being a dick won't make yours bigger, you know.' I smile sweetly.

His glower deepens until he looks in danger of popping a vein. Victory blooms in my chest. It's immature, but it still feels good enough that I'm beaming as I step inside the lift beside Dove, who's distracted by a message on her phone.

She looks up at me as she types. 'I love that top on you.'

'Thanks.'

I adjust the thin strap of my gold-sequined camisole. It's a copy of a vintage piece that belonged to my mother. The original one, which was seized, along with the rest of my father's and my possessions, was worn by a famous British actress. She gave it to my mother as a thank you after she looked after her wardrobe when she was filming a movie in the Cotswolds.

That was my mother's passion, working in the wardrobe and costume department for films and TV. She was just starting out, working as a general dogsbody, when she found out she was pregnant with me. But my father said she always left an impression on those she met, not only from her sheer love and joy of the work, but for how determined she was to chase her dream of running wardrobe for an entire production herself one day. She never made it. But I'm going to live that dream for her. And for my father. For both of us. I had it all planned out. After I finished university, I'd applied for internships at production companies. It took a while, but I managed to get one all set up. Then

Dad was arrested. I've put everything on hold until he's free, focusing on the fashion vlog instead. I want him to be here to witness me do what Mum always dreamt of. I want him and Mum, wherever she is, to be proud of me.

I was wearing her original gold top in the first vlog of mine to go viral. It started as a bit of fun a year ago, a way for me to share my love of clothes, fashion and maybe show those production houses my skills. But I've built up a following and now I'm gifted items from fashion brands from time to time.

The imitation top is lighter and cheaper, but wearing it reminds me of her. Reminds me I can do this. That no matter how dire things can seem, there is always that possibility, that chance, that things can get better. One day it's wearing a favourite top. The next it's overthrowing an unjust court ruling and freeing an innocent man.

I just have to keep going and never give up.

I glance back towards the reception desk, feeling smug, but there's no sign of Rafael.

Reaching into my purse, I pull out a red lipstick and turn to touch my lips up using the mirrored wall on the rear of the lift.

The closing doors jerk as large fingers curl around them. They slide back open to reveal Rafael. He stands there, all six foot something of solid arrogance.

'I'll send a car to pick you up. Where are you going?' he snaps, making the offer sound more like an accusation.

Dove looks at him in suspicion. 'I'm twenty-seven years old. I'm perfectly capable of getting my own cab home.'

He ignores her, his eyes meeting mine in the mirror.

'Just looking out for you, sis. There are all sorts of' – his nostrils flare – '*unscrupulous* people about.'

I narrow my eyes at him as his attention drops over my body with a look of derision.

'You're acting weird. Piss off,' Dove says, half-joking. She's never needed looking after, so I know she won't be about to let her older brother start now.

But this little display of theatrical concern wasn't for her benefit.

It was for mine.

Rafael's eyes meet mine with a finality like he thinks he's won. But my returning smile has the corners of them pinching just a fraction with confusion. If he thinks I'm bothered by his pathetic dig then he's mistaken. Because now I know my comment got to him. It got to him so much that he had to come over and stop our lift to perform his weak comeback.

'See you tomorrow,' Dove tells him as the doors start closing again.

'Bye.' I hold a hand up and wave to him using just my pinkie, making sure to give it an extra wiggle to accentuate my point.

The resulting line between his brows is so deep you could park a plane in it.

I smirk.

His eyes burn into mine until the doors meet, and I hold them without faltering.

I found a new favourite sight to add to my mental image bank: Rafael Fairfax being pissed because he knows I got one up on him.

It's even more satisfying than I imagined.

Chapter 3

Rafael

The thin strap of the lemon-coloured floral sundress slips, exposing her shoulder. She doesn't notice and keeps chatting to the camera. Her face is animated and glowing as she talks through her outfit, twirling in a circle to show the way the hem kicks up in the air as she spins.

I shift in my seat, my rock-hard dick crying out for attention. Instead of touching it, giving it the much-needed friction it's desperate for, I pick up a pen from my desk and balance it on the table, sliding my fingers down, then pausing, before I spin it on its head and repeat the move.

Her eyes glitter as she casually loops the wayward strap back up over her smooth shoulder whilst talking about ways to dress the outfit up or down. It pulls the fabric higher over one breast, and the extra few millimetres of curved skin that were exposed disappear.

I bite my lower lip, concealing an unwelcome groan of disappointment.

She's a problem. A huge fucking problem.

She leans forward to pick up a pair of heels to show to the camera. My pen goes flying as I scrabble to grab my phone and wind the video back.

I hit 'play', and watch again as she leans down, showing the briefest flash of cleavage from her perky little tits.

My hand is on my dick before I can control it, and I squeeze, sucking in a breath as she straightens and starts wittering on about heel heights.

'The fuck am I doing?' I drop my throbbing dick like it's a hot poker and pause the video.

Aurora's face freezes on the screen in a wide smile like she's taunting me. I scroll down, not trusting myself to watch any more. Instead, I head to the comments section.

You look amazing!

I want that dress! I'm saving up. Two more pay days to go.

Simply beautiful.

Looking for a boyfriend? 😉

The last one makes me grit my teeth. But it's not the one that should bother me the most. They *all* should. Every single one is admiring her, *justifying her* prancing around in designer outfit after designer outfit like she doesn't have a care in the world.

Bet her followers don't know she paid for all those frilly little dresses that cup those pert tits of hers with money that doesn't belong to her.

I wonder how much of my two hundred and forty million Daddy dearest spent on his precious daughter's love of all things designer.

Enough that I own the entire dressing room she's filming in, and every item of clothing in it.

I even own the little panties she's wearing beneath that dress. *Maybe I should insist on taking them back.*

'Dammit,' I hiss, tossing my phone on to my desk and raking my fingers through my hair.

Aurora Thorne.

Daughter of George Thorne, a man who, when he stole funds from the company he worked for – a company *my* insurance firm invests heavily with – didn't just steal from them, he stole from *me*.

It wasn't only the two hundred and forty million I lost.

It's the fact I almost lost it all.

George Thorne nearly cost me Fairfax Guardian.

The whole firm could have crumbled if I hadn't dipped into my own pocket to save us.

I almost lost it once, years ago, when I first took over from my father. The fact it almost happened again is an act that simply cannot go unpunished. The authorities might have been unable to recover what I lost, but George Thorne will return it to me, one way or another. A man clever enough to gain the trust of a huge firm and be granted access to that amount of money in the first place is a man clever enough to hide his assets during a criminal investigation.

My eyes flick to my phone.

His daughter obviously didn't inherit his brains. If she did, she wouldn't be flaunting her brand-new designer wardrobe online, even if she does use a fake name for her online persona.

I pick my phone up again and can't resist hitting 'play' once more.

My dick jolts back to attention immediately, but I ignore it.

She tucks a strand of blond hair behind one ear before smoothing the front of the lemon dress down with a loving caress.

'Enjoy it, Beauty,' I murmur. 'I'll find Daddy's secret hiding place. And when I do, you'll be lucky if you can afford to shop in Primark once I'm through with you.'

She looks at the camera like she can hear me. Her pouty lips glisten and her aquamarine-blue eyes stare right at me. Memories of a dancer's darker blue irises flash to mind. I was so close that night to finally taking the edge off this . . . *obsession*.

But not close enough.

I let out an irritated snort. The strippers are getting to be an addiction. A high I chase but can never grasp. Because nothing will compare to the real thing.

I want to scrape back every penny that belongs to me from George Thorne.

And that should be enough.

But for some goddamn reason that defies logic, I want *her* too.

I want to punish Aurora Thorne for being his daughter. For knowing what her father did, yet still claiming to anyone who will listen that he's innocent. For waltzing around with my sister, tainting her with her company. For living in the five-bedroomed house in Chelsea Dove told me about.

All whilst wearing clothes *my* money paid for.

My dick hardens to the point of pain. I despise her. Yet every time I see her all I can think about is how it would feel to have her tell me she's sorry.

Beneath me.

Have her cry it out as I thrust inside her.

See the tears run down her cheeks as she begs me to forgive her.

I'd mark her as mine. Fill her with my anger.

She should feel guilty. Ashamed. Not defiant. Not look at me on the rare occasions we've been in the same room as though *I'm* the problem. This is *her* fault. Her's and her father's, their cosy little crime duo.

And she definitely shouldn't blink those doe eyes at me in a way that makes my palm twitch with the urge to spank her arse until it wears my handprint.

I want to ruin her.

I *will* ruin her.

One way or another I'll get what I need from her. She must know where her father's hidden all the money. And the fact she's not given it up to the authorities makes her my enemy as much as her father.

The day I make Aurora Thorne beg is coming.

And I can't bloody wait.

Chapter 4

Aurora

'Was it an accident?'

I scoff, grabbing another couple of crisps. 'No! He stopped midway to let it out.'

Dove throws her head back with a cackle, the red wine in her glass sloshing about and narrowly missing spilling out over her cream velvet couch.

'Oh, babe.' She sighs, wiping at her eyes. 'I'm sorry, but that's . . .'

'I know, really sexy, huh?' I can't help but smile at the way her eyes light up as I regale her with the sex-fart story, which was too much to share at the fancy place she took me for dinner last time we met.

I don't see her happy often enough.

I swallow a mouthful of cheese and onion crisps, then take a sip of my own wine, savouring the taste of something that hasn't come from the discount section in Tesco for a change.

I sink into her sofa with a sigh.

'It was refreshing with Charlie in the beginning. He doesn't know about Dad, so I got to just be me. It was an escape, and it was nice spending time with someone who didn't look at me differently. Like they're trying to figure out if I'm about to steal their bank details.'

Dove takes my hand in hers, squeezing it.

'And now . . .' I wrinkle my nose. 'Now it's farting during sex and no orgasms.'

'And that's only three months in. Imagine what it'll be like in another three,' Dove says.

I turn my head towards her, and she gives me an apologetic look.

'It's fine. You're right. I should break up with him, shouldn't I?'

'That's your call. But you need to ask yourself what you really want and what will make you happy.'

'Getting my father out of prison,' I tell her, earning my hand another reassuring squeeze. 'Having him there to see me live out my dream – my *mother's* dream. Together.'

She searches my eyes. 'Can I do anything?'

I shake my head, grateful for her offer. She's been offering her help ever since I told her about my plan to look at my father's case notes. I don't know what I'm looking for. Something. Anything that will help prove he's innocent. But Dove has her hands full with all the insurance clients she's taken on. Her role in the business requires her to travel a lot to meet with them.

'Actually, you could pray?' I suggest.

She laughs. 'You need my brothers for that. I could flap my arms around for you instead or pick you an olive branch?'

I snort, and we fall into an easy silence. Dove always jokes about her name being a bird, while her three brothers were all given angelic names, thanks to her mother – a spiritual woman with a love of all things 'woo-woo'. Dove told me her mother is the polar opposite of her father, a man who would be more likely to bulldoze a sacred place of worship if he thought it would make him money. But regardless, they've been happily married for decades. And now her father's retired, they're off on spiritual retreats around the world half of the time, leaving their four children to run the family business, with Rafael at the helm as CEO.

Dove doesn't know what I overheard Rafael saying about my father that day. I haven't told a soul. I don't know what's stopped me. A mixture of anger and embarrassment, I think. Because I know a lot of people agree with him. Not Dove; she's been my rock through it all. But she'd rip Rafael a new arsehole if I told her, and as fun as that might be to watch, he's still her family. And she needs her family. We all need our support network.

My throat grows scratchy as I picture the anchor of my support network sitting in a cell right now. Alone.

'I did discover something in the case notes,' I tell her, eager to share the tiny scrap of information I've uncovered, reading through documents long after midnight last night.

'And?' Her eyes widen in anticipation.

'Apparently, as well as an electronically sealed file I haven't been able to access, there was a copy of an email draft from a woman who worked at the firm with my father. She . . .' I swallow the lump in my throat, hating what I'm about to say. 'She accused him of sexual harassment. She was going to report him to HR.'

'What?' Dove's disbelief is so genuine that I want to throw my arms around her.

'I know, right? There's no way—'

'Your father is the *sweetest* man. He helped when I was ill,' she says.

'I know.'

My chest swells as I think about Dove calling scared and in tears one night after she had passed out. The emergency helpline told her to go to A&E immediately. My father and I went with her. She was scared and in a lot of pain. It ended up being appendicitis. She recovered but it could have been a lot worse.

'You think the company made it up to try to smear his character?' she asks.

I shrug. 'I don't know. It was never sent, and she doesn't work there any more. I can't find a trace of her. But . . . maybe. She's definitely lying.'

Dove's phone chimes. She checks it and rolls her eyes.

'Yes, I bloody called them,' she mutters, tapping out a reply to the text message. 'Sorry,' she says to me. 'It's Rafe. He's micromanaging again. They're my clients, not his. Yet he can't seem to stop himself from checking in.' She shakes her head, but her face softens. 'If he wasn't such a rake, only dating women once or twice before moving on, then he might actually have something other than work to occupy his mind at ten o'clock on a Friday evening.'

'He still sends them all the same bouquet of red roses you told me about. I overheard him talking to AJ,' I add, cringing.

Dove scoffs. 'Figures. He's thirty-nine and never been in a serious relationship. Plenty of women, none that he's ever brought home to meet our parents. He's not going to change now.' She pauses. 'You know he's friends with Dominic Ainsworth?'

'Is he?' I grimace at the name of one of the board members at my father's old company. I'm not sure my father had much to do with members of the board. But any name connected with that company sends a shiver down my spine.

'Maybe Dominic knows about this woman?' Dove suggests.

'You think he might be able to help me?' My chest lifts as hope surges through it like electricity. I've been trying for months and barely got anywhere.

'It's worth a try. I can ask Rafe to ask Dominic for you?'

The thought of Rafael being involved makes the red wine churn in my gut.

No way that arsehole would help us.

'No, thank you. I can do it.'

'Okay,' she replies easily, unaware of how deeply etched into my bones my hatred towards her brother is.

I drum my fingers around my wine glass, my mind racing at a million miles per hour.

I detest Rafael Fairfax.

But if there's a sliver of possibility that he could get me access to information that could help my father, then . . . But that would mean actually talking to him. And I don't mean the odd insult and scathing look I like to toss his way.

I'd have to be – I shudder – *civil.*

My father's voice fills my head. '*You catch more flies with honey.*' That's what he used to say before life knocked him down with the force of a sledgehammer to the temple.

'It *is* worth a try,' I agree, already running scenarios in my head of how I can get what I need from Rafael with as little interaction as possible. Maybe I can even hide who the information is for . . .

Dove lifts the wine bottle and motions to my glass. I smile gratefully as she decants a generous top-up.

I'm going to need it if I have to think up ways to approach Rafael Fairfax. Especially after I called him a dick, then insinuated that he has a small one.

I take a large gulp of wine, determination running through my bloodstream alongside the alcohol heating it.

I've never been afraid of a challenge. And I'm already doing some questionable things in order to find out whatever I can to help my father.

I'm not about to stop now.

Chapter 5

Rafael

'Mr Fairfax? You have a visitor.'

'Send him through, AJ,' I tell him.

I hover my thumb over my screen, preparing to stop the video.

She's modelling gym wear today. Snug-fitting workout leggings and cropped tops showing off a snatched little waist. She does some little wiggles to demonstrate the outfit's built-in support.

I lick my lips.

My momentary pause to drink her in one final time before I stop the video is enough for Dominic to stride into my office, a wide grin stretching over his face as Aurora's voice echoes from the speakers.

'What are you watching?' he asks, his eyes zeroing in on the screen as he approaches my desk.

'Nothing,' I say, turning my phone off and face down on the desk.

He arches a brow, pushing his hands into the pockets of his pinstripe suit trousers.

'Is it one of those websites where she sends you videos without the workout gear on too?'

My jaw clenches and I curse myself internally. My ludicrous obsession with Aurora Thorne means that I couldn't even shut my damn phone off quick enough to prevent Dominic from getting a glimpse of her. Not that it should bother me. She posts online multiple times per week. Any number of men could be leering over the curves of her arse in those leggings right now.

Sourness swirls in my gut.

'Hey.' Dominic throws his hands up in a chuckle. 'No need to get jealous. I'm a happily married man. I can't be looking at some beautiful *young* blonde who's commanded your attention.'

'She hasn't. She's no one,' I lie through my teeth, ignoring his emphasis on the word 'young'. I know Aurora's too young for me. She's twenty-five, I'm thirty-nine. I don't need Dominic reminding me of the fact whilst wearing a shit-eating grin on his face.

'Whatever helps you sleep at night,' he says, sinking into the chair on the opposite side of my desk.

'I have a date tonight. With a brunette,' I announce, like I have to justify myself.

Dominic rests his hands over his stomach, leaning back in the chair. His eyes glitter beneath his swept-back silvery hair. 'Fine,' he concedes with a smirk. 'Let's talk business. How's the Beaufort account?'

I relax back in my seat, mirroring his position, much more at ease talking multimillion-pound contracts than I am discussing Aurora Thorne.

'Great. They've taken on more mines in Botswana. Their share prices have risen as a result. And Sullivan is announcing a new line that's already got a long waiting list.'

'Diamond jewellery business is thriving then?' Dominic quips.

'They'll be busier than a one-armed hooker giving out two-quid hand jobs,' I reply, the tension evaporating from my muscles as we discuss one of Fairfax Guardian's biggest clients. Their headquarters are in New York, and over the past few years working together, their CEO, Sullivan Beaufort, has become a friend as well as business associate.

Dominic chuckles. 'Glad to hear it.'

'Things are back on track . . . finally,' I say, my momentary reprieve meeting a premature end as thoughts of what could have been push to the front of my mind again.

'George Thorne is nothing but a bad memory,' Dominic says, giving me a levelling look.

'You say that so easily,' I grumble, my molars grinding together – a sign that he is not a memory to me, not by a long shot.

'The guy's in prison, Rafe. What else do you want?'

To know what he did with my two hundred and forty bloody million pounds, that's what.

Has he got it stashed somewhere? Ready for when he's out in a few years' time? To retire to some Caribbean island with? Minus what his darling daughter has already squandered on designer workout gear, that is.

The memory of her face getting into the lift last time I saw her niggles at me. Thinking she got one up on me. She might act the cute and innocent daddy's girl, but underneath it all she's a shrew. A cunning and devious accomplice to her father's misdemeanours. She has to be. You'd have to be an idiot to watch a parent go to prison, continue to live alone in your mansion in Chelsea with your clothing allowance, and not ask where the money came from.

I bring my hands together and crack my knuckles.

The fact she's Dove's friend is the only thing stopping me from going after her already. Despite everything, before this all happened, Aurora was a good friend to my sister when God knows Dove needed one. Under ideal circumstances, Aurora would have distanced herself after her father's conviction. Not subjected my sister to the hounding from the press following them both around in those early days after the verdict. Dove was still recovering from the appendicitis that resulted in her going to hospital. If Aurora really cared, surely she would have kept her distance? Realised that environment wasn't healthy for my sister when she was healing?

I gave the menace a little nudge, making sure she overheard me vocalising my less than stellar opinion of her father when I ran into her at the office one day. But even that wasn't enough to deter her.

Aurora Thorne seems intent on staying in my world.

So she had better be prepared for the consequences.

'You still worried they'll find out?' Dominic says, lifting his brows in understanding.

My mouth flattens into a grim line, and I nod.

'This investment was supposed to show my father that I'm perfectly capable of doing things without him.'

Dom grimaces. 'I'm sorry. It was a sure thing. I wouldn't have suggested you invest otherwise. I didn't know some bastard was going to drain the company's account.'

'I know, I know.' I nod. Dom's right. It was a sure thing. Just like previous investments I've made through him with Fairfax Guardian's money. Only this time we went big. *Two hundred and forty million big.* 'They can't find out. None of them. My father handed the business over to me when he retired, and I almost ran it into the ground within the first three months. Doing it again would be the cherry on the bloody cake.'

'That other time wasn't—'

'My fault?' I look at Dominic from beneath my brows. 'Spare me the mercy. We both know the truth. I could have lost the company because of what I did.'

'But you didn't lose it,' Dominic reminds me.

'No.' I pinch the bridge of my nose with a sigh. 'I didn't. Thanks to you.'

He gives me a reassuring smile. 'It's what friends do for one another, right?'

I swallow the thick lump in my throat. 'Yeah, it is.'

My father's disappointment back in my early days as CEO, when I had to tell him I'd lost a huge client that he'd always dreamt of bringing onboard, is etched into my soul.

I cannot have him look at me like that again.

Like a failure.

Like I'm weak.

It's bad enough that he's dropping in every couple of days when he's in the country, phoning when he isn't, and checking up on things. Checking up on *me*. He's never trusted me as CEO. A fact I can handle, but it doesn't mean I can stomach him looking at me like I'm this incompetent, *broken* little boy, which I swear is what he sees.

'Listen, Rafe. Your family don't need to know you lost company money that was invested with the firm after what George Thorne did. You replaced it. As far as they're aware, the money you gave me from Fairfax Guardian was never held in the same account that he drained. My name's on the deposit. And when the insurance pays out, you'll get it back. Everyone who lost money to that bastard will. It's fine. Things are good now.'

'I should have seen it coming. I should have done something.'

Dominic thumbs his nose with a sniff. 'Bloody hell, I get it. I feel the same way. But all we can do is move forward and leave that piece of work in our rearview mirror, okay? Let it go.'

I scrub a hand around my jaw. 'Okay,' I agree, my eyes sliding to my phone, knowing Aurora's video is still on there.

Dominic might be able to move on from what George's actions cost the business he's a part of, but I can't. Not when he made me look like a fool, and his daughter is now flaunting it right under my nose.

When I find out how he did it, and where he's hidden my money, *then* I'll be able to let it go.

And only then.

There's a knock at my office door, and my brother, Gabe, enters.

'Hey, Dom,' he greets, before looking at me. 'Sorry to interrupt. I thought you'd want to know the police called.'

'Angelo? Again?' I groan.

Gabe's grimace is all the confirmation I need.

'Bloody hell.' I push my chair back, blood pounding in my temples. 'Sorry, Dom, I'm going to have to raincheck on lunch.' I rise and button my suit jacket with one hand. 'Seems I'm off to bail out my little brother.'

'Want some company?' Dom asks as he stands.

I shake my head, glancing at Gabe, who looks as tired of this shit as I am.

'Nah. He's all mine.'

◆ ◆ ◆

Two hours later, a stern warning, and another 'agreement' reached with our local police station, and I'm standing beside my little arsehole of a brother, riding the lift back up to my floor in the Fairfax Guardian offices.

'Come on, Rafe. It wasn't that bad.'

'You broke his nose. He could have done you for GBH.'

Angelo shrugs, the gleamy black of his leather bomber jacket glinting beneath the lights. I keep requesting he wear a suit. Sometimes he complies, but this is Angelo; most of the time he does whatever the hell he wants.

A smug smile plays on his lips. 'Did the guy a favour. Now he can get plastic surgery.'

I slam my palm against the 'emergency stop' button and the lift shudders to a halt.

Angelo's eyes slide to mine before he rolls them. 'Come on, bro. No harm done.'

'No harm done?' I hiss. 'Despite the fact I just parted with a huge amount of cash to help compensate your "victim" to keep this off the record—'

'Yeah, Jake did us a solid.' Angelo grins.

'*Sergeant Howard* did you a solid!' I snap. 'You're the luckiest idiot I know, to have a mate answer the call to arrest your arse.'

'Jake said the guy deserved it.'

'Fuck!' I slam my fist against the inside of the lift, inches from my brother's ear.

The move finally evokes a reaction from him, and he squares up to me, tipping up his chin.

'Little brother,' I seethe. 'You want to get into it with me and see where that gets you?'

Angelo's nostrils flare, but he remains silent, indicating I'm finally getting somewhere.

'I can't keep bailing you out like this. You've got to get a grip on yourself. You represent this family. You represent our business.'

'You sound just like Dad,' he spits.

I tilt my head, boring my eyes into his. 'The man who built this company from the ground up, you mean? The man who raised you, fed you?'

'The man who never wanted me.' Angelo holds my eyes defiantly, but I see it. It's always there.

His Achilles heel.

I screw my face up, dropping my fist from the wall.

'He loves you, even if he has a hard time showing it,' I say, all the anger dissipating from my voice and being replaced by brotherly love in an instant. I'd die for all of my siblings, but especially Angelo. He's my kid brother. The youngest. Barely twenty-five. I was fourteen when he was born. I've fed him, changed his damn nappies, wiped his goddamn arse.

He'll always be a little kid to me, no matter how old he is.

'You standing up for him now? You two best buddies all of a sudden?'

'Yeah, best bloody pals,' I mutter, my chest tightening the way it inevitably does whenever I think of our father.

He throws me an apologetic look, and I brush it off. There's no real malice in his voice. He doesn't blame me. He blames himself. It's Angelo's default setting – self-blame and loathing.

'He didn't want to get rid of you, though, did he? Sorry, bro, but you can't understand how it feels to catch your father looking at you, knowing he's wondering if life would have been easier if you didn't exist.'

'That's not true,' I say, not adding, '*I know how it feels for him to look at me like I'm a failure, though. Like I'm weak.*'

'Come on, I'm not stupid.' Angelo screws his face up, losing all the bravado he had when I picked him up from the police station with bloody knuckles and the leftover adrenaline from a fight he could have avoided but sought out anyway.

I know exactly what's making his dark eyes flash with a look that makes my heart fall to my feet.

'Hey.' I pull him to me, and he tries to resist, but within a few seconds he's sinking into my arms, burying his head into my shoulder as I grip the back of his head inside my palm, letting the silky dark strands spill out between my spread fingers.

'You know it's true,' he mumbles, thinking he's hiding the waver in his voice. But this is my kid brother; I hear it loud and clear.

'It's not,' I rasp.

'He said it himself.'

'One stupid, moronic time when he was pissed out of his goddamn head.'

'Alcohol brings out the truth,' Angelo mutters.

I suck a breath in through my nose. I could have decked my father that night. Gabe and I hoped Angelo was too young to remember it. Even my father was so pissed he doesn't recall it and has never mentioned it since.

But as it turns out, an eight-year-old never forgets hearing his father's slur to himself late one night about how his youngest son was an accident. One he'd asked our mother if she was sure about keeping.

I pat him on the back with my free hand, the motion acting like an injection of strength that has him squeezing me back before easing out of my embrace.

'I'm sorry you had to bail me out again,' he says, avoiding my eyes.

'Next time you need to let off steam, call me first, okay? I'll be there.'

He side-eyes me, his lips lifting into a hint of a cocky smile. 'Yeah? You down for that again?'

I shake my head at the growing gleam in his eyes. 'It'd be a lot easier if your vice was women instead of fighting.'

'Who says it isn't both?'

I smirk, unable to stay mad at him for long. This is Angelo. He's always had this infectious, cheeky bravado about him. A sense of freedom and fun. He's magnetic. That's how people describe him. And he's smart when he isn't busy acting like an idiot and getting in trouble.

It's why he's so good at bringing new clients onboard. They like him. And he knows the family business. Even if he questions if he belongs some days.

'How about you? You taking anyone home to meet Mum and Dad soon? Get them off your case?' He elbows me in the ribs as we stride out of the lift and into the foyer.

I don't dignify his ridiculous question with an answer. He knows how I feel about taking a woman home to meet my mother, who will then suck her into a world of wedding organising before she can even get through the door.

AJ turns, stuffing a magazine behind his back where he's straightening up the waiting area.

'Brought some light reading, huh? What is it? Housewives or naughty doctors? I'm not picky,' Angelo jokes, walking over and whipping it out of his hands.

His eyes widen as he takes in the front cover, before he bursts into laughter.

'Some children visited with a client this morning,' AJ flounders, trying to rip the magazine back out of AJ's clutches. But he's no match for my brother, who holds it up in the air as he continues laughing at whatever it is he's finding so amusing.

'Man, I love kids.' Angelo beams, thrusting the cover into my chest and patting me on the shoulder. 'Suits you, bro.' He winks before heading off towards Gabe's office with a swagger, having bounced back from our conversation in the lift already.

AJ's eyes are wide as he watches me peel the magazine from my shirt and study the cover. It's the interview from last month.

'I'll get it replaced straight away,' he splutters.

I frown as I take in the thick black marker, drawn on with angry, hurried slashes, like the artist's hatred was bleeding out with the ink.

It's the cover photo of me in a suit.

Only with the addition of giant horns, a tail, and a pitchfork.

And a monobrow.

'I don't have a bloody facial hair problem,' I spit, crumpling the magazine inside my fist.

'Of course not, Mr Fairfax,' AJ agrees. 'It's kids being kids.'

'Yeah, right . . . kids,' I echo.

I give him a tight smile and storm into my office, the ruined magazine in my fist.

Locking the door behind me, my phone is out of my pocket, and her profile is up before my arse even hits the seat behind my desk. I scowl at her face, ready to unleash a barrage of abuse. But then an unfamiliar pink frilly neckline makes my breath catch. She's in a new blouse today. One that's sheer and shows her lace bra through it.

I lick my lips and narrow my eyes, homing in on a slight darkening of the fabric where her nipple is.

'Fuck,' I murmur, pulling my belt free and unzipping my trousers with lightning speed before my brain can register what I'm doing.

Stuffing my hand inside my boxers, I wrap it around my dick and squeeze. *Hard.*

'Fuck, Beauty,' I rasp. 'Look at you. Goddamn look at you in that see-through little thing.'

I stroke myself with quickening jerks of my wrist, wasting no time in getting my heavy, aching balls drawing up to my body, desperate to unload.

'*And it has these adorable pearl buttons, look!*' she exclaims in a breathy voice, moving towards the camera to show them close up.

The angle elongates her neck, and I salivate like Edward fucking Cullen at the pulsing vein in her neck.

'Jesus,' I murmur, my body shaking. 'Jesus . . . fuuuccckkk.'

I release with a rough grunt that's much louder than I expect it to be. Thick white ropes of cum spurt out of the end of my swollen cock. I manage to yank my shirt out of the way fast enough that they splatter over my lower ribcage, saving it from getting ruined.

I keep stroking, eyes pinned on her as she moves about on the screen.

'*Perfect date night outfit*,' she says with an innocent smile.

Squeezing the final hot drops from my cock with a groan, I rake my eyes over her, drinking in every inch. 'You can't fool me, Beauty. We both know you're far from innocent. And one day, I'll have you admitting it.'

I drop my dick and grab a wad of tissues from my desk drawer to clean up the mess I swore I would never make in my office. Swiping up my cum, I curse at the fact my dick is still throbbing from the sound of her voice. I could wank over her again right now, I know I could. And it still won't be enough.

Only one thing can cure me.

I lift my eyes to the screen, licking my lips.

'Soon, Beauty,' I rasp. 'One day real soon.'

Chapter 6

Aurora

My knuckles turn white as I centre all of my strength into the sponge and scrub.

'Come on, you bastard,' I huff as the stain fades.

I lower my head to the gleaming white surface of the dressing-room drawers and squint at it. It's nearly invisible. But nearly won't be good enough for Tanya. I know she'll notice.

I scrub again until I'm satisfied even a forensic scientist can no longer find evidence of the chocolate-coloured nail polish stain I found smeared over the glossy surface like a particularly offensive skid mark.

'Finally.' I straighten and swipe the back of my hand over my clammy brow, pushing the loose strands of hair from my eyes.

I grab the vacuum and whip it round, then stand back and survey the walk-in wardrobe. It's immaculate. Every surface is gleaming. Shelf after shelf of designer shoes and bags are lined up at perfect forty-five-degree angles to showcase them. The oversized dove-grey velvet pouffe sits in the centre of the room like an inviting cloud, and the entire space smells like I've burnt a year's supply of Diptyque candles.

I inhale deeply and let it out, closing my eyes for a moment and allowing calmness to wash over me.

The low hum of voices coming up the stairs has me glancing at my watch. *Shit.* I didn't realise how late it was. I should have left over an hour ago. I'll just apologise and get straight out of here. I told Charlie I'd go over to his place tonight. If I can gather up the courage, then it's time we talk about the situationship we've got into.

I pause behind the door that leads into the master bedroom as the voices spill into the room.

'Take off your suit,' Tanya purrs.

A rich chuckle accompanies the sound of rustling clothes.

'Patience, sweetheart. I want to take my time with you.'

'You do, huh?' she says.

'I do,' he murmurs. 'I'm going to taste every inch of you.'

The sound of his voice is like warm butter on hot toast. Confident. Dreamy . . . *Sexy*.

God, this woman is so lucky. She has a wardrobe to die for, and her husband sounds like he adores her.

Kissing sounds travel from the room, and I hover by the door, a flicker of embarrassment preventing me from opening it. Maybe I can just wait until they really get going so they don't hear me leave. Then I'll be able to tiptoe around the edge of the room so I don't disturb the fresh vacuum lines in the plush carpet that Tanya gets so precious over, and ease open the window. I can escape down the fancy balcony that wraps around the house. I've been out that way before once when Tanya had dinner guests and said she didn't want to risk them seeing 'the cleaner'.

There's a reluctant, masculine groan as he pulls away from her. 'But I do need to use the bathroom first. Give me a moment.'

'Don't be long,' she coos.

Heavy footsteps move closer, and I look around in panic. I should have walked out and said hello the moment they came in. Not stayed behind the door and listened like some creepy eavesdropper. And there's not enough time for me to open the window and get out now. The wardrobe provides absolutely no places to hide. Not unless you're a Birkin bag or a Louboutin.

Shit, think . . .

The footsteps grow closer, so I dart inside the bathroom and climb into the shower. It's a giant one with a built-in seat, and it has a mound of clean, fluffy towels hanging on the outside of its glass door. If I tuck my feet up on the bench and keep my head low, I can hide behind them.

Planting my butt on the cold tiles, I wrap my arms around my legs and breathe as quietly as I can as her husband walks inside. His shiny black shoes are visible through the bottom of the glass screen as he strides to the toilet. The scrape of a fly being unzipped cuts through the air, followed by the sound of liquid hitting liquid as he relieves himself.

I should put my fingers in my ears. Listening to someone pee seems like a gross invasion of privacy. Sliding my hands up my shins, I reach for my ears, but that's when I see it.

The shower door is moving.

My heart rate kicks up, stealing my breath.

It's creeping open, the weight of all the clean towels hung on the door too much for it to remain closed. Or maybe I didn't shut it properly.

Bloody hell . . .

I stare at it in horror as it inches open further like it's in slow motion.

The guy's broad shoulders come into view first in his dark grey suit. His head is tilted back, like he's savouring a few moments' peace whilst he empties his bladder.

The gap widens, and I clamp my lips together to stop myself from squealing as more of him comes into view.

I don't look away fast enough.

His dick, in all its glory, fills my vision.

My mouth drops open.

I didn't think dicks could be beautiful. But my God, this man has a work of art between his legs. Long, thick, and highlighted by a ridged vein that runs up to a smooth, broad crown that's glistening as he squeezes the final drops from the end of it.

I'm even more jealous of his wife than I was before. I bet he doesn't fart mid-sex. And that dick is a multiple orgasm giver, there's no way it isn't.

'Hurry up! I need you inside me!' Tanya calls from the bedroom.

Instead of hurrying, the man lets out a long sigh and curses under his breath like he's mentally preparing himself. I don't get it. They were all over one another moments ago.

My attention drops back to his dick, and I tilt my head, admiring the way his hand looks wrapped around it. He grips it with purpose – skilled fingers cradling the weighty shaft, thumb sliding towards the wide, fat tip as he prepares to tuck it away.

I lean a little more and my head catches on something.

A shampoo bottle dislodges from the inbuilt shelf above my head and crashes to the floor.

The guy jerks, his gorgeous dick bouncing in his palm at the sudden movement.

My stomach flies into my throat as the offending bottle rolls across the floor of the shower, the sound echoing off the tiled walls.

I look up and my eyes collide with a pair of rich brown ones, like molten bronze, in the mirror above the toilet. I rip them away fast, my heart pounding and cheeks blazing with embarrassment.

'I'm sorry, I . . .'

I can't help it; I glance down at his dick again before my brain registers something.

Molten bronze eyes highlighted with amber flecks.

Thick, wavy brown hair.

Oh God, no.

I move my attention back to the mirror. But he's not looking in it any more. He's spun ninety degrees and is facing me full frontal.

My breath flies out of my lungs in a gasp. 'You have got to be kidding me!'

His expression turns thunderous, and he shoves his dick back inside his trousers hastily.

'*Rafael fucking Fairfax*,' I hiss.

He clears his throat. 'Francis, actually.'

'What?'

'My middle name,' he snaps, tugging his zipper up roughly.

I stare at him, and he stares back, his eyes darkening.

'What are you doing here, Aurora?' he growls.

'Rafe, darling, what's taking you so long?'

Her whiny voice cuts the air between us like a knife. I clamber off the shower seat and step out into the room.

'Alice?' she scoffs, screwing her nose up as she walks into the room and spots me. 'What are you still doing here?'

She's taken her clothes off and is standing in black lace lingerie, complete with stockings and suspender belt. I flick my eyes towards Rafael, but his attention is glued to my face, like she isn't even here.

'Alice?' He scowls. 'She's not—'

'Not supposed to be here, you're right,' I say quickly, widening my eyes at him with a 'please shut the hell up' look.

He closes his mouth, and I let out a shaky breath.

'I'm so sorry,' I say to Tanya, who's standing with her hands on her hips, glaring at me. 'The list you left took longer than—'

'So you being incompetent and unable to get all of your work done on time is my fault?' Her brows shoot up her forehead.

Yes. If you weren't such a goddamn unreasonable witch. That list would have taken two people an entire day to complete, and you expected me to do it in a few hours.

'No, of course not, but—'

'You know what.' She holds her palm up, silencing me. 'I don't care about your excuses. You're fired.' She looks at Rafael and rolls her eyes. 'So hard to find good help nowadays.'

I stay rooted to the spot as she walks to him and runs her index finger down his tie, giving him a flirty smile.

I clear my throat.

She arches a condescending brow at me as if to say, *What are you still doing here?*

'My . . . wages,' I prompt.

She sighs theatrically like I'm a huge inconvenience, then waltzes into the dressing room.

I purposefully keep my eyes averted from Rafael, my cheeks burning with anger at the way she's talking about me, like I'm nothing. But I need that money. I worked for it. I'm not leaving without it.

Tanya returns a few seconds later and holds out some folded notes.

I reach for them, but she yanks them away before I can take them, giving me a dirty look. 'Uh-uh,' she tuts. 'Not so fast. I think it goes without saying that I expect your discretion. You'll never work in this neighbourhood again otherwise.'

I swallow the burning insult that's threatening to spill from my tongue. I give her a sweet smile instead, noting that she's removed her wedding ring. Once the money is safely in my hand, I say, 'Absolutely. You can count on me not to say anything to anyone about what you do when your husband's away on business.'

Her mouth drops open, and she turns to Rafael, excuses spilling from her lips. I don't wait to hear them. I stomp through the dressing area, swiping up my bag and shoes on the way. Then I pause for a moment before sweeping out my foot and messing up the perfect vacuum lines in the carpet.

Feeling marginally better, I run down the grand staircase. I pull my shoes on at the front door then yank it open.

'Wait!' a deep voice booms.

I glance back and Rafael is descending the stairs, his face taut and red like he's in danger of popping a vein any second.

'Seriously? You're chasing after her?' Tanya yells, appearing at the top of the stairs.

Rafael halts a few steps from the bottom. He doesn't move closer, and I pause, wondering if he's about to turn back and get what he came here for. He sure looks ready to fuck. Chest expanding with deep breaths. Fingers twitching by his sides like he needs to grab on to flesh and sink them into it. Eyes filled with a wild . . . *heat.*

Ready to pound the woman waiting for him into the mattress. Husband or not.

'Come back here!' Tanya screeches.

'Give me a minute,' he hisses at her, his eyes locked on mine.

'You want to chase my cleaning girl out of here, be my guest,' she says with an air of smugness, like she knows he won't do it.

The corners of his eyes pinch at her tone, and I snort.

'You're being summoned,' I tell him, before I step out of the door and slam it behind me.

Racing down the darkened driveway, the gravel crunches beneath my feet. My heart's pounding, the sound of it like a deep bass in my ears. I want to get as far away from here as possible and pray that Tanya doesn't tell all of her rich friends about me. That could ruin everything.

The door slams again, and the sound of heavy footfall beats down behind me.

'Aurora!'

I ignore him, speeding up.

'Aurora!' he bellows again.

I pass a fancy-looking Bugatti car in inky black – his, I presume. I fully expect him to get in it and race past me, and that be the end of it. But instead, he continues his pursuit, following me out on to the main tree-lined street.

He reaches for my elbow, grabbing it so I have to stop and face him.

'What are you doing working for Tanya?' he demands, like he has any right to know anything about me.

I scoff, shaking out of his grip. 'Excuse me? I should be the one asking you what you're doing shagging married women.'

'I'm not,' he grits, jaw clenching.

I stare back into his blazing bronze irises. He would be an insanely good-looking man if it weren't for his personality. And then there's that beautiful monster of a dick . . . *What a waste.*

I roll my eyes in disgust. 'What is it? The thought of being caught? Having something you shouldn't? You need those extra risks, huh? Is age making it hard to get it up?'

He steps closer, towering over me and I'm assaulted by his rich, earthy cologne.

'I don't have any issues getting it up, Aurora. I assure you.'

The way he growls the words with such rich, husky conviction has an unwelcome tremor running up my spine and leaving a tingling heat in its wake. I don't want to picture Rafael Fairfax fucking. Not now. Not ever.

'Whatever,' I huff, spinning away.

'Where are you going?' He catches my wrist this time, pulling me to a stop and whirling me to face him. I almost crash into his broad chest.

'None of your goddamn business!' I snap.

'Where's your car?' he grumbles, scanning the street like one might magically appear.

'Ever heard of a thing called "the Tube"?' I throw him a condescending sneer and tug at my wrist, but he has it in a strong grip and doesn't seem in a rush to let go.

'You're not getting the Tube at this time of night.'

He exerts a little pressure on my wrist, his thumb massaging my pulse point, which I don't think he realises he's doing. It forces me to take a step closer to him, so I don't lose my balance. I look up at his set jaw and furrowed brow. He isn't going to drop this.

'Listen,' I say, trying a different tactic and aiming for something resembling gratitude in my tone. 'It's admirable that you're concerned over the safety of a woman whose wellbeing is none of your business. But this is a nice neighbourhood, and I've done it lots of times. I'll be fine.'

His eyes slide from mine, and he assesses the large mansions set back from the street on their large plots, complete with manicured lawns and driveways overflowing with luxury cars.

'Loaded people have loaded secrets,' he says darkly, making no sense whatsoever.

I attempt to extract my wrist from his grip again. 'Fine, whatever—'

'I'll take you home.'

'What?'

His eyes return to mine. 'I said, I'll take you home.'

'I heard you, I just . . . No! No, thank you.'

'Aurora.' He huffs, like I'm testing his patience. 'It wasn't a question.'

I hitch my brows. 'Used to getting your own way, are you?'

'When my way is the correct one, yes,' he replies, manoeuvring us so his hand is no longer around my wrist but is on my lower back, and he's steering me on to Tanya's driveway.

He leads me to his car, then opens the passenger door for me. I slide in wordlessly, glaring at him as he closes the door, then rounds the bonnet and sinks into the driver's side. I could spend all night arguing with him, but it's not worth it. Might as well just let him think he's won and put up with being in his vicinity a little longer.

A rich hum surrounds us as he starts the engine, then drives out on to the road effortlessly, one hand on the steering wheel, the other resting on his broad thigh. I glance around the interior of his car. It's immaculate and smells divine.

It only makes me hate him more.

I stare out of my window so I don't have to look at him. My head is spinning with a million different comebacks I should have used in order to prevent myself from being stuck in his car with him.

'It shouldn't take long to get to Chelsea,' he says.

I glance at him. 'My boyfriend lives in Shoreditch.'

No way do I want Rafael Fairfax seeing where I live. The thought makes me shudder. Rafael's eyes flick to mine, then he reaches for the heating controls and turns the temperature up.

'You have a boyfriend?' he asks, his tone weighted with something I can't put my finger on. Almost like he can't believe anyone would actually want to date me.

'I do.' I force a fake smile.

One that stops to fart mid-sex, but, hey, at least he's not married like Tanya.

Technically, after tonight, Charlie might not be my boyfriend any more. Not if we have the chat I'm planning. But that information has nothing to do with the grisly hulk of a man sitting beside me. And I don't feel like discussing the failures of my relationship with him.

Rafael steers around a junction one-handed. He's such a smooth driver. So in control. It would be sexy if he weren't such a prick.

'Put his address in,' Rafe commands, keeping his eyes glued to the road.

I watch him for a moment, then sigh as I tap Charlie's address into the satnav. Rafael glances at the screen, then scrubs his hand around his jaw. He's wearing a five o'clock shadow that suits him. Makes him appear less polished than usual.

Almost human.

'Who the fuck is Alice?' he asks after an awkward silence threatens to build between us.

I sink into the plush seat a little more and hum the tune of the hit song 'Living Next Door to Alice' by Smokie. Rafael gives me a sharp look and I roll my eyes.

No sense of humour.

'I made her up. It's not like I can give my real name. If people run a background check on me then they'll never hire me when they find out my father's in prison.'

'Your father,' Rafael hisses under his breath, as if the mere mention of Dad angers him.

The acid in his words come back to haunt me. How he thinks my father is scum and got what he deserved.

'Yes, my father, who is innocent,' I snap.

'Says his daughter, who is deceiving her employers so she can unlawfully gain access to their homes,' he fires back.

My mouth drops open, and I stop my disgusted scoff before it leaves my lips.

'It's a white lie. No one's getting hurt. And needs must,' I reply, quietly seething.

I spend the rest of the drive staring out of the window. Rafael seems more than happy to drive in silence too. Then again, he must be used to it. The man is a fortress. All real emotions kept inside.

It wouldn't surprise me if outside of his family he has no friends at all. Except . . . the one Dove told me about.

I dig my nails into my palms, cursing myself over how stupid I am. This would have been the perfect opportunity to ask Rafael about Dominic Ainsworth. But now I've ruined my chance by getting into an argument with him, then ignoring him for the best part of twenty minutes. There's no way he'll help me now. He'll probably laugh in my face if I bring it up.

He pulls the car over in front of Charlie's apartment building and turns the engine off. He unbuckles his seatbelt, and I whip my head towards him.

'What are you doing?'

'Getting out to open your door.'

Oh, hell no. I'm not letting Rafael Fairfax act like a gentleman and pretend he's anything other than a snake in the grass, waiting to bite.

'I can manage,' I say, throwing my door open and climbing out. 'Thank you for the lift,' I add, before I close the door and round the car.

'Aurora?'

Rafael's rich, husky voice hits my back, and I turn. He's resting his elbow on the open window frame, his attention glued to Charlie's building as he cranes his neck to look out of the car and study it.

'Are you sure you'd not rather go home?' he asks, eyes narrowing on the broken light above the main entrance, then sliding over to some peeling paintwork on a sign. He grimaces like he's concerned he could catch fleas just by looking.

Ugh, he's such a snob.

'I'm fine,' I clip. 'Thanks for the lift.'

I head inside the building, and it's not until after Charlie buzzes me in and the front door closes behind me that I hear the angry roar of an engine outside, speeding away.

Chapter 7

Rafael

Staring at the thumbnail of the video, I grind my teeth together, before shoving my phone into my pocket without hitting 'play'.

I'm not watching any more videos of Aurora Thorne.

I want my money back. And watching a video of Aurora in a little black dress isn't going to get me any closer. At least, I'm assuming that's what she's wearing in it, judging from the title – *The Perfect LBD.*

A tight, short little thing, I bet. One that fits snuggly over her hips and arse and probably pushes up those perky little tits until her cleavage spills out. Maybe they even bounce a little as she walks, a tiny glimpse at the way they'd move if she were on top, riding a cock.

Riding my cock.

'Bloody fool,' I mutter, more annoyed with myself than ever.

After the unwelcome stress of bailing out Angelo again a few days ago, I was planning on screwing that brunette into the mattress all night before I found out she was married. I don't condone liars of any kind, which is ironic, considering I'm lying to my family by keeping the company finances surrounding George Thorne a secret.

I paid back every penny from my own bank account, buying time until the insurance would pay out and Dom could return the investment. So my problem with George Thorne and his daughter is now entirely personal.

Aurora. Damn . . . What was she doing there?

Cockblocking me, for one . . . I mean, I was going to at least *try* to screw Tanya. Things have been . . . somewhat uncooperative in that area recently. But I'm not losing it. I'm not *'too old to get it up'*, as Aurora so eloquently phrased it.

I have no problem getting my dick as hard as steel and coming in an amount that makes Niagara Falls look like a trickle.

I just need to watch her videos to do it.

There's nothing wrong with that.

Nothing wrong at all.

'Jesus Christ!' I snarl, slamming my flattened palm against my desk.

She's right. I'm a goddamn limp-dicked thirty-nine-year-old who can't get it up unless I fantasise about a woman I don't even like.

What the hell was Aurora doing, hiding in the shower like that? Was she going to stay there and listen to us? Would she have got off on hearing us if I'd managed to get a boner? Would she have touched herself whilst listening?

I lick my lips, my dick stirring at the memory of her face when she saw me. At the defiance on it. At all the unconcealed disgust in her aquamarine eyes. The closest I got to getting aroused at Tanya's house was the second my eyes connected with Aurora's. What the hell does that say about me?

I drum my fingers on my desk. But *why* was she there? Her and her father live in a five-bedroomed house in Chelsea, for God's sake. And she's always flaunting her latest fashion purchase in her vlogs. She doesn't need money. Unless . . . No, it's out of the question. I saw the evidence myself. Her father is as bent as they come. Nothing more than a low-life crook, intent on taking what doesn't belong to him. And he's smart. The authorities might have seized his assets, but they didn't get everything. He made sure of it. The house is probably in Aurora's name so they couldn't touch it. The bulk of the money too. She's probably laughing at me right now, with her boyfriend.

I grind my teeth until a pain shoots up my jaw and I reach up to rub the sting away.

A fucking boyfriend. She's got a goddamn boyfriend. One who gets to touch her, kiss her, taste her. One who probably has no idea about the sneaky little minx he's sleeping beside.

I bet she laughed all the way into his grotty building, thinking she is so much smarter than me. The job at Tanya's was likely a cover. To explain where her money comes from since her father went to prison. Every penny she's been getting for months belongs to some poor bastard that's been screwed over.

Rage burns in my veins.

Two hundred and forty bloody million.

Yanking my phone from my pocket, I bring her video up and hit 'play'. I'm entitled to watch. It's my goddamn money that's paid for what she's wearing, after all.

I devour the opening seconds like a starving dog salivating over a prime steak as Aurora moves around on camera. I was right. The black dress is tight. And her tits are presented on a fucking platter, jiggling a little as she moves about, creating the perfect channel to slide my dripping dick through. Yeah, I could fuck those tits. Come all over them, while her pouty little lips gasp in surprise at how good it feels to be covered in my cum.

I'd bloody well drown her in it.

My hand is in my boxers in a flash, and I give in to the inevitable urge to wank over her again. It's becoming a daily occurrence, like I need it to function. Wake. Workout. Coffee. Wank. Et cetera.

'Beauty,' I rumble, like she can hear me. Like she's on the receiving end of my low rasp of appreciation as she turns, and I cop an eyeful of her curvy arse.

It's as she spins back, and I wait to see those magnificent tits again, that something else catches my eye. A coat hanging on the rail behind her. A floral fabric. A distinct pattern. One I've seen before but can't place.

She says something to the camera, and I turn my attention back to her face, tugging on my dick with increased urgency as the need to come overtakes everything else.

She's a goddamn problem.

She's fucking divine.

I bought that dress she's wearing, and I'd rip it off her if I could.

Her father stole from me.

And she's laughing at me . . . with her fucking *boyfriend*.

She shouldn't be with anyone. No one should be touching her. No one except . . .

I come with a grunt, thick white ropes splattering across my palm as I rush to catch them.

I hate her.

I clean myself up and tuck my dick away. It'll be appeased for a few hours, at least. Until the urge to watch her again hits.

I rewind the video, the floral fabric niggling at something buried deep in the recesses of my memory. But it's no use, I still can't place it. Can't figure out why it's familiar. One thing I do know is that it's not Aurora's. I zoom in on the background, something sparking in my mind. I quickly select another of her videos, then another, then another.

'You clever girl,' I muse as I relax back in my chair.

She always films so you can't see much of the dressing rooms behind her. Just the odd item of clothing on a rail. Maybe a shelf of bags or shoes. No one would notice anything wrong, unless they were looking.

Unless they were me.

I pick up my pen and slide it between my fingers as I think. Aurora's filmed her content in at least three different dressing rooms, if not more. She's up to something. And if I'm going to find out what that something is, I need to engineer a way to spend more time with her. Give myself an opportunity to discover the secrets and lies she's hiding behind those deceivingly innocent-looking eyes.

Never mind dreaming up getting into her panties and punishing her.

I need to get into Aurora Thorne's head.

I check my watch. I have fifteen minutes until my next meeting. Rolling my lips, I take my dick back out leisurely and click 'play' on the video again. My grip isn't angry this time, like after I found the magazine with the devil horns on. And my strokes aren't urgent, like a few minutes ago, picturing her with her loser boyfriend.

This time I'm measured and controlled.

Because finally I have something on her. Somewhere to start digging.

And it feels fucking fantastic.

'Mm,' I groan, stroking myself slowly as I watch her face light up modelling the black dress. 'That's it, Beauty. Sit on my cock and ride it. Let those little tits bounce in that dress I paid for.' I chuckle darkly. 'Enjoy it. Because once I'm done with you, you'll know exactly how it feels to be well and truly fucked.'

Chapter 8

Aurora

'You can do it. Just rip it off like a wax strip. Quick and painless.'

I snort at Dove's description and shove another ready-salted crisp into my mouth.

She eyes me through my phone's camera. 'I thought you said you were meeting Charlie for dinner?'

'I am,' I say around a mouthful, then lick the salt from my lips. 'It's nervous snacking, okay? Plus, I don't think I'll be able to stomach any food once I'm sitting opposite him.'

She nods in understanding.

Tonight is the night I break up with Charlie. Dove and I have gone over it. I wimped out the other night, too flustered from having to share a car journey with Rafael.

But tonight is the night I end things with Charlie for good.

No sex is better than fart sex with a man who, if I'm honest, isn't my type at all. I mean, Charlie isn't terrible, but he doesn't make my heart race. He's happy to keep things casual, sex at his place, the occasional date. And he never wants to know anything about me. In the beginning, that's what drew me to him. That he didn't really care. I'd ask him about his job as a manager at an imports company, but he barely asked a thing about me in return. It was perfect because I never had to talk about my father and the pain of having him taken away. I got to be distracted.

Only now, I'm not even getting that. I find my mind wandering to my dad every time Charlie opens his mouth. I can't even force myself to be interested in what he's saying any more.

Him and I together are just . . . meh.

'Okay, I'm going in,' I tell Dove, tossing the empty crisp tube into a bin as I approach the restaurant.

'You've got this, babe. I'll call you in an hour in case you need an excuse to leave.'

I smile gratefully. 'Thanks.' I take a deep breath. 'Okay . . . Love you. Bye.'

She rings off and I smooth my hands over my dress as I walk through the fancy glass doors. The woman at the front of house is busy greeting the couple ahead of me.

The place has a trendy feel to it, low lighting and rich colours, and sexy RnB music pumping through the speakers. The candlelit tables look intimate and are filled with couples gazing at one another and clasping hands over the black tablecloths.

It's the worst place to break up with someone.

I swallow, pulling back my shoulders and forcing myself to smile as the woman at the desk greets me.

'I'm meeting my boyfriend here,' I tell her, giving her Charlie's name and already feeling like the villain in a film, knowing that in around thirty minutes – less if I can manage it – Charlie will no longer be my boyfriend, and we'll probably be leaving separately and never see one another again.

'Great.' The woman grins after checking her tablet. 'He's already here. Follow me.'

'Great,' I echo weakly, trailing along behind her.

◆ ◆ ◆

'You . . . wow, you really do look good tonight, Rory,' Charlie says, his eyes roaming over me appreciatively.

'Thanks,' I reply for the fifth time. He's been unable to stop staring at me since I arrived, making this whole evening and what I have to do much harder.

'Yeah.' He pulls his lower lip between his teeth as he eye-fucks my cleavage again. 'Really good.' He screws his face up, glancing away. 'But there's something we need to talk about. And I don't . . .' He looks at my breasts again. 'I don't want to bring it up tonight, but I can't . . .' He licks his lips, eyes glued to my chest. 'Damn it, it can't wait. It's probably a misunderstanding, though.'

'What is?'

He gives my cleavage one final mournful look before tearing his eyes away.

I shouldn't have worn a push-up bra, or actually, maybe this is a good thing. Breaking up with him might be easier if he's looking at my boobs instead.

'Something I heard. I was telling the guys at work about you—'

'You were?' I ask in surprise.

'Yeah, about your make-up blog.'

'My fashion vlog,' I correct.

He shrugs. 'Yeah, that. Well, one of them asked what your name was so he could tell his girlfriend about it. She wastes loads of time watching that stuff.'

I straighten in my seat, choosing to take another sip of wine instead of commenting. There's no point getting into an argument over Charlie's total lack of understanding and respect for what I do.

The server brings our mains out and places them on the table with a flourish. I force a polite thanks as I eye the lobster thermidor, then Charlie's steak. I didn't want to order such expensive things, but Charlie insisted.

'More wine?' the server offers.

'Another bottle, please,' Charlie replies.

The back of my neck heats as I mentally add up the cost. Charlie suggested this place tonight – insisted, really. Maybe because it was his idea he'll offer to pay, but I can't count on it. He's been more than happy to accept my offer to go halves when we've dined out before.

The server disappears and I stab a piece of lobster. The aroma makes my mouth water, and I take a bite. Damn, it is good. Maybe I shouldn't have eaten so many crisps. Even the sourness in my stomach, knowing I'm about to dump Charlie, can't ruin the dish for me.

I take another mouthful, moaning around my fork.

'Steady on, it's not going to swim away.' Charlie chuckles, cutting into his steak.

I lower my fork to my plate, cheeks heating, and nod gratefully when the server returns and offers to refill my wine. I lift my glass and knock a giant swig back, earning myself another judgemental look from Charlie.

Maybe I won't feel guilty breaking up with him after all.

'As I was saying, I told one of the guys at work your name.'

'He wouldn't have found my vlog; I use a different one.'

Charlie chews his steak, his brows rising as he swallows. 'Why?'

'Why what?'

'Why the fake name?'

I shrug. 'A lot of people don't use their real name online. Not their full one at least. For privacy.'

'So people don't find out stuff about you that you don't want them to know?' Charlie says.

The hairs on the back of my neck prickle and I avert my eyes from his questioning ones.

'That, and for personal safety.'

He lifts his glass and leans back in his seat, studying me as he takes his time drinking. I shift in my seat. I preferred it when he couldn't stop staring at my boobs.

I look around the restaurant, feigning interest in the artwork on the walls to avoid his gaze. My eyes land on a couple sitting at a table on the far side of the room. The woman is talking animatedly to her dinner companion, hands gesturing, before she pushes a curtain of glossy hair over one shoulder.

But the man . . . his dark eyes are fixed on me.

My breath stalls.

'No bloody way,' I scoff quietly.

Charlie frowns, then turns to see what's captured my attention. 'He a friend of yours?'

I press my lips together and narrow my eyes. Rafael fucking Fairfax raises his glass of wine, his eyes fixed on mine as he takes a sip. His date excuses herself and picks up her clutch, heading towards the bathrooms. Yet he never breaks eye contact with me.

'No,' I reply. 'Definitely not.'

'He should keep his eyes to himself then,' Charlie grunts, glaring at Rafael before turning back to me. His attention immediately drops to my breasts, and he reaches for my hand like he has to stake his claim.

'He's not looking at me,' I lie.

Charlie doesn't seem convinced, but he lets it go, squeezing my hand. We eat in silence for a few minutes before he speaks again.

'So, my friend . . . when I told him your surname was Thorne, said something really weird.'

Rafael's eyes are still burning through me like lasers, making every millimetre of my skin heat. He hasn't looked away from me once.

'Oh, really?' I murmur, pretending to be listening. But I needn't worry about being convincing because Charlie is too distracted by the way my nipples have tightened to stiff peaks and are poking through my dress.

Rafael takes another sip of his drink, and his gaze notches up in its intensity.

Why does he have to stare so hard? He looks like he's about to cause himself an aneurysm.

'Yeah. He said there was a guy who went to prison for stealing millions from the company he worked for or some shit. His name was Thorne too. And he has a daughter called Aurora,' Charlie says.

'George,' I reply absent-mindedly as Rafael's date returns and leans down to whisper something in his ear before taking her seat.

He breaks eye contact with me and gives her a slow, sexy smile, transforming his face into a version of him I never would have believed existed, let alone think I'd ever witness.

'Yeah, George Thorne,' Charlie continues.

'That's him,' I murmur, watching as the raven-haired beauty reaches over to Rafael and brushes her thumb over the corner of his mouth like she's wiping away an imaginary crumb. He catches her hand in his and turns it, pressing a kiss to her inner wrist. But his eyes return to mine, like it's all a show for my benefit.

'Bastard,' I whisper, hating how he's sitting there, flaunting his date, making her fawn all over him like he's some kind of catch. I wonder if she knows he's a cold-hearted, judgemental arsehole. Then again, knowing his type, she's probably married.

'That's what I said,' Charlie gushes. 'What a bloody bastard. I told my mate it was just a coincidence. You'd have told me if your father was a criminal. Checked if I was okay with it before we—'

I snap my eyes away from Rafael. 'Before we what?'

Charlie tilts his head, grimacing. 'You know . . . before we started sleeping together.'

'Right.'

'It's kind of important, don't you think? To know what kind of family your girlfriend comes from before you start bringing her back to your place and . . . you know? I mean, what if you got pregnant by accident, then I found out? Anyway, doesn't matter, it's just the same names. Weird, though, right?' Charlie blows out a relieved chuckle.

I take a deep breath. *Rip it off*, that's what Dove said. And Charlie's giving me the perfect opportunity.

'George Thorne is my father.'

Charlie laughs. 'Rory, come on, that's not funny.'

'You're right, it's not. It's not funny that he's been locked up for something he didn't do.'

Charlie gapes at me.

'I actually wanted to talk to you about something too,' I say, seizing my opportunity. 'You and me . . . I don't think this is work—'

'You're joking, right?' Charlie leans across the table, glaring at me.

'No, I'm sorry. I've been thinking it for some time and—'

'I meant your father!' he snaps, causing me to recoil at the venom in his voice.

'Why would I joke about that?'

'You mean to tell me I've been dating the daughter of a goddamn crook? Do you have any idea what that could do to my professional reputation if people found out?'

I frown. 'You're an imports manager. You don't work in finance. I doubt anyone would care if—'

'Stuck-up bitch!' he scoffs, throwing his seat back and standing so fast the bottle of wine on our table topples over and falls on to the floor, glugging out its contents.

'*I'm* stuck up?' I gasp. 'You're the one telling me you wouldn't date someone because of who their family is. Even if what people say about them is complete and utter bullshit.'

'I can't believe this.' He pushes his hands back through his hair, dragging in deep breaths before his eyes narrow and he leans over the table towards me, pointing a finger into my face. 'You're a lying—'

'That's enough,' a deep voice thunders.

Charlie screws his face up in pain as he's hauled backwards. He fights to turn so he can get a look at who's got him dangling like a worm on a hook.

'That's no way to talk to a lady.'

His face reddens as Rafael drops him like a sack of shit and he falls into the table, setting the cutlery and plates clanging.

'I suggest you apologise and then get the hell out of here. She was about to dump your arse, anyway.'

'What?' Charlie gapes at Rafael, who's calmly adjusting his shirt cuffs and smoothing them down.

'She's clearly too good for you. Even an idiot can see that.'

Rafael's blistering gaze roams over me, and my mouth goes dry as his attention lowers briefly to my rock-hard nipples, then back to my face.

'I bet you don't even know what to do with her.' He smirks. 'Tell me, Beauty . . .' He tips his head towards Charlie, his gaze fixed on me. 'He ever made you come without you having to fake it?'

'Um . . .' I falter.

'Who the fuck are you?' Charlie rages.

'A man who never has to wonder,' he replies with ease. 'Now, apologise.'

Charlie's eyes slide to mine as the server approaches and places the bill down hesitantly, before retreating. Even he knows we aren't staying for dessert.

Charlie picks the black folder up, and I can't help it, my shoulders soften in relief. Then he tosses it on to my plate, splashing my dress with the remainder of my lobster.

'I'm sorry I ever fell for your lies. Have a nice life, Rory.'

I spin in my seat and watch him storm out.

That went . . . *Holy shit*, that went terribly. I wanted things to end, but this isn't quite what I had in mind.

I turn back to grab a napkin, but Rafael's already holding one out to me.

'Send me the dry-cleaning bill.'

'Excuse me?'

His eyes drop to my dress as I wipe at it in vain. It's no use; the cream in the sauce has left ugly oily patches on it that might not come out.

'I said, I'll pay for the dress.'

'It's fine,' I mutter, abandoning my clean-up efforts and opening up the bill instead.

The numbers burn into my eyes and my palms prick with sweat. I don't have enough to cover it. I'm going to have to offer to wait tables, or clean up in the kitchen, or—

'How much?' Rafael asks.

'I—'

'How much, Aurora?' He sighs, sounding bored.

I force a swallow. 'Two hundred and forty.'

'Hm.' He grunts at the figure like it amuses him somehow. 'I'll take care of it.'

'No, I—'

'Wait here. I'll let Seraphina know I'm giving you a lift home.'

I snap my eyes back to his table. His date is sitting there patiently. She gives me a sympathetic look. I dart my eyes to the other tables. People avert their gazes politely, but I see it in all of their faces: pity, and morbid curiosity. The same looks were on everyone's faces in the courtroom when my father's verdict was delivered.

My throat grows tight. 'I'm fine.'

'Aurora—'

'I said, I'm fine. I don't need you pretending to be nice to me because I'm Dove's friend, okay? We both know what you really think of me and my father, so cut the crap,' I hiss, my cheeks burning with humiliation.

Rafael's brows lower, and if anything he looks impressed at my bitten reply, rather than offended.

'Okay,' he says slowly. 'I'll cut the crap. You'll let me pay for dinner, and your dress. And if you don't want me to drive you home myself, then you'll also take this for a cab.'

He pulls a diamond-encrusted money clip from his pocket and I almost snort at the pretentiousness of it. He holds out two fifties to me and I wait for him to snatch them back like Tanya did, in a pathetic display of twisted control. When I don't move to take them, he takes my hand in his and presses them into my palm, leaning down until his lips brush my ear.

'Now close your fingers.'

I do as he says, curling them around the crisp paper until I have a firm grip.

'Good girl,' he rasps.

A shiver runs up my spine and I glare at him as he moves back so he knows I still hate him.

'Now, if you'll excuse me. I've kept my date waiting long enough.'

I flick my eyes to the woman, who's watching Rafael with lustful eyes that convey every dirty plan she has for him at the end of their meal. Nausea swirls in my gut, threatening to resurface my dinner.

'Thank you,' I whisper, despising myself for saying those words to a man I hate.

I don't look at him again. I can't.

I take his money, and I get out of there as fast as I can.

Chapter 9

Rafael

'Leads were up ten per cent, but we can do better.'

I rest my ankle on my knee, reclining in my seat as Gabe leads the marketing meeting.

Heads bob along the table in agreement like those nodding dogs. My gaze wanders to the graph Gabe's put on the screen at the front of the room as he points at something on it.

I wonder if she got straight in a cab like I told her to.

I tilt my head, the graph swimming in front of my eyes. Her boyfriend's a prick. Who the hell raises his voice to a woman like that? Calls her a bitch? The memory makes me ball my hand into a fist. I might want to squeeze information out of Aurora Thorne, but I'd never dream of shouting at her. Knowing her, it would only make her clam up, anyway. Increase that stubborn defiance in her eyes.

No, if I want to get what I need from her, then I need to be smart about it.

It was a stroke of luck that Dove let slip the name of the restaurant Aurora was going to be in last night so I could rearrange my dinner plans. But I can't rely on luck. I need a strategy. A plan.

'So, what have we got?' my brother continues, addressing the room.

The table of suits, a mix of experienced marketers and so-called prodigies we got fresh out of university, stare back at him blankly.

'Ideas?' he presses, doing a great job at hiding his frustration. If it were my meeting, I'd have probably burst some eardrums by now if I'd received such a piss-poor response.

Guardian Fairfax is a global leader in corporate insurance. They should be damn well coming in their pants to have a seat at this table. There're a few hundred applications for every job we post.

Silence will not be tolerated.

'Someone must have an idea. What's working on social media right now?' I bark.

A guy halfway down the table clears his throat nervously as I pin my eyes on him.

'Human connection, Mr Fairfax,' he says meekly.

'Go on,' I encourage.

He clears his throat. 'Real people, real connection. Seeming less . . . formal, and more relatable.'

'We insure FTSE companies, and leading global brands around the world. How do we make that relatable to Joe Bloggs?' another member of the team pipes up.

I hold a hand up, silencing him, and he shrivels in his seat.

We don't only insure FTSE companies. We also provide the best personally tailored insurance policies for those companies' CEOs. For elite businessmen and businesswomen. The best brains in every multimillion-pound industry. More often than not our reputation precedes us, and new business comes from personal referrals. But from time to time we run marketing campaigns, aimed at attracting exclusive clients who have the kinds of assets we specialise in protecting. Superyachts, private jets, priceless art collections.

'Carry on, Justin,' I instruct.

The first guy looks a little less like he's about to piss himself once he realises I know his name.

'Have you spent much time online watching vloggers, Mr Fairfax?' he asks.

I purse my lips as images of this morning's 'coffee with a friend' outfit spring to mind. Snug jeans and a cute little t-shirt that showed a peek of her stomach.

'Can't say that I've spent long enough,' I answer.

'Well, they build up a rapport with their audience first. You feel like you know them the more you watch. Like they're talking directly to you and you're their only focus. Like you have a relationship with them. When in reality millions of viewers could be having that same experience.'

I crack my knuckles, heat flaring across the back of my neck. 'Your point?'

'I'm not suggesting we vlog. But I think we could learn something from that approach. Make potential clients feel like they're the only ones we're talking to. That it's all for them.'

'Interesting,' I muse, my mouth curving into a smile.

He's given me exactly what I need.

'I've got some ideas, Justin. We'll make it happen, and if it's a success there'll be a bonus in it for you.'

'Yes, Mr Fairfax,' he splutters, looking shell-shocked.

'Great. That's all for now.' Gabe claps, grinning, no doubt eager to draw the meeting to a close. He hates this stuff. He'd be much happier back in his own office with his computers for company, and only emerging to talk to his small, select team about cybersecurity.

But we all have to lead meetings like this from time to time. Show a united front. Remind everyone that this is a family business, and that by working here, they are one of the Fairfax Guardian family too.

Dove leads plenty, and even Angelo has stood up in front of the team on occasion.

Everyone collects their things and files from the room.

Gabe turns to study me. 'You've got that look in your eye.'

'What look?'

He folds his arms across his chest. 'The one that says you're up to something.'

'You heard the team. It was Justin's idea.'

'*What* was, exactly?'

'That we should hire a professional social media expert for a touch of consulting.'

'Oh.' Gabe nods, thoughtfully. 'Okay. I have some contacts over at—'

'Dove's friend, Aurora,' I interject.

Gabe's brow scrunches. 'Dove said she specialises in fashion.'

I wave a hand in the air. 'It's still a product people buy. No different to an insurance policy.'

'If you say so.' Gabe frowns.

'We've got nothing to lose. Give her a call. Offer her a short-term contract. And we'll see how it goes.'

'Okay. I'll speak to HR. Get them to draw up the standard offer.' He closes his laptop and tucks it under his arm.

'Double it,' I say.

He pauses, before bending to retrieve Benedict from one of the many cat beds strategically placed around the building.

'All right,' he says, knowing better than to question me once I've made my mind up about something. He tucks Benedict under his other arm, saying something to him in a low voice before kissing the top of his ginger head.

'Actually,' I call as he reaches the door, '*triple* it. Make it impossible for her to say no.'

He gives me a quizzical look, but nods. 'You got it.'

I pause, before adding, 'Just . . . keep an eye on her. She might be Dove's friend, but we don't know her that well. I don't want her having unsupervised access to any company files.'

'I'll run a full background check on her before we reach out. I know there was that stuff with her father.'

'No,' I cut in sharply. 'That won't be necessary.'

I hate lying to my brother, but the thought of him digging into George Thorne runs the risk of him finding out that I invested company money with his old firm. A fact I've successfully kept hidden and have no intention of sharing. No one can know my own stupidity almost cost us the company for a second time.

They still don't know what really happened the first time around.

I'd like to keep it that way.

'All right. Well, I've got some data scrapes to run.'

He leaves with Benedict, and I steeple my hands over my chest as I spin in my chair. The city comes into view, forty floors below. My mouth goes dry at the sight, and I quickly turn back around so I'm looking through the glass wall into our offices instead.

It's the perfect plan.

I can gain her trust. Get close to her. Know where she is at all times.

She was obviously working at Tanya's to maintain her façade of being penniless, so she'll need to keep up the pretence of earning her own money. She won't be able to turn down the figure in our usual package, let alone triple it, if she wants her cover to remain intact. No one in their right mind would turn down an offer like the one Fairfax Guardian is about to extend to her.

I'll have her exactly where I want her, and I'll finally get my money back. Every last damn penny.

'Mr Fairfax?' AJ asks, peering through the open doorway.

'Yes?'

He walks over and places a pink envelope on the desk. My name is written on the front in loopy handwriting.

'What's this?'

'I'm not sure. Miss Thorne left it for you. She said she owed it to you.'

'Of course, thank you,' I say, plucking the smooth envelope from the table and sliding it inside my inner jacket pocket.

The thing burns against my chest for the entire walk back to my office. Angelo stops me to talk about the new client he's come back from having lunch with. But even the sight of him wearing a suit for a change and taking his role in the business seriously isn't enough to quell the incessant urge to get into my office so I can see what she's left for me.

The moment I step inside, I flick the lock and hit the controls that turn the inner glass wall opaque.

Striding to my desk, I pull the envelope from my pocket and lift it to my nose.

The scent of something rich with a flowery depth hits me. It's the same scent left inside my car after I gave her a ride to her boyfriend's place.

Ex-boyfriend.

My chest rumbles with a warm grunt.

I tear the envelope open, taking care not to damage any of the writing on the front. It's the first time I've ever seen her handwriting. And she's written my name.

Mine.

I pull out a pile of notes. Two crisp fifties sit on the top of a pile of twenties, totalling three hundred and forty pounds.

She's paid me back everything from the restaurant, plus what I gave her for a taxi home.

'Stubborn girl, aren't you, Beauty?' I murmur, using my thumb and forefinger to open up the envelope further.

Disappointment tugs at my gut when I see it's empty. No note. No words that I can play over and over in my head, putting her voice to them as I picture her thinking about me as she wrote them.

I toss the money to one side on my desk and place the envelope in front of me, smoothing it under my palm.

'What were you thinking when you wrote this? What were you *wearing*?' I purr, tracing the curves of her letters making up my name.

I jab the intercom on my phone.

'AJ? Did HR send Miss Thorne's offer to her yet?'

'Not yet, Mr Fairfax. I only just saw the email from Gabriel myself, and—'

'Go down to their floor right now and ask them to do it. Stay there and watch until it's done. Then tell me as soon as it is.'

'Okay,' he replies.

I lean back in my seat and glance at my office door. HR are three floors below us. AJ won't be back for at least ten minutes, and that's if he rushes.

I pull my phone from my trouser pocket and bring up her channel, hitting 'play' on today's video before propping it up on my desk where I can see it.

Then I lift the envelope to my nose and inhale as I tug down my zipper with my other hand.

The stiff brown envelope is tucked safely inside my jacket pocket as I reach for the ornate fleur-de-lis knocker on the door. The pink one that still holds her scent is safely locked away inside the top drawer of my desk, despite the fact that keeping it puts my dick in real jeopardy of being worn away by friction.

I purse my lips, urging the swell of sour anger to retreat back down my throat.

It's a nice house for a criminal to live in. Aurora must be laughing herself to sleep in it every night, stretching out in Egyptian cotton sheets, dressed in some silky little nightwear.

I bang harder on the door again, my patience thinning.

A woman opens it, her brows hitching as she takes me in.

'Hello? Can I help you?'

Her gaze travels down over me slowly, then back up, a glint of interest in her eyes as she gives me a polite smile.

I frown, subtly checking the name of the house on the wall-mounted plaque to my right.

'I'm here to see Aurora.'

'Who?' The woman frowns.

'Aurora Thorne, the young woman who lives here.'

Maybe this lady is her friend, or the housekeeper or something. Figures: Aurora probably has a whole host of staff she's paying with my money.

'Thorne?' The woman's brow scrunches, before smoothing out. 'Oh! You mean the previous owners. Do you know them?'

Previous owners? What the hell?

I clear my throat, stalling for a few seconds so I can think.

'Yes . . . And this is a private matter, which I would appreciate your discretion with.'

'Absolutely.' The woman's eyes widen, eager for gossip.

I pull out my Guardian Fairfax ID and flash it at her quickly, pocketing it again before she can get a good look.

'I'm actually Miss Thorne's parole officer. She hasn't attended her last two check-in meetings, and I'm concerned. She's been making progress that I'd hate to see go to waste.'

'Parole officer?' The woman's face drains of colour. 'Is this to do with her father? I heard that's why the house was repossessed before we bought it. He's in prison, right?'

'George Thorne was convicted of stealing millions of pounds from his employer,' I confirm, making her gasp.

'And his daughter has followed in his footsteps, then? Sounds about right. These people . . . Oh my goodness, they're despicable.' She shudders and I can almost see the cogs of disgust turning in her head. 'I met her once when she came to collect some post. She looked so sad to see the house again that I invited her inside for a cup of tea. I should have known the innocent act was a ruse. I left her alone with my handbag when I went to the bathroom.' She looks at me with panicked eyes. 'Do you think she could have cloned my cards or something? You hear about these scammers, don't you?'

'I very much doubt that.'

'She seemed a bit common, come to think of it. Had a tube of crisps stuffed inside her handbag. No class,' she mutters. 'Are you sure you want to waste your time on her? These sorts of people can't be rehabilitated into anything remotely useful to society.'

'"*A bit common*"?' I arch a brow, an illogical anger heating my blood at the judgement in her tone. Aurora has more class in her little toe than this woman has in her entire body. She looks stunning in the outfits she styles for herself on her vlog. And the times I have spoken to her she's been able to convey her – uncalled for – abhorrence of me with unwavering poise.

'Miss Thorne is my concern, and mine alone,' I clip, my patience rapidly thinning. 'It's very important that I find her. As soon as possible,' I emphasise, letting the insinuation that she would be wise to let me deal with Aurora myself hang in the air.

'Of course, of course.' The woman chews her lower lip. 'I might have an address!' she says suddenly. 'One minute.'

I wait on the doorstep until she returns, flustered, brandishing a piece of paper.

'Here. I knew I'd written it down to forward any letters that might arrive.'

I take the note and flash her a tight smile. 'Thank you. And don't worry. Once I find her, I'll make sure she doesn't leave my sight.'

'Oh, yes, of course. Thank you.' The woman visibly relaxes, giving me a grateful smile.

'Aurora Thorne is my problem, no one else's,' I say, turning and climbing into my car.

Chapter 10

Aurora

'So good,' I hum around a mouthful of crisp shards.

I've combined prawn cocktail with ready salted in a six-layer stack and am merrily crunching away as I watch *Gladiators* on TV.

I swallow and suck my fingers as Legend prepares to take on a contender on the climbing wall.

There's a knock at the door and I peel my eyes away from the screen, crossing the room to answer it. It's probably my neighbour asking me to turn the volume down again. The walls are paper thin, a fact the middle-aged guy loves to remind me about whenever he can. I don't like to point out that if he can hear my TV, I can also hear his phone calls.

I wiggle the door because it always jams.

'Hey, Mike,' I sigh as I manage to get it open.

The space where Mike's face would be is filled with the perfect knot of a forest-green silk tie.

'Oh.' My gaze climbs up a thick neck and over the bump of a strong Adam's apple before sliding over a sharply cut jaw, lips that are set in a grim line, and finally . . . deep bronze eyes that are pinched at the corners, studying me.

My stomach drops to my feet. *How the hell did he find out where I live?*

'What are you doing here?' I balk.

'Expecting *Mike* instead?' Rafael clips, his gaze boring into me.

'Yes,' I splutter. 'Actually, that's exactly who I was expecting.'

His lips thin into a grimace.

'Why are you here? Is Dove okay? Did something happen?' My heart races.

'Nothing's happened. She's fine. May I come in?'

His eyes hold mine, his broad frame filling my doorway like a huge shadow that's sucking the air from the space.

'Um . . . sure,' I say, standing aside to let him enter.

He steps inside the room that makes up my lounge, kitchen, and bedroom, and scans it coolly, before his gaze tracks over to the only other door – leading to a tiny bathroom with a toilet, sink, and shower so small I can barely lift my arms to wash my hair. There's an open box of tampons sitting on the side of the sink in full view and a muscle in his jaw clenches as he stares at them.

I cross the room in a few small steps and pull the door shut, leaning back against it like I'm standing guard over what's behind it.

'So, why *are* you here?'

His attention turns to the TV, where the camera is spanning the view from the top of the wall the gladiators and contenders just raced to climb. He screws his face up like he's tasted something sour and turns away.

I get it. He probably only watches boring insurance programmes that no one with any personality would find remotely interesting. But he doesn't have to be so damn obvious over his clear disdain.

'I came to return this.'

He reaches into the inner pocket of his jacket, and I get a flash of forest-green silk lining that matches his tie. He looks so out of place in my bedsit in his bespoke suit that it's laughable.

Sliding a brown envelope out, his eyes snag on my face. Instead of taking it straight away, I look back at him in challenge. *Doesn't he know it's rude to stare?*

'Those . . .' He lifts his free hand and gestures to my face with his index finger. 'Is one supposed to be that far down your cheek, and the other beneath your eye?'

I reach up to the cheek he's pointing at.

'Yeah, that's how they're designed,' I lie, quickly peeling the bright green under-eye pad from where it's slid down my cheek like a blob of snot. I grab the other that's still in place and yank that one off too, squishing them into a ball and stuffing it in the pocket of the pyjama shorts I'm wearing.

Rafael's attention drops to the shorts, sliding over my thighs and making my cheeks heat.

I tilt my chin up, waiting for him to pass a comment on the potato print that's all over them. They were a birthday gift from my father – a joke because of how much I like crisps.

'It's yours,' he says, his jaw tightening as he holds the envelope out to me.

I take it and lift the unsealed flap up. 'Why are you returning my money? I owed it to you.'

'Did I say it was a loan?'

'Um . . . no, but you didn't say it wasn't either.'

He pushes his hands into his trouser pockets, his lips curling down in disapproval as he looks around the one room that I exist in when I'm not working, seeing Dove, or visiting my father in prison. At least I made my bed, which is squashed into an alcove so small I have to climb into it from the foot end.

Silence engulfs the room, and I swear I can actually hear his thoughts, about how he can't wait to escape back to his immaculate Bugatti that smells like a walking cologne advert. Maybe he thinks he'll need a tetanus booster when he leaves.

'My sister said you lived in Chelsea,' he says finally, his eyes fixing on my gold sequinned top that's hanging on the end of the exposed rail that serves as my wardrobe. I got it from a charity shop, and it leans to one side, but as long as I don't overload it then it works just fine.

'My father and I did. Until it got seized.'

I cross my arms, waiting for him to finish his scrutiny of my home. It might not be much, but it's clean, and filled with my favourite photographs of my father and me. Years ago, before Dad started doing well at his job and got headhunted to work for his old firm, we were doing okay. We weren't wealthy, but it wasn't bedsits like this one, or big houses in Chelsea, either. That only came in the last few years.

But we had enough. And we had each other.

'Are you safe here? There isn't even a doorman.' Rafael's upper lip curls in disgust and I could roll my eyes at how pretentious he sounds.

'It's fine.'

'Fine?' he echoes, like he isn't convinced at all.

I wait for him to say something else demeaning about my home.

Muffled voices on the other side of the wall grow louder.

'You're a dirty little liar,' a woman scorns.

'Oh yes. Yes, I am. I'm sorry, Mistress.'

'You told me you had money, but the only thing big about you is your ego. What's fifty quid? It's nothing. Send me more, you disgusting little cockroach. I deserve much more for having to talk to you.'

There's a deep groan, followed by a feminine drawl. 'It'll do . . . for a start. You're not touching that ridiculously sad excuse for a dick, are you?'

'I-I'm sorry, Mistress.'

'If you're going to do that and make me listen then you'd better send more money right now.'

Another groan.

'My neighbour, Mike,' I explain as Rafael looks at me with horrified eyes, like he just licked the bowl of a public toilet.

'Mike?' he growls, glaring at the wall through which Mike's moans of clear enjoyment are audible. 'You have to listen to this shit?'

'Yeah, but I mean . . . she's actually very skilled. Her name's Mistress of Mockery, and I don't think I could do what she does and keep a straight face. She called Mike a selfish little turd last week. He really liked that.'

I've never seen Rafael look flustered before, but the wide flare of his nostrils tells me he's one breath away from marching next door and telling Mike to quieten the hell down. Which would be ironic seeing as that's what Mike's always telling me to do with the TV.

'He's done this before?' he growls.

I nod. 'Twice a week since I moved in. Then the other nights he listens to the replays.'

'Replays?' His rich bronze eyes widen, which I take as an invitation to continue, although it's second-hand embarrassment that keeps me talking as a way of covering the sounds of Mike's laboured pants coming through the wall.

'Yeah. It's all online. He pays to video call with her. And when he can't, he watches the replays . . . on repeat.'

Rafael stares at me. 'This guy plays recordings of the same woman every day . . . so he can wank to them?'

My cheeks burn at the way 'wank' sounds being growled from his lips.

'Yeah. But she only wants his money.' I shrug. 'Bet you think that's kind of . . . sad?'

His mouth drops open, and he takes a breath like he's about to say something, but then decides against it.

'Oh, Mistress,' Mike moans.

Rafael's eyes bulge. 'I'll damn well insult him for free!' he snarls, striding to the wall. 'Hey, arsehole!' He hammers on it. 'We don't want to hear you bashing one out.'

'A-Aurora?' a confused voice calls back.

'It's fine, Mike,' I shout.

The last thing I need is for him to find a reason to complain to the landlord about me. Mike's been here longer than I have, and even though it's not The Ritz, living here is better than having to rent a room in a house-share with strangers. Ones who might ask questions about my father.

Rafael whips his head and gives me a warning look. 'It's not bloody fine,' he hisses, before turning back to the wall and banging on it again.

'Who are you?' Mike asks in a strained voice.

'I'm her bloody boyfriend, *Mike*,' Rafael snaps, making sure to bite out Mike's name with extra wrath. 'So you'd better damn well keep the sounds of you and your dick to yourself unless you want me to rip it off and choke you with it.'

There's a female purr from the other side of the wall. 'You heard the sexy-sounding man. Even he thinks you're pathetic, you sad little toad.'

'I'm sorry, I can't stop it, I-I . . . Oh God,' Mike gasps out a choked cry, Mistress's final insult hitting the spot.

Rafael's eyes take on a wild sheen. 'That bloody—'

I grab the cuff of his suit before he can storm out of my front door and bang on Mike's.

'It's not your problem!' I hiss. 'Why'd you tell him you're my boyfriend? You think that'll make him stop?'

'It better,' Rafael snaps. 'You shouldn't have to listen to that.'

'It's not that bad. He has to listen to me too.'

He reels back, his brows shooting up his forehead.

'Not like that,' I splutter. 'My TV. He's always complaining it's too loud.'

He presses his lips together, his eyes flicking to the wall like he's still deciding whether to go and rip Mike's dick off like he threatened to.

'You probably ruffled him. Maybe I'll get a few days' peace. Mistress probably won't thank you, though. He's putting her kids through university,' I say.

'You do realise . . .' he says, his voice a rich, deep growl with a bite of something that I can't put my finger on. 'That if he can hear your TV, he can hear everything you do in here. All your phone conversations. Whether you talk in your sleep. What you sound like when you . . .' He swallows thickly. 'When you take a goddamn piss.'

'I'd rather not think about it, thanks.'

I'm still gripping on to the sleeve of his jacket, so I let go. But as I do, my fingers graze his palm.

He stiffens, sucking in a breath. 'Does Dove know you live here?'

'Was there anything else you wanted?' I ask. I don't want to explain how I haven't been able to admit to my best friend exactly how bad things have become since my father got convicted.

The brown envelope burns inside my other hand. I want to shove it back at him, but I know that'll get me nowhere with the giant tosser. I don't want his money. It might not have been pity money when he put it in this envelope, but it sure as heck will be now.

'The offer?' he drawls. 'HR informed me you haven't returned the signed agreement yet.'

'I don't want to work with you.'

If my bluntness offends him, he doesn't let it show.

'You won't be. You'll be working with the marketing team, and maybe Gabriel. Dove said your social media skills are impressive.'

'I have a vlog. A fashion one.'

His expression remains impassive, like he doesn't give a toss whether I post about the intricate workings of the London Stock Exchange or sell vials of belly button fluff.

'Don't you want to see it before you offer me a job?'

'It's a temporary contract,' he clips.

'Fine, I won't be one of the prestigious Fairfax Guardian team,' I huff, understanding his insinuation that I will be an outsider, not good enough to be considered one of them, 'but don't you at least want to see what it is I do to decide whether it's what you're looking for? You're the CEO.'

'What's your answer, Aurora?' he presses.

I grab my phone and scroll through my videos. 'Look. This is my profile. Are you sure I'm who you want? Dove didn't . . . She didn't make you ask me, did she?'

'I don't need to see your little black dress video.' Rafael sighs like he's bored. 'And Dove has no idea about us hiring you yet. She's been out of the office in meetings all day.'

'Well, I don't—'

'Say yes.'

He holds my eyes in challenge, and I stare back, wondering where he gets all his arrogance from. I bet he's never had anyone say no to him in his entire life. And as much as I really want to, just to see his reaction, I can't turn down that kind of money, and not only that . . .

I can't turn down the opportunity.

Dove said Rafael and Dominic Ainsworth are friends and that he visits the office frequently. If I'm working there I might hear or see something that could help my father, or even get the chance to talk with Dominic myself and ask him how the hell the board of directors thought that my father – one of the company's highest-performing employees – was the one who stole from them.

Being in the same building as Rafael Fairfax is the fly in the ointment that I'll have to suck up if I want the chance to see what I can find out from inside the walls of his company. And God knows the money will help when I get the next bill from the solicitor I've asked to assist with my father's appeal.

But I hate that if I say yes, I'm giving him exactly what he wants.

'I'll think about it.'

'No, you won't,' he replies smoothly. 'People don't *think* about working for our company. They'd give up an organ for the chance.'

I wrinkle my nose at the image as Rafael pulls his phone from his pocket and taps something into it.

'Your contract.' He turns the screen towards me. 'Sign it.'

'I—'

'Aurora, you're living in a box unfit for vermin to reside in. Don't pretend you don't need the money. We're being very generous.'

I hold his eyes. *He knows he's got me.*

I hate him more in this moment than ever.

Without saying a word, I use my finger to sign my name on the screen.

He looks at it, studying my writing for a second, then pockets his phone.

'Good girl. Wasn't so hard, was it?'

I shake my head with a scoff. *Condescending prick.*

I open the front door to let him out, waiting until he's in the hallway before I ask, 'Why didn't you rat me out me to Tanya?'

He tips his head. 'Tanya? Ah, yes,' he says, like he can barely remember her. 'Didn't see the point once she fired you. It's not like you'll be going back again.'

'I wouldn't have had an opportunity to tell her husband about you, you mean?'

'It crossed my mind. I'd prefer not to take a punch over a woman I didn't actually—'

'Have sex with?' I scoff.

'Like,' he clips.

I swallow, trying to ease the rough dryness in my throat.

'If I'm going to get into a fight over a woman . . .'

He leans closer until his warm breath fans my ear. I hate that I shiver on reflex. And I hate that my pulse rate kicks up at the scent of his cologne, warm on his skin.

'. . . then she won't be just anyone. She'll be . . . *mine*,' he growls. 'You understand?'

He moves back, holding my eyes for a beat.

'I'll expect you first thing Monday morning.' His attention drops to my pyjama shorts and bare legs. 'Try to find something appropriate to wear. You will be representing Guardian Fairfax, after all.'

I bite back the urge to say something that'll wipe the infuriating smug look of an overinflated ego from his face.

'Of course.' I smile back thinly. 'Perhaps a little black dress.'

Realisation hits me as the words leave my mouth, and something in Rafael's eyes heats before his expression turns grim.

'I'll leave that up to you. Good night.'

He storms down the hallway and disappears into the emergency exit stairwell rather than waiting for the lift.

I close the door and lean back against it.

He knew one of my videos was titled 'The perfect LBD'. How would he know that unless he's seen it? Which he claims not to have done.

Heat flares up my spine, even though I hate the man with a passion.

It means he's lying about watching them.

But why?

Chapter 11

Aurora

Stepping out of my studio flat, I check my bag one more time to make sure I have the essentials. Tube of crisps. Check. New treats for Freddie. Check.

I'm leaving early for my first day at Fairfax Guardian. I want to walk Freddie before I go. There's no way in the world Rafael Fairfax is getting between me and that adorable little silky hairball. Cleaning for Freddie's owners came with the added benefit that I get to walk him a few times a week too. And I love it. I'd have my own pet if my place wasn't so cramped.

Rafael's comment about it not being fit for vermin to live in makes me pull my front door closed with extra force. He's such a rude prick.

I take the stairs after seeing that, no surprise, the lift is out of order again. As I round the last corner of the staircase that leads into the grimy lobby, puffing catches my attention.

'Mike?'

He stops his struggle towards the main doorway, turning to face me. His cheeks are flushed and his forehead shines with a layer of sweat.

'You're leaving?' I ask, taking in the two suitcases he's pulling, one in each hand, and the stuffed rucksack on his back.

He nods, trying to catch his breath. 'I am.'

I stare at him, dumbstruck. He's lived here for decades. A fact he announced proudly to me the day I moved in. He swore he was going to die here and sounded rather happy about the fact.

'Why?'

He shakes his head and readjusts his grip on the suitcase handles.

I rush forward and hold the main door open for him.

He tries to smile, before it's stolen by a cough.

'Ask your boyfriend,' he wheezes.

He shuffles off down the path, dragging his luggage to a waiting taxi.

My boyfriend?

Realisation stabs me in the gut, followed by a surge of white-hot anger.

'Believe me, I will,' I seethe, hitching my handbag up on my shoulder and marching towards the Tube station.

'Good morning, AJ,' I greet.

'Aurora?' He jumps up from his seat. 'Welcome to your first day.'

'Thank you,' I say, mustering as much enthusiasm as I can, considering I spent Freddie's walk, and then the entire journey here, picturing pushing Rafael Fairfax's head against his desk and stapling him to it by his ear.

'Take a seat. Gabriel's going to—'

'I actually wanted to thank Rafael for suggesting me for the position before I get started. His office is that one, right?' I point at the closed door leading to what Dove told me is the largest corner office in the building.

'Yes, but—'

'I promise not to disturb him for long,' I say, flashing AJ a smile.

I stride to the door and knock before he can stop me. The glass is opaque, so I can't see inside, but I know the bastard is in there. Dove told me he's at work by 7.30 a.m. every day. A total workaholic.

'Come in,' a deep baritone voice calls.

I open the door and step inside, closing it behind me. Then I take a deep breath, ready to unleash. 'What do you—'

Bronze eyes spark beneath thick brows as he cuts me off with a raised palm. I stare back, clamping my mouth shut as another voice – a sharper one – stabs out from the speaker on the desk phone.

'I'm glad things are okay. Not as well as they would be if we had the Wyndham account, of course, but—'

'Everything's fine, Dad. You don't need to worry,' Rafael says, his eyes fixed on mine as he gestures for me to take a seat in the chair opposite him at his desk.

Mr Fairfax senior grumbles something on the other end of the call about how he doesn't believe him, then asks, 'How are things with Harold's daughter?'

A muscle in Rafael's cheek clenches as he watches me slide into the seat, before he flicks his gaze away, cracking his knuckles.

'Fine,' he clips.

'Are you bringing her home to meet your mother soon?'

'Seraphina's busy. She's away at a conference,' Rafael says.

'When she gets back then. We'd like to meet her. Harold can't stop talking about her and the things she's been doing with her advertising company.'

Rafael grunts. 'I have to go. My new social media consultant just arrived.'

'All right, son. I'll be in to visit the office as soon as your mother and I land.'

Rafael hangs up without answering him.

'Seraphina's definitely not married, before you start,' he says, leaning back in his chair.

I swallow, hating that he knows me well enough to tell that it crossed my mind after catching him with Tanya. But the way he says 'definitely not married' instantly conjures up an image of the two of them having sex. I saw the way she looked at him in the restaurant when I was at dinner with Charlie. There's no mistaking the fact she was going to be climbing Rafael like a tree the moment they left.

I bet he whispers filth in your ear when he fucks you. Fucks you with that work-of-art dick he's got in his trousers. I swallow, the back of my neck growing hot.

'Your love life doesn't concern me. But what does is what you did to Mike.'

'Mike?' He frowns, and I want to reach across his desk and shake him for having the audacity to look confused.

I fight to keep my voice from betraying just how angry I am. 'I don't know how you did it. But I know it was you.'

'He's my tenant. I can do what I want.'

'Excuse me?' I splutter.

He has the balls to check his watch and then sigh like he doesn't have the desire or the time to listen to me. But the bastard needs someone to tell him what an arse wipe he is. New boss, or not.

'Your tenant? You mean, you own my building?'

'Technically it's my building, not yours. But yes, as of today, I do.'

'What?' I stare at him, my head growing light and making me glad I'm sitting. 'Why? Why would you . . . ? Did you buy it just so you could kick Mike out because you don't like him?'

'How could you tell I don't like him?' He snorts like I'm an idiot, and I stuff my hands underneath my thighs as my gaze moves to his stapler.

'But no,' he adds. 'Contrary to how highly you place my interest in inconveniencing your neighbours based purely on my personal opinions of them, I didn't purchase your building for any other reason than it's a good investment. The land will be worth millions if I get planning permission to knock those grotty flats down and replace them with luxury ones.'

'Wow. I knew you were a . . .' The word 'prick' freezes on my tongue as he arches a brow at me. I need to remember the reason I'm here. To find out what I can from Dominic Ainsworth. I can't let my father down. I inhale slowly, forcing my tone to soften. 'I never expected you to . . . *do this*. He loves that place. It's his home.'

'If you're missing him that much then you can visit him at The Savoy. He'll be there until the soundproofing installation is completed.' Rafael's eyes pinch a fraction at the corners as he studies my reaction. I refuse to break his gaze, wanting him to look away first. It's childish, but I want to win something with him.

'What?' I whisper.

'Do you have it installed in your ears? I said—'

'Why are you having that put in his place?'

He presses his lips together, his eyes burning into mine. 'You're my employee. I can't have you showing up for work, running on air because your neighbour kept you awake with his unique choice of hobby.'

'Oh.'

His attention drops to my mouth, and any glimmer of victory I could have at him looking away first is overshadowed by the sudden heat in the room.

He tilts his head in thought. 'Or perhaps I won't knock them down. I haven't decided yet. I like to keep my options open.'

There's a knock at the door, preventing me from throwing something at him.

'Aurora? Good morning.'

I turn away fast to greet Gabriel.

'Good morning,' I reply, trying my best to get my flushed cheeks under control.

I hate that it's day one and Rafael Fairfax is already getting to me.

'Are you ready to be introduced to everyone?' Gabriel asks.

'I sure am.' I give him a bright smile, climbing out of the seat, grateful to escape.

I make it to the door before Rafael's deep, husky voice hits my back.

'Aurora?'

I turn and meet his eyes.

'How did you know it was me?'

I stall as he stares intently, waiting for my answer. 'Mike, um . . . he told me to ask my boyfriend what was going on,' I admit, my mouth going sour at the use of the word in reference to Rafael Fairfax.

His eyes burn with a darkness that makes me shiver.

'I see. Well, don't let me hold you up. I'm sure my brother has lots to show you.'

Chapter 12

Rafael

Walking into Gabriel's office, I throw myself into one of the couches he has in his seating area. Dove looks up from her laptop beside me, and Angelo lifts both brows at me in question from the couch opposite.

'Your face suggests you just got off a call with Dad,' Gabe comments, glancing up from his computer screen before he continues typing at a million miles per minute. I'll never understand how he can code so fast or do whatever genius tech whizz stuff it is that he's so damn good at, without steam coming off his keyboard.

'That bloody obvious, huh?' I scrub a hand around my jaw, exhaling with a muttered curse. 'He wanted to get me before our meeting.'

This is what the four of us do every Monday morning, usually before anyone arrives. Sit in Gabe's office and go over our plans for the week. My office would be the more logical choice because it's the biggest. But Gabe's doesn't have floor-to-ceiling windows beside his seating area like mine does. A fact that made me want to choose another office when I became CEO, before my father insisted I take his old one. I can't stomach a view that high this early in the morning, or any time of day, for that matter.

'What did he say?' Angelo asks, trying to keep his tone casual.

My heart bleeds for my kid brother, because I know what he's really asking. *Did Dad ask after me?* Did our stiff-upper-lipped father show an ounce of tenderness towards his kids, and actually ask how *we* are, rather than just how business is? Gabe, Dove and I have grown to expect nothing less, but Angelo still holds out hope.

'Same as usual. Wanted figures. Gave his opinion on which clients we should be trying to sign. Told me the latest staff bonuses were unnecessary, and they'll think I'm a bloody soft touch if I'm that generous.'

'That's our father,' Dove tuts. 'Always about the money.'

My spine prickles with unease. As far as they're all aware, our investments were never affected by George Thorne's actions, but her words strike a nerve. I've been so hellbent on finding out what George Thorne did with my money that it's become an obsession.

Maybe I'm more like my father than I care to admit.

Angelo sniffs, looking away. 'Can we get this moving? I didn't have breakfast yet and my stomach's eating itself here.'

'I've seen you hangry, and it's not pleasant,' Gabe says, screwing up his nose. He pulls open his desk drawer, grabs something out, then walks over, taking a seat beside Angelo. 'Here. Bacon flavour. Knock yourself out.' He scoops Benedict up off the floor, where he's rubbing at his shins, and cradles him in his lap as he sits back.

'Nice.' Angelo nods, popping the lid off a tube of crisps.

'Whose are those?' I ask, my gaze fixing on Angelo as he crunches down three at once.

Dove smirks. 'Don't tell me she got you hooked on those too?' she says to Gabe.

'She's trying.' Gabe smiles.

'Who?' I snap.

'Aurora,' Gabe says.

'Give them to me,' I bark, holding out my hand.

Angelo grabs a handful of crisps before passing me the tube. I sniff them, then read the ingredients. 'These aren't food.'

'Taste good,' Angelo moans through a mouthful.

'Why is Aurora bringing you these? We're not paying her to cosy up over lunch with you. She's got a goddamn job to do.'

Gabe's eyes slide to mine, narrowing. 'Would you rather she eats lunch with you?'

'Don't be so bloody ridiculous,' I scoff.

He smirks and I fix him with a glare as I shove the lid back on the crisps. I've barely seen Aurora since she began working here one week ago. Gabe's kept me updated on her suggestions to our PR campaigns. Enquiries are up thirty per cent as a result. She's clever. Too clever.

My plan to unearth where my money is might have stalled somewhat with how busy I've been with new clients, but I haven't forgotten. I'll still get exactly what I want from her, one way or another.

'Let's get this bloody meeting started,' I grumble.

'I'm sho sworry, Mr Fwairfak.'

I wince at AJ's swollen cheek as he cradles a heat pack on it.

'It's fine. Get yourself to the dentist. We can't have you greeting clients like that.'

'Yesh, swir.'

I should have known when he started complaining about his toothache this morning that this could happen.

'Bugger,' I mumble as he leaves my office. I guess it doesn't matter if he's not here to take notes for the meetings this afternoon,

I can keep track of everything we discuss. I just like AJ to sit in because the man is a walking sponge. He'll recall every detail, down to the number of times the client blinks. It's surprising how useful his small observations can be during negotiations.

I open my calendar and check my schedule. I have a couple of calls booked, including one with Sullivan Beaufort.

Getting up from my desk, I exit my office in search of Angelo to get an update on another of our clients – a woman with a private collection of Italian artwork she wants to insure.

Female laughter rings out from the staff lounge as I head down the corridor. Reaching the doorway, I glance in. Steve, one of the underwriters, is leaning against the counter with his hands in his pockets, looking all too bloody comfortable chatting with Aurora as she uses the coffee machine.

He grins at her, and I don't miss the way the fucker's eyes drop to her arse in her pencil skirt as she reaches for the sugar.

'Trust me, it's a great film. We should watch it together sometime.'

'Okay,' Aurora answers innocently, unaware the leech is licking his lips, thinking his dick's about to get wet.

'Steve!' I bark. 'Where's the file for Ruperts?'

His eyes widen as he takes me in, and he straightens from the counter. 'Mr Fairfax, I didn't see you. Um . . . Ruperts?' he questions, confusion knitting his brow. 'That only came to me this morning.'

I usually give him a few days to look over a new client in detail.

'If you've got time to plan a movie night when I'm waiting on something for a new client, then I'm obviously paying you too much,' I say, watching the colour drain from his face.

'Of course.' He swallows thickly. 'I'll get right on it.'

'You do that,' I grunt.

He scurries past me and Aurora watches him go with a frown.

'What?' I snap.

She turns her attention to her coffee and stirs it. 'I didn't say anything.'

'But you're thinking it. I can tell,' I say, moving to stand beside her at the coffee machine.

I place a mug underneath and click it on. She side-eyes me like she's wondering why I'm using the machine here when I have a better one in my office. The scent of her perfume dances up my nostrils and I place my hands on to my hips so I don't reach out and *touch* her. It's sweet, feminine, and adds a whole new layer to what I already know about her from watching her vlogs. In those I can watch every tiny expression she makes, hear every little lift in her voice when she likes something. Savour the sparkle in her eyes when she really *loves* something.

My dick thickens in my trousers, threatening me with the possibility of a raging hard-on in the goddamn staff lounge.

'You might be a shrewd businessman, but you can't tell what I'm thinking,' she says.

'You're thinking I'm an unreasonable arsehole.'

Her brows rise and she lets out a small, surprised laugh. 'Okay. You're good.'

I take the opportunity as she glances away to admire the pale blue silk shirt she's wearing. Her blond hair is tied up and a loose strand has fallen against her neck directly over her fluttering pulse.

'But not great,' she adds. 'I was thinking "demanding".'

I lick my lips. 'I don't need to make demands, Aurora. I always get what I want.'

She chances a glance at me and her pupils dilate the moment our eyes meet.

'Excuse me. Gabriel's waiting for me,' she says quickly, heading for the door.

I stuff my hand into my pocket and rearrange my dick, urging the bastard to chill out. It's perfume. That's all.

I can't help but drink in the curve of her hips. I've never seen her wear this skirt before. Plenty of other skirts and tight dresses in her videos, but never a navy-blue pencil skirt and light blue silk blouse before. It's a new combination.

One I like. *Very much.*

'I need you,' I announce as she reaches the doorway.

She snaps her eyes back to mine. 'But we're about to—'

Images of my brother and Aurora taking lunch together has heat creeping across the back of my neck and my fingers flex with the urge to crack my knuckles. I'm pretty sure Aurora isn't Gabriel's type, but that's not the point. Plus, I need to spend more time with her to find out what I need.

'Gabe's a big boy. And he told me you're making great progress. So he can cope for the afternoon,' I tell her. '*I* want you.'

She frowns, biting her lower lip like she's considering whether she can decline or not.

'I have client meetings. I need you to take notes,' I add, motioning to AJ's empty desk.

'Oh.' Her expression clears, pricking with interest. 'Okay. Absolutely.'

'Good.' I take a sip of my coffee, holding her eyes over the rim.

I wince. The stuff's barely palatable. First thing AJ can do when he gets back is order a replacement machine. I'm not having my staff tell people I'm an arsehole who also makes them drink crap coffee.

I tip it down the sink. 'Let's go.'

I lead Aurora to my office and gesture towards the meeting table.

'Take a seat there. The first call I have is with Beaufort Diamonds, one of our biggest clients. Biggest jewellery brand in the world.'

Aurora nods and obediently slides into a chair at the table where she can see the large flat-screen monitor that's fixed on the wall. It's currently displaying the Fairfax Guardian logo of golden wings.

'They're in New York, five hours behind us. We've got ten minutes until I need to call them.'

'Oh, okay.' She casts her attention around my office like she'd rather be anywhere else than in a room with me.

'How are you finding working here?' I ask, leaning back against my desk and crossing my legs at the ankle as I study her.

'Really good. The work's challenging. And your brothers are great, and so's Dove, obviously. Actually, everyone I've met has been.'

She glances at me, then looks away again. Heat prickles over the back of my neck. *Except you.* I can sense the afterthought flying from her head towards me like a punch.

'Don't forget your new friend Steve?' I retort, crossing my arms.

'He's a colleague, nothing more—' She looks past me, and her eyes widen. 'They're good, aren't they?' Her face transforms into a beaming smile.

I twist my head to see what's got her so animated. The tube of crisps sits like a proud trophy on my desk. I meant to throw the stupid thing away after the meeting this morning.

Turning back, she's still smiling. And it's the first time it's ever been directed at me. Unease bubbles in my gut.

Two hundred and forty million. I'm not a fool, Beauty. A nice smile isn't going to make me forget about that.

'If your idea of "good" is processed starch coated in artificial powder and salt,' I reply.

She snorts. 'Of course. Your body's a temple. Did you not eat anything fun when you were younger?'

'When I was younger?'

She shrugs. 'Yeah?'

I hold her gaze. There's no fire in it. None of her usual defiance. She's genuinely curious. She thinks I'm goddamn old. That I choose to watch what I eat because of the threat of middle-aged spread looming over me. I purse my lips. I was thirty-nine two months ago. Yet, judging by Aurora's face, that makes me a fossil.

I swipe the tube from the desk and flip the cap off. Holding her eyes, I decant a couple of crisps into my waiting hand, then open my mouth and put them in.

Her eyes widen as she watches me.

The things are vile and taste worse than the sludge disguised as coffee in the staff lounge. I force myself to swallow, then look at her pointedly.

Her lips twist in amusement. 'You need to eat at least five to really appreciate the flavour.'

My jaw clenches and I suck in a breath through my nose. She looks at me, waiting, and all I can see in her eyes is that she thinks I'm goddamn old. But with age comes experience. And fuck, if she knew the ways I could ruin her until she begged me to stop because she couldn't take any more.

I glance at my fingers. They're covered in a fine orange, bacon-flavoured dust. I clench my teeth to stop myself from grimacing in disgust.

'Fine,' I grit, tilting the tube again. 'I hope you paid for these,' I mutter under my breath, hating that she's got me eating shit to prove some kind of point.

'Pardon?'

She flies to her feet and marches over to me like a blond tornado. Her cheeks are pink as she glares at me.

'Listen. I know what you think about my father. And what you no doubt think about me as well. But what I don't understand is why you have to make these snide remarks. For a successful man, you behave like a child. How about, instead of muttering things, you say them to my face?'

I stare at her. 'You think I behave like a child?'

'Everything I just said, and that's the part you focus on. You're . . .' She huffs, glaring at me, her eyes on fire and her chest heaving in her silky blouse.

And if it isn't the hottest bloody thing I've ever seen.

Blood floods my dick at an alarming rate, pumping the bastard up until my zipper digs into the hardening length.

'I'm what?' I lick my lips, and her eyes drop to my mouth.

'You're angry with the world. At least, it sure seems that way.'

'Go on,' I urge, my veins coursing with heated blood as she wrinkles her little nose up and scowls at me.

'You're . . . you're uptight. Look at you. You can't even eat a bloody crisp without complaining.'

Uptight and old. Her words make me puff out my chest.

I stuff my hand inside the tube. 'I can eat one. I'll bloody eat ten!'

She stares at me, a mix of hatred tinged with interest swirling in her light blue irises, like she doesn't want to give me her attention, but at the same time can't tear herself away.

I lean closer, unable to resist riling her further. 'Contrary to what you think, Aurora, I'm a man who loves to eat.'

Her cheeks flush and I know my hidden meaning isn't lost on her.

I try to remove my hand from the tube so I can eat the bloody crisps and make my point. Make it while I hold her eyes and let her wonder if I'm really picturing devouring something else entirely.

Nothing happens.

The tube remains suctioned to my hand like an over-enthusiastic blow job.

'It won't . . .' I tug my arm. The blasted thing is covering my wrist and is partway up my forearm. 'It won't come off.'

'What do you mean?'

Aurora's frowning at the tube as I glance at her.

'I mean what I bloody said. It won't come off.'

'Just pull it.'

'I'm trying,' I hiss through gritted teeth.

It's no use, the thing is stuck like it's been welded to me.

I place the tube between my thighs and clench around it, pulling with everything I have. My shoulder twinges and I bark out a curse.

'Let me try.' Aurora grabs the tube and pulls it as I twist my arm.

'It's not budging. I think my hand's swelling up inside.'

'Do you have anything we can slick your arm up with? Like lube?' she asks, her eyebrow quirking just a little.

'You think I have a top drawer filled with lube in my office? Why would I have that?' I hiss.

'I'm just trying to help,' she bites back.

I clamp my lips together. The number of times she's had me wanking at work, I should need lube. Only, she makes me so bloody hard that my dick leaks before I can even get it into my hand. The thing's slicked itself up and is raring to go the moment I click on one of her videos and hear her voice.

'Let me try like this,' she says.

Before I can protest, she's turned her back to me and is pressing her body against mine while trying to prise the tube off.

'Stop,' I grit.

But it's too late, she moves straight back, and her arse grazes the front of my trousers, right over my straining erection.

I suck in a sharp breath through clenched teeth. 'Aurora—'

'Hey,' a smooth American voice says.

The large screen above the meeting table fills with the image of Sullivan Beaufort, sitting alongside his father, Sterling Beaufort, in their meeting room in New York. The Manhattan skyline fills the windows behind them.

I whip the arm trapped in the tube behind my back and clear my throat.

'Good morning to you both. This is Aurora Thorne. She'll be joining us to take notes while AJ is away from the office.'

I lead us to the table, keeping one hand behind my back.

'Nice to meet you,' Sterling replies, giving Aurora a warm smile as the morning sun catches the silver strands in his hair, making them glisten.

'Aurora,' Sullivan repeats as she smiles politely at them and takes her seat. 'Nice to meet you.'

He catches my eye, an undercurrent of understanding in his. He's the one person I've confided in about Aurora, but he doesn't know it's a deep urge for revenge that's driving me. He only knows she's the woman who's been stealing my attention for months.

Stealing being the opportune word.

'Nice to meet you both too,' she replies before flicking her eyes to me briefly. If I'm not mistaken her gaze drops to my crotch. But that situation is under control. For now.

'Let's get to it, shall we?' I say as I take a seat at the head of the table, keeping the crisp tube concealed beneath the desk.

Twenty minutes later, after discussing some new mines they've acquired, and the location of five new stores they're opening worldwide, I'm preparing to close up the meeting.

'Is that the new award you guys won?' Sullivan drawls.

He points to the bookcase near the door, where a selection of industry awards gleam on the shelves.

I crack my neck. 'It is.'

'Can we take a look?'

'Sure. Aurora, do you mind?'

'Why don't you get up and show us, Rafe?'

I narrow my eyes at him, and he looks back, his lips twitching. The guy never used to break a smile before he fell in love with his daughter's nanny. Right now, I wish he was still the serious, moody bastard he used to be. Because I know exactly what he's up to.

'Fine,' I grit, taking my time to rise carefully from my chair.

I keep my arm behind me as I walk backwards towards the bookcase.

Sullivan leans back in his chair, watching me. The bastard will pay for this. I'd rather he didn't see me with a goddamn crisp tube attached to me like a pink cardboard limb. But we're friends; I can tell him to fuck off if he laughs. Sterling Beaufort? Not so much. He's a man I don't want to lose respect from. Fifty-one years old and a goddamn legend in the business world. Being caught looking like a ridiculous pillock by him would be the most embarrassing thing that could ever happen. I'm a bloody CEO of a corporate insurance firm, for God's sake. I deal with billion-pound companies every day. My reputation is everything.

And I currently have a tube of bacon-flavoured crisps melded to my arm.

'You all right there, son?' Sterling asks, watching the awkward way I'm moving across the room.

'Fine, thank you.' I force a smile as I reach the bookcase.

I pick the crystal award up. Aurora's eyes catch mine and she presses her lips together like she's trying not to laugh.

'You know, the doctor can give you fibre tablets for that.' Sterling chuckles as I return, clasping the award in my free hand, holding it up so they can see.

Sullivan leans forward, squinting. 'Hold it steady with both hands. It keeps moving, I can't read what's on it.'

I pull my shoulders back and thrust it closer to the screen, still in one hand.

'Still moving,' Sullivan quips.

'Better?' I grit, my smile tightening.

'Nope.'

I try again and he shakes his head.

'Still can't read it. Just get your other hand, Rafe. What are you doing with it? Got it in your pants or something?'

'Of course I bloody haven't!' I snap, throwing my arm out in frustration.

Cool air whooshes over my hand as the crisp tube detaches itself and flies across the room at an alarming speed. The relief of having full blood flow restored to my hand is immediately interrupted by a loud crack.

I snap my head in its direction at the same moment a siren screeches from the broken panel on the wall.

'Is that the fire alarm? Everything okay?' Concern instantly fills Sterling's voice.

'The panel broke, that's all. There's no fire,' I reassure him.

'What broke it?' Sullivan asks.

I glare at him, the alarm piercing my ears with an incessant hammering to my eardrums.

'Sorry, can't hear you,' I lie. 'We'll get this sorted. Speak soon.'

I swear the bastard's smirking as I cut the video feed.

'Is it the whole building? Can we reset it?' Aurora shouts, already on her feet and looking out into the hallway, where we're attracting attention from the staff.

'It's only my office. It's zoned. If I reset it in time it won't spread to the rest of the floor. Go and wait outside, where it's quieter.'

'I'm fine,' she calls over the noise. 'Let me help.'

A click above is the only warning we get before the sprinkler system kicks in and water sprays out over us both.

'Bloody hell! Grab my laptop!'

I stride over to the control panel as Aurora fetches my laptop from the table and rushes into the hallway. Then she runs back inside.

'What are you doing?' I snap.

'Everything's getting wet!' she cries, running over to me. 'Give me your jacket.'

I shrug it off and hand it to her, and she rushes to drape it over my desktop computer and keyboard.

Water runs down my face as I turn my attention to the fire alarm controls and type in the override code.

Nothing happens.

'Come on,' I urge, fighting the desire to drive my fist through the blasted thing.

I try again, and there's a delay before the siren stops, followed by the sprinklers shutting off.

'Oh my God!' Aurora gasps.

She's standing in the middle of my office, staring at me. Her hair is plastered to her head, and her blue shirt has glued itself against her skin, showcasing the pattern of her lace bra underneath it.

'Oh my God,' she says again. 'That was . . .' She looks down at her drenched clothes, then back at me. 'You're soaked. We're both soaked.'

Her gaze is locked on to my white shirt. It's stuck to my skin, showing my short, dark chest hair beneath it. Even my goddamn nipples think it's a party they're invited to.

Aurora clasps a hand over her mouth, her shoulders trembling. I step towards her, concern etching itself into my bones. Perhaps she's in shock, or cold or—

She bursts into laughter.

'You think this is . . . funny?' I stare at her.

She tries to stop, but she can't. Her face is lit up, her eyes glowing as she snorts out another laugh that has her clutching her stomach like she's in pain.

'Kind of,' she pants.

'Kind of?' I echo, placing my hands on my hips.

'I mean, no . . . Sorry.' She bites her lower lip and looks at me.

That's when I see it.

Her with her guard down.

She's open.

Unapologetic.

Free.

So bloody beautiful.

My heart races and my mouth goes dry. Any anger I had disintegrates. She looks at me, her eyes alive with bubbling energy and pure goddamn magic.

I stare back into aquamarine blue.

I picture her wearing gold sequins as her laughter fills my ears. Picture her gazing up at me as I slide inside her. Not with punishment in mind for once, but with the consuming urge to worship her. The overpowering urge to sink inside her as she looks into my eyes and kisses me, my name a pleasured plea on her lips.

'Aurora,' I breathe.

She blinks, the water droplets clinging to her lashes as her lips part and she steps closer.

She stops toe-to-toe with me, and I stare down at her, my breath coming in slow, steady drags as I force myself to regain composure. I'm so close to pulling her to me and bringing my mouth down over hers until all thoughts of my money are gone.

Until all that exists is the thought of making her mine. Forever.

Memories of my mother crying at my bedside when I was nine years old force their way to the front of my mind, and I wince.

'What is it?' she whispers.

I swallow, shaking my head at her. 'Nothing.'

I need to be careful.

I need to be so damn careful.

Chapter 13

Aurora

'You need to get out of those clothes. Dove might have something in her office. Wait here,' Rafael all but barks at me.

I stand, dripping, in the centre of his office, and he returns moments later, holding a pair of leggings and a t-shirt.

'My bathroom's through there.' He jerks his chin at a closed door.

'Um, thanks,' I say, unable to meet his eyes as I take the clothes and scurry to the door, closing it behind me, sealing myself off from the heat of his gaze.

I'm in a small entryway. On one side there's a small walk-in dressing area with rows of shirts and suits lined up on matching wooden hangers. And in front of me is another door, leading to the bathroom, complete with giant walk-in rainfall shower and long inbuilt vanity area. It's all modelled in dark grey marble – the walls and floor, even the ceiling. There are a couple of large ferns fanning their leaves out over the counter beneath a giant mirror that reaches to the ceiling. The overall effect is dark, sexy, and masculine.

And the whole place smells like him. A heady, intoxicating scent that's earthy and spicy, and makes my mouth water.

I step inside the bathroom and close the door.

'Fuck my life,' I mumble. 'Good-looking, rich bastard. Good-looking, rich, *impossibly awful* bastard.'

I peel my clothes off quickly; the idea of being in his personal space like this is too unsettling. I don't want to glimpse Rafael Fairfax's private life. Seeing him at Tanya's was bad enough. Hearing the way his voice sounded when he was talking dirty to her . . . seeing the impressive dick he's concealing beneath his suits.

No, thank you.

I pull the leggings and t-shirt on then gather my wet clothes into a pile. Movement in the dressing area as I step out catches my eye.

Rafael's standing inside, pushing his arms into a clean, dry shirt.

'They fit,' he comments, his eyes dropping over me.

'Yeah,' I mumble, staring at him.

He pulls his shirt together across his chest, but not before I get an eyeful of short, silky-looking chest hair coating his pecs. His fingers work fast to do the buttons up, and a faint flash of red in the centre of his chest disappears from view.

Frowning, he tucks his shirt into the waistband of a new pair of trousers, and I can't help my gaze dropping to them. When I was trying to get the tube off his hand, I swear I felt . . .

'Of course, you can't wear them around the office. You'll need something more suitable.'

I lift my eyes to his and he's scowling at the t-shirt of Dove's like it's the first time he's ever seen it. I glance down. The front is covered in a large logo I don't recognise.

'Is it from one of her clients?' I ask, trying to decipher the image from my upside-down angle.

'No,' Rafael grunts. 'Thankfully.'

His brusque tone shuts down any further questions I might have asked.

'I can go home and change.'

He huffs. 'It'll take too long to get back to that place you live in.'

That *place* I live in? I hold back my scoff at the disgusted way he says it, like I inhabit a junkyard.

'We'll go out and get you something. We can make it back for my next meeting and take it in one of the conference rooms while maintenance dry out my office.'

'We'll go out?' I stare at him as he expertly fastens his tie in a perfect knot.

'We'll get you a dress or something. We can't take long. There won't be time for a fashion parade.' His lip curls into a slight sneer and I bite back any comeback I'd like to ram down his throat.

'Fine. But I can go by myself.'

He sits on a bench and puts on a pair of fancy shoes and ties the laces. 'Let's go,' he announces, standing and grabbing a new jacket from a hanger.

'I said I can go by myself,' I repeat, chasing after him as he strides out of the dressing room and back into his office, leaving behind a waft of his cologne in his wake.

'And I said, "*let's go*",' he says with a gravelly grunt like I'm testing his patience. 'My time is usually billed at three thousand pounds an hour, Aurora. I suggest you keep up.'

I balk at the back of his head as he strides into the hallway, reassuring the members of staff who ask about the alarm that maintenance is already handling it. Rushing to keep pace with him, I practically jog into the empty, waiting lift.

'There's a store at the end of the street that—'

'Huxton Atelier will have what we need,' he clips, cutting me off.

I clamp my lips together. Huxton Atelier stocks the style of clothes I used to love wearing. I can't even afford to look at their window displays now.

We exit into the lobby, and Rafael finally slows his pace enough that I can walk beside him without panting. The doorman holds the main door open for us and Rafael indicates for me to go first, before gesturing to a sleek black town car.

'Good morning, Mr Fairfax,' the driver greets, opening the back door. 'Good morning, Miss Thorne.'

'Good morning,' I reply, dumbstruck that he knows my name.

'Get in,' Rafael clips.

I do as he says, shuffling along the leather seat of the immaculate interior as Rafael slides in beside me and the driver closes the door.

'You have a driver?' I ask, watching the man walk around the car.

'I'm a busy man. I don't have time to wait on cabs, or . . . the Tube,' he says, flicking a cool gaze in my direction. 'I pay people to wait for me, so I never have to wait on them.'

The arrogant way he says it has one word pushing to the front of my brain. *Prick.* I can't believe I'm stuck in a car with him and his irritatingly mesmerising cologne. I only agreed to take notes in his meetings this afternoon because I hoped spending time with him might afford me the opportunity to find out when Dominic Ainsworth's next visit will be. What a waste.

Crossing my arms, I stare out of the window instead of making small talk with him. What's the point? He'll only use it as an opportunity to swing his dick around and tell me how rich he is, or how valuable his time is again.

'I'll be here once you're ready, Mr Fairfax,' his driver says after pulling up alongside a fancy storefront.

'Thank you, Kyle.' Rafael nods.

Kyle exits the car and is at the door moments later. Rafael climbs out and then offers his hand for me to take. I stare at it in horror.

'We've got fifteen minutes. I suggest you don't waste any by making yourself too comfortable in my backseat,' he snips.

I grab his hand, offering him a 'thanks' through gritted teeth. His fingers curl around mine and I hate how strong and confident his grip is. Like a man who knows he'll always get what he wants. I bet he's never been anxious over anything in his life.

The moment I'm out of the car I extract my hand from his.

'I'll be quick,' I say, making a beeline for the store.

I reach for the tall brass handle on the elegant door, but long fingers curl around it above mine. The heat from his body is like a force slamming into me from behind as he leans closer. His breath hits my temple as I incline my head over my shoulder.

'I'm not waiting in the car, Aurora.'

My stomach drops to my feet. I thought I was about to get space to breathe, but I should have known better. I search his darkened eyes as I scrabble to think of a reason why he should wait outside. 'Because I think you're an egotistical dickhead' probably won't go down well.

'Fine,' I say instead, letting him open the door for me.

The place is beautiful, and I can't stop the way my stomach dances as I admire the racks of beautiful new season designs.

Rafael's already got his phone to his ear on a business call, so I wander around, lovingly running my fingers along racks of silk, cashmere, and linen. I subtly check the price tags. My stomach knots. I can't afford a single thing in here.

'Excuse me.' I catch the attention of a sales assistant. 'Do you have a clearance rack? Or . . .' I give her a friendly smile. '. . . any damaged items?'

I can fix holes, remove stains. That doesn't bother me.

'Oh.' She looks taken aback by my question as her gaze flits to Rafael, who's pacing on the other side of the store. 'Of course. The sales items are over there.'

I leave her admiring Rafael and walk to the sales rack. There are some smart dresses in my size. Lifting one from the rack, I check the tag, and my stomach constricts like there's a whole tangle of knots inside it. Even at fifty per cent off, I'll still struggle to afford one.

'Try it on.'

I turn at his gruff voice, my fingers tightening around the hanger. 'I—'

Rafael extracts the hanger from my grip, his gaze dropping over the black dress with disinterest. 'Can you put this in a fitting room, please?' he says into thin air.

As if by magic, two sales assistants appear, throwing him dazzling smiles. 'Of course, Mr Fairfax.'

They whisk the dress away, and he's back on his phone on another call. He flicks his fingers at me in a shooing motion towards the fitting rooms.

I escape into them. Sliding the dress on, I fasten the gold zipper that runs from the hem all the way up to the base of my neck. Turning to the mirror, I smooth my hands over my hips.

And grin.

This. *This* is what I love about fashion. The way an outfit can make you feel. The dress is a simple fitted shift style, but the gold zipper on the back, and the way the fabric sits, accentuating every feminine curve, makes me feel both elegant and powerful.

I'll have to worry about how I'm going to pay for it after I get my credit card bill. And I can always re-sell it – I've been doing that with brand gifts for the last three months. It's the only way I can cover my rent.

Folding Dove's clothes, I carry them out of the fitting room. Rafael lifts his head, his gaze sliding over me from my feet to my head. He's on a call but tells them he'll call them back before pocketing his phone.

'You're going to wear it now? Let me remove the tag for you,' the sales assistant says.

'Thank you.'

Rafael watches as I smooth my hair away from my shoulder so she can gently snip out the eye-watering price tag.

'Ring it up, please. We need to leave,' he says gruffly, his eyes narrowing on me.

I feel like a bug under a microscope being scrutinised. No doubt he'll find fault. Deem me unworthy to grace the halls of his precious company, even in such a beautiful dress.

'Certainly, Mr Fairfax,' the sales assistant sings.

'Actually, before you do that,' he adds, causing her to freeze halfway to the checkout desk. 'Pencil skirts. Do you have any?'

'Yes,' the sales assistant replies brightly, beaming at him.

But his eyes are still burning into my dress. I knew it. He hates it. He's going to insist I buy something else. Something even more expensive.

I hug Dove's clothes to my chest like a shield.

'Show me,' he commands.

The sales assistant rushes about and plucks a selection of skirts from the full-priced rails.

'She'll take those too. All of them.'

'Of course. And what size would you like?' The sales assistant smiles, directing her question to him.

'Twelve. She's a twelve.'

The sales assistant nods and goes to switch the skirts for my size.

The fact he got my size right must be a lucky guess, but that's all the thought I can give to it as the sales assistant scans the skirts and bags them up. I wipe my sweaty palm on my dress.

'I can't . . .' I swallow, moving closer to Rafael, embarrassment spreading heat up my neck as I prepare to admit I can't afford them if I want to eat for the next two months.

'Put them on my account,' he instructs the sales assistant, sounding bored as he pulls his phone back out of his pocket and types something into it.

‘What?’ I squeak, lowering my voice so only he can hear. ‘Why are you paying for them?’

His lips curl down in a scowl. ‘It’s my money, either way.’

I have no idea what he means. I take the bag the sales assistant is holding out, thanking her.

‘I have a dress. I don’t need three skirts as well,’ I point out as we walk to the exit.

‘I’m replacing the one that got wet. That’s all.’

‘With three?’ I scoff. ‘Anyway, it’ll dry.’

‘Perhaps. But it could be ruined and rendered unwearable.’

‘So?’

‘So that would be a shame.’ He clears his throat. ‘A waste, I mean. That would be a waste.’

‘Why? It’s only a skirt.’

He opens the door for me, his eyes hard and impenetrable as he looks down his nose at me.

‘We’ve taken long enough. Let’s go.’

Chapter 14

Rafael

'How about the Leyton account? Did you get that one?'

I lean back on my office couch, urging the blood in my veins to cool to a simmer, instead of the inferno that's threatening to ravage through them.

'It's being handled,' I tell my father, keeping my voice calm and even. A hint of hesitation and he'll be on it like a shark with a drop of blood. Not that he has any need to be. The Leyton account *is* being handled. There's nothing for him to pick fault with. Yet I'm still tense to the point of discomfort as I wait for him to find something to criticise.

He leans forward in his seat opposite me, eyes of a brilliant and ruthless – albeit retired – businessman gleaming back at me.

'You made sure they signed? Got it all watertight?'

'Of course I did. I learnt from you, didn't I?'

'You did, son.' He smiles for the first time since he waltzed into my office, freshly back from another spiritual health retreat.

My mother told him when people retire their chance of a sudden death skyrockets unless they keep themselves busy. My father would have happily used it as a reason to return to the family business, but

Mum said she'd waited long enough to spend some quality time with him. It was bougie-sounding trips together, or divorce. And for all my father's bullish personality in business, with my mother he's a puppy dog. He adores the earth she walks on and insists he only ever worked as hard and as long as he did because he wanted to give her everything she dreamt of, and for his children to learn how to excel in life.

It doesn't stop him 'checking in' on me every chance he gets, though. My siblings escape his in-depth interrogations about the business because they're neither the eldest, nor the CEO.

'Rafe has it handled, Stan. Stop fussing,' my mother chides. 'They're all doing a great job. Have more faith.'

'Faith. Hm.' My father grunts at her word choice.

'I do love what the designers have done!' my mother exclaims brightly, looking around the room.

I press my lips tightly together, following her gaze, avoiding the giant windows to my left that show the view all the way from here to the Thames. Forty floors up, it's a view that costs millions. And it's one I loathe. If I had my way, the shades would be permanently closed. But not when my father's here. When he's here, they're wide open, despite the fact the view makes my stomach roil.

I can't give him any more reasons to think I'm incapable, or worse . . . *weak*.

'I fancied a change,' I say. I've had enough of seeing disappointment in my father's eyes. I don't need him to know my newly designer-renovated office is the consequence of a tube of crisps, and the urge to prove a certain infuriating blonde wrong.

I've not seen much of Aurora since the fire-alarm incident. I've been out of the office for much of the time, meeting with clients. She only has three weeks of her contract left, and I'm no closer to getting my money back.

My mother brings her hands together, the bangles on her wrists jangling. 'And how are things with you, darling? How's Seraphina?'

The hope in her eyes makes my gut churn. I'm used to my father being disappointed in me, but I'd do anything to keep that same look out of my mother's eyes. Do anything not to cause her pain. *Again.*

'Seraphina's busy being Seraphina,' I reply, keeping my tone non-committal.

My mother beams, and even my father joins in.

'It's incredible how well she's doing,' she continues. 'So wonderful to see intelligent women being celebrated for their achievements.'

'She's a very smart woman,' I agree.

'Indeed.' My mother's cheeks glow as she gives my father a knowing look. If I didn't love her so much then I'd scrape the hope straight from her face without hesitation.

'Harold says she's excited for the wedding,' my father says.

I shift forward in my seat. 'Wedding?'

'The Beaufort one,' my father adds. 'It's in South Africa, right?'

'That's right.' I look between the two of them as they exchange more knowing glances.

'Harold said you'd invited Seraphina,' Mum says.

My poker face comes into full play as I digest this news. I mentioned the wedding to Seraphina at dinner a couple of weeks ago, and she said she'd love to go with me if I needed a plus one. But I never accepted her offer. I was too busy watching Aurora across the room with her loser ex.

'Maybe you'll be coming home with your own news.' My father hitches both brows.

They've wanted nothing more than for me to get married and start producing grandchildren. My mother's made no secret of the fact she can't wait to do the whole bedtime story and baking cakes thing. And my father no doubt sees it as a second chance to this time successfully mould a miniature version of himself of whom he can actually be proud. But I've vowed never to get to that point with anyone. Dating, sex, it's all fine. Anything that keeps women at arm's length, where they won't cry over me if something were to happen with my—

'Ooh, yes!' my mother squeals excitedly. 'One of these days soon a woman will have your heart, darling. Mark my words.'

'Maybe.' My smile is tight. If she knew I hadn't so much as kissed Seraphina anywhere other than her cheek, I don't think she'd be looking so ready to dust off her wedding hat.

Movement in the corridor outside my office catches my attention. Aurora walks past with Steve from underwriting, her head tilted back, laughing at something he's said. I grind my teeth together and suck in a breath through my nose. Even the sight of the powder-blue pencil skirt I bought for her, artfully wrapped around her hips and arse, can't dowse the flare of outrage that seeing her *laughing* with him has brought.

'*You're angry with the world.*' That's what she told me. Her words that resulted in me getting my hand stuck in a bloody crisp tube in order to prove a point. She thinks she knows me. But if she's so bloody smart she'd know I'm not a man who's angry at the world. Why would I need to be when my anger is so much more effective when it's aimed towards myself instead?

Aurora Thorne has no idea of the lion's den she's walked into by working here. It's time I stopped allowing myself to become distracted by blue eyes and tight little skirts and start remembering what she did. I have two hundred and forty million reasons to remember. Who the hell cares if Bad Suit Steve makes her laugh? The only interest I have in her is vengeance. It's time to make her pay. The begging starts now. My dick stirs and I ignore it. The idea of her begging has become an obsession that's threatening to take over. To derail the one thing that actually matters.

My money. And finding out what happened to it.

Recovering my dented pride is the bow on the package. I'm not so pig-headed that I don't understand that it's also about that – my pride. Reaffirming to myself that I can do this. I can be the CEO Fairfax Guardian needs me to be after the colossal fuck-up I made in my early days. And making sure that my father never has a reason to look at me again like I'll be this firm's downfall.

Like I'm *weak*.

This stops now. An obsession for revenge is one thing, but an obsession with Aurora Thorne in general? That's just madness. I need to stop watching bloody fashion vlogs and wanking alone in my office like a sad loser. It's time I had actual sex again. With a woman I don't hate.

I turn my attention back to my parents, matching their smiles with one of my own.

'I'm looking forward to some time away with Seraphina. I'm sure she'll love Cape Town.'

Chapter 15

AURORA

'How are you?' I try to keep the anguish from my voice as I slide into the plastic chair opposite my father.

'Good. They've had me out gardening all week. We'll have the best veggies in the country at this rate.'

He smiles at me, his silvery stubble already beginning to show from where he's shaved.

'That's impressive. You didn't have a clue about growing anything before.' I laugh a little, but it trails off.

My father reaches for my hand, then stops himself, glancing at a guard. Physical contact is limited to arrival and departure only. His solicitor told us that we're fortunate because this place is low security. And my father's allowed to wear his own clothes and do things like gardening whilst he serves his sentence.

But I don't feel lucky.

Only seeing my father for ninety minutes once every weekend when visiting hours permit makes it feel like I'm serving the sentence with him. We manage phone calls during the week, but I used to live with him. I'd see him every day and eat dinner with him most evenings. It's always been him and me, with the occasional girlfriend of his sometimes, for as long as I can remember.

My father chuckles. 'You're right, I wouldn't. Not a green finger on these hands. Until now.' His eyes crinkle at the corners as he smiles. 'You need to stop worrying, sweetheart. Your old man's fine. I get three cooked meals a day here. I eat better than before. And bedtime's a thing – no more staying up late trudging through investment documents. No rat race in the mornings.' He opens his hands, palms upturned. 'Why, it's like being on holiday in here.'

I love him for trying to make light of this whole situation. For trying to make me feel better.

I roll my eyes with a smile. 'All right, fine. It's The Ritz.'

'Exactly.' He winks at me.

'I thought . . .' I reach down to my bag and pull out some paperwork I printed off to show my father. 'I thought we could take a look at these together. They're copies of things I asked your solicitor for.'

'How's Dove? Have you two been out much? You wanted to watch that new movie, didn't you? Did you go?' he deflects as I slide the papers across the table towards him.

I know he wants to avoid this, but I won't let him. I especially won't be drawn into a conversation about Dove. Because that would mean admitting to my father that I'm working temporarily at Fairfax Guardian. And he knows me well enough that one look into my eyes and he'll be able to tell that my motives for doing so are not completely pure. Although the way things are going, I'll be lucky to find out anything from Dominic Ainsworth, or my father's old firm. I haven't seen him visit the office once whilst I've been working there. No one's even mentioned his name. And Rafael is far too uptight to let anything about his personal friendships slip. I need to find a way to get him to loosen up and talk to me if I want to find out anything useful.

'Please, Dad,' I urge, noting his sigh and slumping shoulders. 'I'm not giving up on this, whether you like it or not.'

He sighs, smiling. 'Stubborn, just like your mother. Okay, show me what you've got.'

'Great.' I sit forward in my seat, energy brimming in my voice. 'So, these are two files that the prosecution tried to submit as evidence. One was a statement from an expert witness that supported your old firm's claims, which was seen by the judge. I still haven't got anything more on that yet because for some reason it's sealed. But the other one' – I tap the top sheet of paper with my finger – 'the other one I did manage to get hold of a copy. They weren't allowed to enter it as evidence because its authenticity was called into question.'

My father frowns as he reads the document.

I soften my voice. 'Did you know about this?'

He shakes his head. 'I had no idea.'

I let out a slow breath, relieved that my suspicions are confirmed.

'Apparently the woman left the company shortly after writing the email. She never sent it. They found it in her drafts. And none of the HR team knew a thing about it.'

'You found all of this out by yourself?' he asks, running a hand around his jaw as he reads.

I shrug. 'It's what I do when I'm not working. Even more so now that Charlie and I broke up.'

My father puts the paper down and looks at me. 'You okay?'

'More than okay. He was . . .' The look in Charlie's eyes as he called me a 'stuck-up bitch' at the restaurant and acted like any connection to me or my father would tarnish his reputation still stings. But not because I miss him. Because I'm angry that I wasted so much time on a man like that. 'He was an idiot. I'm better off single,' I finish.

My father pushes the papers back towards me.

'I don't want you spending your time on this, Rory. You're young. You should be out enjoying yourself with your friends.'

I bite my lower lip, not wanting to admit that only Dove has stood by me through all this. Any other 'friends' slowly distanced themselves from me after my father was found guilty.

'But you're innocent, Dad. You shouldn't be in here.' My vision blurs, tears gathering along my lower lashes.

'Hey,' he coos. 'Don't go getting upset. It's not so bad. I'll be out before you know it. And maybe soon they'll let me apply for that day release thing.'

'Release on temporary licence,' I mumble, swiping at my eyes. I know all about it. I've looked up everything I can about my father's time here. But he won't be in with a chance of being granted it until the final few months of his sentence. That's still years away.

'That's it.' He smiles. 'I'll be out and growing my own veggies for you before you know it. Might even learn how to cook them.'

I laugh through my tears, and he winks at me again, making my heart swell with how much I miss seeing him every day. I live for the weekends. For these precious minutes.

'Sounds good, Dad.'

Chapter 16

Rafael

'Your turn next, hey?'

I take my eyes from Seraphina, where she's talking to another wedding guest on the other side of the outdoor terrace.

'I don't think so,' I reply, knocking back my gin and tonic and signalling to the bartender for another.

'You sure about that?' Jenson, a baby-faced member of the Beaufort's security team, quips from further along the bar, where he's nursing a glass of something dark with his colleague, Killian. The two guys are off duty, invited as guests instead of in a professional capacity, but Killian's eyes still drift to the stand-in security team who are dotted around Sterling Beaufort's beach house, where Sullivan's wedding is being held.

'Positive,' I reply grimly, running my tongue over the edge of my teeth as Seraphina moves through the sea of guests, swaying her hips in her tight red dress.

She's head of department at a successful advertising firm. She's smart and beautiful and can hold a conversation. But the second we stepped on to my private jet, I realised I'd made a grave error. London to Cape Town is more than eleven hours' flight time. She spent every available minute informing me of the kind of wedding she's dreamt of, and asking where I'd want to honeymoon.

Then she started hinting how fun it would be to join the mile high club.

My dick's lack of reaction told me everything I needed to know.

I won't be breaking my abstinence anytime soon.

At least, not with her.

'I don't know, man. A woman like your date looks like she'd need a ring on her finger if you want to keep hold of her.' Jenson whistles, admiring Seraphina in a way that should make me want to smack him in the jaw. But I feel nothing.

She approaches, giving me an assessing smile as she stops so close to me that her breasts brush against the front of my shirt.

'How's your head?' she asks, reaching past me and lifting my drink off the bar and bringing it to her lips. She sips it, watching me over the rim.

'Still pounding,' I lie.

'Poor baby,' she hums, reaching up and cupping my cheek. 'Maybe you need to go and lie down.'

My shoulders bunch with tension as she leans even closer, pressing the length of her body against mine.

'Come on. Why don't we go and get you settled in bed?'

I step back, shrugging off her touch. 'I'm fine. The fresh air is helping.'

Her eyes narrow and she huffs. 'You don't have a headache, do you? Is it to do with that girl?' She hitches her brows at me impatiently, pressing for an answer.

'What girl?' I ask, feigning ignorance.

'The one you were talking to on the plane?'

'I told you, I wasn't talking to anyone.'

My headache might have been fabricated as a means to decline her invitation to join her in the plane's bedroom for some in-flight entertainment, but I'm being honest when I say I wasn't talking to anyone. I was *watching* someone. A certain blonde who's dug herself so far under my skin that even six thousand miles isn't far enough away to stop her hijacking my thoughts.

I could have ignored Seraphina's constant wedding talk for a good fuck, but my dick didn't want to know. The moment she went to sleep in the plane's bedroom, I found myself searching for Aurora's videos as an experiment.

My dick was hard and leaking before the video reached a play time of ten seconds.

So, it's official.

I can't get a hard-on for any other woman.

Only Aurora bloody Thorne.

'I don't believe you,' Seraphina snaps, drawing attention from a few guests close by. 'Show me your call history.'

'What?' I balk at her. 'I'm not doing that.'

She throws her hands up in the air. 'Then you're hiding it because I'm right.'

'I wasn't talking to anyone,' I hiss, hating that she's turning us into a spectacle.

'You know, I was warned about you. Rafael Fairfax, the serial bachelor. But I thought I'd give you the benefit of the doubt. You seemed like a decent guy on our dates. I didn't have you down as a conman, playing me for a fool.'

'Conman?' I seethe. 'I'm not a bloody criminal, Seraphina.'

She purses her lips. 'Hardly trustworthy, though, are you? If you don't have anything to hide, you'll show me your phone.'

Heat flares up the back of my neck, bringing with it an unwavering compulsion to prove her wrong. I'm not a goddamn criminal. Not like people who steal millions of pounds from the company they work for.

Blood pounds in my ears as I rip my phone from my pocket, unlock it, and thrust it at her.

'You want to check. Go ahead. The last person I called was my brother about some cybersecurity upgrades we're making. And before that it was a client who makes rocket engines. And before that it was my mother. In fact, the only women you'll find I've called on that phone in the last week are my mother, my sister, or two female CEOs whose business we insure. And they're both married . . . to each other!' I snap.

Seraphina narrows her eyes, and I hold my hand out, expecting her to return my phone to me. But instead, she twists her lips and scrolls through it. My gut tightens as she opens up my internet app, and Aurora's smiling face fills the screen. The caption across it reads, 'Cute Swimwear for the Perfect Beach Break'.

Seraphina's brow wrinkles as she presses 'play' and listens to Aurora's bubbly commentary spilling from the video as she showcases the pale blue bikini she's wearing.

She doesn't do swimwear videos. It's the first she's ever filmed.

I drink her in, watching the way she moves on screen. The way her fingers skate over the skin either side of her belly button as she talks about the cut of the bikini bottoms. The way she shivers and goosebumps prick up along her arms like a breeze has blown on her as she's filmed.

I lick my lips, my dick stirring to life.

Seraphina shoves my phone into my chest.

'She looks about twenty-two. And you're what? Forty next? For God's sake, Rafe. You're a walking cliché. Is this what you do? Get off to young women rather than get into a relationship with a woman your own age?'

'She's twenty-five,' I snap, making Seraphina's eyes widen.

'Oh God, it gets better. You've googled her. Fed into your pathetic fantasy. You've . . .'

Her mouth drops open suddenly, and she stares at me.

'Wait . . . she's the girl we saw at the restaurant. The one fighting with her boyfriend.'

I don't make it any worse by trying to deny it.

'Her name's Aurora. She's a friend of Dove's.'

Seraphina reels back. 'Oh my God. You're ridiculous. I can't believe I came here with you.'

'It's nothing. I don't even like the girl.'

I don't know why I'm bothering to try to explain.

'Does your sister know you watch videos of her friend?' she sneers.

My jaw hardens, 'Now, wait a minute. It's not—'

'Not what? Not like that?' She scoffs. 'So, you're telling me that if I call up your sister right now then she'll be perfectly fine with you watching her friend's videos in secret?'

I stay silent, and she snorts. 'To think I wasted time on you, believing you were actually one of the good guys, when you're just an insecure man lusting after a woman who you shouldn't even be looking at.'

She spins and every drop of blood in my body vibrates with pent-up anger. No one makes me this angry. No one except . . .

'Aurora!' I snap. 'Don't walk away from me.'

Seraphina turns and pins me with a dark, menacing glare. 'Excuse me?'

I stare back at her, forcing myself to breathe slowly through my nose. How the hell am I so stupid? I've never called a woman the wrong name in my life. Even when I've forgotten their name.

Jesus Christ.

'You know what?' Seraphina says. 'You deserve this and more.'

She grabs my glass off the bar and hurls the contents into my face. An ice cube cracks me on the nose.

She slams the empty glass down on the bar. 'I'll get my own flight home.'

Storming off through the guests, she attracts more than a few curious glances.

'Ah, bloody hell,' I hiss, turning back to the bar.

'Here you go, buddy.' Killian hands me a towel he's got from the bartender.

'Thanks,' I grunt, wiping my face.

'Sister's friend, hey? I reckon you might have more of that coming if she finds out,' Jenson says.

He chuckles as I toss the towel on to the bar.

'I need another drink,' I rasp, not wanting to think about how accurate he might be if Dove were to realise I have my own private stash of every video Aurora's ever made.

Forget workaholic, she'll discover I'm a goddamn wankaholic. A bloody fiend. Unable to stop bashing one out at every opportunity.

I should be disgusted at myself.

I *should.*

But fuck, the only thing I can think about – the only thing that would make me feel better right now – is if Aurora bloody Thorne was kneeling at my feet. And if I was feeding her my cock and making her gag on it.

She's Dove's friend.

I don't even like her.

She's a goddamn thief.

I scrub a hand around my jaw, letting out a low curse.

What the hell's wrong with me?

Killian claps me on the back. 'Get the poor guy another drink,' he says to the bartender. 'He looks like he needs it.'

Chapter 17

Aurora

The office is blissfully quiet when I arrive at 7 a.m. It won't be like this for long. The first people will start arriving soon, along with Rafael.

I huff as I approach the staff room. With any luck he'll be out at client meetings today and I won't have to see him. I head to the new coffee machine that's been installed and grab a mug.

'Ugh, seriously?'

The empty bean container taunts me.

I knew I should have picked up a coffee on the way in. I was too occupied thinking about Freddie's owner, Kate, and what she must be going through since I found something I wasn't supposed to in the coat pocket of her dry cleaning I collected yesterday. I've never met her husband face-to-face, but from all of their photos around the house they look like they have the picture-perfect life. What was it Rafael said? '*Loaded people have loaded secrets?*' Turns out, he's right about something.

I drum my fingers around the empty mug. Rafael usually has fresh beans in his office beside his coffee machine.

Hesitation swirls in my gut, but the need for caffeine quickly outweighs it.

He won't know if I borrow a few beans. And even if he realises, the guy's an arse, but he isn't going to begrudge me for wanting to start the day with a coffee. Or maybe he will. But I'm prepared to take that risk.

I head to his office, relieved to find it empty with the door open. The coffee machine is on a fancy sideboard on the far side of the room by the dressing-room door, so I cross the newly laid carpet quickly and glance around to check I'm still alone before I flick the machine on and place my mug underneath it.

'*Jesus Christ.*'

The muffled words come from inside the dressing area. A crack of light spills out from beneath the wood.

'Fuucckk.' Another drawn-out groan rumbles from behind the door.

Oh my God. There's no mistaking it's Rafael. He sounds like he's in pain. What if he's slipped in the bathroom and hit his head? It's earlier than he usually arrives. What if he's been in there all night, waiting for someone to find him?

I can't stand the man, but I don't wish him to meet a grisly end on his bathroom floor alone, either.

My heart flies to my throat as I rush to the partially closed door and ease it open carefully in case he's lying behind it. I get it far enough to poke my head through before I look inside.

He's not on the floor. Or inside the walk-in wardrobe area.

But the inner door to the bathroom is wide open.

I freeze.

Rafael's standing stark-bollock naked in front of the marble basin, one hand gripping the edge of the counter like he's about to rip it off the wall. And the other . . .

. . . the other is furiously working his dick.

'Bloody hell,' he hisses like he's angry.

I suck in a gasp. The solid, carved muscles that are usually concealed beneath his suit fill my eyes.

I can't look away.

He's huge, and solid, and . . . so *obnoxiously* handsome.

He's an arsehole.

A hot, sexy arsehole who's masturbating with such vigour that it's as if his life depends upon it.

His bicep bulges as he tightens his grip on his dick, adding his hips into the fray, and thrusting into his palm with determined jerks. His ass cheeks clench, two solid globes of marble as he fists his dick so fast and hard that it looks painful.

'Just once,' he groans. 'I need to be inside you. *Just. Once.*'

I can't breathe, let alone move. He's no more than a few metres away. Close enough that the wet sounds coming from his dick as he attacks it curl through the air like they're coaxing me closer. Inviting me to watch.

He curses and swipes his phone, turning the volume up on what he's watching, then props it against the mirror over the basin.

My mouth goes dry, and I squeeze my thighs together, hating that my panties are damp.

I don't even like him. I certainly don't want to watch him get himself off to porn.

But I can't deny he's the most beautiful man I've ever seen. My head might hate him, but my body's not immune to the sight.

Everything about Rafael Fairfax is so . . . *virile*. From his thick, rich brown hair, to the sharp jaw he's currently clenching as he breathes out in a jagged hiss. To his giant shoulders, and the smattering of dark, silky hair decorating his pecs. Even his torso is thick. He's pure muscle. I'd ache if I had to wrap my legs around his waist.

Not that I'd ever want to. Not in a million years.

He grunts, his bitcable arse tensing as a female voice flits out from his phone.

'The sweetheart neckline on this is so pretty. And if you look closely, it's got this beautiful, embroidered detailing.'

That sounds like . . .

Bile rushes up my windpipe and blood rushes in my ears. I stare at his phone, trying to focus on the screen. It's too far to see properly, but the moment she speaks again, I suck back a gasp.

That's *my* voice.

It's the video I uploaded last night.

How would that even come up on Rafael's phone? I'm so specific about how I advertise my vlog. There's no way one of my videos would have made its way on to the ads banner on a porn site.

Oh my God, this is mortifying. Maybe he'll think I'm affiliated to the site or—

'Fuck, yes,' he rasps, eyes glued to his phone.

The urgency with which he's stroking his dick doesn't cease. He doesn't break pace. He doesn't even seem surprised, or bothered, that my video has appeared. He just keeps touching that giant, angry-looking dick of his with quickening strokes.

I need to back out slowly and pretend I was never here. I will my feet to move, but they're glued in place like I'm standing in cement.

'Aurora,' he hisses.

Oh, shit.

My heart stalls, steeling itself for the wrath he's about to deliver for me being in his personal space and spying on him, and—

'That's it,' he groans, working his dick so fast there should be smoke coming off it.

His eyes are still pinned to his phone. His entire torso expands as every muscle in it swells and goes rigid.

My pulse thunders. In my chest. In my ears. My fingertips. My *clit.*

He wasn't talking to me.

He hasn't noticed me.

His teeth clench and he slams a flattened palm down on the counter like he's livid.

'Aurora,' he growls like I'm right in front of him and he's chastising me for something I've done.

His lower abs flex, and his jaw goes slack.

Then cum fires from the end of his cock with force.

'Jesus Christ.'

He grunts as it lands heavily, splattering all over my image on his phone.

'Uh, yeah,' he groans, fisting harder and aiming the head of his cock at his phone as though he wants to cover it in cum.

My voice chirps out happily as I say something about hemlines, and he shudders as a new wave seems to overtake him.

More glistening liquid fires over the counter and shoots across the mirror before his shoulders soften. He keeps stroking, the desperation gone and making way for a rich groan of satisfaction as he sinks his teeth into his lower lip. He squeezes up his shaft slowly, encouraging the last drops out from the end of his dick. They leave a trail from the slit on his crown to the shiny marble beneath before it breaks and he drops his head back.

He closes his eyes, dragging in a deep breath. A look of bliss settles over his face as my video continues playing in the background, filling the air with my voice.

If I stay here a second longer the chance of him catching me . . . *watching* him increases.

And there's no way in hell I want that to happen.

What I just saw I . . . God, I can't even begin to make sense of it.

My heart thuds against my ribs as I back away.

Rafael's head is still tipped back, his eyes are still closed . . . and his hand is still on his thick, semi-hard cock as I turn and flee from his office as quietly as I can.

'Why don't you take a break and grab a coffee?' Gabriel suggests.

'Oh, um, thanks. Do you want one?' I ask.

'I'm good.'

He bends down to scoop up a meowing Benedict, who's rubbing himself around his legs. I'm going to have to ask Dove what the deal with his cat is. I'm sure Dove said he rescued him from somewhere. The way he dotes on Benedict is sweet. He doesn't baby him, but instead talks to him like he's talking to a business partner, explaining all the cyber-stuff he's doing. I don't understand half of what I've overheard him saying.

'Okay. I'll not be long,' I tell them both, already used to addressing Benedict as well because he's constantly glued to Gabriel's side.

'Take your time. We have some things to check on,' Gabriel answers, spinning his chair back to face his desktop computer. His fingers are already flying over the keys at lightning speed whilst Benedict sits comfortably in his lap when I leave his office.

Heading in the direction of the staff lounge, I can't prevent my steps from slowing as I near Rafael's office. The door is wide open, and his rich, deep voice is floating out whilst he talks on the phone.

I never thought about the huskiness of his voice before. The way it's rough enough to send a shiver up your spine and set your pulse racing.

The way it sounded when he growled my name.

Walking past the door, I'm unable to resist peeking inside. He's sitting at his desk, reclined in his chair, phone glued to his ear, and one ankle resting on top of his other leg. The pose screams arrogant, big-dick energy.

I don't turn away fast enough, and he catches me looking. His eyes heat before he drags his gaze down and back up my body with an entitled air, like I'm *his*.

I hate that my pulse quickens and my cheeks heat. I *hate* it.

But what I hate most is the way my nipples stiffen against the thin silk of my blouse at the exact moment Rafael looks at them. Like they're doing it because of him. Like it's all *for him*.

I tear my gaze away and stride down the corridor.

'Get a grip,' I mutter under my breath.

I need to shake off the weird feeling I've been having since I saw him in his office bathroom this morning.

He was watching *my* video. He was groaning *my* name. He came all over his phone. He *wanted* to watch it. It wasn't a mistake. That much is clear, the more I've thought about it.

Rafael Fairfax has my videos in his wank bank.

And I have no idea why.

Neither of us has made a secret of the fact we'd rather stick pins in our eyes than spend unnecessary time in one another's company. I'll never forget the comments he made about my father. Maybe that's what this is to him – a perverse power play. Perhaps he laughs behind my back when I look at him, all innocent, with no idea about the sordid little sexual fantasies he might have had me acting out in his imagination with that stupid giant dick of his.

But I'm not oblivious any more. I'm not going to do nothing. I'm going to use Rafael Fairfax's secret to my advantage.

I've been unable to concentrate on anything except how I can do it. No wonder Gabriel told me to take as long as I want on a break. I'm too preoccupied to be useful. To him, at least. But to my father . . . to him I might finally be able to get somewhere.

I've been approaching it wrong, waiting for an opportunity to find out something that could help me. Hoping that Dominic Ainsworth might visit so that I can ask him about the client my father had started working on just before he was arrested. But I need to *create* an opportunity. I need to distract Rafael so that he's not paying attention to what I'm asking him. If he and Dominic are as close as I'm led to believe, then maybe Dominic's mentioned this client, or told Rafael something useful. And if he has, I need to find out exactly what that something is. I need him to be so consumed that his brain doesn't register that he's telling me exactly what I need to know.

I'd rather kiss roadkill than flirt with Rafael Fairfax.

But sometimes we have to do things that make our skin crawl in order to survive.

And I don't just want my father to survive in prison.

I want him free.

Chapter 18

Rafael

There's a knock at my office door.

'Come in!' I call, tapping out the final line of my email and hitting 'send'.

'Do you have a minute?'

I glance up. Aurora's hovering by the door.

'You need me?' I ask.

She straightens her shoulders. 'I do,' she says, fluttering her eyelashes at me.

I stare at her for a moment, trying to figure out her angle. She gazes back, attempting to look friendly. But I can still see it – her derision for me, thinly veiled behind another flutter of lashes and a soft, forced smile.

The back of my neck heats as her gaze turns knowing . . . accusing. Like she's the one in control here. But if there's one thing she needs to learn about me, it's that I will always be the one in control when it comes to her.

'I've always got time for you, Aurora,' I say smoothly, injecting warmth into my tone.

Amusement dances in my chest as she falters and a flush creeps across her décolletage.

I've never been so welcoming towards her before.

But I've also never found her coffee mug, complete with a trace of her lipstick on the rim, underneath my coffee machine first thing in the morning, either.

The sight of it posed one question in my mind.

How much did she see and hear?

'Oh . . . good. Um, thank you,' she says, keeping hold of the door handle like it will offer her support.

The blush creeps into her cheeks.

And now I know.

The little minx heard enough. Perhaps she even stayed and watched the entire show. Because now, here she is, in my office, an extra button unfastened on her blouse, trying her best to act as if she doesn't despise me.

It's almost too good to believe.

She wants something. And she thinks that by catching me *enjoying* her video, she has a chance of getting it. But she's mistaking basic carnal desire for something else entirely. Something that would result in me actually *wanting* to help her.

And she's about to be sorely disappointed, because as easily as I can shoot my load thinking about Aurora Thorne, I can just as easily pass her in the street without blinking.

But still, seeing whatever little charade she has planned will be fun.

'Of course,' I say.

She hesitates, smoothing the front of her blouse, which only pulls it tighter over her breasts, highlighting the curve of them beneath the fabric.

Those perfect little breasts that would fill my palms.

My dick throbs at the memory of this morning's video, and that cute top she was wearing. The one that hugged them perfectly. That was a good video. A new favourite I'll no doubt watch again later.

'Take a seat.' I gesture to the chair on the other side of my desk.

She glances back out into the hallway, like she's questioning if she should be here. But then she steps inside, closes the door and walks to my desk.

'Your office is lovely,' she says, her pulse fluttering in her neck.

'I take pleasure from lovely things,' I reply, leaning back in my chair.

She flicks her eyes to mine. 'The view especially, it's stunning. You can see so much from this high up.'

I keep my chair pointing forward, refusing to turn it towards the wall of windows behind me. I'd much rather look at her getting all flustered.

Her eyes dart back to mine as I let the silence stretch. 'I just thought I'd come and thank you again for the opportunity to work here. I'm enjoying it.'

'You are?'

She nods, then walks to the edge of my desk, her steps clumsy and uncoordinated.

I rest my elbow on the arm of my chair and lift my thumb to my lips. I swipe it over the lower one as she rounds the side of my desk and comes to stand beside my seat, resting her pencil-skirt-clad arse against the desk.

'Yeah, really enjoying it,' she says, wrapping her fingers around the edge of the desk and leaning back a little.

The position is a flirtatious one, there's no doubt about it. And my dick thickens in my trousers as I allow myself a slow sweep of her body.

She shivers under my scrutiny, but I'll give it to her, she holds her nerve as I take my time drinking in her curves, making no attempt to hide the fact I'm eye-fucking her.

Her eyes are expectant the moment I lift them to her face.

'You came in here to thank me for giving you the position?'

'I did,' she replies, her voice coming out breathy.

'I do appreciate gratitude,' I rasp, loving the way the blush in her cheeks has deepened.

She looks away quickly. 'Um, maybe I could buy you lunch as a thank you? Unless you already have plans, that is? Gabriel said you might be having it with a friend, Dominic Ashworth?'

'Dominic *Ainsworth*?' I correct.

'Oh, is that his name?' She blinks innocently.

I smirk internally, applauding her for her acting. So that's what she's after. Dominic. The innocent act might work on others who just see a pretty face, but I know a determined gleam when I see it. And Dove's let slip before about how hellbent Aurora is on appealing her father's conviction.

The question is, how far will she go to get what she wants?

I always fantasied about her begging for my forgiveness.

But I never considered her begging me for help.

'It is. He's an old friend. We go way back,' I tell her, tilting my head and noting the way her eyes light up.

I hide a smile. I don't want to make it obvious that I'm on to her little ploy. Especially when there's nothing for her to learn from me, or Dominic. But I could use this to my advantage. Maybe if I play my cards right, I might learn where my money is.

'Really? That must be nice. I bet you know all sorts about one another,' she says, trying to sound casual, but I can see the desperation in her eyes.

'Pretty sure I've seen every skeleton in Dom's closet,' I say.

He knows all of mine too, of course, but there's no way in hell I'm telling Aurora that.

'Wow, really?' She inches closer along the desk until her leg brushes my knee. She fights to school her reaction, but there's no mistaking the small intake of air passing her lips as we touch.

I keep my leg in place, allowing hers to rest against it.

'My father met him years ago through business. Dominic knew them back when my mother had her accident.'

Aurora's gaze shoots up from where my knee is touching her leg, and her brow wrinkles.

'The one where—'

'We both almost died because she was pregnant with me at the time? Yes, that one.'

A look of genuine concern crosses her face. 'Dove told me. It sounded awful. That's why your mum called you Rafael, isn't it?'

I study her. She's watching me, an eager curiosity in her eyes despite it no longer being Dominic we're talking about. Perhaps she thinks getting me to share something personal with her is the start to getting me to tell her whatever else she wants to know.

'It is,' I reply, deciding to toy with her, lull her into a false sense of security, to think we're sharing a moment. She might think she can find out something that'll aid her crook of a father, but she won't. Because George Thorne is a guilty son of a bitch. He stole from his company. He stole from me.

I spread my thighs, pushing my leg harder against hers. Her fingers tighten around the edge of my desk, but she doesn't move away.

'My mother believes her guardian angel was looking over us that day. And that it's the reason she walked away with barely more than a scratch, when our car, on the other hand, was reduced to a mangled wreck. It's why she gave us all angel names. Except Dove. My brothers and I made her sick throughout her pregnancy. But Dove didn't. Her "little slice of calm", she said.'

A soft smile tilts Aurora's lips. 'I was the opposite. Apparently, my mum had morning sickness the entire time.'

She looks at me and I ignore the sudden pang in my chest at the sadness in her eyes. Dove told me Aurora's mother died from complications shortly after giving birth to her. But I shut down the surge of sympathy; she's not going to get me falling for her innocent act.

We're silent for a few moments before Aurora clears her throat. 'So, do you? Have plans for lunch?'

'I'm not meeting with Dominic today.'

Her face falls and I make a show of checking my watch.

'But I am expecting a call from him soon, now that you mention him.'

'Oh. Should I go?' she asks, her voice lifting a little like there's the offer of something else at the end of her sentence.

I shake my head. 'No. You should stay right here.'

She bites her lower lip and gently moves her leg so it brushes along my thigh. 'Okay, um—'

My phone rings with perfect timing, and I could kiss Dominic for always being such a punctual bastard.

'Dom?' I answer cheerfully after bringing it to my ear. 'I was just talking about you.'

Aurora's eyes widen and she pales like she might be sick.

'Should I be concerned?' he chuckles.

'Of course not,' I answer, holding Aurora's eyes, knowing she can't hear him on the other end.

'Listen, it's just a quick call. I wanted to check if you're up for golf with Hillingdon on his course?'

I purse my lips, mulling over the idea, even though I already know my answer. So many of these CEOs want to do business on the golf course, or over a poker game. I'd rather do it in my own meeting room. But this is business, and if Fairfax Guardian want to keep landing the big clients, then we need to be prepared to accommodate them.

Sourness coats my tongue, because I know first-hand what can happen when we don't. It can risk the entire business. And that cannot be allowed to happen.

Lifting my eyes back to Aurora, she's listening intently.

'Absolutely. One second,' I tell him, reaching around Aurora and grabbing a pad and my pen from beside her. 'Did he seem interested in our quote, then?' I ask Dom.

Aurora sucks in a little breath as I draw back, and the back of my hand grazes the front of her skirt.

'After he called you an up-yourself twat, yes.'

I smile. Hillingdon, a sportswear mogul who needs insurance following a suspicious fire at one of his factories where some employees were injured. He wants to keep it out of the press, and I want to make Fairfax Guardian money.

Desperation attracts a higher premium.

'Give me the details. I'll look forward to beating his arse on the course before I take his money,' I tell Dom.

I take the lid off my pen and write something on the pad, keeping it angled away from her. I'm not even listening to Dominic any more as I place the pad face down on my desk.

'I'll see you then,' I murmur in response to his instructions about when and where to meet him. He's a good friend to have, both in life and in business. He sends as much business our way as we send his.

It's win-win.

I end the call and place the cap back on my pen.

'How was he?' Aurora asks, her gaze boring into the upturned notepad.

I bite the inside of my cheek to stop myself from chuckling. She has the subtlety of one of Benedict's farts after he's gorged himself on the special brand of tinned salmon that Gabriel insists on buying him.

I hold the pen, running my thumb up and down its smooth surface. 'He's having some issues, nothing major,' I say, studying her reaction.

'Oh really? What kind?'

She inches a little closer, reaching up to toy with her necklace so my eyes are drawn to the opening of her blouse and her smooth, bare skin.

'Why did you really come into my office, Aurora?'

She drops her necklace like it's on fire. 'I told you. I came to say thank you.'

I lean back again and study her. Liar. Just like when she told the authorities she didn't know where her father put the money. When she insisted that he was innocent.

'Sit on the desk,' I growl.

'What?' Her eyes widen.

I lick my lips, dropping my attention back to her blouse and the hint of lace bra that's visible through it.

She thinks she can come into my office like this, bat her eyelashes at me a little, and what? I'll tell her something that'll re-write history and save her criminal of a father from facing his time? She's deluded.

But it'll still be fun to see how far Daddy's little princess is willing to go. She's spent long enough playing with me. It's time I played back.

'Sit on my desk,' I repeat, dragging my eyes up her chest to her face.

Her cheeks are pink, but there's a flash of determination in her eyes as she hitches one hip in preparation for sliding herself up on to the desk.

'Not there. Here.'

I push my chair back just enough that there's a space in front of me.

I can practically hear the nervous thud of her heart as she hesitates, before squeezing into the gap, and slowly lifting herself on to my desk.

For a second I just soak her in, sitting there in her tight little pencil skirt and silky blouse, blond hair pulled up into a high ponytail, begging me to wrap it inside my fist.

I could fuck that little pretty mouth. Stuff it so full she couldn't spout any more lies.

She fidgets and I pull my chair even closer until her legs are practically in my lap.

'Are you uncomfortable?' I say, a perverse satisfaction rumbling in my chest as she shakes her head and lies to my face. Again.

'No. Of course not. It's nice talking to you.'

The look on her face is akin to someone being told they'll need a rectal exam with a barbed-wire glove. She might be a terrible liar, but she's also a terrible flirt. The latter brings a sense of calm to me. She's obviously never tried doing this to get what she wants before. I like that I'm the first man she's done this to. That I'm the *only* man she's ever done this to.

'I'm enjoying myself too,' I tell her, watching her reaction.

She brushes away imaginary lint from her skirt.

'Sit still, Aurora,' I instruct, a quiet bite in my tone.

She sucks in a breath, and her aquamarine eyes dart up to meet mine. I drink them in. The innocence that I know isn't to be believed. The sheer beauty of them. A weaker man would fall for it. But when it comes to her, I know all of her expressions.

I know all of this is her pretending.

'Quite the little wriggler, aren't you?' I muse.

She blushes and a flicker of something I've never seen in her eyes before comes to life.

Heat, mixed with denial.

Well, I'll be damned. *She likes this.* She might not want to admit it to herself, but it's in her eyes and the pink of her cheeks. Not to mention the way her nipples have stiffened into little suckable peaks and are pointing at me through her shirt, fighting for my attention.

She doesn't just like this, she's turned on by it.

I lick my lips and hold my pen up between my fingers for a few seconds until I know she's watching. Then I slowly bring the end down, making contact with the bare skin on her kneecap.

'You're the first woman to ever sit on my desk,' I say, sliding the capped end of my pen down the front of her shin.

She sucks in a little gasp, and I pause, looking at her from beneath my brows.

'You like that?'

Her eyelids hood as I run the pen down to her ankle.

'No . . . Y-yes,' she breathes, her brow knotting in confusion at her confession.

Her breathing quickens as I repeat the move on the other leg. I study her face the entire time. Study the way her lashes flutter, until she finally gives in and closes her eyes, tilting her head back a fraction and surrendering herself to the sensation against her skin.

My dick's hardened to the point of pain in my trousers, and I adjust myself while her eyes are closed, my attention glued to her chest rising and falling with laboured breaths.

'I . . .' She swallows.

I don't give her time to make up an excuse. To say something to end the moment. She walked in here looking for something. And I intend to show her just what she's going to get if she thinks she can play me.

Reaching forward, I take hold of her feet, lifting them until I can bring each of her high heels down on to the armrests of my chair.

She snaps her eyes open in shock.

I hold her eyes as I drag my chair forward. The move causes her skirt to rise up her thighs as they're pushed wider. It's a filthy angle that places me inches from her exposed white lace panties.

'That's better,' I purr.

Leisurely, I lower my eyes to between her thighs, making a show of admiring what I see.

'Do you want to leave?' I ask, eyes glued to her lace-covered pussy.

She pauses, before her breathy answer has me licking my lips. 'No.'

'Good.' I lift my eyes to her face and inhale slowly, purposefully. Her cheeks flare bright pink. Because she *knows* which scent has just reached my nostrils.

Hers.

She's wearing her arousal like a goddamn perfume.

I narrow my eyes at her, and she stares back, her lower lip quivering.

She walked in here pretending, but there's no mistaking the scent of real, hot and needy arousal that's seeping through the dampened lace of her panties like an enchantment calling my name.

'Rafael,' she whispers, shaking her head slightly like she's telling me to stop.

'Aurora,' I counter huskily, loving the way her arse jumps off the desk as I place the end of my pen behind her knee.

I run it up her inner thigh with painstaking slowness until I reach the edge of white lace. Aurora sucks in a sharp breath as I trace the tip over the patch of fabric that's darkened in colour from her wetness. I roll my wrist, teasing her clit beneath the damp fabric.

'S-stop,' she whispers.

I drag the pen lower until it meets the dip of her entrance. The fabric is even darker. *Soaked.*

'You want me to stop?' I halt, but keep my pen pressed against her, watching the way her pussy lips fit snuggly around it like they're trying to suck it inside.

It could be my tongue in its place. *My cock.*

'I don't . . . I don't know,' she whimpers, screwing her eyes closed and shutting me out.

I reach down and give my dick a squeeze, before pressing a little harder with my pen. The fabric only allows me so far, so I move it back to her clit instead, stroking in deliberate circles.

Never in my life did I think when I woke up this morning that I'd have Aurora Thorne spread out on my desk, her pink, manicured nails gripping the edge of it as I played with her cunt with my pen.

Her scent intensifies and my mouth waters. What I'd give for one taste. One touch. And to hear her moan as I push inside her for the first time and make her stretch around my cock.

I stroke faster, mesmerised by the way the hints of pussy lips I can see either side of the white lace are flushed with blood as I push her closer to the edge.

'How about you stop overthinking, and let me make you come?' I growl.

'Oh my God,' she gasps, so quietly, like she doesn't want me to hear. Like she's saying it to herself. Trying to reason with herself. Asking herself why she's enjoying the man she thinks is an arsehole rubbing her needy little clit through her soaked panties.

'I know you don't like me, Aurora,' I say, rubbing more determinedly with my pen. 'And despite what you think you know about me, I don't care much for you, either. But it would make the sex between us even better, don't you think? I know your ex never made you come.'

'What?' She jerks up, her eyes flying open like she's realised where she is and *who* she's with.

I lean back in my chair and bring my pen to my mouth. Holding her eyes, I dart my tongue out and flick it over the end.

'Your cunt tastes like it agrees with me.'

She lets out a tiny whine as I push the pen past my lips and suck it with a rich groan. Her eyes drop to my tented trousers, my erection providing an impressive bulge in them.

She frowns. 'I . . . How do you know that about Charlie?'

Just his name makes my blood boil.

I stand and step closer. She parts her thighs around my legs instinctively, letting me in, but her frown deepens like she's fighting an internal battle.

'It was obvious that night at dinner when I saw you with him.'

'You're wrong,' she argues, the lustful haze clearing in her eyes a little to make way for disgust. 'You know nothing about me. You think you do, but you don't.'

'Beauty,' I rasp, reaching up to take her chin between my thumb and forefinger. She doesn't fight me. She stares back, her breath hitching like she can't help herself. 'Such a lovely little sleeping princess. Oblivious to the real villains. Or perhaps not. Perhaps you know where it is, hm?' I allow my question to burn into her through my gaze.

My two hundred and forty million.

'What are you talking about?'

I shake my head. 'Now that's convincing. You're getting better.'

I tilt her chin up, bringing my mouth to within an inch of hers. She looks into my eyes, her lips parting.

'Do you want me to kiss you?'

'Never,' she hisses.

We're so close that as her breath fans over my lips I can taste a hint of sweetness radiating from her lipstick.

She moves. It's imperceivable. But it's there. A fraction of an inch in my direction.

She wants this.

She wants *me.*

I allow myself another slow inhale, tasting the breath she's expelling, before I run my thumb over her lower lip, watching the way she opens them, inviting me in.

I smile wickedly.

'Good, because I have work to do.'

I prepare to go in for the kill, determined to teach her a lesson for walking in here and pretending with me.

I reach down and curl my hand around the curve of her arse, giving it a firm squeeze. My cock leaks in my trousers as I get my first real feel of her body. And fuck, if it's not a billion times better than I ever dreamed.

'Time to go now. There's a good girl.' I flatten my palm and pat her bottom condescendingly.

She scoffs, a look of indignation quickly making way for disgust as I step back, giving her enough room to leap from my desk.

I bite back a rough chuckle as she stomps across the room.

'Oh, and Aurora?' I call as she reaches the door.

She whips her head back over her shoulder, her ponytail flicking with enough force to take out an eye.

'What?' she snaps.

I lift her coffee mug from my desk.

Her gaze narrows on it, and I can pinpoint the exact moment she recognises it.

I clear my throat, choosing my words carefully. 'Next time you flirt with me to get something, be prepared for what would happen if I were to give it to you. Because if this was real, I'd have hitched that little skirt I bought you up over your arse and fucked you on my desk. Understand?'

'You're an arsehole,' she spits, her usual hatred for me back in her eyes.

I can't help my smile stretching. 'I'd have fucked that too if you'd asked nicely.'

She throws open the door and storms out.

I wait for it to shut before I reach in into my pants and grab my throbbing dick.

Jesus Christ.

Chapter 19

Aurora

'Are they always this wanky?' I ask, knocking back my champagne.

Dove snorts out a giggle, before doing the same with hers. 'You mean all the dick measuring? Yeah, pretty much. This is why I needed you here with me. A couple of circuits in order to network, and then we can get the hell out of here.'

I follow her gaze around the mansion's large living space that spills out into a fancy orangery on the other side of the room. It's teeming with men in tuxedos, standing in groups, talking about money and their businesses, pretending to be impressed while mentally calculating the other guy's wealth to see whose is greater. *Dick measuring*, like Dove said.

'The lack of women in this room makes me sick,' she says.

'Yeah,' I murmur, my eyes flitting to Rafael.

He's on the far side of the room, tall and devastatingly handsome in his tux as he talks with a group of older men. He hasn't brought a date tonight. I expected to see Seraphina, but Dove said he's not mentioned her since he got back from his friend's wedding in South Africa.

He's also not mentioned the incident in his office, either. But that could have something to do with the fact that I've avoided him like the plague for the past two days.

I tilt my head back, admiring the giant crystal chandelier above our heads. Dove's informed me that the man who lives here is Fairfax Guardian's newest potential client. I don't recall exactly what she said his business was. Something big that involves *a lot* of money. This evening's soirée is being hosted by him in order to alleviate concerns about restructuring and reassure partners and investors that it's business as usual.

'You know Poppy, the stepdaughter? It was her mother who started the business. Apparently, the husband didn't want her to work after they got married and encouraged her to let him manage it all, thinking he could do better. Bet she didn't expect him to be almost running the company into the ground,' Dove says.

'Things can happen that you least expect,' I reply as I look around the room.

A shiver runs up my spine as my eyes collide with rich, molten bronze ones. Rafael holds my gaze for a few seconds, and I glower at him before he's pulled back into conversation again and looks away.

'I'd love to meet Poppy,' Dove adds. 'I'm going to go and see if I can find her.'

'Okay. I'll catch up with you. I need to use the bathroom.'

'Okay.'

I watch her walk away, passing Rafael as she does. He's still deep in conversation. *Bastard.* I've been running through a lengthy list of insults in my head over the last two days that I'd love to use on him. The man is insufferable. He knew the moment I stepped into his office that he was going to mess with me. The arsehole got a kick out it, I know he did. He toyed with me like a cat with a mouse, belittling me for his own perverse pleasure.

Almost making me come on his desk, with a bloody *pen.*

My cheeks heat with a cocktail of shame and anger as I recall the heat of his broad body leaning over me.

I hate that I was turned on by him.

I hate that I wanted him to kiss me.

I hate all of it.

I hate *him*.

Weaving through the sea of dinner suits and tuxedos, I exit the main living space and cross the marble-floored foyer.

'Could you please tell me where the bathroom is?' I ask a member of the wait staff as they approach with a silver tray of canapés.

'That way, madam,' he says, gesturing towards a small group of people waiting outside a closed door on the far side of the grand entrance hall. 'Of course, there is another bathroom down the hallway, fifth door on the left, should you wish.'

'Thank you.'

The hallway is wide, stretching on with closed doors on either side. A door on the right opens and Gabriel walks out, quietly closing it behind him.

'Aurora!' he greets, his brows shooting up behind his glasses like he's surprised to see me.

'Hi.' I smile, forcing myself to breathe. 'I was just looking for the bathroom.'

He clears his throat. 'Me too. Wrong door. Are you having a nice evening?'

'I am. It's . . . interesting.'

'Indeed it is,' Gabriel replies, glancing up the hallway as voices float down from the main entryway. 'Excuse me. Enjoy your evening.'

He strides off in the direction I came from as if he's forgotten he was looking for the bathroom. Something about it makes me wait for him to be out of sight before I carefully open the door to the room he came out of. Poking my head in, it's a cute little library with floor-to-ceiling bookshelves and one of those ladders to reach the high ones. A comfy-looking sofa with threads hanging from its cushions sits in the centre of the room. The most interesting thing is the window. It's huge, arched, and beautiful, complete with a cosy window seat. The moonlight shines outside, illuminating an extravagant circular fountain in the garden.

Closing the door gently, I move along the hallway, locate the bathroom, and step inside.

Standing at the basin afterwards, I fish for my lipstick inside my purse. My phone pings and I pull it out to read the message.

Dove: OMG! He's here!!!

'What the hell?' I murmur. There's only one person Dove would use that many exclamation marks for. The man who didn't just break her, he *destroyed* her. The one we never ever speak about. Not unless we're really drunk. And even then she won't tell me exactly what happened. Only that he lied to her and left her heartbroken.

Her next message comes before I can reply.

Dove: He's back from Singapore for a long visit!

I hit 'call'. This conversation requires more than a text.

'Are you okay?' I ask in a rush the moment it connects.

'I'm . . .' Her voice wavers. Dove never sounds unsure about anything. 'I don't know what to do.'

'Has he seen you?'

'No,' she whispers.

'Okay. Here's what's going to happen. You're going to get the valet to call you a cab right now, you're not going to look back, okay? I can find your clients. Tell them you got ill. No one needs to know why you left.'

'It's okay, I . . . I was with them when I saw him and . . . and I told them I needed air. I don't think they'd find it strange if I don't return.'

'Good.' My voice softens. 'You'll be okay. I'm in the bathroom; I'll be right out. I'll come with you.'

'No,' she fires out, her usual strength returning to her voice. 'No, Rory. I saw Dominic. He's here. You need to speak to him. See if he knows anything that can help your father.'

'What?' I stutter, my heart leaping into my throat. Dominic Ainsworth, the one man I have wanted to speak to for months, is here?

'Talk to him. Dad's known him for years. And he's Rafe's friend. I'm sure he'll listen once you explain who you are and what you've found out.'

I love her optimism, but suddenly I'm flooded with doubts. What if, once he knows I'm the daughter of the man who supposedly stole millions from the company he works for, he doesn't want to help at all? While I'm slowly uncovering more scraps of information that suggest my father's conviction has no evidence to support it, what if Dominic doesn't want to hear it? A sudden, painful realisation drops into my mind. If my father's innocent, then that means whoever stole the money could still be working there . . .

'But I want to come with you and—'

'I'm fine, I promise. I'll call you tomorrow. Now go,' Dove urges.

'Thank you,' I choke back, wanting to hug her more than ever in this moment. I can hear in her voice that she's anxious, yet here she is, thinking about me and my dad.

Sliding my phone away, I reapply my lipstick, then smooth down my dress and take a deep breath.

Here we go.

The moment I exit the bathroom, strong male cologne hits me.

'Oh, excuse me,' a man's voice purrs, as he almost walks straight into me. He takes hold of my bare upper arms to steady me. 'I was looking for the bathroom. The queue up there was too long after five champagnes.' He chuckles.

My gut twists as I look into cool grey eyes.

'Are you okay, young lady?'

'I'm . . .' I swallow, staring back at Dominic Ainsworth as his hands stay curled around my arms. 'I'm fine. Just a little hot.'

His attention drops down my body. I'm wearing a tightly fitted evening gown in deep pink charmeuse silk that a brand sent me to film. It's a stroke of luck they did, because I wouldn't have anything suitable to wear tonight otherwise. Even with the money Fairfax Guardian is paying me, I'll still need to sell it to pay for Dad's solicitor.

'So you are.' His mouth lifts into a wolfish smile, and he runs his hands down my arms before he lets me go, leaving prickling goosebumps behind. 'Why don't I accompany you to the terrace? You can get some air.'

Before I can protest, his hand is on my lower back and he's steering me to the end of the hallway and through a set of double doors that open out on to a small seating area. It must join up to the main garden area where I've seen people mingling, but here, around a darkened corner, and separated by a giant hedge, it feels miles away from everyone else.

He gives me a concerned-looking smile, and I force myself to pull it together. He's just being friendly, and I wanted to seek him out anyway. This is the perfect opportunity to talk to him, just like I wanted.

'These parties are always full of people yapping on about business. Gets a bit much, doesn't it?'

'It does,' I agree, raking my eyes over him. He looks exactly like photos I've seen of him. Only in those he isn't half as intimidating as he is in the flesh.

'Do you work with Phillip?' He says the host's name so easily, like he's a friend of his.

'No, I don't. I came here tonight as a plus one.'

'I see. How are you feeling? Still hot?' He lifts the back of his hand to my forehead in a move that's way too familiar.

I step back quickly to create space between us. The bite of branches from the bush behind me dig into my back.

His eyes crinkle at the corners like he's amused, and he leans in close. 'Don't be shy, young lady. I don't bite. Unless you want me to.'

He moves back with a wink. I stare at him, my breath coming in shallow pants. All these months wanting to get to speak with this man. Wanting to be close to him. And now I'm paralysed as his eyes drink me in.

'I'm Aurora Thorne,' I blurt.

He looks blank, his brow furrowing like he's trying to place the name but isn't quite there yet. *Bastard.* He never came to court. None of the board members did. There was one lone representative from the company, and that was it. It was as if they didn't even deem my father's case worth their time. As long as he was convicted and they had a scapegoat to blame then they didn't care.

They washed their hands of my father the day they fired him and handed their suspicions over to the authorities.

If Dominic Ainsworth had been in court, then he'd recognise me. Remember my name, my father's name.

'George Thorne's daughter,' I add with a hint of bite in my tone.

A flash of recognition passes across his face briefly before he clips, 'I see.'

'I've been hoping we'd meet.'

'Have you now?' He chuckles, but something about the sound makes the hairs on the back of my neck prick up.

'Yes,' I press on, determination burning in my veins. 'I've been looking into my father's case. And I believe the company might have more information that could help him, and—'

'Who did you come with?'

'Sorry?'

His eyes roam over me hungrily as he admires me in my dress. The thing feels itchy suddenly. I wish I'd worn something less fitted. Something with a higher neckline.

'My father is innocent. He—'

'Whoever it is, they've abandoned you in this large house,' Dominic continues. 'If you were my date, I wouldn't have taken my eyes off you for a second.'

I swallow. 'I've seen some records that—'

'Tell me, young lady, who's the lucky man?'

The spiky bush seems inviting again as he lifts his eyes to mine.

'That'd be me,' a deep voice interjects.

Rich brown hair appears a couple of inches above Dominic's head before Rafael steps around him, placing himself by my side. The heat of his body spills from him like a furnace as he snakes a possessive hand around my side and grips my hip.

I hate him, but at the same time, I've never been so glad to see him in my life.

Dominic reaches out and claps Rafael on the shoulder. 'Makes sense,' he says, looking at me. 'A beautiful, young blonde.' He smiles and turns to leave. 'Well, have a good evening, you two. I'll catch up with you later, Rafe,' he calls over his shoulder.

'How can you be friends with a guy like that?' I exhale with a mixture of relief and regret as every dream scenario I'd had of interacting with Dominic Ainsworth goes up in smoke.

Rafael's jaw is clenched hard, and he's glaring into the house with narrowed eyes as Dominic's cologne disperses into the night air.

'He's married,' he states flatly.

'And?' I shudder. 'Doesn't mean he can't be a leery prick.'

'Are you okay?' He turns so we're facing one another head on.

'Like you care,' I retort, too unnerved by Dominic to be civil. I shrug out of his grip. 'You told me that, remember? In your office.'

'I recall what happened in my office.'

He holds my eyes, and I hate him for having such beautiful, mesmerising ones.

'Exactly,' I huff. 'So don't claim to be bothered now, just because your pervy friend was—'

'Did he touch you?' he growls.

'What?'

He moves closer, and instead of moving towards the bush, I find myself leaning into his space, staring up at him towering over me.

'Did Dom touch you?' he repeats, his voice a rough husk.

'No, he . . . Well, yes, technically, on my arms and my face. And it was weird . . . I didn't like it.'

Rafael sucks a sharp breath in through his nose and a muscle in his cheek clenches. 'Stay by my side.'

He holds his hand out to me and arches a brow when I don't move.

'What? No way!'

'Aurora,' he growls, his darkened gaze boring into me. 'I'm not asking. Take my hand, or have it wrapped around you. Either way you're not leaving my side until I take you home.'

His sudden protectiveness is like whiplash. Dove told me he's like this, always wanting to know everything about every man she ever dated. Before everything that happened with the one we don't talk about, that is. Apparently, with him, Rafael's brotherly protectiveness soared to even greater heights.

But I'm not his sister. There'll be another reason he's being so bossy when he's usually such a dick.

I study him, noting the bunched-up tension in his shoulders and the deep line etched between his brows as he stares back at me with startlingly focused precision.

'You're not to leave my side, understand?' he says, like he's explaining something to a child.

I snort. 'Why do you care if I get hit on? Are you worried I'll embarrass Fairfax Guardian by insulting a pervy client if I tell them to fuck off?'

He steps closer, his eyes blazing. 'You think I'm worried about you embarrassing me?'

'Why else are you acting all weird? Like you actually give a toss. You know what? I've had enough of trying to figure you out.'

I move to walk past him, but he blocks my path with his giant body.

'What I "give a toss about",' he hisses, 'is that I might jeopardise a multimillion-pound business relationship and end up in prison like your father when I rip the hand off any man who touches you. So, please, Aurora, don't fight me. Not on this.'

I gape at him, hating how he has to have another dig at my father, like he can't help himself. 'You're an arsehole, you know that?'

He lowers his voice to a rough warning. 'No one touches you, understand?'

I look down at his hand that he's wrapped around my hip like he thinks he's actually going to win this.

'*You're* touching me right now.'

'No one except me.'

'What makes you so special?'

'Better the devil you know, isn't it?' He arches a dark brow, and I hate that he has a point, because as much as I despise him, he seems the safer option right now.

'You figure, huh?'

'I know. You can trust me not to do anything you don't want or ask for.'

I huff out a humourless laugh. 'I can't trust you!'

'Aurora.' He steps closer and my nipples pebble like they're magnets being drawn to him. 'You have no idea the restraint I have. I didn't kiss you in my office when you said not to, did I?'

'What? You were screwing with me in your office . . .'

He draws in a slow breath, eyes pinned on mine. 'Don't act so innocent. You knew damn well the moment you saw me watching your video.'

'Just let me go. I wouldn't want to distract you,' I say sweetly, but it's filled with a wrath that's seeping from me, dark and unforgiving.

Rafael slams to a halt, whipping back towards me.

'You're already distracting me! I don't do this with anyone! You think I want this? Having my thoughts taken over by you? Seeing you with another man and feeling like I'm—'

'Like you're what?'

'Like I'm going out of my bloody mind!'

He moves so fast I have no time to react. He pins me against the wall, both of my wrists firmly inside his bruising grip on either side of my body.

'How does it make you feel? Knowing I've watched all of your videos. Multiple times. That I'm addicted. That I couldn't stop even if I wanted to. Believe me, I've tried. But you're under my skin. You're . . . Fuck . . .'

He exhales, leans closer, until our faces are inches apart. I can't help but trace the path of his tongue as he runs it over his lower lip, my breath hitching as it slides back behind his perfect teeth.

The next confession leaves him in a gravelly whisper.

'And I don't just want to watch. I want to touch . . . taste . . . *savour*. I want to do unspeakable things that your pretty little head can't even begin to imagine.'

My breath stalls. I expected some embarrassment, a level of denial even. Not brazen honesty. Not from him.

'But you don't like me. And I don't like you.'

His gaze drops to my mouth. 'And it'll be much simpler if it remains that way.'

He releases one of my wrists, and dusts my cheekbone with the backs of his knuckles, a deep edge of regret in his voice.

'I'm a man who knows what he wants, Aurora. Even when what he wants is no good for him.'

I turn my cheek into his touch without thinking, but he lets go of me before I can soak in the warmth of his skin.

'Are you saying I'm not good enough for you?' I bite back quietly.

Rich molten bronze swims back into focus as he holds my eyes.

'I'm saying I shouldn't be this close to you.'

'Because of Dove,' I say in understanding, feeling the soft flow of his breath against my lips.

I'm not entertaining the idea of me and him for one second. Despite the fact my panties are damp right now and he smells . . . damn, he smells amazing.

I still hate him.

He frowns, his gaze dropping to my mouth. 'Because of *me*. Because of who I am. And who I will never be.'

He pushes away from the wall and holds his hand out to me. I don't know what makes me do it, but I slide mine into his waiting palm.

He swallows thickly, looking at our entwined fingers. 'Now come on. The sooner tonight's over, the better it'll be for everyone.'

Chapter 20

Rafael

Aurora's stiff in my grasp as I lead us back into the main ballroom, where a band is now playing, and people have taken to a dancefloor in the centre of the room.

My thumb has a bloody mind of its own, rubbing gentle circles on her lower back, and I know I need to put a stop to this. I lean in close to whisper in her ear. 'Come on. I know what a good actress you can be. You can pretend you like me for twenty minutes.'

She turns inside my arms, sliding her hands up my chest to my bow-tie. She takes her time adjusting it, her smile sickeningly sweet.

'Fuck you,' she says ever so gently under her breath.

'Now, now,' I purr. 'Flirt with me like that and I'll start to think you do want me.'

'I'd rather lick a badger's arsehole,' she hums.

'Lucky badger,' I muse, pulling her closer with one hand on the base of her spine so she can't escape. 'Now if you're a good girl, you might learn something. I know every man and woman in attendance tonight. Including the one who used to work with your father and is on their way over. I'll introduce you. Perhaps *she* can be of some use in your father's case?'

'You'd do that for me?' she breathes.

My mouth goes dry as she gazes up at me with something akin to gratitude in her eyes. But it wouldn't be there if she knew my offer is nothing more than an empty box wrapped up to look like a gift. A mere distraction to prevent me from crossing more lines tonight if I'm left alone with her for too long.

'Of course,' I reply, as she gives me a genuine smile.

I feel like the biggest bastard in history when Aurora returns from another fruitless conversation fifteen minutes later. I knew she wouldn't get anywhere when I introduced her to people who would have worked with, or done business with, her father. Yet I did it anyway. Because I wanted to. Because I knew it would snuff out any hope she has.

Because I yearned to see her suffer like I have.

But where I've lost money, I've forced her to confront something much greater. I've made her lose faith. I took it away from her purely because I could.

Sourness swirls over my tongue.

'Dance with me,' I find myself saying.

'What?'

'Dance with me,' I repeat. 'Then I'll take you home.'

She sighs, 'I don't feel like dancing.'

'Then do it so you can stamp on my feet and hope you break a toe.'

A small halo of glitter ignites around her pupils in response to my words. 'Don't tempt me.'

Before she can protest again, I take her hand in mine and lead her towards the centre of the dancing couples. She follows me easily, much more easily than I expect. Guilt tugs at my gut. I've destroyed her fight. Sucked the energy from her.

I turn and pull her into my arms, gently drawing her body in until it's flush to mine. 'Start with the big one. It'll cause the most inconvenience when trying to walk,' I say in a low voice.

She lets the softest of laughs escape her lips. 'Thanks for the tip.'

'Anytime,' I rumble as she snakes her arms up around my neck.

The move brings us closer to one another. Her breasts push against the front of my shirt, and the scent of the perfume sprayed on her wrists transfers on to my neck. Branding me like I'm hers.

I swallow hard.

'I only have to pretend for a little longer, right? I figure you get one song, and then we go back to hating one another,' Aurora says.

'Sounds perfect,' I reply, my eyes glued to her face.

We dance in silence for a minute, my feet unscathed.

She feels like perfection in my arms.

I can't help myself. She's the perfect height for me to lean a touch closer so that my lips rest in her hair as we move. She keeps dancing like she hasn't noticed, and I push my luck further by inhaling slowly, drinking in the scent of her. The softness of the blond strands are like golden silk against my skin.

The song changes, flowing into a slower one.

She sighs in my grasp, her head turned to one side as she watches the other dancers. 'My father taught me to dance to this song. He and Mum used to dance to it in the kitchen at night when they first moved in together.'

I stay silent, scared that if I speak, if I alert her to the fact it's me she's talking to, then she'll stop talking. Because despite knowing this is dangerous territory, I'm hanging off her every word like a starving dog being handed a scrap of meat.

'And that's where he taught me too. Not that we could do it easily. That kitchen was tiny. The whole house was.' A small laugh falls against my chest from her lips. 'Dad always promised that when we moved we'd have a huge kitchen. And he kept his word. The one in Chelsea made our old one look like a postage stamp.'

'I'm sorry you lost it,' I say.

But of course, I don't mean it, do I? People like George Thorne, who steal others' hard-earned money, deserve to lose everything. And being his daughter, who can't have been blind to it all, Aurora deserved to lose her home. They have my money stashed away somewhere, hidden in an offshore account, or somewhere the authorities can't find it, just waiting for the day he's freed and they can cash it all in. The two of them will probably be laughing all the way to the Cayman Islands once he's released.

Laughing at *me*.

Regardless, I still wince as the words land heavily on my tongue, because the lie feels like the most honest thing I've said all evening.

Aurora sighs. 'I'm not. Not really. I'd trade anything to go back to our old house. Before my father got his new job, before he started earning good money, if it meant that he'd not be where he is now. He tries to tell me it's not so bad when I visit him, but I know he's only trying to make me feel better. I wish more than anything I could dance with him again now and not have to wait years until he's finally free.'

She twists her face up to look at me. 'I don't know why I'm telling you all this. I think it's because you don't look at me in pity like most people do when I tell them my father's innocent. Like they think I'm delusional. At least with you, I know what you think of us both. You're an honest arsehole.'

I gaze down at her. 'A complimentary insult. How did I get so lucky?'

She snorts. 'Keep behaving like you do. I'm sure you'll get more.'

As she looks around the large room, her brow creases. 'It's weird being somewhere like this. That's how I felt in the house in Chelsea. Out of place. Like I didn't really belong. You know, my father and I went on holiday to Menorca when I was ten. He saved for months to take us to this three-star hotel and was so excited.

Then when we got there the hotel had been downgraded so the tour operator had to offer us an alternative at no extra cost. We ended up in a five-star resort. They served these really delicious posh fish cakes that we ate every night. My father kept saying how lucky we were. He couldn't believe it.'

She pulls her lower lip past her teeth, biting it, like she's channelling all of her anxiety into that single move. And I want to gather it all up and toss it into orbit, where it can never reach her again.

But instead, I do something reckless. Something stupid. Something that suggests I'm moved by what she's telling me. That a part of me actually bloody *cares*.

I look into her eyes and open my heart a little.

'And it made you think you *were* lucky. That you shouldn't have been there. That you didn't belong,' I say, understanding Aurora Thorne more in this moment than I ever have before.

She looks at me like she's both surprised and impressed that I get it. That I get *her*.

She nods. 'Exactly. Because I didn't belong there.'

'No . . . Aurora.' I take her chin between my thumb and forefinger and tilt her face up.

'What?' She searches my eyes, and I tighten the grip I have on her lower back, melding her to me.

I need to stop this. I need to . . .

She leans into me, feeling so right inside my arms.

'You belong wherever the hell you want to be, okay?' I whisper softly.

She licks her lips, gazing at me. 'Easy for you to say, Mr CEO of a multibillion-pound company.'

I frown. 'You think I always feel at ease? Like I'm not bloody winging it some days? Like I'm not constantly under the scrutiny of my father, for whom nothing is ever good enough?'

I clamp my mouth shut, having said too much. But Aurora homes in on my words, a bloom of tenderness warming her voice.

'You're amazing at what you do. Dove tells me so. Your brothers tell me so. And the way every employee at your company talks about you, it's obvious. They respect you. They admire you.'

'Pretty sure they think I'm a demanding prick.'

'You can't have it all,' Aurora says, her eyes glinting.

The beginning of my smile falters. 'No. But I wish I could.'

She falls silent, her eyes narrowing like she's trying to read me. Like she's seen a glimmer of something worth looking at, hidden deep down.

'You want your father to be proud of you?' she says after a moment. 'I'm sure he is, Rafael.'

I swallow, my chest growing tight at the memory of sirens and pain, so much pain. *Of my mother's screams when she saw all the blood.* And then of the look in my father's eyes years later when I had to tell him we'd lost the Wyndham bid. The one he'd been working on for months before he retired. The culmination of his life's work. The deal was worth billions. He'd set it up; all I had to do was get the contracts signed. My first triumphant act as CEO. A walk in the park. A job a monkey could have done.

One I fucked up royally.

The worst part wasn't that I'd destroyed everything he'd worked his entire life for. It was the way he had turned away, *unable* to stomach looking at me when I told him.

Some things you never forget.

Aurora looks at me, waiting for me to continue. To open up old wounds that I'd rather not let resurface. Dancing with her was a mistake. An indulgence I should never have allowed myself. One that has gone far enough.

'It's been twenty minutes,' I announce, bringing our dance to an abrupt end. 'It's time I took you home.'

Chapter 21

Aurora

I stomp up the stairs as Rafael stays one step behind me, insisting he walk me to my door.

That was the longest car journey of my life. He clammed up the moment his father came up in conversation while we were dancing. Which is a shame, because for the first time I was enjoying his company. But I need to forget about how *much* I was enjoying it – namely the feel of his hands on my back, and the heat of his body pressed against mine as we danced.

This is Rafael. I still loathe him.

'Home sweet home,' I announce at my door. 'Good night, then.'

He's towering behind me like walking tuxedo porn, eyes burning.

'Invite me in.'

'What?' I splutter. 'Why would you want to come inside my "*not fit for vermin to inhabit*" place? Checking on your investment, are you? Still can't believe you bought it.'

'I bought it to ensure you wouldn't be forced to listen to men wanking next door.'

'You just gave me a job at your office so I could watch them doing it instead. To my videos.'

Everything inside me freezes. I cannot believe I just said that out loud to him. Mortification slithers up my spine.

'So you did watch?' His voice lowers to a rich purr like he's amused.

'I didn't say that. I just saw, that's all. For *one* second.'

He shrugs. 'Didn't do it for me, anyway. Too . . . *bland*.'

'As if!' I scoff. There's no way I'm going to sit here and let him insult me like that. 'Your phone probably needed drying out, the amount it got covered in!'

His lips curl into a ghost of a smirk. 'Thought you didn't watch for more than one second?'

Irritation bubbles inside me. I walked straight into that one.

'You're a wanker,' I seethe.

'Evidently. But only to your videos,' he replies drily.

I hate that his words send a shiver up my spine. One with a fiery heat that spreads out through my veins and threatens to infect my blood until it pulses to his command. One that has me immediately picturing being railed into next week by him on my tiny bed that'll probably break with the way I bet this man fucks.

'I want you,' he says calmly. 'This evening has proved to me that I . . .' He tilts his annoyingly handsome head, his gaze narrowing on me in thought. '. . . *need* you. Just once. You can pretend it never happened tomorrow if that's what you want, never talk to me again.'

The hallway falls silent enough to hear a pin drop. I've never wished for Mike to be on one of his calls to Mistress so badly, just to provide a distraction. Something, *anything*, other than having to stand here staring at Rafael Fairfax with my mouth hanging open like I've just witnessed him turn water into wine.

I fight to regain control over my body, because my panties seem to have forgotten that we hate him and are rapidly dampening under his heated gaze.

'Why on earth would I ever—'

'Before you say no, let me kiss you like we both wanted in my office.'

'What?'

My jaw isn't just on the floor, it has left the building and is halfway down the street.

He licks his lips subtly, like he's preparing.

'You think it's going to be so good I won't be able to say no? Is that it?'

He tips his chin, arrogance personified.

'Oh my God, you do!' I scoff.

'I'm going to kiss you now, Aurora.' He moves closer, and I gape up at him, as my core flutters with heat like a traitor. 'But you can tell me to stop,' he rasps, all deep and husky and delicious.

I blink. 'Oh, so reassuring—'

He slides his hand around my neck, cupping it gently, pausing for a beat, his molten irises searching mine for hesitation. Then he lowers his mouth and covers my lips with his. They brush mine oh so gently at first, like he's giving me a chance to back out. But when I do nothing other than question if I'm about to have a heart attack from the way it's fighting to escape my ribcage, he presses them more firmly against mine, drawing me into a kiss.

It's warm, soft, confident.

And all hope of me ever being able to deny him obliterates with the rich groan that comes from his mouth and pours straight into mine.

Everything fades around us. His cologne washes over my senses like a warm wave, and the sound of his breath mixing with mine fills my ears.

I'm inside his bubble. Under his spell.

It's a kiss that's painstakingly tender, and in complete contrast to what I'd expect from him. He kisses me the way a lover would if they were told it was their last moment together. His hands sink into my hair, and he holds me in place, my head tilted back with such care, like he's scared he could break me.

'I've thought about doing this for so bloody long,' he whispers against my lips.

He sinks into me again with more insistence, a rougher groan escaping from the back of his throat as he slides his tongue out to taste me. I gasp as the feel of him inside my mouth sends my core into meltdown.

I'm kissing Rafael Fairfax.

I hate this man. But even as my mind wages a war with itself, my body arches into his, fighting to get closer, to fuse with his like it's the only acceptable outcome. I kiss him back like it's instinctual. Like I both want and need him.

'Please,' a voice whimpers, and it takes me a moment to realise that it's mine.

I'm begging Rafael fucking Fairfax.

'Beauty,' he chokes, running his thumbs over my cheeks before he surges forward with vigour, stealing my breath from me like it's his.

That one word. The way he says it, like it means *everything* . . .

It sparks a fire in my soul, smashing the final thin barriers that remain.

I grab the lapels of his dinner jacket, hauling him to me. His balance falters and we slam back against my front door, our kiss growing frantic.

'Tonight never happened,' I gasp against his lips.

They curve with a flash of a dark smile. 'Finally. Something we agree on.'

I kiss him back with explosive desperation, and he matches me stroke for stroke, breath for breath. It takes everything in me to tear my lips from his and turn to put the key into my front door.

Commanding, warm kisses cascade up and down my neck from behind, and I moan as he grabs my hips and yanks them towards him, grinding his erection into my arse.

'Hurry up before I fuck you right here,' he hisses, sucking on my skin, then grazing it with his teeth and sending heat racing up my spine.

There's no mistaking it. The man is a certified big-dicked arsehole.

But right now, I couldn't care less. Common sense has deserted me, waved off by my conscience, which has happily boarded the Rafael Fairfax fan club train.

I open the door and he spins me, hoisting me up into his arms and barging through it like the entitled prick he is.

Wrapping my legs around his waist, he slams the door closed with his foot and crosses the room in two strides, until he's standing beside the tiny alcove that contains my bed.

'You have to get on from the foot end,' I pant against his mouth. 'Because it's a tight fit.'

'Jesus,' he groans, sinking his hands into my arse as I grind over the solid dick in his trousers.

I tug on his hair, deepening our kiss and tightening my thighs around his torso.

He pulls his lips from mine. 'You need to stop, Aurora. I . . .'

'Why?' I pant.

He kisses me again like he can't control himself, sliding his teeth over my lower lip in a final, lingering tug before he withdraws and places me on my feet.

'Can I use your bathroom?'

I blink at him in surprise. 'Now?'

'Right now,' he says in a strained voice.

'Um . . . sure.'

He stalks into my bathroom, cursing to himself, and closes the door without looking back.

I'm left, standing alone with soaking panties, and a chest heaving with lust-fuelled pants as I wait for a man I don't even like to exit my bathroom. Tanya's house creeps out of the recesses of my memory. This is what he did there. Sounded really into it with her, then escaped to the bathroom, acting like taking a piss was a more enjoyable experience than going back into a room with a woman who clearly wanted him.

He's going to flush the toilet any moment, then walk out of there, declaring he's changed his mind, and this was all a mistake.

And I'll be left here like an idiot.

The toilet doesn't flush. Instead, a roughly bitten curse echoes through the closed door, followed by the sound of the tap running.

A moment later the door flies open and Rafael strides out. He makes a beeline for me, his eyes blazing.

'You're wearing too many clothes,' he growls, his eyes drinking in my dress as he rips off his tuxedo jacket then his bow-tie, like he's fuming.

Oh my God, I'm about to get fucked, and I'm fully here for it.

The guy might be an arsehole, but it's been a long time since I had sex with a man who knew what he was doing. *Really* knew what he was doing. In fact, I'm not sure any man I've slept with has ever—

Rafael's hands land on the back of my dress, grabbing the zipper.

'Be careful!' I warn, scared my monthly rent payment will fly out of the window if it gets ripped.

He arches a dark brow at me, holding my eyes as he slowly slides the zip all the way down to where it ends, just above the curve of my arse.

'It's a nice dress,' he rasps. 'You look beautiful in it. But it still has to come off. I'm far more interested in the beauty beneath it.'

Hearing such words of admiration from him has my core tightening with arousal.

'I filmed it for my vlog earlier,' I blurt, over-talking like I'm nervous. 'It'll be posted tomorrow.'

He runs his tongue over the edge of his perfect teeth, his tone lowering to something dark and filthy. 'Is that so? In that case, my schedule for tomorrow is already looking promising.'

My breath hitches as he lets go of the silk and it slides down my body like an expensive curtain at an art unveiling, letting my breasts spill free, and leaving me standing in nothing but a lace G-string and heels.

Rafael purses his lips, his eyes roaming over me appreciatively from head to toe and back again, settling on my breasts.

'You're even more exquisite than I imagined.'

I shudder as he reaches out and cups the underneath of one breast in his large palm. He assesses its weight, brushing his thumb over my painfully hard nipple.

He cups the other breast, and I stand, completely on show and at his mercy as he strokes my nipples and palms my breasts in a way that makes me whimper and arch into his touch, believing I could actually come like this. Just from Rafael Fairfax playing with my tits like some magically fingered bestower of orgasms.

'Hm, perfection,' he murmurs to himself, his eyes glued to my tits like I've passed some secret test.

He continues to admire and caress them until I'm squirming in my heels.

'Don't worry. It's coming,' he says, eyes and hands still on my breasts. 'I'll give every perfect inch of you the attention it deserves.'

I hate that I whimper at his words, like I'm desperate for more of him. But I am. I want to snatch his hands away and shove them between my thighs. Ride those long, skilled fingers until I come all over them and my arousal drips into his palm.

Then I want to sit on that infuriatingly handsome face and do it again. And again.

And that magnificent cock of his?

I want to ruin it.

I want to take it so hard and deep inside me that he'll never forget the feeling of being inside me for as long as he lives.

I want to fuck Rafael Fairfax like my life depends on it.

Even though I still hate him, obviously.

I don't wait for him to set the pace, I grab his shirt, unbuttoning it, slamming my lips to his at the same time.

'Feeling impatient, Beauty?' he groans, coming to me easily, yanking his shirt from his trousers and tearing the rest of the buttons open for me.

He rips down the zipper on his trousers as we kiss, then shoves them off along with his boxers and socks, before pulling me back into another devasting kiss that's all tongue, heat, and sex.

Hot, velvety skin presses against my stomach, bringing with it the mouth-watering hardness of a giant cock. The type that will make my jaw ache, but that I can't wait to see what it's like to choke on.

'I want . . . Oh, fuck,' I moan as my panties are skilfully pulled to one side and strong fingers glide over my clit.

'You want me to fuck you?' he groans into my mouth. 'I want that too. I want your perfect little cunt wrapped around my cock as I wring every last drop of your orgasm out of you. I want to hear you moan my name as I stuff you full of it until you're scared you'll split in two.'

'Oh my God,' I whine.

'Good girl. Pray. Because the things I'm going to do to you, you'll need all the help you can get to take them.'

He pushes two fingers inside me, his other hand flattening against my lower spine and keeping me upright against him.

'Why are you so wet, Aurora?' he asks, his sharp eyes intent on mine.

He curls his fingers, hitting my G-spot and making my entire body shudder in his arms.

'I asked you a question.'

'Because . . .' I pant. 'It feels good.'

'My fingers inside you feel good?'

'Y-yes,' I moan as he fucks me with them in slow, deliberate strokes.

'Do you want to come on them?'

I nod frantically, my orgasm coiling tight beneath the surface. That night at the restaurant, when he told Charlie he's a man who doesn't have to wonder about whether a woman comes with him, makes perfect sense. It's been approximately five thrusts of his thick, skilled fingers, and I'm already close to finishing all over them.

'Not yet,' he says, removing them and leaving me feel empty.

I wilt into his arms at their loss, blinking at him through a horny haze as he brings them to his mouth and sucks.

'You taste even better on my fingers than you did on my pen.'

All I manage is a strangled whimper as he walks me backwards until the edge of my bed hits the back of my legs.

'Lie down,' he instructs.

I sit on the bed, kicking off my heels, then scoot up it, reclining on to my back and gazing up at him. He stands at the foot of it, naked, hand wrapped tightly around his dick like that morning in his office.

'Show me,' he grunts.

'Show you what?'

'Show me where I get to put my cock tonight.'

His filthy words send a shot of unbearable heat through me, and my lips part on a moan as my thighs fall open on the bed.

'Your mouth and your pussy? Why, thank you, Beauty. I'm going to enjoy filling both.'

I blink at him, shyness threatening to overtake me. When we were kissing before I didn't feel so exposed, so *vulnerable*. But lying here while he looks at me with an animalistic wild sheen in his eyes is as terrifying as it is hot.

'Rafael,' I whimper.

He dips his chin and spits on his cock, lubing it up.

Dark eyes rise to meet mine.

'You've no idea how long I've wanted you,' he groans, his bicep straining as he tugs on his cock.

I lower my eyes, taking it all in. He's huge. Bigger than I remember. His balls look full and ready to burst, bouncing heavily behind his shaft with every pump of his wrist. And his cock . . . My eyes widen at its length, coated in a mix of his saliva and precum as the fat head glistens in a shade of deep red like it's furious.

He climbs on to the bed, between my thighs, working his dick as he braces himself on his other arm and leans down to kiss me.

It's deep, consuming, and makes my breath leave me in tiny little gasps like I can't believe this is happening.

He lets go of his dick, and then his fingers are sliding inside my pussy again, forcing it to stretch around him.

'You're so bloody perfect. Look at you.' He captures a nipple between his teeth and sucks down on to it as he holds my eyes. 'Your body was made to drive me goddamn insane, Aurora.'

He sucks ravenously on my breast, kissing and biting it, pulling as much of it as he can into his mouth as he lets out a low hum of appreciation.

'Jesus Christ.'

He fingers me harder, and I wriggle up thc bed at how deep inside me he feels.

Grasping my hip, he drags me down beneath him. 'Come back here. I'm nowhere near done with you.'

His fingers leave my body, and he slides down the bed, bringing his head level with my pussy. He studies it, like he's savouring the moment, before he presses an open-mouthed kiss against my lace panties.

'Bloody hell.' His eyes fall closed in ecstasy.

Determined fingers slice under the fabric by my hips and peel my G-string down my thighs with agonising slowness.

I'm practically vibrating with need as Rafael unhooks them from my ankles and strokes the lace between his fingers with a frown.

'These are drenched, Aurora,' he scolds.

'Are they?' I reply innocently.

Sharp, cool eyes cut up to mine, melting into something hot and possessive as soon as we lock gazes.

'All wet for me?' he rasps.

I nod. 'For you.'

'Jesus,' he groans.

Then he dives between my legs like he's scared I'll disappear. My thighs are pushed wide by his broad shoulders rippling between them, demanding space for him to be able to eat my pussy like he's been starved.

The moans that leave my lips rival those of a casting couch audition. But I can't help it. The man is a certified fiend. Just as I think I can't possibly feel the heights of any more pleasure, the angle of his mouth changes, and his tongue flicks at a different speed, and my toes are curling all over again. I wriggle and writhe against the duvet.

'Rafael,' I pant. 'Oh wow.'

'Bloody delicious,' he mumbles around a mouth full of my pussy before he zeroes in on my clit and circles a flattened tongue over it like he knows it's guaranteed to drive me wild.

Arousal runs from me, coating his chin as I puff and whimper, making an involuntary sound show that's no doubt massaging his ego to sky-scraping new heights.

But I can't stop even if I wanted to.

The man is literally making me see stars with his sinful mouth.

'So good,' I whine, fingers tangling in the duvet cover like it'll somehow help me as the torturous pleasure of an orgasm as hot as the sun threatens to burn through me.

Capable hands extract the material from my vice-like grip, and guide my hands to thick, rich brown waves, waiting to anchor me.

'Good girl. Get a tight grip,' Rafael groans as he closes his hands around mine, forcing me to scrunch his hair between my fingers until the tug against his scalp must feel like I'm trying to rip it from his skull.

His groan deepens into something primal and dangerous.

My clit throbs in response, and I pull harder.

'Eat me out, then. See how hard you can make me come,' I goad, a bloom of confidence surging inside me as Rafael doubles down on his efforts, fucking me with his tongue.

'Dirty girl,' he murmurs, sucking up a load of slick wet heat as it runs out of me into his waiting mouth.

'Yes.' I throw my head back and let loose, yanking at his hair as he winds me tighter and tighter.

'Come on my face, Beauty. Soak me in it.'

Something about his filthy words have me arching up and moaning embarrassingly loud.

Everything about this is wrong.

I don't even like him. He's my best friend's brother. He's fourteen years older than me.

He's about to make me come harder than I ever have in my life.

'Rafael,' I squeal, as I lift heavy, lust-hooded lids to gaze at him between my thighs.

I could get used to seeing him there, all big and broad and muscular. Thick, dark hair twisted unapologetically between my fingers, dark brows set in concentration as if his sole focus is to get me off, and dark eyes . . . dark eyes looking at me with such intensity that it's like he's looking deep inside me at my soul.

'Fuck!'

I come hard, mouth flying open, body trembling, thighs tightening around his head.

He holds my eyes through all of it, his pace never faltering.

My orgasm sends me reeling, crying out and thrashing beneath him, not knowing what to do with myself.

Until it explodes into another, making tears spring from the corners of my eyes.

'Rafael,' I choke, as wave after wave of pleasure hurtles through me.

Deep aftershocks ripple through my pussy, pulsating as it tries desperately to clench on to something that isn't there.

'Please,' I whimper, knowing that two isn't enough, that I won't be sated until I've come on that big, glorious dick of his.

Movement on the bed makes my eyes flutter open.

Rafael's moved to straddle my chest. His hand is working his engorged dick as precum leaks from the end of it, dripping on to my tits.

'My perfect Beauty,' he murmurs, his other hand curling around my breast and squeezing it. His thumb skates over my nipple, making me whimper with need all over again. 'You've no idea how many times I've watched you. How many times this beautiful body of yours has starred in my fantasies.'

His gaze remains fixed on my breasts as he licks his lips, the evidence of my orgasm gleaming all over the lower half of his face.

'You're a goddamn work of art. A perfect distraction.' He sucks his lower lip past his teeth as the end of his cock swells and a fresh wave of precum oozes from the end, forming a non-stop, thick, shiny strand, all the way from his slit to my nipple. He watches it land. 'A thief,' he muses, 'stealing my thoughts. My attention. *My goddamn sanity.*'

I moan at how degrading the position is – him, all dark and brooding, straddling my chest, eyes fixed on where his cock is leaking all over me.

I love it.

My clit throbs, aching for him to fill me up. He's going to move in a moment and fuck me. He has to. I *need* him to.

'You owe me this,' he says, his eyes rising to meet mine.

'What—?'

He rises on to his knees and pushes his cock into my mouth.

It isn't deep, but the shock makes me gag around him.

'That's it,' he groans. 'Good girl.'

He pulls out, and a string of saliva connects us for a second before it breaks.

His eyes fix on mine in challenge. 'Now give it a little kiss.'

I hold his gaze as I lift my head, pressing a soft kiss to the tip of his cock. His chest goes rigid, and he sucks in a sharp hiss like he's barely maintaining control.

'Again,' he grunts, his voice strained.

I repeat the move, my attention snagging on his chest, on the pale red scar running down the centre of it, mostly hidden by short, dark, silky strands.

'Hold them together,' he barks at me, making my attention snap back to his face.

I cup my breasts, pushing them together to form a channel.

The groan that leaves Rafael's chest as he slides his cock through it, watching with rapt attention, has me clenching my thighs together with need.

'That's it,' he husks, clasping the back of my head gently and lifting it so the tip of his cock slides past my lips on each forward thrust. 'You were made for sucking my cock, Aurora. Look how well you take it.'

I gurgle around him as he fills my throat, holding himself still for a few seconds before he retreats with a grunt.

Sticking my tongue out, I wrap it around the underside of his crown until he moves close enough that I can suck him back into my mouth like I want to.

'Jesus,' he groans, his breath stuttering as he watches me. 'You like that, don't you?'

My response is to suck harder, loving the way he fights to keeps his eyes from closing in pleasure.

'You need to stop,' he urges. 'Bloody hell, Aurora, you need to stop before you make me come.'

I suck harder.

Rafael has always thought he's had the control when it comes to me and him. It's been so obvious, from his cutting, snide remarks, to his obvious disdain for me whenever he's seen me. Now I'm the one in control, bringing Rafael Fucking Fairfax to a trembling mess with my mouth. And it's a welcome switch of power.

His eyes flash with warning, and he wraps his hand around my throat, fingers gently applying pressure to my windpipe as he thrusts deeper than before, then stills.

We stare at one another, a battle of silent wills as his cock fills my windpipe and he strokes my throat, feeling himself claiming that part of me as his own.

His eyes burn with a possessiveness as one side of his mouth curls up. 'I'd happily lose every penny again if I knew it'd lead to this.'

I frown, no idea what he's talking about as he pulls out, letting me breathe again.

He moves away and forces my thighs wider as he brings his thick, giant body between them. The head of his slicked-up cock brushes my clit, and I practically lurch off the bed with a needy sound that should be embarrassing. But I'm past the point of caring. I need him inside me. Now.

'Don't want any surprises,' Rafael growls as he reaches to his trousers on the floor, then sits back on his heels and rolls a condom down on to his thick cock.

He leans over me, arms braced against the mattress.

'Legs wide,' he growls.

I do as he says, parting them around his torso. He doesn't wait for me to finish before he thrusts in deep, like it's his God-given right to be inside me.

The intrusion is a shock. One that sends curls of white-hot pleasure searing through me at an alarming rate. I ripple around him with a moan, stretched deliciously wide and full to take him.

'Aurora,' he tuts like he's angry as I clench around him and moan again.

He stills inside me, dragging in a couple of deep breaths like he needs to control himself. Then he pulls back and sinks inside me again. My body sucks him back in greedily.

He's so thick that it's like I'm being stretched for the first time again.

'More!' I gasp. 'I want more.'

'Fuck,' he grits. 'Dirty girl, you like having my cock inside you, huh?'

He sets a punishing pace, his muscular arse driving his cock into me with a series of gravelly grunts and groans. He holds my eyes the entire time as he pounds me into the mattress with the stamina of a sexual athlete, barely breaking a sweat.

Meanwhile, droplets gather between my breasts and slick my brow as I fight to match his pace, arching my body towards his and lifting my hips to meet his as I sink my nails into his biceps and grip on to him.

He feels so good above me, covering my body with his, hips driving with incessant urgency like he can't get deep enough, hard enough. It's hot and desperate. Impatient.

It's exactly what I need.

'Rafael,' I gasp as one thrust lands deliciously deep, teasing my G-spot.

'Good girl, moan my name,' he growls, spurred on as his thrusts drive deeper and faster.

Blinking, I search his eyes. We've been locked in a heated gaze since he first pushed inside me, his face hovering above me, his lips so close to mine, his heavy breathing matching my own.

It's intimate. *Too* intimate.

But I can't tear my eyes away. I don't want to. And neither it seems, does he.

'Aurora,' he grits, his biceps straining underneath my touch. 'It's not . . .' His jaw clenches. 'It's not enough.'

He pulls out sharply and the snap of rubber fills the air.

He flings the condom across the room like it's personally insulted him.

'What about surprises?' I say as he looms back over me, the naked crown of his dick swiping through my wet skin.

He holds the base of it in one hand, his other bracing himself above me.

'Have you been tested recently?' he grinds out, looking at me from beneath his brows with a desperate hunger like his reserve is hanging on by a thread.

'Yes. I'm fine, but—'

'So am I,' he says.

'But—'

My argument dies on my tongue as he slides back inside me with a deep groan of euphoria that I feel all the way to my toes. Everything is so slick and warm and wet. Impossibly addictive.

'You shouldn't . . . you shouldn't be inside me bare,' I pant.

'I disagree.'

He circles his hips, his hot, thick dick filling me and making me pulse around him. His balls nestle against my arse, and I let out a mewl of appreciation at how good it feels to be skin on skin.

'You're so wet. Admit it, Aurora. You want me to fuck you bare. You want it as much as I do.'

He pulls out and slides back in again, *deep*. His eyes glint with victory as a whimper escapes my lips and my pussy ripples around his length, gripping on tight like it's trying to strangle him.

'We shouldn't,' I protest weakly, at the same time my thighs widen of their own accord, allowing him to drive deeper.

He grits his teeth with a rough hiss. 'Fuck, I'm leaking inside your perfect cunt right now. Dripping right inside it.'

His words are filthy and so wrong. Yet something about them has my nipples hardening and my clit screaming for more friction.

He pulls back and drives inside me again, catching a nipple inside his mouth as it bounces up my chest towards his mouth in invitation.

'I'm not on birth control,' I pant.

That stops him. His head snaps up from my breast and he stares at me.

'You're not on the pill?'

'No.'

'What about the injection? The coil? Anything?' He grimaces.

I shake my head.

'Where are you in your cycle?'

'What?' I gape at him.

'Where are you in—'

'My period's due any day now.'

'I see,' he growls.

He retreats, and I exhale shakily as his dick slides out of me.

Then he thrusts it back in more violently than ever.

'What are you doing?' I cry.

Rafael's eyes carry a determined gleam as he pulls out, then slams back inside me again.

'You better make sure you come before I do if you're worried.' His lips press into an arrogant line as I stare at him in horror.

'You're a bloody insurance CEO,' I gasp. 'You're risk averse!'

He drives inside me harder, his jaw clenching with the effort. 'The chance of pregnancy at this point in your cycle is slim at best.'

'Oh my God.'

I force myself to breathe. But it's okay, it's fine. He's not going to get the chance to finish inside me because I'm so close . . . I'm practically there. The man might be a nightmare in a suit, but he's a goddamn delight between your thighs. Every inch of him feels like it was crafted specifically to bring me the most pleasure possible.

We just fit.

'Rafael,' I moan, tilting my head back as my orgasm slides into the edges of my consciousness, rapidly racing closer and closer.

'Aurora,' he counters. 'Damn it, Beauty, come on it, you know you want to. Come. On. My. Cock.'

Each word is backed up by a delicious thrust that has me pinned into the mattress beneath him. Dear Lord, this man can fuck. I'm going to ache so much tomorrow. But he looks like he could go all night and still execute multimillion-pound business deals over breakfast without batting an eye.

I tremble as he bottoms out inside me again. Everything tightens. Everything draws in until all I can focus on are his eyes, watching me like he's entranced.

'Good girl,' he whispers.

And it's the final push I need.

I come around him in pulsing waves, crying out as my pussy clamps on to his length like it's trying to fuse us together forever. He covers my mouth with his, kissing my gasp straight from my lips, matching it with his own as his hips buck wildly.

It's dirty, desperate.

Dangerously close.

'Look at you,' he growls. 'Perfect, aren't you? Snug little cunt that feels like heaven. Aquamarine eyes that I see in my goddamn dreams. You were sent to ruin me, weren't you? Sent to take everything from me.'

'What are you talking about?' I moan, another orgasm threatening to burst from me.

He grabs one of my thighs and hitches my leg up around his waist. The new angle allows him to push even deeper, and my eyes roll in my head.

'It's your fault that I'm addicted to you,' he growls.

My eyes squeeze shut as another orgasm rips through me.

Rafael grunts as my thighs tighten around him and the sound of increasing wetness spills through the space between us.

'Open your eyes and look at me when you come,' he orders.

I force my eyes open, and his gaze softens a touch as our eyes connect.

'There you are, Beauty. Don't leave me,' he murmurs.

I whimper, the pulses of my orgasm strong enough to steal my breath.

Rafael watches me the entire time with an intensity that should be unnerving. But all it does is make me feel desired. So *powerful.*

He keeps his pace, sliding in and out of me as he waits for the final tremors of my release to fade. I exhale happily. He didn't want to stop before I was done. He was waiting for me to finish first.

'My turn,' he groans, like he's barely able to hold it back.

He keeps thrusting but every muscle in his body has gone rigid. 'Say no and I won't,' he hisses, seeing the panic on my face.

The word is on the tip of my tongue.

But that's where it stays.

'You want to come inside me?' I whimper. But rather than sounding panicked, my voice comes out husky, like a sultry invitation.

'Fuck, yes,' he groans.

The tendons in his neck pop out as he jerks his chin forward, eyes burning into mine. Even if I could form the word, it's too late to say no now.

'Do it,' I urge suddenly, irrationality overtaking as the desire to feel what it'll be like overcomes me. 'Fill me.'

'Jesus,' he hisses.

His cock thickens, jerking with the telltale sign of an orgasm pumping through it. He keeps driving his hips fast and hard, spilling deep inside me.

I stare into his eyes, witnessing him coming apart.

He groans like he's experiencing a soul-altering release, one that will change him forever. His pupils dilate as I moan his name, like a burst of starlight in an otherwise pitch-black sky. He fucks me all the way through his release, mouth hovering over mine, eyes reaching inside me and taking everything he can. His breath entwines with mine like everything starts and ends with this moment.

With me and him. Us. Together.

I stroke his hair back from his brow, unsure why the need to touch him so tenderly overtakes me.

He shudders to a stop, sweat finally shining on his brow.

'Aurora,' he murmurs, dropping his forehead to mine, smiling against my mouth as he kisses me. 'Fuck.'

Chapter 22

Aurora

Rafael Fairfax is a cuddler.

I wriggle, trying to stretch my legs, but they're pinned in place by the equivalent of a giant lazy cat, languishing its long limbs all over me.

I settle back into his grasp instead, my arse grazing against his semi-hard dick as he plays big spoon behind me. He mumbles something incoherent in his sleep before tightening his arms around me and nuzzling his face into my hair.

It's not like I invited him to sleep over. Or expected him to be so . . . snuggly. But after the epic sex where, quite frankly, I thought I might actually pass out from coming so hard, he'd kissed me the same way he did on my doorstep.

Soft, tender, unhurried.

I'd kissed him back for far too long, losing myself in the fantasy of him actually being a man I like.

I still can't get over how he – the man who, Dove told me, breaks out in hives at anything remotely *risky* – not only seemed happy to fuck me without a condom but did it with even more enthusiasm than when he was wearing one.

The guy is a walking contradiction. Rude to me one minute, complimenting me as we dance the next. Talking about me like I'm beneath him. Then *fucking me beneath him* and looking feral while doing it.

The many confusing layers of Rafael Fairfax, doing a stellar job of keeping you wondering which one is the real him. And if that wasn't enough, when I returned from the bathroom, fully expecting him to be back in his expensive tuxedo and halfway out of the door, he was right where I left him.

In my bed.

Fast asleep.

And looking like an undressed model from *GQ* magazine.

I sigh contentedly, giving in to the cosiness. I never found it comfortable sleeping with exes before. But this, even though it should be overwhelming with how he has me pinned, is somehow ridiculously relaxing. His legs are wrapped around mine like he doesn't trust his arms to do the job of keeping me glued to him by themselves. And his breath is falling in a gentle rhythm against my hair.

It's . . . unnerving how different he is in his sleep.

The Rafael I'm used to is cold and calculating. Okay, recently I've seen lighter flashes of him, maybe even a rare bolt of humour, showing that he is, in fact, a human like the rest of us. But sleeping Rafael? Sleeping Rafael is a hot bubble bath on a cold winter's night – all warm and cuddly and safe.

My phone pings nearby, and I crane my neck to peer over the edge of the bed. My clutch bag is lying haphazard on the floor in the tiny slice of space at the side of the bed, half of the contents scattered out of it where I tossed it down as he unzipped my dress last night.

I shuffle inside Rafael's firm grip, but his arms tighten around me and he pulls me back against his chest with a sleepy grunt like

I'm an errant prisoner attempting escape. I wiggle inside his arms and turn on to my back. I gaze at him, all dark hair, chiselled jawline, and full, parted lips as he breathes in and out evenly, lost in a dream.

'I need the bathroom,' I whisper, delivering the gentlest dust of a kiss to his mouth.

His breathing alters and he grumbles something, his grip on me loosening. I slide out from beneath his arm. I can't believe that actually worked.

Sitting up in bed, a large, strong palm lands on my hip, giving it a squeeze.

'Don't be long, Beauty.'

The half-asleep request slips out easily, all deep and rich and husky. Heat blooms between my legs, making my clit ache.

Stop it. It's just sleep-talking. He'll be gone as soon as the sun's up. Back to his fancy world and arsehole remarks.

He won't be looking back. And neither will I.

I scoop up my phone.

Dove: He called me! Can you believe the nerve of him?

I hit 'call' immediately.

'When?' I ask the moment it connects.

'About ten minutes ago,' Dove says, sounding breathless. 'I let it go to voicemail but he didn't leave a message.'

This is so unlike Dove. I've never seen her get flustered over anyone. Except him. That one older man from her past who she's never been able to fully leave behind and move on from.

I shuffle on the bed, keeping my voice low.

'Do you think he saw you at the party?'

'I don't know. I don't think so, but maybe . . .'

'I wonder what he wants.'

'Why are you whispering?'

'I . . .'

'Oh my God!' Dove gasps, seeming eager for a distraction. 'Did you hook up with someone after I left?'

'Um . . .'

'Tell me the truth. Is there a hot-blooded male in your bed right now, Rory?' she teases.

I glance over my shoulder at Rafael's sleeping form, looking like some kind of Greek god statue carved from marble. The sheets have got tangled beneath us, and his glorious thick thighs and arse are on full display, taut and muscular, and practically screaming to be bitten.

'Yes . . . He's, um . . . asleep.' I wince, unable to lie to my best friend, even if I did spend the night getting thoroughly dicked by her eldest and grumpiest brother.

Please God, don't let her ask me who.

'Okay,' she hums knowingly, like we're in on a fun secret. 'In that case I'll let you go. Just tell me one thing . . . Fart sex?'

'Oh God, no!' I splutter. 'The opposite, like as far from it as you can possibly imagine. I think I witnessed the afterlife and came back after my orgasm,' I blurt, then immediately cringe.

God, if she ever finds out I'm saying these things about Rafael . . .

He shifts in the bed behind me, then a large hand wraps around my waist, splaying across my stomach and pulling me backwards.

'Aurora,' he mumbles sleepily.

'Go.' Dove giggles. 'Sounds like you're needed.'

I slump forwards in relief, dropping my phone on the carpet. The strong hand on my stomach tugs again, encouraging me to lie back down.

Far too easily, I sink back inside Rafael Fairfax's arms and let out a sigh as they wrap around me, his forearms flexing as he gathers me up inside his grip. Only this time his semi-hard dick isn't just semi any more. It's fully engorged, standing to attention, ready to go . . . much like the warm set of lips that are kissing a trail down the side of my neck with increasing determination.

His rich, deep voice makes his chest vibrate against my back.

'Open your legs,' he purrs.

A whimper breaks from me at the same moment as long, skilled fingers graze my clit. I should resist. *I should.* But technically it's not morning yet, and . . .

'Oh,' I moan as he rubs my clit with the perfect amount of pressure that I know I'll be coming with in minutes.

'That feel good?' he whispers, kissing my neck. 'Let me make it even better.'

I manage a breathy mumble of agreement, then his legs are entangled with mine once again as his glorious, thick dick slides inside me.

His other hand grabs my breast possessively, squeezing it as he fucks me, slow and deep.

I thought it was just in his sleep, but it seems until dawn, at least, Rafael Fairfax has no intention of letting me go.

And I am more than okay with that.

Chapter 23

Rafael

Cool cotton carrying the scent of something light and floral cradles my head as I crack my eyes open. Best night's sleep I've had in a while. Rolling my shoulders with a groan, I smile.

Aurora Thorne.

Bloody hell, that girl can moan. I think my ears are still ringing from her eager cries of my name.

My name.

I smirk. It's a shame her neighbour, Mike, will be enjoying his new soundproofing. The guy could have done with getting a taste of his own medicine. But then that would have meant another guy hearing the way she sounds when she unravels . . . when she *really* comes.

My jaw tightens. *No bloody way.* Those sounds are where they belong – *with me*, not with any other bastard.

Sitting up, I rake a hand through my hair. Aurora's no longer beside me, and one quick glance around, and I can tell she isn't in the tiny living and kitchen area either. Climbing out of bed, I look at the closed bathroom door.

'Aurora?' I call.

No answer.

I take in the state of the place as I wander across the small room. It's neat and tidy, with little in the way of personal possessions apart from a few framed photographs of her and her father. Makes sense. If she's trying to maintain the appearance that this really is how she lives, then no wonder there's barely anything of any real consequence here.

Still, I'm impressed she's managed to uphold the façade for so long. I wonder where she stores everything that her and her father hid from the authorities. A rental lock-up, perhaps? Because all of those fancy designer outfits she wears in her vlogs are noticeably absent. Her meagre wardrobe is hanging on a flimsy rail that looks like a blind monkey assembled it.

A dazzle catches the morning light that's trying in vain to push through the old, broken blinds at the window. Walking over, I pull the chain, opening them.

'Hm.' I grunt, spotting the source.

Gold sequins glitter on the rail between two dark pencil skirts – ones I bought for her, if I'm not mistaken. I slide them apart so I can admire the garment between them. The gold is bright, obvious – like it wants to blind me for having the audacity to look at it.

I caress the neckline of the top with the pads of two fingers. I've seen Aurora wear this multiple times. Both in photos Dove has taken, and in person. I feign disinterest every time, but really, I know every damn sequin on this top like I sewed it on myself.

She looks beautiful in it.

And now I know she's even more beautiful beneath.

'Aurora?' I call again.

I told her last night was a one-off. That I needed to have her. Just. Once. But of course, that turned into twice. And if she didn't have this disarming effect of making me so relaxed that I sleep like a log in her bed that smells of her, then it would have been more than twice. I'd have made damn sure of it.

It's perfect. I don't know why I didn't think of it before. I've always kept women at arm's length. I can't risk one caring about me enough to spill tears over me. My mother's cries *that day* are dug so deeply into my soul that I swore I'd *never* be in a position to hear a sound like that again. But sex with Aurora? A woman who's always held disdain for me? It's win-win. There's no chance of hurting her if my heart ever . . .

I rub at the centre of my chest as it twinges, the dull pain serving as a reminder for me not to get carried away. Not to expect or covet having the things most men my age already have and take for granted.

Aurora's antipathy towards me is the biggest damn aphrodisiac I could hope for.

A distant birdsong creeps in through the window. It's early. Early enough to argue that the day hasn't started yet, not really, and that this is just a mere extension of the night. My dick twitches between my thighs as I dip my head and inhale the faint ghost of her perfume lingering on the small gold discs.

'You in there?' I purr as I make my way to the bathroom door and rap my knuckles against it.

I push open the door when there's no answer.

The shoebox-sized bathroom is empty.

No naked Aurora waiting for me to drag her back into bed with me.

No Beauty that's taken up permanent residence in my head, to help me out with the aching situation I have going on between my thighs.

No bloody sign of her.

I walk to the sink. A small note has been taped to the mirror above.

Thanks for the dance last night, because that's all that happened.
A
;)

'All that happened?' I snort.

Of course she'd like to take my words last night as gospel, toss them back at me. A deluded part of me thought one night with her would be enough. The part that controlled my mouth last night. But now I understand, one taste of her will never be enough. Not even close.

One night can't rid me of this maddening obsession with her. And now I understand she's safe to get close to, I can indulge this overwhelming need to be near her. To fuck her until she admits what she knows. Until I finally get the truth. And whilst I take delight in George Thorne's infuriatingly beautiful daughter's body, I can quell some of this anger inside me whenever I think about how much her father cost me.

I need Aurora. I *want* her. Not just for what she might know, but for everything else. Her way of getting under my skin with her snarky little comments. The way she acts like she wants to fight me but then submits like a goddamn angel. The way she looks when she's arguing with me and it makes me burn inside with hunger, rather than hate. The softness of her voice when she's confiding in me, even though she admits she doesn't know why she's telling me things.

And most of all, the way her perfect aquamarine eyes light up when she sees me – even though she'll swear they don't. But I see it. They light up like she's looking at a man worthy of her attention. Of her admiration.

Aurora Thorne looks at me like she sees a man she could be proud to know – if she didn't claim to hate me, that is. And fuck, the idea of *her* being proud . . . The ramifications are too huge to digest right now.

I turn my focus to the note and squint at it. The little smiley face beams at me with smugness, its eyes staring right at me like it knows something. Beneath it, pushed up against the skirting board, is a small rubbish bin without a lid. There, sitting alone inside it, like a glaring beacon, is a wad of tissue, thick with my cum.

I knew I'd never last with her if I hadn't taken matters into my own hands last night when I stepped through the door. Her scent was everywhere in here. I was a condemned man the moment I crossed the threshold.

Where the hell are you, Beauty?

I walk back into the main room, gather up my crumpled clothes from last night and pull them on. As I shake out my jacket, a stack of mail falls off the small table beside me.

Bending, I gather up the documents.

Final notice.

Missed payment.

Last warning.

The pile of demands goes on and on. Phone bill, heating bill, credit card bill, a bank statement showing she has exactly thirty-seven pounds and fifty-one pence in her account. She even has a goddamn unpaid parking ticket for overstaying in a supermarket car park.

What the hell is this? The numbers – or lack of them – swim in front of my eyes. I check the company headers on each paper. These are real. They aren't a part of some elaborate plan to make out she's poor, when in reality she's sitting on hidden piles of stolen money.

I glance around the bedsit, seeing it through new eyes.

This really is all she has left.

She's goddamn skint.

The back of my neck grows clammy, sickness washing over me. I step backwards clumsily and drop on to my arse on the end of the bed, the papers crumpling inside my white-knuckled grip.

I've spent months assuming Aurora knew what her father did with the money. That she was his accomplice, or at the very least a silent enabler. I've never allowed myself to consider that she wasn't involved in some way. But what if she wasn't? What if she knew and tried to talk reason into George Thorne? Scared she could lose her one surviving parent? The way she talks about him, it's obvious they're close.

But if that were true, then how can she be in this situation? How can a man with all the money he's stolen stand by and allow his only daughter to live like this? She's barely making ends meet. Is it all to maintain the appearance of his innocence? Would he really do that? Leave his daughter to fend for herself for all those years he's inside, so that when he does get out, the money is safe, ready for them to disappear together, no questions asked?

If that's true, then my hatred for the man has just increased ten-fold.

George Thorne will be living in conditions better than his daughter. No one's threatening to cut his heating off. No one's shoving payment demands through his door every day. His 'debt' ended once they slammed that cell shut.

I shuffle through the papers until I get to her bank statement again. Multiple entries for payments made to the same business come up over and over.

'Bloody hell,' I hiss, recognising the name of the specialist law firm. The one I vaguely recall Dove asking me about once in passing, specifically wanting to know if they were good at taking on criminal appeal cases.

Aurora's not hiding a bloody thing. Except the fact she's living on the goddamn breadline. She's spending every penny she has fighting for her father.

Can I really have been this wrong for so long?

I hang my head and rub at my temples with my free hand.

'Jesus Christ,' I mutter.

I stand and place the papers back where I found them.

There's only one man who can clear this up for me.

Chapter 24

Aurora

'Heaven,' Dove hums, taking a sip of foam from the top of her latte.

'Yeah,' I murmur, trying and failing to summon her enthusiasm for our favourite coffee place.

'What's wrong? You have that look again.'

'What look?'

'The one you get when you've hit another dead end. Is it your dad's case?'

I shake my head. Dad's case is exactly as it's always been – going nowhere. Every time I think I've got something, I get knocked right back to the beginning again. I can't find anything out about the woman who drafted the sexual harassment email. It's like she's disappeared off the face of the planet. And the other sealed file from the court remains just that – sealed.

'I'm sorry, I was just thinking about one of my clients,' I tell Dove.

'The one you said found evidence her husband is having an affair?'

'Yeah. Freddie's mum. I keep thinking about that hotel receipt and photo of him kissing another woman I found in the pocket of her coat. She must have suspected something and hired someone to follow him. I hope if she leaves him then she'll get to keep Freddie. What if they have a custody battle over him, and he gets doggy depression as a result of all the stress?'

Dove smiles. 'Not that that doesn't sound awful for him, but I think you're worrying too much. You said that receipt was dated over six months ago, right? If she was going to leave him, she would have done it by now. Maybe they've worked it out.'

'Yeah, maybe.'

I'd like to latch on to Dove's optimism. Kate's always been lovely to me and is a brilliant dog mum to Freddie. She doesn't deserve to be married to a lying shithead who can't keep it in his pants.

'Are you sure that's all that's on your mind? You've seemed different this past week.'

'Me? I'm fine.' I flash her a smile, but am unable to hold her eyes, and drop my gaze to my coffee instead, fiddling with the mug handle between my fingers.

I can't admit to her that I'm thinking about how I spent the night of the networking event getting completely and utterly fucked by her brother. And that he hasn't called or texted me since. It's exactly what we both agreed to that night. It never happened. I never have to talk to him again. That's what he said. That's what I wanted.

So why does it bother me so much?

'What's been happening at work?' I ask, needing to take the spotlight off me, because I'm pretty sure my cheeks are flaming right now as my brain threatens to recall the filthy things Rafael whispered in my ear when he screwed me from behind in my bed that night.

Those particular flashbacks need to be reserved for when I'm alone.

'Don't tell me you miss us all?' Dove grins, taking another sip of her coffee. 'Well, things are moving ahead with a new client I have, so that's good news. Gabe bought Benedict this giant cat tree monstrosity and put it in the conference room. And Angelo's gone to Italy to meet with one of our clients who owns hotel chains. So, it's business as usual.'

'And, what about . . . *him*?' I ask. 'You haven't mentioned him since the party.'

Dove blows out a breath and puts her cup down with a clang. 'Fuck, I have to talk about it, don't I?'

'It might make you feel better?' I offer.

She gives me a tight smile. 'He keeps calling me,' she says quietly.

'But you won't answer,' I finish, because this is Dove, and I know her.

'I don't know if I can. It's been a long time, Rory. Years. It's all in the past. Maybe it should stay there.'

'Aren't you curious about what he has to say? The way things were left. You said it was all so abrupt?'

She sighs, her shoulders sagging. 'It was. One day he was there, and we were making these amazing plans together. And the next he was gone. No explanation. No apology. Nothing.'

She looks out of the window and frowns, faint lines creasing the middle of her brow. I hate the way her voice loses its fight when she talks about him. And the way she still looks so hurt.

'We weren't even together, not really.' She huffs out a strained laugh. 'It's ridiculous that I let myself be so affected by him.'

'Stop. It's not ridiculous. You had a connection.'

'I thought we did. But I didn't know him, not really. Not the big stuff. Not what his relationship with his family was like. Or whether he wanted kids.'

'You knew his dreams. You knew what he was passionate about. What you had was real, even if it ended suddenly.'

'Thanks, Rory.' She gives me a soft smile, then sips her coffee again. 'Mm, I think this place gets better all the time. This is delicious.'

That's Dove-speak for 'this conversation is too raw, and I can't talk about it any more'.

'So, a cat tree?' I ask, changing the subject.

'The thing's bloody massive.' Dove laughs. 'Rafe went nuts when he saw it.'

My throat thickens at the mention of him.

'I warned Gabe he wouldn't want it in there, but I didn't expect him to be quite that pissed off. He's been a moody bastard all week.'

'Really?' I squeak, my cheeks heating.

'Yeah, I'm wondering if it's got anything to do with Seraphina.'

My stomach sinks at her name. I never considered they could still be together when I spent the night with Rafael. I just assumed they weren't. What if he cheated on her with me? What if I'm party to his deceit?

I take a sip of my coffee to do something with my hands, but all I can taste is sourness as I swallow it.

'You know he took her to the Beaufort wedding in Cape Town,' Dove continues. 'Well, get this, I just found out she flew home alone after he called her by another woman's name.'

'Whose?' I blurt.

'I don't know.' Dove frowns. 'My source wasn't close enough to hear. But she saw Seraphina throw a drink in Rafe's face after shouting something about videos of this other woman being all over his phone.'

I stare at her. 'Videos?'

'Yeah.' She laughs. 'I don't want to know. But I don't feel sorry for him. He's my brother and I love him, but he's a total arsehole when it comes to women. He dates them, fucks them, then moves on to the next.'

I push my coffee cup away, unable to stomach another drop.

What Dove's saying isn't news. I've always known what Rafael is like. So I have no idea why there's this niggly little voice in my head stamping its foot that I didn't even get the date first. I just got the fuck, then the ghosting. Even if it was really great sex, something about the whole situation makes me feel dirty and used. I'm just one in a long line of Rafael Fairfax's bedpost notches. And he's my best friend's brother. How stupid can I be? Catastrophically, tragically stupid, it seems. Because as much as I've tried not to, a tiny part of me wonders what it would be like to be in a relationship with him. To be held in his arms every night. Like you're something precious to him that he'd lay down his life to protect. And what it would be like to talk to him all the time, like I did when we were dancing, and for him to gaze down at you and just . . . *listen.* Like he was hanging off your every word, and wanted to commit them all to memory, learning everything about you that he could.

And of course, to be kissed like you're his reason for everything.

Because that man can kiss.

He holds your eyes like he's trying to see your soul when he fucks you.

But he kisses you like he's sharing his right back.

My mind must be playing tricks on me and remembering that night with rose-tinted glasses. Because this is Rafael Fairfax we're talking about. A man who doesn't even try to hide his disgust of my father. One who I never have to speak to again. Just like he said.

And I should be happy about it. I should be bloody ecstatic after all the times I've had to endure his company and wished I hadn't.

I should be punching the damn ceiling over the thought of never having to speak to him again.

I really should.

Chapter 25

Rafael

The vending machine coffee grows cold, a layer of oil floating on its surface within the flimsy Styrofoam walls.

'Something tells me you didn't request to come and see me so we could sit in silence. Although, I can keep pretending, if that's what you want?'

George Thorne relaxes in his plastic chair on the opposite side of the small, cheap table. If I wanted to reach right across and wring his neck, I could. I could flip the bloody thing over, then smash his head against the floor.

I could make him tell me what I want to know.

I roll my lips, glancing away. The thought of Aurora getting a call telling her that her father's been taken to the hospital is the only thing stopping me. She'd be worried. She'd be upset. The thought of either of those things is more unpleasant to me than the man sitting opposite me. The man who's wearing an open expression, like we could actually have a conversation, man to man.

I clear my throat.

'This is how it's going to work. First, you're going to tell me what you did with the money you took.'

He laughs, actually goddamn *laughs*.

'Okay. And then I'll tell you I'm Santa Claus too.'

'You think this is funny?' I glare at him.

'How much did you lose?'

'How much did I have *stolen*?' I correct. There's no point in beating around the bush, so I get straight to it, studying his reaction carefully. 'Two hundred and forty million.'

He shrugs like it's mere pocket change. 'Some lost more, so better get in line. Although I have to warn you, you'll be waiting a long time. I don't have a clue where your money is.'

I suck in a sharp breath through my nose. It took a week to get my visitor request granted. And for what? So this arsehole can play with me?

'Well, that's unfortunate, isn't it? Because I'm sure a little . . . *cooperation* would be useful, if I were to, say' – I tip my head, eyes dropping over his crumpled clothes – 'have a word with the prison governor about getting you some . . . additional home comforts.'

He rests his forearms on the table and leans over eagerly. 'You can do that for me?'

'Mr Thorne. I'm a resourceful man with friends in high places. I can do just about anything.'

He nods, his eyes narrowing like he's mentally compiling a list.

I smirk internally. Some better bed sheets, magazines, a cuddly fucking teddy bear. If it makes him give me what I need, then I can make it happen.

'Do you know what they took? When they bashed in our front door?' He doesn't wait for me to answer. 'Everything,' he hisses. 'They took bloody everything. Even my dead wife's clothes. They ransacked the shit out of my house! They weren't theirs to take. My daughter wanted to keep them, to remember her mother. They restrained her when she tried to stop them.'

My blood boils and I bite back my grimace at the image of Aurora seeing all of that. Of them *touching* her.

'Give me the officers' names. I'll make sure they're fully investigated if they used unnecessary force.'

George sits back in his chair, shaking his head. 'What's the point? It's not going to undo the damage, is it? It's not going to erase that memory from my daughter's head.'

My jaw clenches. He's right.

'I'm worried about her. She's too trusting. Too naïve.'

Something in his tone has me listening more carefully. 'And?' I encourage.

'And she was always this bright, happy young woman. She lit up every room she walked into. And now she's visiting me here. I see the way it affects her. My daughter's everything to me. It's always been just me and her. You think I wanted to get locked up in here? Away from her?'

'I think you didn't want to get caught,' I answer.

He snorts, turning away, then asks, 'How's Dove?'

'Leave my sister out of this,' I say with a deathly calm to my voice.

'She's been a good friend to Rory,' he continues. 'She's the only one who's stuck by her through all this. The only one who believes I'm innocent.'

'My sister makes questionable decisions at times,' I reply, forcing my arse to stay in the cheap plastic chair so I don't launch myself at the bastard and drive my fist into his face.

'You wouldn't want anything to happen to her? Would you?'

He doesn't see me coming. The coffee flies to the floor and I'm fisting the collar of his shirt before he can even blink.

'Are you threatening me?' I hiss.

He doesn't look worried. In fact, the arsehole looks pleased, like this is exactly the reaction he wanted.

A guard rushes over, but George waves them away. 'We're fine. Just a misunderstanding.'

The burly guard eyes me in warning, and I let go of George's shirt and slowly lower back into my seat.

'Don't bloody test me,' I warn in a low voice as the guard walks away, keeping his eyes on us. 'I can get you sent to another prison that makes this one look like Buckingham Palace.'

George straightens the front of his shirt. 'It wasn't a threat. I just needed to know if you were the right man.'

'Right man for what?' I spit.

'To keep an eye on my daughter.'

I reel back. 'You're joking. Why the—?'

'I know your sister well. I probably saw more of her before I got put in here than you did. My daughter adores her and trusts her, and I trust my daughter's judgement.'

'Spare me the bullshit. What do you want?'

'Dove says you're a good man.'

'Debatable,' I grit.

'You're a man who loves his family. Who would do whatever it takes to help them. I can see that.'

I don't like where this is going . . .

'Leave my family out of this,' I snarl.

He inhales slowly, eyes pinching as he studies me across the table.

'I have no intention of doing otherwise.'

The tension in my bunched-up shoulders eases a fraction.

'As long as you bring mine into it,' he adds.

'What the hell does that mean?' I snap. But as I look into his eyes, I get it. 'Aurora?' I whisper, her name coming out softly.

'My daughter,' George confirms. 'She's struggling. With money and bills and things. She won't admit it to me, but I know her.'

'What do you want?'

'You said yourself: you're a well-connected man. Make some calls. Get them off her back.'

'Her rent's already taken care of,' I tell him. *Perks of being her new landlord.*

'And the rest.' George grimaces. 'She's not . . . she's not eating enough. I wouldn't put it past her to be living off the samples at Tesco. She used to love that as a kid. Trying all the freebies they'd have out on the counter.' He tries to smile, but it falls straight from his face. 'She won't tell me if she's struggling.'

'And you think she'll tell me?'

'Not unless she thinks you're something bloody special, she won't.' He snorts. 'She only lets people she really cares about get close to her. But I think you can help her anyway.'

'And if I do?'

He levels me with a look that cuts right through me, his bloodshot eyes boring into mine.

'Then I'll tell you where it is. Every. Damn. Penny.'

I lean my head back against the Bugatti's cool leather headrest.

'Dammit!' I curse, punching the steering wheel.

He wants me to watch over Aurora. Act as her what? Goddamn guardian angel?

I snort, our company's name taunting me.

Guardian Fairfax. Protecting the priceless. Providing you peace.

My mother's whimsy over the way she and I were saved in that car accident led to my father's name choice for the business. *Guardian Fairfax* because of guardian angels. And my mother's choice to name me Rafael. The slogan came later, once Dove was born. She was the 'peace'. The calm baby. The one that completed our family, my father said. And then we got Angelo too. A happy bonus for all of us, except, perhaps, my father.

I crack my knuckles, staring out of the window at the uninspiring grey box of a building.

He's in there laughing at me. George bloody Thorne. Mastermind. Blackmailer. *Desperate father.*

I know he's playing the only card he thinks he has. One that will help Aurora. The poor arsehole practically collapsed with relief when I agreed to his proposition.

I don't want to be indebted to George Thorne. I'd look out for his daughter for goddamn nothing other than my own peace of mind since I discovered she's struggling. But now I understand what his offer really means, and it throws a whole new light upon the situation. A whole new light indeed.

I drag in a deep breath and pull out my phone. My thumb hovers over the name, hesitating before I hit call.

'Hello?'

She answers on the second ring, making satisfaction burn warm and reassuring in my chest.

It's been a week, but she wants to talk to me. Maybe she's been thinking about me as much as I've been thinking about her.

'Aurora,' I purr softly. 'How are you?'

There's a pause before she answers. 'Fine.'

I can hear the hesitation in her voice. The suspicion. She isn't used to me calling her, and certainly never with anything less than blame and distrust dripping from my voice.

'How's your week been?'

'Fine.'

I smile. She's going to make me work for it. Good girl.

'I've been thinking about you,' I tell her.

Silence.

'Are you still there?'

'Why are you calling me?' she bites. 'We aren't doing this.'

'Doing what?'

'This. It was once. You said I'd never have to speak to you again. I thought we agreed.'

'It was twice, actually.' I lick my lips at the memory.

'I don't care what it was. It's done. I want to forget about it.'

I sit up in my seat, a flash of unexpected nerves coiling in my gut and taking me out like a bat to the knees. She sounds so sure. How can she be? After a night like that? The threat of her slipping away tugs at my subconscious, engaging my mouth before my brain.

'Where are you? I'll come to you so we can talk.'

'What's there to talk about?'

'Aurora,' I growl.

She huffs. 'I can't. I just had coffee with Dove, and I've got work to do.'

I lean back into my seat again. So that's it. It's not that she wants to forget about that night, it's that she *can't* forget about it. And seeing my sister has made her feel guilty. The knowledge is like a soothing balm cascading over me. Aurora might be my sister's best friend, but I've known Dove her whole life. My sister won't be angry at Aurora for being with her brother.

She'll just come for my balls if I hurt her friend.

'Are you filming more videos?' I ask, unable to conceal the interest piquing my tone.

'Seriously?' she scoffs.

But I hear it, the hint of heat in her voice. She knows I'll be watching as soon as she loads them up. And she knows what I'll be doing as I watch. That's been my only saviour this past week, trying to maintain distance from her until I saw her father. I needed answers before I spoke to her again, concerned that I'd tell her what a pathetic excuse for a father he is, leaving her suffering alone, when he has the means stashed away to help her. And I know she thinks she already hates me after one or two meagre comments I've made. But if I annihilated him like that, I'm not sure there would have been any coming back from it.

And now I've seen him, it changes everything.

'I'm always serious when it comes to you and your career, Aurora,' I say.

And I'm *seriously* looking forward to her new videos. I've devoured the ones she's already posted this past week. Although none of them are a scratch on the real thing. Not now I've felt her beneath me, tasted her, heard the sounds she makes when she comes undone.

Looked into her eyes as she's come all over my cock.

She snorts. 'You don't think it's a stupid hobby?'

'Why would I think that?'

'Charlie always said . . .' She stops short as a rough grunt leaves my throat at the mere mention of her idiotic ex. 'It doesn't matter,' she finishes.

'I want to see you,' I clip.

'No.'

'Yes.'

'No.'

'Yes!' I snap. 'Give me one good reason I can't.'

'I can give you a million,' she argues.

We're silent for a few seconds, just the sounds of two sets of laboured breathing echoing on the line.

But she hasn't hung up.

'Beauty,' I murmur, pinching the bridge of my nose, my voice dropping to a soft exhale. 'I miss you. *Please*.'

'Don't call me that,' she whispers back, her fight making way for something stronger. *Desire*. Desire for me. For us. For the way I'm praying she feels when she's with me. Judging by the way she kissed me and slept so contentedly in my arms, I'd say she does feel it. Even if she doesn't want to.

Because I need her to feel the same damn way I feel – obsessed, out of control, *complete*.

'Rafael, we . . .' She falters, and I hear it. The way she breathes my name, like it feels right on her lips.

'We . . .' I repeat, bringing us together as one, uniting us in a singular word. 'We should talk about things. I want to ask you something.'

'What?'

'Not now.'

'I'm not playing games with you. You want to ask me something, you can ask me now,' she says.

I bring my phone away from my ear and press the screen to switch to video. Mistrusting eyes appear, framed by soft golden strands, blowing around her face as she walks. I study the buildings behind her for clues about where she is.

'You're so bloody beautiful.'

Her cheeks flush and she glances away, her attention on the street ahead.

'Ask me then,' she says.

'I need to look into your eyes. Stop walking.'

She sighs, annoyed.

'Good girl,' I murmur as she comes to a standstill and looks directly at her phone's camera.

'What is it?'

The flush deepens on her cheeks as I take a few moments to gaze at her, admiring each curve of her face.

'I need you to tell me the truth,' I say slowly.

'Okay.'

Wide, innocent aquamarine eyes blink at me as I lose myself in their depths. Sunlight on top of a glistening, calm ocean.

'Do you know where it is?'

'Do I know where *what* is?'

Her brow furrows in confusion. I've never asked her outright. And I know the answer now, after visiting her father. But I need to hear it from her. After all these months, I need to look into her eyes and hear it from her.

'The money I was investing with your father's old firm. The money that was stolen from me. Aurora, do you know where it is?'

Chapter 26

Aurora

'Arsehole!' I screech, stomping through my front door and tossing my bag on my old tatty sofa.

Who the hell does he think he is?

I'm vibrating with anger as I storm over to the tiny kitchen and wrench open the refrigerator. I grab a carton of orange juice and tip the dribble that's left into a glass, before slamming it back like it's tequila. I wish it was. Getting off-my-face drunk feels quite appealing right now.

I hate him.

I actually hate the man. I can't believe I had sex with him. *Twice*. I can't believe I cuddled him after. Let him hold me inside his arms like he actually cared.

'*The money that was stolen from me when he was convicted?*'

Those were his words. I had no idea that the theft from my father's old firm affected Rafael financially. He's blamed my father this entire time. Why would he even spend the night with me in the first place if that were true?

A sharp rap vibrates my door. I take my anger out on it as I rip it open.

'You have got to be kidding me?' I seethe.

Rafael stares back at me, his mouth set in a grim line. 'You hung up on me.'

'Of course I bloody did! You accused my father of stealing from you!'

'My opinions of your father's innocence have never been a secret,' he replies, his attention fixing on something behind me.

I glance over my shoulder. I've forgotten to close the fridge, and its lack of contents screams like a glowing neon sign.

'When did you last eat?' Rafael demands.

'Earlier,' I snap. 'How much?'

'Where?' he presses.

'Doesn't matter. How much did you lose? It's obviously a lot if you're so concerned about it that you're swinging accusations around. Ones that have no real evidence to back them up.'

'*Where* did you eat, Aurora?' Rafael says, his eyes returning to mine.

'I went into Tesco on my walk back,' I say in a rush. 'Now tell me. How much?'

'Did you buy food there? Or eat the scraps that every dirty bastard's hands have been on?' he hisses through gritted teeth.

I pull back my shoulders and glare at him. 'How much? Tell me.'

'Tell me first,' he counters.

I muster all of my energy to stop myself from shoving him in his ridiculously broad, solid chest to make him move out of my doorway so I can slam the door in his face.

'I forgot my purse,' I lie.

A vein throbs in his temple and his nostrils flare.

'Now tell me. How—?'

'Two hundred and forty million.'

'What?' I gape at him. 'That's—'

'An amount I'd very much like to recover.' He clears his throat. 'Do you have a suitcase?'

'What?'

'A suitcase?' He arches a dark, thick brow at me, and I gesture vaguely to underneath my bed.

'Good. That makes this easier.'

He slides past me, the front of his suit jacket brushing my chest.

'What are you doing?' I screech as he retrieves the suitcase from beneath the bed, then places it on top of the duvet and unzips it.

'Packing,' he grunts.

He pulls his suit jacket off, tossing it to one side, then rolls his shirt sleeves up his forearms. I hate that my gaze drops to the veins protruding beneath his skin.

'I'll do my best to keep things from creasing, but I'm warning you, I'm about one step away from losing my goddamn shit right now, so I'm not in a gentle mood.'

'What are you talking about?'

He strides over to my clothes rail, widens his arms, then lifts all of the hangers off at once, before marching back to the open suitcase with them.

'Rafael!' I press when he ignores me.

His sinful lips purse as he takes my gold sequined top from its hanger and folds it with extreme care, placing it inside the case.

I whip it back out and he turns, glaring at me with stormy eyes.

'You can't come in here and start touching my things. Who the hell do you think you are? And where the hell do you think I'm going?'

Realisation dawns on me, making anger fire in my gut.

'Oh, I get it. This is because you're my landlord now, isn't it? You think you can evict me because of what my father *didn't* do?' I throw my arms out. 'I'm sorry you lost so much money, okay? I'm sorry you probably had to downgrade from a private jet to first class on a regular airline, and, shock horror, perhaps even have to consider whether you need that sixtieth navy Brioni suit that's identical to all of the others hanging in your giant walk-in wardrobe at your office. But it doesn't mean you can come in here and force me to leave without warning. Ask yourself this? Why would my father ever take that amount of money? He had a good job. He was paid well. We had everything we needed. There's no logical reason he would need hundreds of millions of pounds.'

My words cause him to pause, his jaw clenching like he's thinking.

'Oh. Am I saying something that makes sense? Am I getting through that thick skull of yours?'

'You're being a brat,' he grumbles, continuing to pack.

The calm way he keeps folding my clothes makes me see red.

'And you're being an arsehole! I hate you!' I scream.

He turns so fast, pulling me to him by my upper arms, that my breath flies out of my lungs and leaves me panting.

'And I bloody *care* about you!' he thunders. 'I care about you far more than I'd like to admit. Far more than I ever saw coming.'

I stare into his wild eyes as he pants, holding me against him. Our faces are inches apart, and his eyes drop to my mouth.

'You're not living in this shithole any more. You're coming home with me,' he barks.

'What?'

Him turning up here to throw me out makes more sense than this.

'I want you, Aurora. I *need* you. And that's precisely why I'm here. This place isn't safe.'

'It's fine. I'm not in any danger here.'

He slams his fingers against his chest. 'It's not under *my* roof with *me*. Therefore, it is not *fine*. And as for danger? I'm in danger of losing my goddamn mind if I have to sleep another night without you.'

I don't know what makes me do it. Madness, I guess. Being caught up in the heat and explosive energy of the moment. But I lean towards him, just a touch. A tiny little movement, accompanied by my gaze dropping to his mouth.

And he swoops on it like an invitation.

His lips crash on to mine and he kisses me like it's not been a week but a century since he was last permitted to touch me. My body ignores the voice in my head screaming at me to get as far away from him as possible. Instead, I moan into the kiss, sliding my tongue into his mouth and grabbing at his shirt. He pulls me closer and his rock-hard dick presses into me.

'This is madness,' I pant, breaking away. 'Why are you doing this?'

He shoves his hands on to his hips like he needs to physically restrain himself from pulling me back to him. 'Because I have no damn choice.'

'What? Why?'

He frowns as if what he's about to say both irritates and confuses him in equal measure. 'Because it's *you*, Aurora. It's only ever been you, no matter how much I've tried to convince myself otherwise. I thought it was because I blamed your father. That this . . .' His nostrils flare and his voice drops to something low and dangerous. '. . . this *obsession* would be gone once I knew the truth. Only, it's not an obsession any more, it's something that's become goddamn essential to my survival. And it hasn't gone. It multiplied by a billion the moment I knew.'

'Knew what? What are you talking about?'

'That he's innocent. That your father's innocent.'

'Y-you b-believe me?' I choke, clinging to his words, desperate for someone, anyone, to know what I have all along. That he didn't do it. That my father's a good man.

Rafael's eyes soften as he steps closer to me.

I can't help it, I let out an ugly, strangled sound. 'Are you just saying that so I'll come with you? Is this some cruel joke?'

'Aurora,' Rafael says, cupping my face inside both palms. 'I would never joke with you. Not about this.'

'You really believe me.' I sniff, searching his eyes for hesitation, but there's none. He looks back at me with the same confident assurance he has in his eyes when I've seen him negotiate multimillion-pound deals at work.

'I believe your father,' he says.

'I don't understand.'

He inhales slowly, sliding his lips to my forehead before pressing the gentlest of kisses there.

'Let me finish packing, Beauty.'

Chapter 27

Rafael

Aurora's unusually quiet as I give her a tour of my house. I'm so used to her snarky backchat that her silence is making a niggle of dread squirm in my gut.

I'm used to people being speechless when they see the extent of my property. Six en suite bedrooms, all with walk-in wardrobes, home office with its own giant meeting room, private cinema, pool house with gym and boxing ring.

The place on The Bishops Avenue set me back a cool fifty-three million when I bought it. Worth every penny, the agent assured me. And she was right. The lack of neighbours only served as a bigger draw. It's not that there aren't other houses, but half the time the owners aren't here. It's a ghost street, partially made up of billionaires' second homes, visited only by the staff on their payroll who maintain everything between visits. But something tells me this isn't that.

What if she won't agree to stay and insists I let her leave?

'Your home is beautiful,' she says finally as I lead her back into the kitchen.

'Use the gym and pool whenever you like. It's maintained daily, so you may meet Jeff coming into the pool house to check on it,' I say.

'Jeff?' Aurora echoes, her face pale as her eyes ping-pong around my giant open-plan kitchen and dining room that overlooks the garden where the pool house sits.

If she didn't look like a scared little bunny in headlights then I might feel jealous at the sound of another man's name leaving her pouty lips.

'Help yourself to food, drinks. Anything you like. I want you to feel at home.' I walk over to her, studying the deep line that's settled between her brows. 'Aurora?' I say, gently lifting her chin so she meets my eyes.

She swallows. 'Yes?'

Her blond locks are trying to escape her ponytail. Her pink lips have been parted in surprise ever since I packed that suitcase and carried it out to my car. And her eyes. Bloody hell, her beautiful clear blue eyes are gazing at me with such uncertainty.

'I have six bedrooms, but I'd very much like you to unpack your things in mine.'

'Oh.' She stares at me, her frown line deepening.

I want to kiss her right now. Pull her to me and lose myself in her taste. But one wrong move and I can sense she'll pull away from me. Hard.

'Why don't I make you something to eat? While you go upstairs and unpack?'

It'll take everything in me not to log on to my home security system and watch her whilst she's upstairs without me. To see which room she chooses.

'Um . . . sure. Thanks.' She stares at me like she's trying to figure something out.

'Oh, this is for you,' I say before she leaves the room.

I reach inside my jacket pocket and take out the piece of paper.

'What's this?' she asks, unfolding it.

'The alarm codes. And instructions for the front door. It works on biometrics, so we can set that up in the morning.'

She stares at the paper, before glancing at me. 'So, it's like the key for the front door?'

'Exactly.'

'You're giving me a key to your house?'

'Yes,' I say slowly. 'Is that a problem?'

She shakes her head, her eyes popping. 'No problem, I guess. I just . . . Aren't you worried I'll steal something?'

I hold her eyes, noting the hint of challenge in hers. But it's only thinly veiling her real emotion – hurt. That snide remark I made about her paying for her crisps, amongst other 'digs', have led to this – she doesn't trust me. She doesn't know whether I was being sincere when I told her I believe her father is innocent.

'Anything you want that's under this roof is yours. You don't need to ask. Now go and unpack.'

She clamps her mouth shut, giving me one more uncertain look before she walks out.

I rest my hands on the counter and exhale.

She's here. That's the main thing. She's where I can see her. The rest I can work on, as long as she's here. *With me.*

I set to work, cooking some fresh pasta while I fight the urge to go upstairs. I need to tread carefully. She might need my help, but she sure as hell won't find it easy to accept. Everything I thought I knew about her situation has been tipped on its head since I sat down in that seat opposite George Thorne. I saw the raw desperation in his eyes. I've seen it countless times in the eyes of people who've lost everything. The people who then come to Fairfax Guardian to make sure that it never happens to them again. We assure them that their assets are protected. But Aurora isn't an asset. She's his daughter. Which made his desperation all the more tangible. It was a living, breathing mass that I could feel and taste across that table.

He's an innocent man claiming he has the one thing I want, in order to get the single thing he needs.

Someone to protect his daughter.

He can't tell me what I want to know about my money. I'll have to re-assess how I deal with that. But he can give me something I want much, much more.

Aurora.

He's a man willing to do anything. The glow of pride in his eyes as he spoke about her could have made it easy to hate the pair of them for how wholesomely they love one another – without condition, without expectation. And for how fiercely they're prepared to sacrifice for one another. Her father isn't concerned for himself, only for her wellbeing. He doesn't have a secret stash of money hidden away to provide for her should she need help. Her bank statements showed that. And the wildness in his eyes confirmed it.

He doesn't have my money. And he never has.

The man is pushing her right to where I want her. Because the past week has taught me one thing: what started as an obsession for revenge has turned into something very different. Something that feels like my heart is in danger of beating out of my chest whenever I see her.

This isn't pure lust. God knows how much easier that would be. But it hit me the moment she opened the door to that grotty bedsit with a fire in her eyes, ready to fight me.

I care about her.

She's *mine.*

In my head she always has been. And now my heart's catching up. I'm in danger of falling in love with Aurora Thorne. And that's fine, as long as she doesn't fall in love with me back.

Because if she did, then that would be a huge risk against everything I've spent years keeping at arm's length.

But for the first time, something deep inside me is telling me to do it.

To take the risk.

◆ ◆ ◆

'There's more if you want it?' I offer, looking up from my laptop, where I'm sitting on the floor beside Aurora as she finishes her giant bowl of pasta.

Her attention flicks from the reality TV show she's watching.

'Thanks, but I'm good.' She gives me a tentative smile.

She's warmed up slowly in my presence since she returned from upstairs. She asked if we could eat in front of the TV, and initially I thought it was to ease the awkwardness she might be feeling being here with me. But the way she's relaxed more with each mouthful and her eyes have lit up as she's listened to the people on her show talk non-stop shit, made me realise – this is how she relaxes at the end of the day. And to not only be privy to that, but to be invited to sit beside her while I work, was an invitation I was not going to pass up. Even if my back might kill me tomorrow from sitting on the floor.

'Thanks for dinner,' she says.

'You're welcome.' I carry on typing, fully expecting her to go back to watching her programme in silence.

'You know I'm not staying more than one night, right?'

'We can talk about tomorrow night tomorrow,' I reply.

She shifts against the sofa, turning so her body's angled towards me.

'You mean, you can try to talk me into it again? What are you going to do? Convince me each day to stay?'

'If that's what it takes.' I frown as I spot a typo in the email I'm composing.

She huffs. 'You know this is crazy, right? I can't stay here forever.'

'I disagree.'

'Rafael,' she scoffs, like I've said something absurd.

My name from her lips has heat running through my veins.

'Stay tonight. Then see how you feel.'

She sighs. 'Fine. I'll stay tonight, seeing as I'm here now. But that's it. And we don't tell Dove about it. At least, not yet. I don't want her knowing that the reason you insisted I stay here is because I'm poor. Because I'm not. It's fine. I'm managing just fine. But if she knew where I lived and . . .' Her nose wrinkles. 'If she knew, then she'd insist I stay with her for free. And I won't abuse her generosity like that. I'm not a freeloader. But you? You'll let me pay you back for anything I use while I'm here. Electricity, water, food.'

It's a statement – albeit a misguided one, so I don't dignify it with an answer.

Her shoulders relax, taking my lack of reaction as confirmation of agreement.

Of course I won't take her bloody money. What's she going to do? Give me her last thirty-seven pounds and fifty-one pence, then write me an IOU for the rest?

'You admit it, then? That you're financially disadvantaged right now?'

'It sounds really weird saying it like that.' She sighs. 'I'm fine. I'm coping. But I'm not booking holidays and opening savings accounts, if that's what you mean.' The tops of her ears tinge pink and she darts her eyes away from mine.

'There's no judgement here, Aurora.'

'Sure there isn't,' she mutters, folding her arms.

'I am an arsehole at times,' I admit, 'but I'll never be one when you're being honest with me. I want to know you better. I want to know everything.'

She looks at me warily. 'No, you don't.'

'Try me.'

'I don't think—'

'Tell me,' I urge.

She shakes her head with a sigh. 'Okay, fine. You want to know what it's like to have the one family member you have taken from you? And what it's like to have the press make out the person you love more than anything in the world is a criminal? Or that people will tell you how disgusting he is and look at you like they expect you to agree with them? You want to know all of that?'

I hold her eyes, and her chest rises with angry breaths as she continues. 'And you want to know what it's like to fight every day since he was convicted, searching for something that will help him? Something that will finally bring him home, where he belongs. But getting nowhere because you're not smart enough? You don't . . . you don't understand what it's like to lose your father.'

Guilt bites low and vicious at my gut as her face falls.

'You've been looking into his case?' I ask.

Her expression hardens and she presses her lips together before nodding.

'And how's that going?'

She grimaces.

'You're resourceful. Not to be underestimated. You'll be making progress, even if you think you're not,' I say.

Her expression softens from my compliment, even though I can tell she's fighting against it. She's a beautiful thorn that they won't see coming. Sideline them with beauty, then slash them at the knees. She doesn't realise the power she has.

'Stop being nice to me, it's weird.'

'You'd rather I was an arsehole?'

'I'd rather you told the truth.'

'The truth is I thought your father was guilty, and now I don't. It's as simple as that.'

She falls into silence as she processes my words, then finally she whispers, 'Thank you. I appreciate that. And for you to finally believe in him gives me hope that other people will too. I thought you were a lost cause because, yeah, I agree, you are an arsehole at times.'

'I like to think I have some redeeming traits.'

'Debatable.' A tiny smile plays on her lips as she returns to watching her programme.

I chuckle, then carry on answering work emails until the closing credits roll.

Groaning, I roll my neck out.

'You okay?' Aurora asks.

'Fine. I just don't understand why you want to sit on the floor when there's a perfectly good sofa behind us.'

'Aww, is it making your old bones hurt?'

The return of her usual snarkiness has heat spreading through my chest.

'Thirty-nine isn't prehistoric, and my bones are fine. But I appreciate your concern.'

Her eyes catch mine and she smirks, making my own lips twitch. She looks at me for a few seconds, then returns her attention to the TV.

'Means you do like me,' I murmur quietly, returning to my work.

'Tolerate,' she corrects. 'And that's being generous.'

This time my lips curl into a smile. 'I'll take it,' I say, opening up another email.

It disappears as the lid is closed by a slender hand.

'You've been working long enough,' Aurora announces.

Her eyes spark with something that sends blood racing to my dick.

'I always work in the evenings,' I say, carefully placing my laptop on the floor and pushing it away, my eyes fixed firmly on hers.

'Even if you have company?'

'I rarely have company.'

Her eyes widen, then narrow in suspicion. 'Are you telling me you don't bring all your dates here? That I'm not about to sleep in a bed that hundreds of women have slept in before me?'

I drag in a slow breath, my voice lowering to a rough husk.

'You unpacked in my room?'

Her cheeks flush. 'I might have.'

'You might have?' I echo. 'Because I asked you to?'

'Because for some reason I can't explain, I . . . *wanted* to.'

'We can work on helping you explain those reasons.'

She shuffles a little closer. 'We can?'

I swallow, fighting the desire to pull her to me. I want her to come to me herself. To give in to what her body's telling her to do. And to accept that she and I are inevitable. That even if she fights it, I'll be here, fighting for her to see it right back.

We've gone from hating, to fucking, to tolerating.

It's progress.

And I intend to keep progressing until I get exactly what I want – *her*. Not just in her videos. But in my arms. In my bed. In my life.

Mine.

I sit completely still, making her do all the work. I want her to understand that she's choosing this. That she wants this.

Like the perfect little beauty she is, she leans closer, parting her lips in invitation.

'Rafael. That night you and I . . .' She pauses, her words coming out breathy and needy. 'I keep *thinking* about it. I—'

'Have you touched yourself?'

Her eyes widen. 'What?'

'Have you touched yourself whilst thinking about it?'

Bloody hell, the thought of her making herself come to the memory of me . . . it's . . . I inhale, my fingers tingling with the need to touch her.

She sinks her teeth into her lower lip. And nods.

Fuck it, my willpower isn't the stuff of legends. I'm a man whose future is in front of him with her little tits straining against her top, the outline of her nipples visible through it, and aquamarine-blue eyes rapidly hazing over with unconcealed lust.

She wants me. And damn it, I *crave* her.

'I've thought of *nothing* else since,' I growl. 'You wouldn't believe how much I've thought about it. Wondering if you were doing the same.'

I grab the back of her head, bringing her mouth to mine and claiming it the way I've wanted to ever since she walked through my front door.

She gasps against my mouth like my urgency has shocked her. But it's all an act, because the moment my tongue slides against hers she's clambering into my lap and straddling me like she can't get the feel of my hard, straining dick between her legs fast enough.

'Oh God,' she mewls, grinding herself down on it.

I keep kissing her, shoving her dress up over her hips roughly, and sliding my hands over her exposed arse cheeks. I sink my fingers into her flesh and bring her down harder on my dick.

'You want to fuck me again, Beauty? Is that it?'

'No,' she whimpers, kissing me back harder.

'You can admit you like me. Admit you want me to slide your little panties to one side and take my cock out.'

'No,' she whines again, grabbing fistfuls of my hair, whilst desperately bucking her hips.

Warmth seeps through my trousers and underwear, and I just know my dirty girl is already soaking for me.

'Touch yourself.'

I wait for her hesitation, but it never comes.

She places her hand over the centre of my chest, using it as a lever to rise from my crotch. The position of her palm burns into my flesh, making my heart rate kick up.

Holding my eyes, she snakes her hand between her thighs.

'Now put your fingers in your cunt. Yeah, just there. That feel good?' I groan, my sharp intake of breath matching hers at the exact moment she buries her fingers in her tight little pussy.

She moans, her lids hooding as I gaze at her in awe.

'In and out now, Beauty. Fuck yourself, so that when you give me those fingers, I'll be able to taste deep inside you on them.'

'Oh God,' she whispers.

She rides her hand harder, and a small gasp falls from her pouty lips.

'Good girl, that's it. Get them nice and covered. I want to be able to see it.'

I tip my chin, holding her eyes as I wrap my hand around her wrist and force her fingers deeper and faster until her body makes wet, squelching sounds.

She's a goddamn goddess, watching me the entire time, like she's getting high on my reaction.

I pull on her wrist, freeing her fingers. She wilts forward, her weight pressing through her hand into my chest.

'You know what I want,' I encourage, bringing her hand up between us.

Her eyes drop to the slippery arousal coating her fingers. It's glistening on her skin like a jewel.

She doesn't move, so I flex my fingers around her wrist, snapping her out of her trance.

'It's all yours,' she breathes, sliding her fingers past my waiting lips.

I hold her hand in place, lunging forward and sucking down her fingers until my nose grazes her knuckles. I slide my tongue over the underside of them first, then roll it around the top, swallowing with a deep, husky groan.

She tastes incredible. Exactly how she did when I made her come on my face a week ago. Bloody hell, that feels like a lifetime ago. It's too long to be denied her taste. To be denied the feel of her, pressed up against me. Hot and needy, and so goddamn perfect.

I grab a handful of her arse, guiding her back and forth over my aching cock.

She watches me, grinding over me with desperate need. A gasp breaks free from her lips as I tilt my hips, meeting her next move with friction against her clit.

'More,' she moans.

I suck up to the tips of her fingers, then let them go.

'Show me.'

'Show you what?' she pants.

'Show me that clit. Is it out for me, huh? Is it all pretty and swollen?'

Her cheeks pinken immediately as if she's embarrassed, but a second later she's hooking her delicate nails through the edge of her pink lace panties and pulling them to the side.

The view almost makes me shoot my load on the spot.

'Aurora,' I growl like I'm angry. 'Look how swollen it is, making sure I see it. Begging for my attention.'

I spit on my thumb, then slide it over her clit.

She jerks, her thighs tightening around my hips.

'You're a dirty girl, aren't you? Aching to be touched like this.'

She whimpers, her eyes glazing over as I slowly rub my thumb over her, keeping my touch featherlight.

'Rafael,' she moans, her eyes falling closed as she tips her head back.

I admire her throat, admire the fluttering pulse in it, her blood pumping harder because of me.

'Take my cock out.'

She reaches down and unzips my trousers.

I wrap an arm around her waist, making her gasp as I lift her high enough that she has space to put her hand into my boxers, and pull my dick and balls out through the gap in the fabric.

'That's better,' I croon, keeping her held high, hovering over my rock-hard dick. It's leaking from the slit, big fat drops of glistening precum that she's about to take inside her.

She wriggles, eager to get friction again.

'Not so fast,' I purr.

'Why?' she pants.

The flush in her cheeks is enough to ruin me as she gazes back at me in innocence.

'Tell me first.'

'Tell you what?'

I smirk. 'Tell me that you like me now.'

'I *tolerate* you, Rafael Fairfax,' she says, dusting her lips over mine in a whisper of a kiss. 'But don't let it go to your head.'

I take her chin between my thumb and forefinger. 'Hm. Good girl. Now you can do it.'

She licks her lips. 'Do what?'

Sitting forward, I bring my mouth to her ear as I place both hands on her hips.

'Make a mess on my dick,' I breathe.

She shivers as I kiss her neck.

'Make a big, dirty mess all over it, Beauty. Don't stop until I'm covered in your cum.'

I sink my face into her neck, sucking on her skin as I bring her down on to my cock, easing her on to it inch by inch until she's crying my name and rippling around me.

'That's it,' I groan, every tendon in my neck and shoulders going rigid as I withhold the threat of an explosive orgasm from cresting.

I can't get enough of her. Of being inside her. Of her scent, her warmth, the feel of her silky little mouth as she kisses me.

'Fuck me, Beauty. Fuck me,' I urge, digging my fingers into the flesh on her hips and helping her to ride me hard and fast.

Her moans are like goddamn music to my ears as she bounces on my dick like she was made to.

I lean back against the sofa, widening my thighs so I can thrust up inside her deeper.

'So good,' she pants.

'Yeah? You like being stuffed full of my cock?'

She mewls as inches of slick-coated skin slide out of her before I drive them back in with a harsh pump of my hips.

My grip is hard on her, forcing her to ride the shit out of me. I flex my fingers to allow the blood to return to them, then reach up and yank the front of her top and bra down underneath her tits.

The perfect little handfuls spill out, bouncing up and down in time with her body.

'You're mine,' I hiss, kneading them and flicking her puckered rosy nipples with my thumbs.

'I'm not,' she whimpers, still choosing to fight with me even as she clenches and ripples around my dick.

I thumb her nipples again, making her moan.

'You are. I'll have you admitting it. I'll have you *loving* it. I'll have you wanting nothing else.'

I pump up into her with brutal force and she sinks her nails into my shirt, biting through the fabric until my skin stings.

'Rafael,' she cries. 'Oh my God, you're insane.'

Her cries turn into breathy gasps as I encourage her to ride me faster.

'That's right,' I groan. 'Those sounds are mine too. It's my cock inside you that's causing you to make them. You're going to come, aren't you, Beauty? You're going to make that mess all over my cock. You're going to mark me as yours. Just like you're mine.'

'Fuck!' she squeals.

A gush of fluid floods my cock, spraying over my trousers and running over my balls.

'Oh g-god,' she pants, struggling to keep pace as her body clamps down on to me.

'Good girl. Let it go.'

She shudders around me, whimpering and trembling as my soaked balls slap against her arse with each thrust.

Her body keeps rippling around me in waves until she finally manages to catch her breath.

'Was that—?'

I grin. 'A much bigger mess than I expected this soon. Such a dirty girl, squirting all over my dick.'

I reach up into her hair with one hand, my other dropping to her hip and gripping on tight so she can't go anywhere. I'm buried to the hilt, not even a fraction of a gap between us as I bring her back down on to me.

I hold her eyes as my cock swells inside her.

'You're mine,' I growl. 'Mine.'

I come hard inside with my eyes pinned on hers, driving my point home as I unload inside her with a curse. She stares back, her lips parting with a moan as I fill her. Fill her so damn deep that she tightens her thighs around my hips and moans like she wants every last drop.

My moans.

My cock.

My pussy.

My Beauty.

Exactly where she belongs.

Chapter 28

Aurora

Strong hands slide around my hips, pulling me back in a wall of solid, suited muscle.

'I'll make you breakfast,' Rafael purrs, dipping his head to kiss the top of my shoulder.

'I don't usually eat breakfast,' I say, pulling what I'm looking for out of my bag on the kitchen counter.

Last night feels like a dream. A hot, sexy one. After the fast and messy sex in the living room, Rafael led me upstairs and waited for me to clean up in his ridiculously lavish bathroom. He was lying in bed when I came out, a curve of a sexy smile on his face as he saw me in my vest and potato-print shorts. Climbing in beside him felt weirdly intimate despite what we'd just done, so I was relieved when he turned out the light and just pulled me back against his chest instead of talking.

Turns out he's still a cuddler.

And I *really* like that.

Even if I'm still getting used to everything else that goes along with spending time with him, I know that once we're in bed, and he wraps me up in his arms like he's scared I'll try to sneak away – that everything will feel . . . *It'll feel right.*

I bite back a goofy smile.

'What you got there?' he asks, stroking my stomach.

I could definitely get used to swoony Rafael. The one who kisses me the moment I wake up, but doesn't try to force anything, even though I felt how hard his dick was against my back when we woke up. The one who walks naked to his bathroom and gives me a spectacular view of his muscular arse before he showers, then leaves me in peace to do the same, like he understands that I need my privacy whilst I'm trying to navigate what being with him in his house – in his bed – *really* means.

And I could especially get used to the one who's kissing my neck in a way that's making me want to go back to bed right this moment and take him with me.

'Just my pill,' I reply, popping the small round tablet out of its foil and placing it on my tongue.

Rafael's kisses cease, but he keeps stroking my stomach.

'You got the contraceptive pill?'

'I did.'

'Why? Do you get heavy periods?'

Once again, his knowledge of female birth control and the related aspects to it surprise me.

'How do you know enough about its uses to even ask that?'

'Dove,' he replies simply. 'Is that why you've got it? You weren't on it last week. You told me you didn't take birth control.'

I turn so I can see his face.

'You're asking a lot of questions.'

His brows lower and the intensity in his gaze makes me shiver.

'Answer me, Aurora,' he says slowly.

'No, I don't get heavy periods. I just thought it might be a good idea, that's all.'

'A good idea?' he repeats.

The deep husk in his tone has me fidgeting.

'Why did you think it was a good idea?'

His eyes bore into mine and I feel like a bug under a microscope.

'In case I was going to start having more sex,' I blurt, folding my arms like a shield. 'Okay?'

'With me?'

I roll my eyes, but he tilts my chin up with two fingers to meet his gaze.

Rich, molten bronze shimmers back at me.

'Beauty, did you go on birth control because you were hoping we'd fuck again?'

'No,' I scoff.

His eyes narrow in amusement.

'I don't know,' I admit. 'Maybe.'

I know my cheeks are flaming. I didn't plan on this – me and him – ever happening again, and that's the truth. But yet, I still went to the doctor's and got a prescription just in case. And I can't explain why I did it, only that I did.

'Hm,' he purrs, and presses a soft kiss to my lips. 'And you still think you're not mine?'

'I'm not,' I argue.

He kisses me again. 'I'm not going to lie, the thought of getting you pregnant has a certain . . . *appeal.* But being on the pill's a smart choice seeing as I'll have you coming on my dick every day from now on.'

'Oh, you will, will you?' I snort at his arrogance, unsure what to make of the pregnant comment.

He smiles against my mouth, and I can't help it, I sink into his next kiss like I'm greedy for it.

'I guarantee it. Now what do you want for breakfast?'

'I told you, I don't really eat it,' I reply as he walks over to the fridge and opens it.

The guy is most definitely walking suit porn. He's wearing a grey pinstripe one today with a waistcoat – *a goddamn waistcoat.* He looks like a chestnut-haired David Gandy, hot-suited chef edition.

It's doing things for my appetite, but not the one for food.

'Maybe just a juice,' I say.

'I'll make you an omelette. Juice isn't going to sustain you until lunch. Did you have plans for it?'

'For what?' I ask, as he gets a carton of eggs out, then pulls a pan from a drawer.

'For lunch?'

I shrug. 'I've got three client houses to visit today. I'll grab something in between.'

'Whereabouts?' He cracks the eggs into a bowl and whisks them with a fork.

'One is in Notting Hill, so I guess I'll be in that area at lunchtime.'

'There's a nice place I know there – you'll like it.'

'Oh sure, what's it called?' I ask, knowing full well I won't be visiting any places for lunch that Rafael thinks are 'nice'. Not if I want to have enough money to eat for the rest of the week.

'Juniper and Jones. I'll meet you there.'

'What?' I gape at him.

He inclines his head towards the cupboards near me. 'Can you please pass the salt and pepper?'

I open a random door, a million questions bubbling on my tongue.

Tubes of crisps stare back at me, myriad flavours lined up like soldiers in varying colours. I whip my head back around.

He doesn't like crisps.

Rafael's eyes land briefly on the crisps. 'Salt and pepper's in that one,' he says, pointing to the cupboard beside the one I've opened before he goes back to whisking like I didn't just find the Aladdin's cave of all things salty and delicious.

I fetch it and walk over to him.

'You really want to meet me for lunch?'

His whisking never breaks pace. 'Yes.'

'But aren't you busy at work?'

'Swamped.'

I frown. 'Having lunch doesn't mean we're . . . you know . . . anything other than a man and a woman having lunch together,' I say, more to convince myself.

Rafael grinds some pepper into the bowl.

'Does it?' I press, waiting for him to agree with me.

'Call it whatever you like,' he replies easily.

I exhale in relief.

'But we both know what it really is,' he adds.

'What?' I stare at him.

He turns and gives me the full effect of the Rafael Fairfax heated look that's guaranteed to melt panties.

'It's not a date,' I say. 'We're not a couple. I stayed last night, but I'm going back to my place today. This is . . .' I wave my finger between the two of us. 'This isn't going to be a regular thing.'

He merely arches a brow like he knows he has all the power without even needing to speak.

'It's not,' I protest.

He cooks my eggs as I stare at the side of his face. He's so handsome and in control. It only makes me contemplate arguing with him more to see how far I can push him.

He plates the omelette up, and I hate to admit that it looks and smells incredible.

'Eat up,' he says, placing it down on the giant quartz island in the centre of the room.

I slide on to a stool, my mouth watering.

'This is going to last me until at least dinner,' I say, eyeing my plate.

Rafael arches a brow.

'It is,' I insist.

'Nice try,' he replies, kissing my head like it's the most natural move in the world. 'I'm still taking you for lunch.'

'On a non-date,' I say, picking up my fork.

He chuckles and the rich sound sends warmth radiating through me.

'Eat your breakfast, Beauty,' he murmurs. 'Before I feed it to you myself.'

Chapter 29

Aurora

'I've kind of been spending time with someone.'

Dove's face lights up and she beams at me across the table of the coffee place we're in. 'Who?'

'It's really new.'

She clasps her hands in front of her face, her eyes gleaming for more information. I swallow the lump of deceit in my throat. Guilt is gnawing at me about last night and the fact I had sex with Rafael again. And now I have plans to meet him for lunch like we're a couple. Not confessing to my best friend just feels wrong on so many levels.

'We're not even a . . . I don't know what we are . . . But I stayed at his place last night and . . . Oh God, I'm not sure what you're going to think,' I say.

Her face falls. 'You're not back with Charlie again, are you?'

'No! God, no. Although he texted me this morning.'

'He did?'

'Ugh, yes.' I unlock my phone and hand it to her, open on Charlie's message.

'He wants to meet you and talk? After the way he spoke to you in the restaurant?' Dove scowls, handing my phone back. 'Tell him where to shove it. Dickhead.'

'I will, don't worry.'

'So, this new guy . . . ?'

I need to confess to my best friend that I accidentally banged her hot older brother. *Three times.* I take a deep breath for Dutch courage. Here goes . . .

Her phone rings in her pocket and she pulls it out.

'It's my brother. Sorry, one sec.'

'Okay,' I reply, sitting back in my chair as she answers the call.

'Hey,' she says brightly.

She listens for a moment, and I wring my hands together underneath the table, wondering which brother she's speaking to.

'Trust Benedict.' She laughs.

My shoulders soften. It must be Gabriel.

'What did Gabe say?' she asks.

I tense again. Angelo? Please let it be Angelo.

'Uh-huh,' she murmurs, glancing at me. 'Actually, Aurora's here with me now. Is there a problem with the campaign?' She sighs. 'Why are you always so bloody cryptic? Fine. I'll ask her.'

She looks at me. 'Rafe wants us all to meet to discuss something. He's asking if this afternoon works? He's got plans for lunch, so after that?'

'Um . . .' My own phone ringing rescues me from blurting out something I can't take back.

Why does he want us all to meet? The knot in my stomach tightens. Does he want to tell Dove about me and him already? Despite that being exactly what I was about to do, the idea of Rafael wanting to do it feels so much more official.

I swipe to answer my phone. The name on caller ID registers too late in my brain as the call connects.

'Rory,' Charlie says, sounding delighted I answered.

'Charlie, now isn't a good time,' I say, catching eyes with Dove.

She frowns. 'Tell him to piss off,' she hisses. 'Not you,' she says into her phone. 'Aurora's ex just called her. I don't know. Wants her back, probably.' She exhales. 'Fine, yep, speak to you later.'

She puts her phone down as Charlie continues.

'Rory? You there? I really want to meet and talk. What about lunch today? I could—'

'I'm busy. I have to go.' I jab 'end call'.

'Why didn't the knob put as much effort into your relationship before it ended?' Dove snorts. 'Maybe you'd have at least got an orgasm out of him.'

I screw my face up at the memory of sex with Charlie. It feels like a lifetime ago.

My phone rings again with a withheld number.

'If that's him again, give it to me,' Dove snaps.

'Hello?'

'Aurora.' Rafael grits out my name like he's angry. 'Where are you?'

I shake my head at Dove. *Not him*, I mouth.

She gestures to the bathrooms and rises from her seat.

I watch her move far enough away before I reply.

'I'm having coffee with Dove. You know that. You were just on the phone with her.'

'Where exactly?' he presses.

I don't know what's got into him, but he sounds like he's about to pop a vein.

'Near my client's house. I'm headed there in fifteen minutes.'

'Send me your location,' he growls. 'I need to speak to you.'

'Why?'

'Please, just bloody do it.'

I do as he says, then put my phone back to my ear. 'What's wrong?'

'I'll be in my car when you're done,' he barks.

The black Bugatti shines in the late-morning sun like a black swan on a lake – graceful and calm. But something tells me what's awaiting me inside is going to be far from idyllic.

He sounded pissed on the phone. *So pissed.*

I open the passenger door and slide into the cool leather interior. Rafael's eyes drift over my legs as I lower into the seat and close the door. It shuts with a deep *thunk*, sealing off sounds from the outside world and trapping us both inside.

The air is thick with tension that makes goosebumps pepper along my forearms.

'I thought we were meeting for lunch?' I say hesitantly. 'It's not even ten thirty.'

Rafael sucks in a sharp breath through his nose, then lifts his gaze from my legs and locks eyes with me.

'That was before I learnt that you're still talking to your ex.'

I snort. 'Hardly. I answered by accident. I've been trying to ignore him.'

'It's not the first time he's called you?' he hisses.

Wow, he sure zeroed in on that information.

'I mean, it's the first time he called me today, if that counts.' I shrug.

The whites around Rafael's eyes shine as his focus takes on a deadly precision, like a hunter's. 'Why didn't you tell me?'

'I hadn't seen you for a week until yesterday, and anyway, why would I? It's nothing.'

'Do you want him back?' he snaps.

I stare at him. He's all tense in his suit, his shoulders practically bunched up to his ears.

'Why would you even ask me that?'

'Do you?' he presses.

This is ridiculous. He's being ridiculous.

'No!'

'Because he can't have you!' he rages, twisting in the driver's seat to face me. 'You hear me? I won't bloody well share you, Aurora.'

'You won't share me?' I scoff. 'What the hell does that mean?'

He flexes his fingers before they curl right back into a white-knuckled fist again. I've never seen him this angry. Not even when I called him out for being rude to AJ, and then the other time I insinuated he had a small dick. How mistaken was I with *that* assumption . . .

'You're mine. No other bastard's. Mine,' he seethes, making the temperature inside the car soar by at least ten degrees.

'I'm no one's,' I correct, anger bubbling inside me as I cross my arms to fight the urge to smack him in his gorgeous mouth for being such a neanderthal.

His eyes flick to my cleavage in my scoop-necked t-shirt and heat pulses between my thighs at the small, tortured groan that rumbles in his throat, like me standing up to him turns him on. But I'm not going to let him get away with this. Who the hell does he think he is? Calling me and demanding I meet him just because he heard something he didn't like?

He at least has the sense to keep his mouth shut as I shoot him a look that would turn any other man to stone.

'You're jealous,' I state.

'Of course I'm bloody jealous. The bastard's touched you.' He swallows thickly, lowering his voice. 'He's been *inside* you. But the worst thing is . . .' He screws his face up and looks away cursing. 'The worst thing is, he *hurt* you.'

The anguish on his face as he works through it, his cheek clenching like he's grinding his teeth to dust, sends butterflies fluttering in my stomach.

That's what bothers him? That he thinks Charlie hurt me? The giant idiot's getting all worked up because what he told me at my place yesterday is true – he cares about me.

'He didn't. I hated what he said to me that night in the restaurant, but losing him didn't hurt. I wasn't in love with him.'

Rafael's brow smooths a little, and the flicker of tentative hope in his eyes makes me want to hug him.

'You weren't?'

'No. Not even close. Our relationship was a welcome distraction after my dad was convicted. It helped take my mind off things. But I never loved him. I don't think I ever saw a real future together.'

Silence engulfs the car.

'Are you going to say something?' I ask.

He stares through the windscreen, his elbow resting on his door, hand scrubbing around his jaw like a storm's still raging inside him, just beneath the surface.

'I didn't love him,' I repeat. Surely we can move on now? And talk about something more fun than my ex before I have to leave for my client's house.

Rafael licks his lips, then speaks slowly. 'Good. It'll make firing him much easier.'

'Pardon?'

He reaches across me, opens the glovebox, and takes out a thick manilla envelope.

'Here.' He hands it to me, and sits back in his seat, regarding me closely.

'What's this?'

'The company where your ex works. I bought it.'

I stare at him in shock. He can't be serious. But I know him well enough now to understand that he never bluffs. This is like him buying my building so he could ensure Mike's soundproofing was installed all over again. Only this is bigger.

'You bought it? Just now?'

He exhales with a humourless chuckle. 'I'm a man of means, Aurora. But even I can't acquire an entire imports company in fifteen minutes whilst driving like a bat out of hell across London to get to you.'

The envelope is a dead weight in my lap. 'Then when? And why?'

'The day after I heard the way he spoke to you in the restaurant. I intended to keep it for myself until I'd finished . . . *dealing* with him the way I saw fit. But seeing as he's still calling you, trying to weasel his way back into your life, I figured, what better way for you to show him you're done with him, than to take over his company yourself . . . and get rid of him.'

He rolls his neck, cracking it, unable to meet my eyes.

And it dawns on me.

This isn't about me. It's about him.

'This is a test,' I say in disgust. 'You want me to go all psycho revengeful ex on him, and for what? Because he's a bit of a prick sometimes? Because he said some nasty things to me? So what? You've said a whole lot worse, and what did I do? I had sex with you, like an idiot!'

'Aurora,' Rafael growls in warning, but I'm on a roll. The arrogant arse sitting beside me needs to hear this. I bet no one's ever stood up to him in his life.

'Don't!' I hiss. 'Don't you dare make out you're doing this for me. You're doing it for you because you're a jealous, insecure man who throws his toys out of his pram when he doesn't get his own way. I don't care what Charlie's doing. Him and I are done. And I certainly don't think about him enough to want to ruin his life in some weird, twisted revenge fantasy. And, frankly, the fact that you would is disturbing! What else are you capable of, huh?'

His lips thin into a grim line. 'You're behaving like a child. Not to mention being ungrateful. Take the company, or don't. But there's no need to start acting like a brat about it.'

'A brat? So we're on to name-calling now? Wow.' I blow out a breath. 'Funny, I thought dating an older man would mean they're more mature. Seems you blew that misconception out of the water. Thanks for clearing it up for me.'

'Are you saying you have a problem with me being older than you?'

I roll my eyes at how dense he's being. 'I'm saying I have a problem with this.' I throw my hands out. 'With you being a dickhead and saying arseholey things. With you thinking you can buy companies because someone you don't like works there. And then give them to me, and what? Expect me to flutter my eyelashes and say thank you? Maybe even suck you off in your fancy-arse car because I'm so grateful?'

'That's not what I—'

'It is, though. You say I'm being a brat. That I'm being ungrateful. But I didn't ask you for any of this, Rafael.'

'Then what do you bloody want?' he hisses.

I look back into his wild eyes, the molten bronze flecks in them rippling like flames, ready to burn if you get too close. This is him. A man I'll never truly understand. Because he doesn't let anyone get close to him. Not really. He tells me he wants me. And the way he touches me makes me believe there's something real there. Something worth holding on to and fighting for.

But when it comes to it, we're too different.

I don't need revenge like Rafael. I just want the truth and my father back.

My shoulders sag. 'I don't want this. Whatever *this* is. I'm sorry.'

'Beauty,' Rafael rasps, his tone turning from angry to pleading.

'Don't call me that. Please. Whatever this was between you and me, it's done. I don't want to sneak around behind my best friend's back with her brother, for God's sake.' I rub at my temples, the threat of a headache making my brain fog. 'And I'm not going to play into any of your weird little power games. Keep the company yourself. Or sell it again. I really don't give a toss.'

I throw the door open before he can argue back and jump out of the car, closing it behind me.

'Aurora?' His deep voice booms as he flies out behind me and rushes on to the pavement.

'Leave me alone,' I call over my shoulder as I march away, tears bubbling in my eyes even though it was always destined to come to this. He's Dove's brother. We never used to even like one another. 'I swear to God, Rafael, if you follow me, I'll scream for help,' I threaten, knowing it's the one thing that might stop him. Because we can't do this. We never should have in the first place.

His low, muttered curse echoes off the buildings behind me as I turn the corner and leave him in my past.

Chapter 30

Rafael

Another sheet of paper receives my wrath. Crumpling it into a ball inside my fist, I fire it across the room, gritting my teeth as it lands alongside a growing pile of identical ones beside the overflowing bin.

'Should I call Greenpeace and tell them why deforestation has increased tenfold?'

'Very funny,' I huff, as Gabe leans against my office doorway. Benedict stands beside him like a furry little henchman, here to witness my demise.

'Who is she?' His lips curve into a knowing smile that I'd like to wipe off his face.

'Who said it's a woman?'

He lifts one shoulder and drops it. 'What else can it be? You don't sweat this much even when one of our biggest accounts is on the line.'

If only he knew how wrong he is.

He bends and scoops up a ball of paper, unscrewing it. His face falls as he reads it. 'Brother?' he groans. 'Seriously?' He screws the paper back into a ball and tosses it into the bin. 'Does Dove know?'

'Not yet,' I grumble.

'Tell her before she finds out another way.'

'I was going to this afternoon . . . with Aurora,' I say.

Just the sound of her name makes my chest hurt. I rub at the centre of it and Gabe looks at me in concern.

'You oka—'

'I'm fine,' I grit out before he can make a big deal out of nothing. 'Just a little indigestion.'

Bloody liar. My heart feels like it's being wrung out like a wet rag, but I can't tell my brother that. He'll assume there's something wrong. Make me go for a check-up. The only thing wrong with me is the fact I'm physically sick from the idea of Aurora meaning what she said. That me and her are done. Her calling me jealous and insecure I'll take. She's not wrong. I am bloody jealous of any bastard who's touched her. And my insecurities revolve around her walking out of my life. Which she did this morning.

'Aurora . . . She's everything I want, she's . . . goddamn it . . . I *need* her, Gabe.'

His brows shoot up at my confession. He's never heard me ever come close to saying anything like this about a woman before.

'Do you love her?' He looks at my miserable face and must see his answer. 'Then what are you doing sitting here, trying to write apology letters, when we both know anything you come up with will sound like an illiterate mole wrote it?'

I snort. 'Thanks for the vote of confidence.'

'Aurora needs to hear it directly from you. You excel at face to face, Rafe. You're good at having difficult conversations with people. It's why you're the best CEO this company has ever had.'

'Don't let our father hear you say that,' I mutter.

I push my finger and thumb into my eye sockets and exhale. My brother doesn't know how wrong he is. Sure, I've made Fairfax Guardian a tonne of money and brought in high-profile clients since I took over from our father. But no one in the family knows the real reason we lost the Wyndham account. None of them know it was my fault. That I fucked it up because I was weak.

None of them know just how screwed up I am.

'I'd rather not look at your sour face for the rest of the afternoon. Go and sort it out with her. Then work out how you're going to tell our sister that you're in love with her best friend.' He frowns. 'I don't bloody envy you that one.'

'Thanks.' I grimace, but Dove's reaction is the least of my problems. Especially if I can't get Aurora to forgive me.

Gabe shakes his head, giving me a withering look before he leaves, Benedict hot on his heels.

He's right. I *can't* fail. I promised myself after what happened with the Wyndham account that I'd never bloody fail at anything again.

And this is Aurora. There's no way in hell I'm going to fail with her.

I drop my head into my hands. *What have I done?*

My phone chimes with an alert from my home security system, breaking into my dark well of self-pity. I open the connected app and select the camera in the hallway. Aurora's stepping inside the front door, her eyes darting around like she's checking I'm not home.

She'll be coming to get her things. Erasing herself from my life.

I can't just sit here like an idiot and watch, knowing I'm about to lose her. I have to do something. I have to convince her to stay.

I grab my car keys from my desk at the exact moment her lips move. I turn up the volume on the camera.

'You had to ruin it, didn't you? Just when I was starting to think you weren't that bad,' she mutters, wrapping her arms around herself like a shield.

I zoom in on her face, catching the wobble of her lower lip.

She's upset.

Over me. Over us.

And as much as the sight of her hurting eats me alive, it also stokes the raging fire in my gut. It means she cares about what she's losing. A dangerous boundary we're getting too close to. I should let her get her things and walk away. It's what needs to happen.

I rub at the centre of my chest, over where the healed line of skin sits beneath my shirt.

It's what I *should* do.

The camera picks up the choking sound she makes, a mix between a held-back sob and a garbled cough, before she shakes her head like she's chastising herself for *caring*.

The pain growing in my chest is greater than any I've ever felt before.

My office door hits the wall with a loud bang as I punch my way through it and storm towards the lifts.

I'm coming, Beauty.

Chapter 31

Aurora

Packing shouldn't take me this long. I don't have many things. It's the fact that I have to keep stopping to wipe my eyes that's dragging out the process. Everything in this room smells of him. It's torturing me. Reminding me of what almost was. But I'm being ridiculous. It was never going to end well between Rafael and me. We're too different. And he's so closed off. I barely know the man beneath the surface, despite how physically intimate we've been together.

This is for the best. He can buy companies for his next girlfriend. Maybe she'll be into that. *Girlfriend.* The word brings a lump to my throat. I wasn't his girlfriend, I was . . . I don't know what I was to him. A mistake? A fleeting itch to scratch? A mere sexual attraction for a woman he clearly held so much disdain for until recently? An attraction even he couldn't understand?

I huff as I pull the lid of my suitcase down and reach for the zip.

'Don't leave.'

I whip my gaze up and it collides with rich, molten bronze, glittering with emotion. Rafael stands in the doorway to his bedroom, looking at me like he's watching the end of the world happening right in front of him.

'*Please.*' The single word is hoarse, exhaled with a ragged breath like he ran here.

I turn back to my suitcase. 'I have to. We were never meant to happen.'

Rafael runs his hand around the back of his neck, hovering in the doorway like he's waiting for permission to enter his own bedroom. 'I'm sorry, Aurora. I'm not good at this.'

'Good at what?'

'Dating.'

'We're not dating,' I fire back, regretting it as Rafael's eyes pinch.

'Spending time together, then. And talking about what we both want. I'm not good at it. At navigating these . . . *feelings*.' He screws his face up. 'Arguing with my . . .' He exhales slowly, leaving me wondering what word he was going to use to describe what I am to him.

The bratty version of myself that he called out earlier in his car surfaces, reacting before I can rein it in.

'You've spent time with plenty of women. I'm sure you can conjure up some advice from your memory. Didn't you argue with Seraphina?'

I fiddle with my suitcase zip. *Now who sounds like the jealous and insecure one?*

'Not like this,' Rafael says.

'Dove said she threw a drink in your face,' I continue, like I'm picking a scab that should be left well alone.

'And?'

'And that sounds like a big fight.'

'I didn't think of it as a fight. More an overdue end to something I should have stepped away from a long time ago,' he says, his voice all deep and delicious and doing things to my core that it shouldn't be.

I shrug. 'Yet here you are, home from work in the middle of the afternoon, thinking about our fight.'

A glimmer of something passes over Rafael's face. Hope?

'Yes, I am here. I've never had a proper fight with a woman before, because I haven't ever cared enough to argue back. But not only am I here, Aurora, I'm prepared to bloody beg on my knees if I have to in order to convince you to stay.'

'Why?'

'Because I'm pretty sure I'm falling in love with you.'

No hesitation. Just spoken like it's a fact.

'What?'

He still hasn't entered the room. Still hasn't crossed the threshold. Yet he's dropped that bomb, delivered so matter-of-factly, like it was inevitable and should have been obvious to me.

He inhales through his nose, eyes locked on mine. 'I think I've already fallen, actually. I'm right down at the bottom of the bloody cliff. Looking up at the most incredible woman I've ever met in my life and hoping she doesn't finish zipping up her suitcase.'

I drop the zip I'm fiddling with like it's on fire.

'We've only slept together three times,' I whisper.

His gaze intensifies, making me shiver. 'And you've consumed every part of me – mind, body, and soul – for over three months.'

'You didn't like me. I was just material for your wank bank,' I say, like saying it out loud makes it true. Makes it all I am to him. Because the idea that he actually *loves* me . . . It makes my mind race at a million miles per minute.

What would being loved by Rafael Fairfax be like?

What would being held in his arms every night like I'm safe be like? What would being kissed like I'm precious be like? What would being looked at and listened to with amused molten bronze irises as I regale him with the virtues of various crisp flavours be like? Being adored enough that he fills his cupboards with them . . .

And what would being loved so much that he's irrational and jealous because he thinks an ex-boyfriend hurt me be like?

Rafael holds my eyes. He doesn't need to correct me, because the way I'm looking back at him – lips parted, pulse racing with desire – it's obvious that I *know* I'm so much more than that to him. And I always have been.

But he does anyway, making light burst from my core like a cascade of glowing stars.

'You've never been *just* anything, Beauty. You've always been *everything* to me. Even long before I realised it. And I'm not asking you to love me back, far from it. I'm just asking you to stay.'

We stare at one another. The air thick with need. But he won't move until I invite him to. He won't come to me without my instruction. I can see it in the way his eyes are darkened and intent on mine. He needs to know if I want this. He's waiting for me to make the next move.

I lick my lips, the need strong to still prove to him, and myself, that I have some control here. That Rafael Fairfax telling me he's in love with me doesn't mean I lose my own voice. That I don't have to bend to his every whim, the way people at his workplace do. If whatever *this* is between us is going to work, then he needs to understand that he can't throw his money around and get his way whenever he wants it. Not with me.

'I'm not sure you deserve to walk in here yet,' I say, allowing my eyes to rake over him from head to toe.

He arches a brow, his question coming out in an inviting growl. 'Then how do you suggest I come to you?'

A vision of something pushes to the front of my mind. Of him. Handing all control over to me. Trusting me to take charge and give us what we both need. If he wants us to work, then he needs to meet me halfway.

'On your knees,' I reply. 'Crawling.'

His eyes narrow and for one beat of my thundering heart I expect him to laugh. To tell me not to be so bloody stupid.

But he jerks his chin, gesturing to me. 'Stand up.'

Heat zaps all around my body, before it concentrates between my thighs, pulsing in my clit like a deep bass as I rise.

Holding my eyes he slowly removes his jacket and tie, placing both on the floor. Then his hands reach for the buttons on his waistcoat.

'Leave that on,' I breathe. 'I like it.'

His eyes blaze and a muscle twitches in his cheek. 'Very well.'

Then he lowers to his knees.

My breath echoes in my ears as he crawls across the carpet, painstakingly slowly, drawing it out like he wants me to remember every second. The broad muscles in his shoulders roll and strain beneath the starched white cotton of his shirt. The closer he gets, the more intense the scent of his cologne, mixed with hot male skin, grows.

I sink my teeth into my lower lip as he reaches my feet and looks up at me from beneath thick, dark brows.

'Aur—'

I silence him, lifting one finger in the air in front of his face like he's a dog I'm training. I don't know who this woman is who's taken over my body, but I'm loving watching what she does. And judging from the glittering heat in Rafael's eyes, so does he.

'Tell me what you want to do to me,' I breathe.

'Taste you,' he answers, not needing to consider it for a second. 'Wear you all over my face for the rest of the day.'

My breath hitches as he bows and presses a soft kiss to the top of my bare foot.

'Let me, Beauty,' he begs, tracing slow kisses up the inside of my calf until he gets to the sensitive skin behind my knee. 'Please don't deny me your taste. I can't survive without it.'

As he kisses the delicate skin, his eyes pinned on mine, my eyelashes flutter and a soft moan falls from my lips.

He kisses higher, rising to his knees and inching my skirt up my thighs with the care and precision a bomb disposal expert would handle something that's in danger of detonating.

'Tell me I can,' he utters, his voice dripping with desperation.

His breath is warm against my panties as he gently brushes his lips over the sheer fabric. It's so thin it might as well not be there. I can feel every soft pass of his mouth over me. It's the sweetest torture.

I let out a breathy whimper. 'Yes.'

'Thank you,' he groans, eyes hooding as he kisses me through the fabric. 'Soaking wet,' he murmurs, licking me in one slow, controlled drag of his tongue.

I bite back a moan, fighting to maintain that I'm still the one in control, when my body is screaming at me to hand it all over to Rafael and let him ruin me in the way only he can.

Strong, skilled fingers hook into my panties and pull them aside. The air hits my clit, sending it into a desperate throb. The first swipe of his tongue over it has my balance wavering and my inner thighs trembling.

Without saying a word, he lifts one of my legs over his shoulder. The thick bulge tenting his trousers makes confidence surge in my core.

He wants to do this for me.

He *loves* doing this for me.

I sink my hands into his hair, nails scraping his scalp as I guide his face where I need it.

'Do it properly,' I instruct. 'Or I won't let you put that big dick of yours inside me after.'

The primal groan that vibrates from his mouth as he sucks my clit is almost enough to make me come on the spot. But I don't want to. Not yet. I want to witness the grown, suited man, kneeling at my feet and worshipping me a little longer. Until the image is burnt into my memory – because, damn, what a hot sight it is.

Rafael groans and hisses, eating me out like a starving man who's been handed a life-saving meal. His tongue traces the lips of my pussy, dipping inside and sucking up my slick arousal with each pass of his mouth.

I try to hold back, but the moment he slides two fingers inside me and circles my clit with the tip of his tongue, my core tightens.

Fingers corkscrewing his hair, I grind my pussy down on to his face.

'Yeah . . . just like that,' I whine.

He eats me out faster. Harder.

Fingers me deeper.

'Rafael!' I come on his face with a sharp cry as I struggle to remain standing.

He drinks it up. Groaning and sucking up every wave and pulse of my orgasm. His fingers curl inside me, drawing it out for as long as he can, until I tug his hair and try to extract my sensitive clit from his mouth.

'Enough,' I whimper. 'I want you inside me.'

I'm feral as I yank him to his feet by his hair and smash my lips to his. I can taste myself all over him as he kisses me back with an urgency I feel in my bones. It makes the need to have him inside me overrule everything else.

'On the bed.' I push him in his chest, and he drops back on to it. Then I kneel beside him, tear his belt open, and pull his trousers and boxers down.

His glorious, thick cock springs free, jutting up from his body like an invitation.

Dropping my mouth to it, I suck up the glittering pearls of precum seeping from the slit.

'Jesus, Aurora,' he groans, palming the back of my head and pushing me down until my throat fills with him.

I pull back, despite how much I'd love to suck him off right now. I'm supposed to be mad at him. I *am* still mad at him.

Hooking my fingers beneath the edges of my panties, I slide them down my legs and take them off. Rafael's eyes widen as he gets a flash of my bare pussy.

'That's it. Come here,' he growls.

He reaches for me, but I place my palm on his chest and push him back down as I straddle him.

'Let's get one thing straight. I've not forgiven you for acting like such a caveman yet.'

'I'll crawl everywhere until you do,' he groans, reaching for me again.

I slap his hands away. 'I'm here because I want to be. Because I don't want to fight any more.'

'Me neither, I—'

His words are cut off as I bring my balled-up, soaked panties to his face and press them to his lips.

His lids hood and he lets out a groan, opening his mouth and accepting them as I push them past his teeth.

I smile at him sweetly. 'I'm not ready to talk to you again yet. I just want your dick.'

His chest heaves with laboured breaths as he watches every move I make, his arousal seeping from his pores like an aroma.

'You've got such a nice one. So big and hard,' I muse, holding the base of it and tilting my head as I take my time admiring it, teasing him.

He groans beneath me, his eyes rolling as I slide my hand up and down it slowly.

'I'm going to use it however I want. And you're going to be a good boy and watch.'

I'm pretty sure the tortured rumble in his chest would be accompanied by a curse word if he didn't have my soaked panties stuffed inside his mouth right now.

His eyes glitter like embers from a fire as I rise up and position the smooth, fat head against my entrance.

I hover, gazing down at him.

'Do you want me to put it inside me?'

'Uuuurrrr . . .'

'You don't. Okay, then.' I pretend I'm about to move away, and Rafael arches off the bed, then throws his body back down again in frustration, screaming around my panties.

I bite back my smile and take hold of his cock again. The tip smears wetness all over my wrist as I slide my hand up and down his shaft.

'Oh . . . you do?' I pout innocently. 'You do want me to put your cock inside my pussy?'

He lets out a whine, his eyes burning with desperate need.

The power thrumming through my body as I lower myself on to him, filling myself with inch after perfect, solid inch of his cock is like nothing I've ever experienced.

His gaze melts and he looks at me like he's in awe.

'Feels so good,' I moan, rotating my hips to help me take him.

Once he's all the way inside me, I tilt my head towards the ceiling with a happy sigh as Rafael groans, his cock twitching.

'You better not come,' I warn. 'Not until I say you can.'

Dropping both hands on to his thighs behind me, I arch my back and ride him. I work my hips at the pace I want, using him as my personal fuck toy. His balls brush my arse, and I whimper with each bounce on top of him.

His deep, husky groans fill the room. His hands are balled into fists, resting on top of my thighs, his knuckles white with the effort of holding back.

'Do you want to touch my breasts?' I moan, slowing to take him deeper.

'Mh-mh!' He grunts, his eyes pleading with me as the soft fabric of my panties bloom from his mouth like a flower.

I hold his gaze as I pull my top over my head, then unhook my bra.

The groan that clogs in his throat as my breasts fall free makes me clamp down hard on to his dick.

His hands are on me like a shot, cupping and kneading my tits like it's the first time he's felt them. He pinches my nipples, and I cry out and ripple around him.

It would almost be worth pulling my panties from his mouth so I can feel his hot tongue flicking over them. But I really want to watch him come undone whilst all he can taste is my cum-soaked underwear filling his mouth.

If he wants to call me 'his' and treat me like he can control me, then we can both play that game.

I increase my pace, spurred on by his feral grunts as he fills his palms with my tits like he can't let them go. Something about fucking him topless with my skirt hitched up around my waist, whilst he's fully suited and wearing a goddamn waistcoat, is so filthy. Like I'm his dirty girl, made to ride his cock and get filled with his cum.

I bite down on my lower lip as a rush of fluid coats his cock, making it slide deeper. I sink back on to it. Rafael groans like he's in physical pain and pinches my nipples as he thrusts up into me.

'Aww, is it getting hard to hold back?' I tease, pushing my tits further into his palms. 'How about if I tell you I'm about to come all over your cock?'

His eyes pin on mine with an intensity that steals my breath. Every tendon in his neck is exposed, tight and taut as I ride him.

His chest heaves with rough breaths and he stares into my eyes, *begging* me to do it.

I fire my hips faster, chasing my own pleasure. Using his cock to get myself off.

My orgasm builds with the intensity of a nuclear explosion, before detonating spectacularly. I fall forward, catching myself with my palms flat on Rafael's chest as wave after wave rips through me, blurring my vision and muffling my hearing.

'Fuck!' I whine. 'Rafael, oh . . . oh . . . *fuck* . . .'

I sink up and down, riding my release out in a tangle of overstimulated nerves that make it stretch on forever.

His hands dig into my hips, and his cock thickens inside me.

'You can come,' I pant. 'Fuck, you can come. Fill me . . .'

I moan as my orgasm spills into another.

I barely register the deep, guttural groan from Rafael as he comes inside me. I just keep riding out the high as warm, wet heat spills inside my pussy, making it so full that some runs out and snakes down my inner thighs.

'Oh my God,' I mewl, focusing on his face as my movements slow, working out every last drop from him.

He gazes up at me with a tenderness that has me pulling my panties from his mouth and slanting my lips over his in a rush.

'Rafael,' I whimper.

I kiss him desperately, grabbing his face in my hands. 'Don't ever be an arsehole like that again, okay? Don't make me fight with you.' I stumble over my words as I kiss him through them.

'I'm sorry.' He sinks his hands into my hair, holding me close. 'I'm so bloody sorry. Forgive me.'

I dive into another kiss, unable to tear my lips away from this man's kisses.

'I will . . . this time.' I smile against his mouth.

'I never want to fight with you again.' He cups my face, kissing me like a man who's been handed a second chance at life. 'But any time you want to stuff your panties down my throat, please, be my guest.'

I can't help it; I giggle. 'You liked that, did you?'

His answer is a groan as his grip tightens and he kisses me like he's sharing his soul with me.

Pulling away for air, I sit up, loving the way he feels nestled inside me, all thick and hot and semi-hard like he's already hoping for round two.

'I really like the waistcoat,' I say.

'Yeah?' he rumbles, gazing up at me. 'Will it get me fucked more if I wear one every day?'

I shrug, my lips curling up. 'Maybe.'

My eyes fall to the neck of his shirt, and I slowly undo the first three buttons, revealing short dark chest hair beneath. There, concealed beneath it, is the scar. I didn't feel like I had the right to ask before.

But now . . .

'What happened to y—?'

Rafael catches my wrist gently before I can trace the scar with the pad of my finger. He brings my hand to his mouth and presses the softest of kisses to my inner wrist, over my fluttering pulse.

'Another time, okay? I don't want to taint this moment with anything other than joy and relief that you didn't leave me.'

My throat thickens at the glassiness in his eyes as they plead with me again, but for completely different reasons this time.

'Okay,' I whisper.

'Okay,' he repeats softly.

The scar disappears as he adjusts his shirt and sits up.

Wrapping his arms around me, he pulls me into a kiss that makes me forget why I was ever mad with him in the first place.

Chapter 32

Aurora

'Are you sure you want to do this?'

'I have to,' Dove replies, peering through the windscreen of her car. 'I was told Vance will be here tonight. It's time I saw him on my terms. No more dodging his calls. No more wondering why the hell he's back. It's time for answers.'

I study the way she's gnawing on her lip. We're referring to the man from her past by his name now. I'm not sure if it's a good thing or a bad thing. But the longer Dr Vance Falcon has been back in England, with no sign of leaving, the more Dove's been talking about him. When I arrived at her house earlier this evening, after psyching myself up to tell her about me and Rafael, she whisked me out of the door before I could even catch a breath.

And that's how we ended up here, sitting in her car in the dark, in a part of the city I've never been to before, and would happily never visit again.

'Are you sure? It looks derelict.' I stare at the grimy building, a shiver running up my spine. I've heard more police sirens going off in the distance tonight than on an episode of *Police Interceptors*.

'There must be a bar in the basement. Look, there's a bouncer,' Dove says, unperturbed by yet another wailing siren a few streets away.

I follow her gaze and, sure enough, a giant, scary-looking bald guy stands beside a concealed door, scanning the alleyway, wearing an earpiece and dressed head to toe in black.

'Come on.' She opens her door and climbs out.

I rush to keep up as she strides to the bouncer with purpose.

'Evening, darling,' he drawls, eyes dropping over Dove's tight jeans and loose, silky blouse. 'You lost?' His eyes pass to me, and he chuckles to himself, drinking in the low-cut dress I'm wearing.

'We're here for the whiskey.' Dove gives him a calculating smile. 'Heard they serve the good stuff downstairs.'

'They might,' big bouncer guy replies. 'You can find out if your friend shows me her tits.'

His eyes return to me, and he drags his thick tongue over his lower lip. Bile rises up my windpipe.

'How about I show you mine?' Dove interjects, a steely look of determination on her face.

'Dove!' I hiss, but she flaps away my concern, reaching for the buttons of her blouse.

The bouncer's eyes widen as the swell of Dove's generous breasts come into view, cupped in a deep maroon bra.

'Fuck, you were hiding that rack beneath that shirt, weren't you, love?' The bouncer practically salivates as Dove stands with her hands on her hips.

'Now let us in,' she says.

'Nipples too,' he says, with another leery drag of his tongue over his lip.

Dove pulls the cups of her bra down for a couple of seconds, and the bouncer groans and adjusts the crotch of his trousers.

'Juicy titties you got there, love. How about a feel and I'll give you the full VIP tour?'

'Fuck off. A deal's a deal,' she says, pulling her bra up and buttoning her blouse.

He chuckles like it was worth a try and wraps his meaty fingers around the large metal pole-shaped handle, pulling the thick, heavy door open.

'Enjoy the whiskey,' he says, his hot breath hitting me in the face as we slide past him.

'What the hell is this place?' I whisper to her as we descend some metal steps, lit by a single bulb hanging from a cord above. The scent of something metallic fills my nostrils as we reach the door at the bottom.

'Well, I think it's safe to say it isn't just a bar,' Dove says, linking her hand in mine. 'You good?'

My heart's hammering against my ribs. We could be about to walk into a drug lord's den, or a brothel, or an organ-harvesting backstreet operating theatre.

I swallow thickly and nod. 'Yeah. You?'

'We're here now. Let's do this,' she says, sounding much more confident than the clamminess of her palm suggests.

I take a deep breath as Dove opens the door and we walk through.

The inside space is dark and cramped. Hundreds of bodies stand shoulder to shoulder, jostling around, yelling and shouting. Glasses are thrust about wildly, the liquor inside them sloshing out and landing on clothing. But no one notices. No one cares. They're all too busy looking at something.

'What the hell?' I squeak, squeezing Dove's hand. She squeezes mine back and weaves us through the heaving crowd.

The scent of male sweat and cigarette smoke tickles my throat as the crowd swells around us, curse words flying, then suddenly replaced by cheers.

We move closer to the source of their attention, and the sound of flesh hitting flesh increases over the raucous yelling.

Dove freezes, her attention fixing on a man standing inside a wide, empty circle on the dank concrete floor. His silver-flecked hair is slick with sweat as he wipes his forehead with the back of his forearm. His hands are bound with gauze, and he's shirtless.

The crowd moves, blocking out our view of his opponent, circling him inside the ring. The older guy spits some blood out on the floor, raising his fists back in front of his muscular torso.

'Vance?' Dove utters, her eyes widening.

There's no way he heard her, but it's like he can sense her presence, because he looks straight up and directly at us both, standing at the edge of the ring.

The momentary distraction provides his opponent a window of opportunity, and he swoops on it. The ripple of tattooed, corded back muscles is all I see before Vance is punched in the jaw and sent staggering.

The crowd erupts into another mass of curses and cheers as he drops to the floor, out cold.

A man calls out, 'Hell's Guardian! Undefeated champion.'

I look at Dove. She's staring at the scene in shock.

A guy behind us roars with anger. 'I lost a grand because of that piece of shit!' he snarls.

I yank on Dove's hand as the atmosphere around us plummets, and angry, liquor-fuelled men yell out threats and obscenities.

'We need to leave,' I shout over the noise of the crowd.

A huge hulk of a man looks at the two of us like a shark that has caught the scent of blood.

'What's the rush, darlin'?' he says, reaching out and pulling me to him with a bruising grip on my hip.

The move makes Dove's hand slip from mine, and I whip my head around in time to see the space between us fill with thick bodies.

'Dove?' I shout, wriggling in the man's grasp.

His grip tightens on my hip, and he pulls me against him. 'Feisty, huh? Save the fight for later. It'll make it more fun.' His other hand drops to the hem of my dress and ice-cold fear slithers up my spine. I can't fight him off. He's twice my size.

He slides his hand up the inside of my thigh and I push at it hopelessly, digging my nails into his flesh with no effect. His thumb grazes the edge of my underwear, and I look into his dilated pupils.

He gives me a leery smile.

'Get your hands off her!'

My throat seizes. *I know that voice.*

The guy's head snaps to the side in a blur of flesh and crunching bone. The tight grip he had on me disintegrates.

'Rafael?' I scream. 'What the hell are you doing here?'

He towers over the guy, who's bending, wiping at his bloody mouth. 'You shouldn't be here,' he says to me, his attention fixed on the guy who's now glowering at him and cracking his knuckles.

'Neither should you!'

He's dressed all in black. Black joggers, and a black t-shirt straining over his broad chest and hugging his thick biceps. But the guy who just tried to feel me up is wider than him and looks like he could get hit by a 747 and not feel a thing.

The crowd gathers around us like they're getting a free show.

'That your girl?' The guy sniggers, his hungry eyes flicking to me. 'Pretty sure I got the scent of her snatch on my fingers when I touched her just now.' He lifts his hand to his nose and makes a show of inhaling. 'Mm. Smells like she likes me.'

Rafael grabs the guy's hand so fast he doesn't have time to react. A sickening snap rings out as he forces his fingers back towards his forearm.

'That's for putting your disgusting fingers on her. I should rip them off and choke you with them!'

He grabs my hand and pulls me through the crowd.

'Wait! What about Dove?' I cry.

'Angelo's got her,' he snaps, punching open the door that leads to the stairs and outside.

I stumble along beside him, trying to keep up. Despite the way his chest's heaving, and his muscles are literally vibrating with adrenaline right now, he has an eerie control about him.

I gulp in the cool night air as we rush up the alleyway. There's no sign of the bouncer any more.

'What the hell were you doing there?' Rafael spits, leading me down the street and around a dark corner. The lights on his car flash and he opens the door, slamming it behind me after I scrabble into the seat.

'What was I doing there? What were you doing there?' I gasp as I struggle to get my hands to stop shaking for long enough to fasten my seatbelt.

Rafael leans across me and clicks it into place roughly, then starts the engine and screeches out into the road.

'Do you fight there?' I ask.

His face is a mask of cold, ruthless composure as we speed through the streets.

'Are you going to answer me?'

'Do you have any idea the danger you put yourself in?' he spits. 'Do you?'

The cold detachment in his eyes as he flicks them to me makes my breath catch in my throat. 'Dove wanted to see Vance.'

Rafael sucks in a sharp breath, his nostrils flaring. 'So you thought you'd play outings with her? For fuck's sake, Aurora.'

'I had no idea what that place was!' I shout back. 'You told me you were going to your parents' house.'

'I did.'

'And then you went there to fight? Why?'

'I wasn't fighting.'

'You get off on watching it, then?'

'No! I was there to make sure my brother didn't get himself killed.'

'Angelo?' I question, because no way can I see Gabe in a place like that.

Rafael's jaw hardens.

'You broke some guy's hand,' I splutter.

'I should have broken his neck,' he seethes.

'What?'

He thumps the steering wheel. 'I love you, Aurora! What the hell do you think I'm going to do when I see a sleazeball touching you?'

I clamp my lips together. He told me he'd fallen in love with me after our fight. But he hasn't said the words since. I didn't trust him then, but now? The way he sounds – so convinced, so *sure* – has my heart racing.

He's in love with me. So in love with me that he'll break a guy's hand. But he's still not telling me everything. I know him well enough to understand there's more to him being there tonight than he's admitting.

We drive in silence, the tension thick and filling the car, until we pull up on Rafael's driveway.

'Why was Vance there?' I ask as he kills the engine.

He stares out of the windscreen, his expression closed off like a vault.

'He broke her heart. I know that much. And now he's back again, and you're what? Playing fight club with him? Was that Angelo fighting him?'

Rafael's jaw clenches, but he gives me nothing.

'Was it?' I press.

'Yes,' he says finally.

'Why?' I splutter.

'Because Vance was there, and they both wanted to, that's why.'

'That's all you're going to give me?'

He climbs from the car and strides around to my side. I take the hand he always offers me to help me from his car, but this time it's covered in another man's blood.

'I'll go and clean up,' he grits, following my gaze.

We head inside and go straight to Rafael's bedroom. He strips off his dark clothing as he looks at me, his face set in a grim expression like a mask of stone.

'Come and shower with me?' he rasps.

My gaze drops to the scar running down his chest. There's still so much he's not telling me. Tonight is just another example of how he can't open up and let me in. How are we supposed to have a relationship if he won't be honest with me?

I shake my head. 'I don't want to.'

'Fine,' he hisses. 'Suit your bloody self.'

He strides past me in just his underwear and slams the bathroom door behind him. I pace up and down in front of the balcony doors in his bedroom. He never opens them, but everything about tonight has got my blood racing. I'm hot and clammy and need air.

Unlocking them, I swing both open, stepping out. The cool night air on my skin is a welcome companion, and I take a couple of deep breaths as I walk to a thick metal railing that runs around the edge between wide concrete pillars. The garden spreads out beneath, the scent of jasmine bushes tinting the air with sweetness.

The pillars are wide with flat tops. Plenty of space to climb up, sit, and soak in the calming silence of the night. I settle myself on one, bringing my feet up and wrapping my arms around my legs as I wait for the sound of the shower to stop inside.

Five minutes later Rafael appears in the open doorway with a towel wrapped around his waist, his hair wet and tousled.

'Get down,' he whispers. 'Aurora, get down and come here.'

I sigh and avert my eyes from his, back over the garden. 'It's so pretty. Why don't you ever come out here?'

'Get the fuck down!'

I whip my head around, ready to give him hell for thinking he can speak like that and order me around. But the sight of him stops me dead.

He's clutching either side of the doorframe, his face contorted like he's in agony.

'What's wrong?' I slide off the pillar to go to him, but he's already coming for me.

He grabs me in his arms, pulling me back on to the balcony. The force of my body crashes into his and he brings us both down on to the ground.

He slumps with his back against the pillar and bundles me on to his lap, the grip of his arms around my torso almost suffocating.

His entire body is shaking.

'You . . . could . . .' His chest heaves against my back as he struggles to speak, like something is tearing him up inside.

'You're holding me too tight,' I wheeze.

'You could have . . . fallen,' he chokes out.

The panic in his voice makes my throat burn. 'What?' I wriggle inside his grip until I can turn and look at his face.

Tears are streaming down his cheeks, and his lips are parted as he drags in rough, uneven breaths. 'Aur—'

'Shh. You're okay. Don't try to talk. Just breathe, okay? I'm here.'

I cup his cheek and look into his eyes. He winces and lifts one hand to his chest, rubbing it.

'What is it? What's wrong?'

He grabs my hand, placing it over his scar. His heart is beating wildly, racing like he's just sprinted for his life.

His face is pale and clammy, his eyes have lost focus.

'Breathe with me, okay?' I instruct, keeping my hand over his chest and my eyes locked on his. I take his hand and place it over my chest so he can feel it moving up and down as I breathe.

It takes everything in me to keep my breathing slow and steady and not panic at the sheer terror in his eyes.

'In,' I whisper, breathing in slowly and encouraging him to do the same. 'And out.' I blow out a slow, long breath, nodding encouragingly as the whites around his eyes become less pronounced and his breathing levels out.

'Again,' I whisper, stroking my thumb back and forth over his chest, tracing the line that he's never permitted me to touch before.

We breathe together until his heart rate slows, and his body relaxes.

'You're okay,' I soothe, stroking his wet hair back from his face. I keep the backs of my fingers resting on his cheekbone and gaze into his eyes. They're glassy and wet, but he's not crying any more.

'I thought you were going to fall,' he says, his voice hoarse.

'I'm fine.' I smile softly.

He stares at me like he's still processing what just happened.

'I couldn't live with myself if anything happened to you.'

The emotion in his voice has tears springing up in my eyes, and I nod, because I don't know what to say.

My eyes drop to his scar, and I open my mouth, wanting to ask, but knowing that he probably won't tell me.

'I feel the same way,' I say quietly.

He takes my hand in his and lifts it to his mouth, pressing a kiss to the centre of my palm.

Then he places it over his scar, right above his heart.

'I had heart surgery,' he breathes.

I nod, tears welling in my eyes as his barriers fall down like a tower of cards. I didn't know what I was expecting to hear. But nothing could have prepared me for the anguish on his face.

'I was nine years old, and I fell from the balcony at my parents' house. A planter broke my fall, but it smashed, and a piece embedded itself in my chest. I needed open heart surgery to repair the damage.'

'Rafael,' I whisper, my vision blurring.

'My heart stopped twice on the operating table, but they managed to bring me back.'

'Oh my God.' I look at the pillar we're leaning against. 'And that's why—'

'Why I'm a goddamn coward who's scared of heights? Yes. You know, every time I go to my parents' house, I walk around to look at that damn balcony before I knock on the door. It's a ritual I perform. For no other reason than to remind myself of who I am. And who I'm not.'

I sob at the way he winces. 'I can tell you who you're not. A coward. Don't ever say that.' I cup his cheek with my spare hand. 'Listen to me, that's a trauma. It's a horrible, awful thing that happened to you. Of course you're going to be affected by it. But you're not a coward! How can you say that?'

'It's what my father says. The day it happened he told me I needed to grow up, that I was becoming a man and needed to act like one. And could start by doing some "man's work" around the house. So I thought I'd show him how grown up I was by stripping the ivy that was growing on their balcony. My mother wanted to remove it all and repaint it. I climbed the rail, and I lost my balance and fell.'

My heart breaks for him. He's never looked lost before. He's always so confident, so in control. But looking at him now, I can see all the years of pain this has brought him.

'You're not a coward,' I whisper. 'You're incredible.'

'I swore the day I heard my mother crying over me that I'd never cause anyone to cry like that. I couldn't handle hearing it again.'

The utter despair on his face makes my heart twist painfully. 'But I don't understand why you'd buy a house with a balcony if you hate them so much.'

'I bought this house after I took over from my father as CEO for Fairfax Guardian. It doesn't serve me to forget, Aurora.'

'Why would you do that to yourself?'

He licks his lips, like he's contemplating how much to tell me. Inside my head, I'm pleading with him to tell me everything. To be honest with me. To let me in. But I can't force it. It has to be because he wants to.

His heart beats steadily beneath my palm and my fingers tingle against his warm skin.

'The Wyndham account,' he says eventually. 'My father worked his whole career towards securing a client like them. He'd set it all up. All I had to do was meet with the head of the company and sign the contracts. It should have been easy.' He blows out a ragged breath, his face pinching.

'What happened?'

'The guy, Montgomery Wyndham, liked to do business in . . . unusual ways. He invited me to his building in London. His offices were on the top floor. Fifty floors up. And he had a roof garden.'

I swallow, nausea swirling in my gut.

'He wanted to talk outside?' I say in understanding.

Rafael huffs. 'Not just that. He was having a charity abseil down the side of his building that day. Raising money for children with cancer because his daughter was being treated for leukaemia.'

'And you had to watch them going over the edge? That must have been hard, I'm so sorry.'

'It was. I started guzzling down champagne to get through it. I just needed to get the contracts signed, then I could get the hell out of there. My heart was racing, Aurora. I thought it was going to give out on me right there. It felt like I was dying.'

His voice cracks and something inside me splits wide open. 'It must have been awful.'

'Mr Wyndham thought it would be a great start to our business relationship, and stellar publicity, if we were to abseil it together.'

'He what?' I stare at him in disbelief, images of a traumatised and panicked Rafael searing into my brain and making me want to burst into tears.

'God-awful idea,' he mutters. 'The safety team there talked him out of it because I had no experience. But I'd already started drinking more to quell the bloody . . . the bloody *fear* that I was going to have to do it in order not to let my father down.'

'He'd have understood. He's your father.'

He shakes his head with a heavy sigh. 'Your father would have understood. Mine wouldn't.'

'So what happened? Why didn't he sign the deal?'

Rafael's gaze drops from mine as his brow knits like the memory is almost too painful to recount.

'I was pretty drunk, though I didn't realise how drunk until I made a comment about it being stupid to throw yourself off a building. He didn't appreciate that, so I went inside and tried to sober up. I found an office with a coffee machine, and I made myself one. But then . . . Fuck,' he curses quietly.

'But then?' I encourage.

He lifts his bloodshot eyes to mine. 'I don't want you to look at me differently, Aurora. I was drunk, it was a stupid mistake.'

Images of him wrecking the office out of frustration or throwing up all over the desk fill my head. 'What did you do?'

'This . . . woman came in. Smart, attractive. She could see I was freaking out, and she offered to help, told me I needed to relax and think about something else. And then she . . . *kissed* me.'

Sourness creeps over my tongue. 'You had sex with her?'

Rafael's silence speaks volumes.

'In *his* office,' Rafael says slowly. 'She was . . .' He swallows. '. . . bent over his desk when he caught us.'

The visual of Rafael fucking another woman is hard to stomach. I press my lips together, ignoring the sting of bile in my throat, even though it happened years ago.

'Right,' I murmur.

He winces. 'She was his wife.'

I snap my eyes up to his, clamping my hand over my mouth. 'You had sex with his wife on his desk? Rafael, that's . . .'

'I lost the deal. My father was livid. And he still doesn't know why. He thinks I just couldn't keep it in my pants. He doesn't know the full story.' He looks at me with shining eyes. 'I'm broken, Aurora.'

'No, you're not! You are not broken,' I sob. 'You're not. You were just a child. You needed help.'

'My mother wanted to take me to a therapist, but my father shut it down. He said men aren't made from talking about their feelings, but from taking action. He made me clear the rest of that ivy from the balcony with him as soon as I was home from hospital. The first time I shook so much . . . I wet myself. He made me carry on without getting cleaned up. He said facing up to it was the only way to get over it.'

'That's just cruel.' Anger surges through my veins, making my blood burn at the idea of a nine-year-old, traumatised Rafael being told to 'man up' and get on with it when he almost lost his life.

'Yeah, well. Didn't work, did it?' Rafael shrugs. 'I'm still screwed up. And he lost the biggest deal of his career because of it.'

'That's not your fault,' I insist when he flicks his eyes away from mine. 'Rafael?' I turn his face back to mine. 'None of it is your fault. You need to stop blaming yourself. And you need to talk to someone about it. This isn't healthy.'

'I'm talking to you.'

I stroke his cheek. 'You are. And I'm grateful you're sharing it with me. But I mean a professional. Someone who knows what they're doing and can help you.'

He rests his head back against the stone column. 'I don't deserve you.'

'Don't say that.'

'I don't.'

I swallow, my throat burning with the words that I've never voiced to anyone before. Not my father. Not Dove.

'I know what it's like to blame yourself for something, even though people tell you it isn't your fault.'

Rafael's brow furrows and he sits forward, searching my face for meaning.

'My mother died after giving birth to *me*. My father lost his wife because of *me*. And now he's losing his freedom because I can't help him,' I choke out. 'I'm not strong enough or smart enough to be able to get him out of there, even though I know he did nothing wrong.'

'Listen to me,' Rafe says, all of his usual confidence and assertiveness returning at once. 'You had nothing to do with losing your mother. Jesus, Aurora.'

'I-I k-know. That's exactly what I'd tell anyone else in my position. But it doesn't stop me from feeling like it was my fault.'

'And your father?' Rafael frowns. 'You could never let him down. Look at all you're doing. All you have done for him. You've never given up, not once. I'm in bloody awe of you.'

I stare at him, unable to speak. No words could ever convey how much hearing him say that means to me. Even if I'm struggling to believe him.

'Let's go back inside,' I whisper.

I help him to his feet, and he readjusts the towel around his waist, then holds my hand. He keeps his gaze firmly ahead until we're safely back inside his room with the balcony doors locked behind us.

'I'm sorry for shouting at you,' he says, pulling me into his arms. 'I didn't mean to scare you. But seeing you on that column, I just—'

'It's okay. I understand. I didn't, but now I do.' My eyes drop to his chest, and I trace his scar with the pads of my fingers. 'Thank you for trusting me enough to tell me.'

'The same goes for you too.'

He hooks his fingers under my chin, tilting it so he can slant his mouth over mine. His kiss is weighted with emotion, and everything about the gentle way he traces my tongue with his tells me this isn't like all the other times. His kisses have always been enchanting. But this one? This one's raw and wounded. Scarred.

'I don't think it's only heights that scare you,' I whisper against his mouth as he takes his time tracing the seam of my lips with his tongue.

'No. Now, I'm more scared of losing you,' he breathes.

He kisses me deeper, sliding his hands into my hair and holding me in place. Our bodies press together, and the solid length of him strains against the towel.

I shake my head against his lips. 'I think you're scared of disappointing your father. Of feeling like he doesn't love you and isn't proud of you.'

'Aurora.' He sighs, pulling back, but I know he hears the truth in my words.

'You should tell him what really happened with the Wyndham deal.'

'I was going to today. But he and Angelo argued, and I needed to get my brother out of there. It's how we ended up at the fight.'

'He doesn't get along with your father?'

Rafael grimaces. 'Angelo's relationship with him is worse than mine.'

He falls quiet and his gaze drops to my hand, still resting over his heart. I hold his eyes and dip my head, sliding my hand away and placing a soft kiss over the red, healed skin. He sucks in a sharp breath, and I lift my lips from his chest to gaze up at him.

'I'm sorry, I won't—'

'Do it again.' His voice is thick like it's an effort to speak. '*Please*.'

I place my lips over his scar again and kiss it gently. He watches me as I carefully pepper tender kisses down to where it ends, then back up again.

'Beauty,' he whispers.

His hand tangles in my hair, and he strokes it back from my face, studying me as I kiss up and down his skin again. The way he's looking at me has me pressing my thighs together. His eyes are intense, darkened with a mix of gratitude, awe, and desire.

'*If I'm going to get into a fight over a woman . . . Then she won't be just anyone. She'll be . . . mine.*'

That's what he said once, the first time he ever came to my flat. And that's exactly what he did tonight when he punched that guy. He risked his own safety for me.

It's time I risked mine for him.

'I love you.'

His eyes widen as the softly whispered words leave my mouth, like he never expected to ever hear them from me.

'I'm at the bottom of the cliff too. You don't have to look up to see me. I'm right beside you.'

'You are?' He searches my eyes. And I see the exact moment my confession sinks in and he allows himself to believe it. 'But you can't, you—'

'I do,' I say, pulling him to me for a kiss.

He hesitates, but as I slide my tongue past his lips he swoops on me, kissing me back until I'm panting. My dress is lifted over my head, and my bra and panties are slid off within seconds. I don't know whose hands are doing what any more. We're a tangle of limbs, touching, stroking, caressing.

'Tell me again,' he urges, his brow knotted as if he's confused as I lie on the bed and he climbs up over me.

My thighs part around his hips on instinct, allowing him to bring his body flush to mine.

'Tell me again, Aurora,' he pleads, his tone filled with a desperate need.

'I love you,' I say as he slides inside me.

'Again,' he begs.

'I love you,' I gasp, submitting to the delicious feeling of having him so close and deep.

'Again.'

I hold his eyes as he moves in and out of me with aching slowness, every cell in my body vibrating with golden energy.

'I love you, Rafael Francis Fairfax.'

He groans. 'You remember that?'

'I do.' I bite my lip in a smile as he pulls almost all of the way out, then slides back deep inside me where he belongs.

My eyes roll and I whimper beneath him.

'Aurora?'

'Yes,' I answer breathlessly as he keeps his pace, moving inside me with perfect strokes.

'I love you too. And I'll love you until my scarred heart takes its last beat.'

Tears prick my eyes as I gaze back into molten bronze that's shining with devotion, warming me from the inside out. 'Promise?'

'On my life,' he whispers, drawing me into another kiss.

We stay tangled in one another, coming at the same time a few minutes later. Two bodies, two hearts, two souls. Each time between us has been passionate, and intense, and electric.

But this time it's simple.

We're two people who have fallen head over heels for one another. Making love like we're desperate to cling on to every fibre of the other's being. Like we need one another to exist, to thrive, to *live*.

'Beauty,' he breathes, dropping his forehead to mine. 'Are you sure you love me?'

His vulnerability cuts me like a knife. He thinks his father isn't proud of him. Maybe that he doesn't even love him.

Looking into his broken gaze, I realise he's never had anyone he truly feels like he's enough for. Rafael Fairfax, ruthless CEO, award-winning businessman, a man people admire and dream of meeting.

And he's never felt like he's *enough*.

I press an achingly tender kiss to his lips, hoping it conveys just how much I mean what I'm about to say.

'I've never felt like this about anyone in my life before.' I search his eyes, holding his face in my hands. 'No matter what happens, I promise I love you, that I will always love you.'

The next crush of his lips on to mine is tinged with salty tears. But he doesn't need to worry. Because I mean every word.

No matter what happens, Rafael Fairfax has embedded himself so deeply into my heart that I could never dig him out even if I wanted to.

Because if I did, there'd be nothing left of me.

Chapter 33

Rafael

'I'm so close. I know I am. I just can't work out what I'm missing.'

I walk up behind Aurora and slide her hair to one side so I can press a kiss on her shoulder. She's been working on her father's case all morning, the sea of paper she's spread over my dining room table a testament to her exhaustive research.

'The solicitor just called. They told me my father's appeal will be denied unless we can find more evidence. If only I were smarter, Rafe. If I knew things about law instead of fashion, then I could help him. But this is useless. I'm getting nowhere. I'm failing him,' she says, her voice trembling.

'Listen to me. You are not failing him. You've never failed anyone. Not him, not your mother. You hear me? You're strong and you're smart. Even the police got this bloody wrong.'

'Thanks. But that doesn't help get my father out, does it?'

'How can I help?'

She turns inside my embrace, the despair in her eyes making way for hope as she looks up at me. 'You'll help me?'

'Of course I'll help.'

I kiss her, pulling my lips from her before I get carried away. Ever since last night's spectacular meltdown on my balcony, things have been different between us. She's been happier. Lighter. It's like she needed us to open up to one another. And if I'm honest, I needed it too. Last night was the best night's sleep I've had in ages. And waking up and sinking inside her as she looked into my eyes and told me she loved me again, confirming it wasn't all a dream, has made me feel like I'm punching the damn sky, despite the niggling voice hissing in my ear that this was never supposed to happen. She was never supposed to love me back.

Me being vulnerable and open to the hurt that love can bring is one thing. But inflicting that on Aurora? *I should have been more careful.* But damn, I don't want to be. If anyone is ever going to love me then I want it to be her.

God, do I want it to be her. I just have to ensure I never make her cry.

'Tell me what you need?' I say.

Her brow furrows and she gnaws on her lower lip.

'Beauty?' I coax.

'I thought Dominic might know something. Or have at least heard something, seeing as he's on the board. But last time I spoke with him . . .' She shudders. 'Can you talk to him?'

I stiffen. Dominic. I haven't seen him since the night I found him on the terrace with Aurora. The slippery bastard has been keeping a low profile, avoiding my calls, not being there when I've visited his office. He knows he fucked up. I'd never have had him down as the type of guy to put a move on a woman and make her feel uncomfortable unless I saw it with my own eyes like I did that night. And it wasn't just any woman. It was Aurora. Not seeing him these past weeks is a good thing. I'm not sure I could have controlled myself.

It's time I had it out with him.

'I'll go to his house later,' I tell Aurora.

'Thank you.' She kisses me, then pulls back sharply as the sound of my front door closing vibrates through the walls.

'All of my family are programmed into the security system,' I explain.

I take in a deep breath, knowing exactly who is stomping down my hallway.

Dove barrels around the corner, slamming to a halt as she spots the two of us.

Aurora flinches inside my arms.

'We were going to tell you, I swear,' she squeaks, her eyes widening with worry. 'Please, don't be angry.'

But my sister's glare is focused on me. 'You shagged my best friend behind my back! What kind of brother are you?'

I run my tongue over the edge of my teeth as she storms over. Aurora tries to step away, but I tighten my hold on her, keeping her firmly in place.

'We were going to tell you yesterday. I'm sorr—' I say.

She scoffs. 'Uh-huh. I speak, you listen. You need to work on your poker face, brother. I could read you like a book last night. The two of you have never liked one another. I'm not bloody stupid!' she rages when I try to interrupt. 'For you to suddenly go charging off looking like you're about to burst a blood vessel at the mention of her name. It was so bloody obvious!'

'Dove—' Aurora starts, but I interject.

Dove is vibrating with fury, but I can see the chink in her armour. All of this fire, all of this . . . hurt . . . it isn't because she found out her brother and her best friend have something going on, it's deeper than that.

'No, I'm sorry,' I say as calmly as possible. 'I didn't know he was going to be there.'

My sister's wince is almost imperceivable. But I see it. And so does Aurora.

'Rafael. I need . . .' Aurora whispers, looking up at me with a stricken expression because she wants to run to comfort Dove. But I keep her firmly in my grip.

'Not yet,' I whisper in her ear. If Aurora goes to Dove now before my sister regains composure, then Dove won't thank me for it. She's spent years forgetting the man who left her functioning like an empty shell of herself.

Dove sniffs, pulling her shoulders back. 'Don't try to make this about anything other than the fact you've been lying to me.'

She looks at me with a piercing clarity in her eyes as the memories from the past fade, and all that's left is cold, hard fury at being deceived.

'Okay,' I answer. 'In that case, ask what you want to know, and we'll tell you.'

My sister opens her mouth like she's preparing to assault us with a barrage of questions. But then her eyes drop to where Aurora's palm is resting over my chest – above my heart – and she sucks in a breath.

'Bloody hell, it's serious, then?' She whips her eyes to mine.

I let go of Aurora, holding Dove's gaze as Aurora runs to her.

'I'm so sorry,' she whispers, stopping in front of Dove. 'Please don't hate me. I never in a million years thought I'd ever like him. I'd have been more likely to accelerate if I saw him crossing the road.'

'Charming,' I grumble.

Dove shoots me a look that tells me to zip it before she turns to Aurora, her eyes sparkling.

'You'd have reversed too,' she says. 'Just to make sure.'

Aurora sobs out a laugh. 'Probably.'

A smile tugs at my lips as I stand back and watch two of the most important women in my life hover by one another, waiting for the other one to make a move.

'He hasn't sent you roses, has he?' Dove asks, suspicion oozing from her.

Aurora shakes her head. 'No. But those arrived this morning.' She gestures to the giant bouquet of lotus flowers I ordered after she fell asleep in my arms last night.

'Lotus?' Dove questions.

'They're the symbol of dawn, like the meaning of my name,' Aurora says softly, turning to gaze at me.

Her eyes shine with the same unconcealed joy they did when the flowers arrived, and I told her that lotus flowers can bloom in muddy water – just like how she's never given up, despite what she's been through.

Dove looks at me like I've grown an extra head. 'Rafe?'

'I love her.'

My sister's eyes light up and then she looks back at Aurora.

'You understand, if you want to ditch him, he'll haunt you like a weird smell? We'd all given up hope he'd ever fall for a girl, but knew that if the day ever came that poor girl would be stuck with him, because once he makes up his mind, that's it,' she adds.

Aurora gives Dove a hopeful smile. 'I mean, I love him too, so I guess I'm okay with that.'

Dove's brows shoot up and she exhales. 'Jesus, okay. Just . . .' She wrinkles her nose. 'I don't want to know . . . *everything*.'

Aurora nods seriously. 'Absolutely. No sex talk.'

'Ugh, please.' Dove covers her mouth like she feels sick.

The two women snort into giggles and then they're in each other's arms, a mix of apologies, sniffling, and tumbling words I can't make out.

'I need to make a call in my office. I'll leave you both to it,' I say.

'Yeah, sure, whatever.' Dove waves me off, not even glancing my way.

Aurora catches my eye and the relief on her face makes my heart swell. She'd been worried about telling Dove, but I know my sister. All that matters is that I treat Aurora the way she deserves, then my sister will be on our side. And I have no intention of hurting the woman I love.

After my call, I return through the kitchen, and their conversation floats towards me.

'Has Vance tried to contact you since last night? He looked right at you,' Aurora asks.

'No,' Dove replies. 'At least, not yet.'

I bristle. My sister's better off keeping far away from Dr Vance Falcon. The guy hurt her once; he isn't going to get the chance to do it again.

'How's the sleuthing going?' Dove asks.

Aurora's exhausted sigh makes my gut twist, and I pause, waiting to hear her response.

'I'm not getting anywhere. I know he's innocent, but I can't prove it. The only thing I've found that seemed weird was about that woman – the one who drafted the sexual harassment email to HR and then vanished into thin air. Well, she mentioned a client in the email. It must have been one she worked with my father on, but I can't find a thing out about them. It's like they don't exist.'

'Weird,' Dove muses. 'What's the name?'

I strain to hear Aurora's answer. Maybe it'll give me a start of where I can help.

'Larkhay,' she replies. 'My father had never heard of them either when I asked him. I found a candle company with that name, who are completely unrelated, but that's all.'

Something cold tightens around my windpipe.

Of course she hasn't found a client with that name.

Because Larkhay isn't a client.

It's a place.

And I know exactly where to find out more.

'Hey. Didn't know you were dropping by.' Dom gives me a wide smile as he opens the front door to his townhouse.

'Would you have been home if you knew I was coming?' I grit.

He laughs and ushers me inside. I follow him to the rear of the house and into the large, bright open-plan kitchen and living area that spans the width of the property.

'Drink?' he asks, opening the fridge and grabbing a soda.

'Not for me.'

I look around the room, my eyes settling on a sideboard with a picture of him and his wife on their wedding day.

'Twenty-five years,' he comments.

'Congratulations,' I reply without enthusiasm.

He slurps the soda from the can, leaning back against the counter.

'How are things?' he asks.

'Things are good,' I reply. 'How about you? You been out to the cottage recently?'

He pushes a hand back through his silvery hair, his eyes crinkling with a smile. 'Nah, not as much as I'd like. We're renting it out as an Airbnb.'

'Really? Since when?'

He shrugs. 'Few months.'

'Is that so?' I murmur. 'You never told me that.'

He chuckles. 'I know you didn't come over here to talk about holiday homes. What's eating you, Rafe?'

'Actually, I did want to talk holiday homes. When did you last go there?' I ask.

Dom's brows hitch with intrigue. 'Is this about that hot little blonde you were with last time I saw you?'

I clench my fists at the way his eyes gleam. 'Aurora.'

'Aurora,' he purrs. 'How old is she?'

'Twenty-five.'

Dom chuckles. 'You lucky bastard.' He puts his soda down and holds his hands out. 'Sure. As soon as the guests are gone, the place is yours. Have some time away from the city with her. Get the champagne out in the hot tub after dark. Must be the bubbles that makes the girls horny. Always works.' He winks.

'Even when they're not your wife, eh? What happens at Larkhay stays at Larkhay,' I say.

He grins like I made a joke. 'Exactly. Aurora will love it there.'

'Did Ella?'

He narrows his eyes, like he's not sure he heard me right. 'Who?'

'Ella,' I repeat, looking him dead in the eye.

It's the name I saw on Aurora's paperwork before I left my house. The woman who was about to file a sexual harassment complaint against George Thorne before she left the company and disappeared.

The one who mentioned Larkhay in her email.

He runs a hand around the back of his neck with an awkward chuckle. 'She, um . . . yeah, she liked it there. How'd you know about her? Does—?'

'Your wife doesn't know. Or if she does, then she didn't hear it from me.'

Dom's shoulders loosen as he blows out a breath. 'Thanks. I—'

'Don't thank me. I'm not keeping it a secret for your benefit. I only found out this morning.'

Dom shrugs, looking uneasy. 'You know what it's like, Rafe. These young women come to work and hang off your every word, eager to learn the ropes. Then they're working late, trying to get ahead. Batting their eyelashes at you and telling you they're so grateful for your help. And they're wearing these tight little dresses, and . . . fuck, you'd have to be a saint not to indulge a little, you know?'

My jaw clenches. 'Pretty sure that's called dedication to their career. One they probably work twice as hard as their male colleagues to earn the same respect at.'

Dom scoffs. 'Come on. You're bedding a twenty-five-year-old. You can't tell me you're immune. I saw her. She's got a body on her, that—'

'Talk about her again and I'll rip your tongue out!' I snarl, advancing on him and grabbing the neck of his shirt in my fist.

'What the hell's got into you? It was a joke.'

'Do you see me laughing?' I spit.

Dom locks eyes with me, and I stare back at the man I once had immeasurable respect for.

'She took the money, didn't she?'

Dom's lips thin into a stern line.

'Answer me!' I yell, shaking him.

'All right! Yes!'

'Why?'

'I don't bloody know!' he splutters. 'I think to get back at me when I told her I wasn't leaving.'

'She thought you'd leave your wife for her?' I snort at the pathetic cliché of it. I bet Dom told her whatever she wanted to hear in order to get his dick wet.

'She did after . . .' He looks to the side, unable to meet my eyes.

'After?' I growl.

His Adam's apple strains against my grip as I tighten it to make him look at me.

He swallows thickly. 'After she told me about the baby.'

Jesus Christ.

I drop him like a sack of shit, in disgust. 'You have a beautiful wife who loves you, with whom you've built an entire life . . . You have grown children, for fuck's sake.'

'I didn't plan on getting her pregnant. Jesus,' he hisses, rubbing at his throat.

'So you let an innocent man take the fall? They had evidence. How did they fucking have evidence, Dom?' I roar.

'I have access to every staff member's log-in. It didn't take much to remove Ella's details as the last one who accessed the company account. I didn't know George Thorne was the last one before her, I didn't—'

'You didn't bloody think! Or care! You just wanted to cover your own arse.' I grip my hips, breathing heavily, sinking my fingers into the fabric of my trousers so I don't stride back across the kitchen and murder Dom with my bare hands.

'The guy's going to get out on appeal soon. The evidence was flimsy at best. He'll be back living his life like none of this ever happened,' Dom argues. 'And you'll get your money back once the insurance pays out. Bet you're glad Fairfax Guardian aren't the ones who cover us,' he adds, attempting a stab at heinously inappropriate humour.

I shake my head in disgust. 'To think I used to look up to you.'

He holds a hand up. 'Listen, Rafe. This stays between us. You know my secrets, and I know yours.'

'Are you threatening me?' I snarl.

'Just reminding you of the facts. We've been friends for years. We've always had each other's backs. After losing Wyndham, I helped you land other clients. Helped bridge the void you'd have been left in without them.'

'For which I'm grateful, you know that.'

He eyes me warily. 'I know. And I'd also be grateful if this stayed between us. Plus, there's that other thing Aurora doesn't know about. She told me George Thorne's her father.'

I advance on him again and he throws his hands up in front of his chest.

'Relax. I'm just saying.'

'You're not *just* anything!' I hiss.

'My lips are sealed. But I'd have thought you wiser than to get involved with his daughter.'

I suck in a sharp breath. I can barely stand to look at him. But he's right. He's bloody right. I have no business starting a life with Aurora until she knows everything. Not just about my accident and how screwed up I am.

But *everything*.

'I'm going to tell her,' I grit.

Dom chuckles. 'Sure. Let me know how that goes. But take it from me, the last woman I upset stole millions from the company I'm on the board for, and disappeared without so much as a "fuck you".'

'Aurora's not like that. I haven't been lying to her and leading her on.' But even as I say the words, I wince. Because it's exactly what I've been doing. It started as revenge, spending time with her to find out where my money went. Then it became obsession. And then it turned to love. I can't imagine even being able to breathe without her, nor wanting to.

Dom sighs like he feels sorry for me. 'Ella was in love with me too. Or so she said. Now she's gone. And she took my baby with her. I don't even know if I have a son or a daughter.'

The sudden emotion brimming in his eyes has a niggle of empathy twisting in my chest. But what Dom knew about the money . . . and how it's affected Aurora . . . what it led to me doing that she still doesn't know about . . .

'And the sexual harassment email? Why not just delete it?' I ask.

Dom shifts uneasily, his hands curling around the countertop either side of his hips.

'Dom?' I bark. 'You son of a bitch!' I snarl. 'You changed it from your name to George Thorne's. Why?'

'Ah, that happened before . . . She told me she'd written an email to send to HR. I think she wanted to have something over me. Well, I couldn't delete it while she was still here; she'd have realised I had access to her account. So, I just changed the name.' Dom looks away. 'But then she was gone. And so was the money. And with all that going on, I forgot about going back to get rid of it.' His voice cracks. 'Rafe, you don't understand. She was so angry, saying I'd used her, that I'd lied to her. But I never lied. She knew I was married. I might have told her I loved her. I mean, I did love her. But, look, I didn't know it was George fucking Thorne who was the last one to access the account. I mean, what are the chances?'

'Pretty fucking high if they're working on the same client together! Jesus! With that and the email, you put the nail in the damn coffin. Because they didn't brush it off, did they?' I yell, fighting the voice in my head that's telling me to go and wring his stupid, lying, cheating neck. 'They convicted him. The guy's in bloody prison!'

'I know!' Dom shouts back. 'Don't you think I know? I don't think Ella even knew him. The client they started working on together wasn't brought up at the last board meeting, and Ella never mentioned it. But their client . . . it was a big one. They both had access to a lot of information, and a lot of money, Rafe. *A lot of bloody money.*'

'Jesus,' I utter, pinching the bridge of my nose. George Thorne took the fall for something he didn't do. He was just in the wrong place at the wrong time.

'I even thought maybe it was him to start with, until I realised Ella had disappeared. I'd never have put his name in that email if I'd known what she was going to do, I swear.'

'What would you have done? Put some other poor bastard's instead?' I snort.

I shake my head as Dom stares back at me, his expression heavy with guilt. It's exactly what he would have done. No matter what, Dominic was always going to make sure he came out of all of this shit without scars. He's pathetic. The man I idolised and considered a father figure is a ruthless piece of shit who only cares about saving his own skin.

Bile rises up my windpipe and I have to press a fist to my mouth to chase it away.

Dom's words are hollow. 'I didn't know what was going to happen. What Ella was planning. You were meant to land a huge payout. That investment was solid. Listen, Rafe . . .'

I wince hearing my name from his lying lips.

'I don't care about the bloody money,' I whisper.

Dom snorts. 'Two hundred and forty million, of course you bloody care. Don't try to act all holy about it. You wanted that money. You wanted to show your father what you were capable of. And like I said, Thorne's in a white-collar prison. He'll be fine. And he'll be out soon enough. But if any of this comes out . . . Just think about it. I'm not the only one who has something to lose here. You're involved too.'

The growl in my chest builds. The threat's there, lying dormant in the undercurrent of his tone. Insidious and poisonous. Dom knows what happened with the Wyndham account. He's the only one who knows the whole story. A story he swore to me he would never tell my father.

But my father's respect isn't the only thing I stand to lose.

Aurora.

Dom's words send a wave of realisation racing through me like acid.

'Fuck!' I snap, pushing my hands back through my hair as the enormity of my other secret hits me like a sledgehammer. How it played a part in Dom's huge fucking charade.

I charge at him, rage boiling the blood in my veins. 'You knew all this! You were the one who put my name forward! Encouraged me to do it! "Stand up for what's right," you said. You bastard! You made me a pawn in your sick and twisted little game. You—'

The front door closes, followed by the scamper of claws on hard floor, and I stop inches from Dom, fist drawn back, ready to drive it into his face.

I stare at him, vibrating with barely contained rage.

Dom's dog jumps excitedly at our legs, but his eyes remain fixed on mine, glossing over with a hardened shutter of self-preservation as he parts his lips and slowly enunciates each word. 'Down, boy.'

I drop my fist, glaring at him as his wife walks into the kitchen.

'Oh, hi, Rafe,' she trills, placing her handbag on the counter, unaware she arrived just in time to stop me from smashing her husband's nose to the back of his skull.

I break Dom's gaze and give her a friendly smile, portraying normality and calm so well it's like I'm working towards winning a goddamn Oscar.

'Hi, Kate.' My eyes drop over her outfit, specifically the floral jacket she's wearing. 'You look lovely.'

'Flattery will get you everywhere.' She laughs. 'Oh, Freddie, get down, you silly boy,' she scolds.

I bend, curling my palm around the little dachshund's head and petting him. 'Hey, boy,' I say, earning myself a lick across the palm.

Kate calls him again and he runs over to her, his tail wagging.

'Would you like to stay and have something to eat with us?' she asks, bright and welcoming, the way she always is.

'No, thank you. I have things I need to do.' I look at Dom, my jaw clenching. 'I'll see myself out.'

Chapter 34

Aurora

It's dark outside as I pad barefoot into the kitchen.

'Here you are,' I say, stifling a yawn as I spot Rafael, standing hunched over the dining table in just a pair of joggers, staring at the paperwork laid out on it.

I curl my hand around his bicep and rest my cheek against his hot skin.

'How long have you been down here?'

I scan the table. Earlier today it was just my notes. Now the sea of paper has doubled. Handwritten comments are hastily scribbled on to Post-its and stuck to new email threads and client contacts I've never seen before.

'Wow! How did you get all of this so fast?'

Rafael jots something down on another Post-it and reaches over the table, slamming it on to a piece of paper. 'I couldn't sleep,' he grumbles.

I run my fingers up his bicep, loving the strength that ripples in the muscle as it flexes beneath my hand like he can't stop his body reacting to my touch.

'Come back to bed. You've got work in a few hours.'

'I'm taking the day off.' His brow is set in a deep frown of concentration as he surveys the papers.

My heart soars at the determination on his face. 'To work on this?'

He turns his head, pressing a kiss to my temple, but doesn't answer.

'Rafael?' I urge.

He keeps working, so I snake my hand up to his cheek and turn his head to face me. His eyes are bloodshot, and he looks like he hasn't slept for a week, let alone one night.

'Come back to bed,' I whisper. 'You need to rest.'

He sighs, looking into my eyes with an adoration that makes warmth blanket my chest.

'Aurora, you haven't rested since your father was convicted. And I'm not going to rest now that I know he's innocent.'

'You're doing this for me?'

'Yes . . . And because it's the right thing to do.' He turns away again.

I can't help it, I break into a wide smile. 'And to think we used to hate one another. And you thought he took your money,' I tease.

He keeps scowling at the papers like they hold the answer, if he can only find it.

'Rafael? Did you hear what I said?'

'I heard,' he clips.

I roll my eyes. I love that he's doing this, but I don't want to see him make himself ill by not taking a break for an hour or two.

'You say it like it amuses you,' he adds, his attention still fixed on the tabletop.

'That we hated each other, and now we're . . .' I snuggle into his bicep with a soft sigh as the heat of his skin warms me.

'And now I'm in love with you and dreaming of the day you're my wife and the mother of our children and share every penny I have to my name?' he finishes.

'What?' My voice clogs my throat.

Rafael looks at me from beneath lowered brows. 'What's wrong?' His expression morphs into worry as he scans my face.

'Um . . . nothing. You sound very sure, that's all.'

'I am sure. I love you,' he replies seriously. 'What else could I possibly need to be surer? I want to marry you, Aurora. But first, we're going to get your father out.'

'We are?' Hope lifts my voice at how confident he sounds.

His eyes flick back to the paperwork and a muscle clenches in his jaw. 'My wife is going to dance with her father on her wedding day.'

I blink at him, unable to speak from the emotion bubbling in my throat. For months no one except Dove has believed me. And now, not only does Rafael believe me, but he's making it his mission to help me.

He isn't going to stop until my father is free.

I take a deep breath, forcing my voice to work. 'I love you,' I whisper. 'I love you so much, Rafe.'

He pauses. 'Rafe?'

I stall. I've always called him Rafael. And he's never said a thing about it. But this time 'Rafe' slipped out so easily, like it was right.

'Do you not like it? I just hear your family call you it, and—'

'Aurora.' He twists his body, wrapping both arms around me and tugging me closer until my chest is flush to his. 'You're my entire world. You can call me whatever you want.'

His eyes glow in the lamplight with a tenderness that makes my legs weak.

'Do you want to call me Rory? My friends do. Well, Dove does.'

His smile is soft, but there's a glimmer of hurt in his eyes, like he hates to hear me admit I have no friends apart from Dove. Not since they abandoned me after my father's conviction.

'Do you want me to?' he asks.

I lick my lips. 'I don't mind. But I . . .'

'You?' He hooks my chin and tilts my mouth up, hovering his over mine.

'Still call me Beauty,' I breathe.

'You like being my sleeping princess?' he asks, rubbing his thumb over my lower lip and tracing its path with his eyes.

'I like being yours,' I confess.

His pupils blow wide. 'You admit that you're mine?'

I swallow, steeling myself for the moment his lips touch mine as he leans closer until his breath fans over them.

'I'm yours,' I whisper. 'As long as you're mine too.'

He brings his soft smile down over my lips and kisses me tenderly. 'I love you, Beauty. Now go back to bed before I spread you out on this table and ruin all my progress.'

'Are you coming?' I ask, unable to resist pressing another light kiss to his mouth.

'Soon,' he replies.

He kisses my forehead and watches me leave the room.

The following morning Rafael's rubbing his jaw as he reads a document. I didn't go back to bed last night. I couldn't sleep knowing he was down here, working tirelessly to help my father. So we've been here, side by side, for hours, doing this as a team.

But I did force Rafael to take a break, despite his protest. He's now dressed in jeans and a t-shirt; his hair is wet from his shower.

'Coffee?' I say, holding a cup out to him.

'Thanks.'

I sit down in the seat beside him. 'What next?'

He hands me a thick folder I've never seen before. 'Press articles from the time of the trial. Pull out and highlight any saying anything other than proven fact. We want to demonstrate public opinion was swayed before your father even set foot inside that courtroom.'

'Okay,' I reply.

The two of us work together in companiable silence for another hour. I keep stealing glances at Rafael, and pitch in where I can. He's intimidating with how intense his laser focus is. But he's brilliant. Completely captivating. Now I know why his staff have so much respect for him.

And he also looks hot as hell.

I stretch my arms above my head, eyeing the way his navy t-shirt hugs his broad chest. We need another break. As determined as I am to find something that will help my father, I know that when I push myself for too long, I make mistakes. I miss things and have to circle back around to them again. Looking at Rafael and how capable he is, I'm not sure he has the same issues. But I still want to make sure he doesn't give himself eye strain or worse.

'I need to film a blog post for some items a brand sent me. Can I use your dressing room?'

He frowns, eyes still on a court transcript. 'Course you can. You don't need to ask. And it's *our* dressing room.'

'It's for a new summer line. Lots of cute dresses. *Short* ones,' I add.

His focus doesn't break.

I twirl a strand of hair around my finger. 'Can you . . . hold the camera for me?'

That gets his attention. His eyes lift to mine with a gleam of interest sparking in them. 'You want me to film you?'

I tilt my head, my tone suggestive. 'That depends. Are you going to touch yourself while you watch me?'

He sits back in his chair, his gaze dragging down over me and hovering on my breasts in my t-shirt.

He licks his lips. 'If I don't, I'll be wishing I was.'

'Come on.' I stand and hold out my hand. He threads his fingers inside mine, following me upstairs to his bedroom and into the large dressing room.

Row upon row of immaculate suits line the walls, but there's a section that's been cleared, which now homes my meagre collection of clothing.

'I'll film with your things in the background. It'll look better,' I tell him, crossing the room to open the box I've been sent from one of the brands I regularly work with.

'We need to take you shopping again,' he grunts, scowling at my clothes like they've personally offended him.

'It's fine.'

'It's not fine,' he huffs. 'You've hardly got any clothing, Aurora.'

'Thought you preferred that.'

I roll my eyes when he keeps glaring at my pathetic-looking rail of items.

'We'll go tomorrow. I have a personal shopper who can help us source everything. Get you some new dresses. New shoes. Handbags. The lot.'

'Why?' I shrug. 'It's not like I'll wear fancy designer things when I'm cleaning people's houses for them and walking their dogs. Unless . . .' My throat burns. 'You're not embarrassed to be seen with me, are you?' My mind flits to Seraphina and how stylish she looked that night at the restaurant. 'I know I'm not polished and wearing all the latest—'

'Bloody hell, Aurora. Who put that idea in your head?'

His outburst has me snapping my eyes to his. His nostrils flare. He looks ready to go into battle.

'No one,' I flounder. 'I was just thinking out loud.'

His face softens. 'Beauty, the only reason I want to take you shopping is because I want to give you everything. Not because I want you to look a certain way. I love you whatever you wear, but . . .' His eyes drop over me as I shimmy into the first new sundress I need to film. 'But that one you're definitely keeping.'

'You like it?' I smooth my hands over the front of the white dress. It's got tiny red rosebuds embroidered all over it, and the chest area gathers and ties in a bow, lifting my breasts up.

'Does it come in more colours?' Rafael asks.

'Pink with white daisies, I think.'

'Order that one as well. And get two.'

'Two?'

'In case I rip one off you.' He reaches down and squeezes the crotch of his jeans. 'Damn, I can't get over how sexy you are.'

I giggle and open up the camera on my phone, ready to film.

'How many clients do you have?' he asks, watching me.

'Only a few who I clean for and organise their wardrobes, that sort of thing. And one whose dog I walk a few times per week.'

'Dog?'

'Yeah, he's adorable,' I gush. 'He's a dachshund.'

'What's his name?'

I flick my eyes up to Rafael's, the back of my neck heating. 'Um . . . Freddie,' I confess.

'Freddie,' he repeats slowly.

I turn my back on him, my cheeks burning as I busy myself with the box of clothes again, so I don't have to look at him.

'Aurora?' he rasps, all deep and gravelly.

'Mm-hm?'

'Turn around.'

I look back at him and he raises both brows. *Damn, why does he have to look so hot when I know he's busted me?*

My mouth dry, I squeak, 'I needed to know if Dominic knew anything. I thought maybe I'd overhear something. It was a stupid idea. But it just felt like fate, or I don't know, a sign, when I heard his wife was looking for a cleaner.'

'It was a genius idea.'

His praise has my cheeks heating further. 'How did you find out? Does Dominic know? Does Kate know?' Panic claws at my throat. Kate's a lovely woman. I'd hate her to find out I'm not who I said I was from someone else. I never thought it through, but I want to be the one to tell her who I really am.

'Neither of them knows.'

'Then how do you?'

'A floral jacket.'

'What?'

Rafael shakes his head. 'Never mind.'

I sigh. 'It was a long shot. But I needed to try. I'll do anything to help my father.'

'We'll get him out.'

The confidence in Rafael's voice is a lifeline I desperately cling on to. 'Maybe we'll find your money as well. I'm sorry you lost so much.'

He exhales. 'So am I. But that's not what matters.'

'The truth is.' I nod.

His eyes pinch before he turns away from me, running a hand around his jaw. 'Yeah. You'll get the truth, I promise. Just remember that whatever happens, I love you, okay? Never forget that.'

I walk over to him and rise on my tiptoes, pressing a kiss to his stubbled jaw. 'I love you too.'

His eyes soften as he gazes down at me, making butterflies swarm in my stomach.

'Are you ready to film me now?' I beam at him and hand over my phone.

'Ready whenever you are,' he replies, his voice husky as he takes a seat on a deep blue velvet chaise.

He holds the phone up and looks at me from beneath dark brows, waiting.

I get into position and nod, indicating he can start recording.

His attention drops to the screen as I plaster on a smile and go through my intro, talking about the brand I'm wearing and their new collection. But the entire time I feel his eyes on me, like he's undressing me through the camera.

'It's called a "milkmaid" style, and it has this gorgeous tie detail on the bust,' I chirp, loosening the ribbons at my cleavage, then re-tying them tighter to demonstrate how you can accentuate your shape. 'There's enough support in this one that I don't need to wear a bra.'

A low groan steals my attention, and I look up. Rafael's gaze is fixed on the camera. He drags in a rough breath, which I know the camera will have picked up. I'm going to have to re-record now I have his background sound in it, but I carry on, regardless, a frisson of energy sparking in my core at the way he's transfixed on me.

'Lots of support, see?' I purr, leaning forwards and shimmying so the movement of my breasts can be seen.

'Bloody hell,' he rasps quietly.

I continue like I haven't heard him.

'And it's got such a cute hemline,' I muse, lifting the floaty layer of cotton away from my legs, then twirling in it, giving Rafael a flash of thigh.

I spin back to the front and my eyes collide with his glorious, thick dick. He's freed it from his jeans, pushing them down over his hips, and is slowly palming the solid length in one hand as he continues to film me.

My mouth waters and I lift my eyes directly to the camera. 'It's a sexy dress. Perfect for date night. Just the right length to be naughty in. To hitch up around your waist and . . .'

'Jesus,' Rafael hisses.

I bite back my smirk as he drops my phone.

'Get over here and get on my cock, Aurora.'

I trot over, squealing happily as he yanks me to him the second I'm within reaching distance. Our mouths collide in an impatient kiss, and his hands roam underneath the dress, grabbing my arse cheeks and squeezing. He hooks his fingers around my panties and slides them down my thighs.

'Get me inside this pretty pussy before I explode.'

He pulls me on to his lap, lining his cock up, and pulling me down on to him in one smooth move.

'Rafael!' I moan as his chest vibrates with a husky groan.

'Fuck yeah, just like that. Take my cock, Beauty. You're so wet already.'

'You make me wet,' I say as he pulls me up, then glides inside me again.

'Yeah? You want my cock inside you so badly that you're already wet before I've even touched you? Just the thought of this cock does it for you, huh?'

'Yes,' I whimper.

'Dirty girl,' he tuts. 'Bet you expect to be allowed to come on it too, don't you?'

'Mm, yeah, I do,' I moan as he controls the pace I'm riding him, with his palms full of my arse cheeks.

'Bet you want to milk it dry. Take my cum deep inside this sweet little pussy.'

'Uh-huh,' I gasp.

He speeds up, bringing me up and down his cock and making my breasts bounce.

'Get those tits in my mouth, Beauty.' He grabs the ribbon between his teeth and pulls, untying the bow. I pull the fabric out of the way and the sound he makes as he sucks one of my nipples into his mouth has wetness running from me, coating his dick.

I ride him hard as he kisses, sucks and nips at my breasts like he can't get enough. Then he squeezes my arse, pulling my cheeks apart and making me clench down on to him.

'I want to fuck you from behind so I can look at this beautiful arse too.'

He lifts me off his dick and it's wet and glistening in my arousal. His lips curl into a smug smile.

'All mine,' he rasps, reaching under my skirt and running his fingers through my wetness. I gasp as he strokes my clit, steadying myself with my hands on his shoulders. 'You're so damn perfect,' he says, gazing up at me. 'Now get on your knees for me.'

I scrabble to do as he says, hating the empty feeling from just a few seconds without him inside me.

Resting my forearms over the velvet chaise, I look back at him over my shoulder.

'Like this?' I tease.

He pushes my dress up around my waist, slamming his palm to my skin in a soft spank. 'Like this,' he growls, driving inside me with a deep thrust.

I'm forced into the velvet cushion as he fucks me hard and deep from behind, one hand on my hip to keep me in place, the other teasing my arse cheek open until cool air dances against my skin.

'So goddamn beautiful,' he rasps.

'More!' I cry, wanting to get lost in pleasure and not think for a while. Not think about the pile of paperwork that's waiting for us downstairs. Not think about what will happen if we don't find the answers we're searching for. Not think about anything else, other than chasing the physical high that I feel when I'm with him.

He bottoms out inside me with a masculine groan that I feel roll through me like a rich wave. I never thought sex could be this good.

'Take that cock, Beauty. That's it. It's all yours,' he growls behind me.

His hips slap into my arse on each forward surge.

'Oh fuck,' I whimper. 'That's so good.'

'Yeah? You like my cock buried deep inside you, don't you? You like being full of me. Stretched wide, ready for my cum.'

'Yes,' I cry out shakily. 'Please, yes!'

'You're mine, Beauty.' He grunts, working his cock into me harder. 'All mine.'

'Rafael,' I moan.

'Uh, yeah, so wet. This tight little cunt loves to be stuffed full of my cock, doesn't it?'

'Only yours,' I cry. 'Only yours.'

'Yeah. Only mine.'

His grip on me tightens, and then he's fucking me. In and out with deep, precise strokes. I cry out at how good it feels, my hand scrabbling against my clit to rub faster. My orgasm barrels towards me, taking me by surprise.

'I'm coming! Oh, God!' I cry.

'Good girl. Come on my cock.'

His arm wraps around my waist, holding me against him as I collapse, my pussy spasming through an orgasm that steals my breath.

'Rafael!' I gasp. 'So good.'

'I love you,' he growls in my ear. 'I'll love you no matter what. Tell me you love me,' he chokes out, burying his head into the crook of my neck.

'I love you too.'

My words are his undoing, and he comes with a deep grunt.

'Jesus,' he chokes, his body shaking against mine with the force of his orgasm. 'Aurora . . . fuck . . . I love you. I love you so much.

I'll never stop. Promise me the same. Tell me you'll never love anyone else. Only me.'

He turns my face, holding my chin as he crushes his lips to mine.

The desperation in his bruising kiss makes my heart bleed for him. I know what he's really asking. Will I love him no matter what? Or will I make him feel alone like his father did? Make him feel like he isn't 'enough'?

'I promise,' I sob, my emotions spilling out into our kiss. 'I promise you, Rafe. I'll only ever love you like this.'

He presses his forehead to my temple, his face screwing up. 'You have all of me, Aurora. Every part of me is yours. I'll love you my entire life, I promise you.'

Chapter 35

Rafael

'You look beautiful,' I say under my breath. 'Don't be nervous.'

'They're your parents. Of course I'm nervous.'

Aurora fusses with her dress as we walk from my car to the front door of my parents' house. I glance to the side, the rear balcony and patio calling to me like an evil spirit in an Ouija board. But this time I'm not going to walk around the corner and torment myself. I'm going to walk in the goddamn front door like a sane, normal man. And introduce my girlfriend to my parents.

Girlfriend.

The word brings a smile to my lips. We haven't had that conversation yet. But Aurora is living under my roof, sleeping in my bed, waking up and smiling at me every morning . . . *telling me she loves me.*

She's my bloody girlfriend whether she realises it or not. She's perfect. She's incredible. *She's mine.* And even though I didn't plan this, never thought I'd ever allow myself to get to this point, I have. Realisation has slammed into me with the force of a nuclear explosion . . .

I'm completely, ridiculously, obsessively in love with Aurora Thorne.

And I want the world to know.

'Should I call them Mr and Mrs Fairfax, or . . . ?'

'Call them Hillary and Stan. My mother will tell you off for making her feel old otherwise.'

'What about your father?' Aurora whispers.

'Don't worry about my father.' My jaw tenses, but the feel of slender, soft fingers threading through mine has it relaxing.

'I'm nervous, but I am excited to meet them,' Aurora says.

'Good.' I squeeze her hand, then narrow my eyes at the smile tugging her lips. 'What?'

She shrugs, blushing. 'It's just . . . you've given me everything I could ever want. I only need my father freed and all my dreams will be coming true.' She gazes up at me like I hung the damn moon. So open. So trusting.

Deceit burns like a wildfire in my gut.

She looks away, her attention fixing on the imposing front door of my parents' home.

I need to give her back her father even if it kills me. She's been working for months to free him, going as far as getting an undercover job at Dominic's house. She's desperate. And she's smart. But she'd never have unravelled everything with Dominic and this Ella woman. Christ, I never even saw it coming and I thought I knew everything about Dom. The only clue was Larkhay . . .

Dom and I have helped one another in the past. He helped save Fairfax Guardian after my catastrophic fuck-up. But most of all, he helped keep it a secret from my father. And then when he came to me a few months ago after the theft from his firm, asking for *my* help . . . of course I agreed.

I just had no idea what doing it meant.

I've spent months chasing after my money when I should have been chasing the truth, the way Aurora has. And when we get home, I'm going to give it to her. The complete, ugly truth. I'm going to confess the one last secret she needs to hear.

It's the hardest one to tell her, but I can't put it off any longer.

The diamond engagement ring I had Sullivan Beaufort make and courier over from New York is burning a hole in my safe at home.

I want her father out of prison.

Then I want it on her finger.

I want Aurora Thorne to be Mrs Aurora Fairfax.

I just hope she still gives me that chance when she finds out what I did.

Taking a deep breath, I ring the front doorbell, rearranging my features into a picture of calm.

'I love you,' Aurora says, seeming to know exactly what I need to hear and when I need to hear it.

I gaze at her, drinking in her beautiful, innocent expression, and committing it to memory. That final niggle, that hesitation I have about what I'm opening her up to if she loves me, is fading fast. But even though this is what I want, there are moments it still scares the hell out of me.

'I love you too.' I lift our entwined hands to my lips and graze her knuckles with a kiss at the exact moment the door swings open.

'Oh!' My mother claps her hands together in front of her face, her eyes glowing as they zero in on Aurora. 'Thank heavens. You're real!' she declares, tugging Aurora from my grasp and enveloping her in a crushing hug.

'I didn't fabricate a girlfriend when I accepted your dinner invitation, Mum,' I say, my lips twitching in amusement at Aurora's shocked expression as my mother lets her go.

'He always says he'll bring someone one day, but he never has,' my mother tells Aurora. 'And then he turns up with you! What a treat!' She grins. 'I've already heard a lot about you from Dove.

I didn't think I'd be seeing you with my eldest son,' she titters. 'Maybe Gabriel.'

'Gabriel?' I bark, making my mother wave away my concern with a laugh.

'He's not as grumpy as you are, Rafe,' she says lovingly. 'You've got a good heart under all that frowning,' she adds, for Aurora's benefit.

Aurora glances up at me, then smiles at my mother. 'He does. A really good one.'

My heart rate picks up as I stare into her eyes, my lips curling into a smile.

'Well,' my mother announces, sounding delighted, 'get yourselves inside. Everyone else is here. Except Angelo, but he's on his way.'

We're ushered inside and Aurora sneaks a sideways glance at me.

Girlfriend? she mouths.

'Girlfriend,' I whisper in her ear, loving the way the pulse in her neck flutters faster at my proximity.

Her smile is bright as my mother closes the door and links arms with her, leading her down the hallway. The two fall into easy conversation, Aurora complimenting the house and how lovely dinner smells as we walk towards the kitchen.

I hang back, one step behind as I watch, my head growing light. Aurora's wearing a new figure-hugging cream dress I insisted on buying her when I took her shopping a couple of days ago. The dressing room at home is now filled with racks of new outfits, all in her size. As well as shoes, bags, accessories. None of which she wanted, but all of which I insisted I buy for her. After helping her unpack it all, I sat her on that chaise and took my time eating her out, surrounded by all her shiny new things.

Turns out spoiling her gets my dick hard.

Everything about her gets my dick hard.

We walk into the kitchen. Dove beams, calling out a greeting from where she's pouring drinks at a sideboard, and Gabe waves from the other side of the room.

I move closer, my hand falling to Aurora's lower back as I sense her hesitation at being faced with my family – or namely, my father. Dove's her friend, and she's spent enough time working with Gabe to be comfortable around him. And she and my mother seem to have hit it off. So that just leaves him – the suited tower of a man rising from his seat on the far side of the room wearing a curious expression.

I dip my mouth to her ear, admiring the new diamond earrings and necklace I bought her, bright and dazzling against her soft skin.

'Breathe,' I instruct.

Aurora shivers. She's nervous, and I know it's meeting my father that's got her wound up tight like a knot. Even taking my time coaxing three orgasms out of her before we left home hasn't loosened her up.

'I know,' she whispers back. 'I just want to make a good impression.' She smooths her dress as my father crosses the room. The uncertainty on her face makes me recall the story she told me about she and her father going on holiday when she was a child and being upgraded to a nicer hotel. About how she felt she didn't belong there.

But here, beside me, is exactly where she should be.

My father stops in front of us. 'Evening, son.'

'Evening, Dad.' I nod at him as his attention fixes on Aurora. 'This is Aurora, my girlfriend. She's moved in with me.' Might as well get straight to the point.

He does a good job of not over-reacting, but I know my father. The slight hitch of his brows tells me he's zoned in on that nugget of information, already dissecting its meaning. I've never lived with a woman before. Sure, some have stayed at my place for a few days here and there, but I've never made anything permanent. Never felt the desire to.

'It's a pleasure to meet you.' He takes Aurora's hand and shakes it, studying her with an interested smile.

'You too,' Aurora replies. 'Thank you for having me join you all for dinner tonight.'

'My son told us there was someone he wanted us to meet. We were intrigued, weren't we, Hill?' he calls to my mother. 'Tell me, what makes you so taken with my son? Because I know it's not his jokes.' He chuckles.

'Quit bombarding the poor girl, Stan,' Mum scolds. 'She's barely walked through the door.'

My jaw tightens. He thinks he's being funny, but I hear the digs, loud and clear. But what hurts most is what he *isn't* saying. He should just ask outright, '*What do you see in my son? A man who almost cost us Fairfax Guardian once?*' Because that golden topic will come up sooner or later. Maybe it'll take a few visits, but it will happen. He won't be able to stop himself.

My father glances at my stony expression and chortles. 'Ah, it's his easy-going nature.'

Aurora hesitates, clearly uncomfortable as she picks up on his sarcasm. 'Well—'

'It's his big dick, isn't it, bro? Runs in the family.'

Angelo walks in, grabbing his crotch lewdly, and despite the vulgarity of his arrival, I could kiss him for arriving in time to stop me from telling my father where to shove his dinner invitation before whisking Aurora back out of here.

'Angelo!' my mother tuts.

'Please don't talk about my best friend and my brother's dick in the same sentence,' Dove scoffs. 'I still have to eat dinner.'

Benedict runs over from beside Gabe and starts rubbing my mother's calves until she bends and feeds him a piece of chicken from the roasted one on the counter.

'Don't encourage the fleabag, Hillary,' my father scolds. 'It'll be doing its business in the garden next.'

'Benedict uses the lavatory,' Gabe chimes in. 'And I've trained him to flush. He has better aim than any of you.'

Dove snorts out a laugh and Aurora's shoulders relax as she flicks her gaze to meet mine, biting back a giggle.

'Welcome to the family,' I grit with a tight smile.

Twenty minutes later, we're sitting at the dinner table, listening to my father talk about some old business colleague of his who died of a suspected heart attack while jet-skiing.

'Got to take chances. Hugh went doing what he loved. No point living like a coward and being afraid to do anything,' my father says.

'Pretty sure ignoring your doctor's advice when you're awaiting surgery is just being reckless, but . . .' I tilt my head, knocking back a large mouthful of wine.

'Of course you'd see it like that,' my father mutters.

'Rafe's right,' Dove chimes in. 'Hugh took a risk against medical advice, and now he's dead.'

'Straight to the point, sis.' Angelo chuckles, draining his glass for the third time since we sat down.

'Ten to fifteen per cent of sudden cardiac deaths in men over fifty is the result of vigorous activity,' Gabe contributes calmly, Benedict sitting in his lap. 'Most occur during running, heavy gardening, or sex. Jet-skiing is an interesting one.' He strokes Benedict's ear, his expression unchanged.

'Was Hugh having sex whilst jet-skiing?' Angelo asks.

'Angelo,' my mother scolds.

'Don't be ridiculous,' my father chides.

Angelo shrugs, refilling his glass with what's left in the wine bottle. 'Thought it was a relevant question following Gabe's statistics.'

I throw him a look to tell him to ease up on the wine, but he shakes his head, lifting the glass to his lips. He drinks to get through dinner with our father. It's his coping mechanism, but more often than not, things get messy if he goes too far. My father's never been one to back down from confrontation with anyone, his own flesh and blood or not.

Aurora shifts uncomfortably in her seat beside me. We're not even done with the main course and the temperature in the room is already approaching arctic conditions.

Sliding my hand on to her thigh, I give it a squeeze, massaging my thumb over her skin reassuringly.

'This is delicious,' she says to my mother, taking another bite of the roast chicken.

'Thank you.' My mother smiles proudly. 'It's Stan's favourite.'

My father nods his agreement as Mum looks at Gabe across the table. 'I've made a plate up for Benedict. He can have it when we're finished.'

'He's a bloody flea-ridden cat,' my father interjects. 'Don't waste perfectly good chicken on him.'

'I assure you Benedict does not have any kind of parasite.' Gabe's expression remains impassive, but his eyes flick down to something in his lap.

My father's phone blares at full volume in his pocket, making him jump.

'Jesus Christ. Blasted thing's doing it again,' he grumbles, pulling the device from his pocket.

The chorus of the song 'Baby Got Back' plays at full volume.

I narrow my eyes at my brother, but Gabe takes a sip of his wine, looking back at me blankly.

Our father jabs at the phone and the song stops abruptly.

'Bloody technology,' he hisses.

'What happened to your hand?' my mother asks, spotting the fading bruises on Angelo's knuckles.

'I knocked Vance Falcon out,' he announces proudly, slurring a little and sloshing wine out of his glass.

Dove drops her cutlery, and it clatters against her plate.

I stiffen, wanting to fly out of my seat and clamp my hand over my youngest brother's mouth.

'Vance Falcon. I thought he was in Singapore?' My mother's face pales, and she glances at Dove, who's pretending to be enthralled with blotting splattered sauce off the white linen tablecloth with her napkin.

'Maybe he'll go back there, now he knows how hard my right hook is.' Angelo grins, chuckling to himself.

'That man was far too old for you,' my father booms in Dove's direction. 'Silly crush you had on him. I don't know what you thought would happen. He must be fifty now, for God's sake.'

Dove pales, blinking rapidly. My sister's a force, but one mention of Vance's name and she looks like she's on the verge of a breakdown.

'Leave it, Stan,' my mother pleads, her worried eyes on Dove.

My father ignores her and waggles his finger in Dove's direction. 'Now, I think you should—'

'Enough!' I clip.

My father's eyes round on me, thinning into slits. 'Pardon?'

'I said *that's enough*. Now's not the time for fatherly advice.'

My father's a bully. I can take him throwing his weight with me. But not with my brothers. And especially not with Dove.

He balks, staring at me with amusement and a flicker of pride that I'm standing up to him. But I know him. It'll only make whatever comeback he's about to deliver all the more brutal.

'No.' He tilts his head, drawing the word out slowly. 'The time for fatherly advice would have been before you screwed up signing the Wyndham account.'

'Stan!' Mum gasps, even though she's used to this type of behaviour from our father by now.

'It happened, didn't it?' he replies in mock innocence. 'Just stating facts. Sorry if my son neglected to tell you about that little piece of history,' he directs to Aurora.

My chest expands as I draw in a deep breath, ready to tell him to leave her the hell out of it.

'Rafe told me about that day,' Aurora says, lifting her chin with confidence.

My father chuckles. 'Did he? Even the part about screwing Wyndham's wife on his desk?'

'Stan, really?' my mother warns.

My father shrugs and I tighten my grip on Aurora's thigh as rage bubbles in my veins. Aurora places her hand over mine, bringing an instant layer of calm to my stampeding pulse.

'That part too,' she replies, a picture of composure as she faces my father.

If I didn't love her already, then seeing her hold her own so eloquently would do it.

'We tell each other everything,' she adds, giving my hand on her thigh a squeeze.

My gulp's so thick I'm surprised it doesn't shake every glass on the table.

Everything.

Once we make it through this dinner and I have a much-needed conversation with her, then it will be everything. But right now, that one last secret is sitting low in my gut, weighing it down like a boulder.

'Lovebirds. Isn't it sweet?' Angelo grins, his cheeks rosy from all the wine.

My father leans back in his chair and regards Aurora with a new-found interest. 'So you know my son well, then? You know all his secrets?'

My spine straightens as Aurora flicks a worried gaze my way. There's no way my father knows about my anxiety episode that led to the events that lost the contract. I've never told a soul, except Aurora and . . . Dominic.

'Son of a bitch,' I hiss under my breath.

'He told me, and I understand,' Aurora says. 'In fact, I think he's amazing.' She glances at me again, her eyes glowing with love.

My father leans his forearms on the table, his eyes pinned on Aurora. 'He is . . . *was*. He was top of his field. It's why he always got called on. But I didn't expect it to happen now he's no longer specialising any more.'

Aurora frowns, confusion knitting her brow. 'I'm sorry, I don't know what you mean. I was talking about . . .' She trails off, understanding we're no longer talking about *that* secret.

Every cell in my body wishes we were. Because there's only one other secret. And that one has the power to destroy everything. Especially if Aurora hears it from someone else first.

Ice threads its way through my veins. How the hell did my father find out?

Placing my napkin on my plate, I look at my mother. 'My apologies, Mum. Aurora and I need to leave.'

'But you haven't had dessert,' Mum says, flustered.

'Escape the clutches of the dysfunctional Fairfaxes while you can, Aurora.' Angelo sniggers into his glass.

'Shut up,' Dove hisses at him.

Gabriel catches my eye with a questioning look. I subtly shake my head. I'm fine. Or at least, I will be as soon as I get Aurora out of here and have this conversation with her in private.

But my father seems determined to continue, his brow furrowed as he studies Aurora.

'Your father's trial,' he says, gauging her reaction. 'Rafael was always the first expert witness they called on those financial fraud cases. I didn't think you did them any more, son?'

Aurora's hand stills on top of mine, her gentle, soothing strokes ending abruptly. 'What?' She lets out a small, disbelieving laugh. 'What does he mean?' she asks, widened eyes rounding on me.

I stare into her aquamarine irises. 'Beauty,' I whisper. 'Let's go home. We can talk there.'

Her gaze bounces between me and my father, a line deepening between her brows. 'Did you . . . Were you at my father's trial? You can't have been. I never saw you there.'

My throat tightens, preventing me from speaking. All I can manage is a curt shake of my head. Aurora's shoulders soften, but confusion is still painted over her face.

'I wasn't there,' I manage to get out, but my voice sounds strained and not like mine at all.

'The solicitors read these things out sometimes if it's more of a formality,' my father continues, seemingly unaware of the magnitude of his choice of conversation topic. 'Like I said, Rafael was the best. Cases like your father's weren't anything special. All in a day's work, eh, son?'

Aurora stares at me, a gut-wrenching, horrified understanding uncoiling behind her eyes like a cancer spreading through the bloodstream, infecting all in its path.

'You gave evidence against my father?' she whispers.

'Not evidence. I just . . .' I glance around the table at the silent, grave faces of my family. 'Please, let's go home and talk about this.'

'Just what?' she scoffs. 'Just what?!'

'I was going to tell you.'

'Tell me now!'

'Aur—'

'Now, Rafael!' she cries.

I clear my throat and reach up to tug at my collar, which is cutting off my air supply. 'I still get asked to provide my . . .' I wince at the words. '. . . *expertise* on occasion.'

'What does that mean?'

'It means I give my professional opinion to the court on whether *theoretically* a crime could be orchestrated in the way the prosecuting solicitors claim it has been.'

Her eyes widen and she shoves my hand from her thigh under the table. 'You gave evidence against my father?'

'Not evidence. Just his professional opinion on whether the methods were possible,' my father chimes in.

It's one of the first times in my life he's stood up for me. But right now, I couldn't want it less.

I couldn't *deserve* it less.

'And what was it? What was your *expert* opinion?' Aurora gapes at me, the blood draining from her face as she blinks rapidly, like she's trying to hold back tears.

'Aur—'

'What was it?' she shrieks.

I tuck my chin and pull in a breath through my nose. 'Yes. I told them that yes, what they were claiming was entirely feasible and could have been carried out by someone with the access and knowledge that your father had.'

'Oh my God.' Aurora trembles in her seat.

I've never felt like a bigger goddamn arsehole in my life.

A low whistle echoes around the room. 'Fuck, bro. You helped bang her dad up?'

'Shut the hell up, Angelo,' Dove snaps, looking at Aurora with worry etched into her face.

'He did his job. He never said the man was guilty. The court decided that,' my father says, waving a hand in the air like this is just small talk, and not something that has the power to destroy me.

I search Aurora's crumpling face, tilting my head to try to get her to look at me.

'Aurora?' I choke in a strangled whisper. 'It's not what you think. I didn't know what was going to happen between us. I answered the few questions I was obligated to, that's all.'

'But you thought he was guilty,' she says in a voice so quiet I have to strain to hear her. 'You told me as much. You thought he was guilty up until I moved in with you and . . .'

I curse Dominic internally. He pushed me to return the favour of his help after the Wyndham deal went south. And I agreed. There was no connection between me and losing Fairfax Guardian's money, and George Thorne's case, because I'd given the money directly to Dom to invest for me. If the court knew that I had a financial stake, then I would have been considered biased and unable to be called as an expert witness.

I could have said no, but back then all I could see was red. And a gaping hole where two hundred and forty million should have been.

I wanted to watch justice be served. Only, they had the wrong bloody person. And Dom set up all the 'evidence'. Now I'm about to pay the price for my own arrogant pig-headedness.

This is on me.

'Aurora, please . . .' I urge.

She finally lifts her eyes to mine and the coldness in them makes my heart freeze.

'This has all been some twisted revenge scheme, hasn't it? Because of the money you lost.'

'What money?' my father booms.

'It doesn't matter,' I toss in his direction, my gaze fixed on Aurora.

'Two hundred and forty million. It'd be enough for most people to want revenge,' she says.

'How bloody much?' My father flies to his feet, his chair toppling backwards on to the floor. 'Was that money from Fairfax Guardian?'

'Was!' I snap, looking at him. 'I repaid it myself. Every damn penny.'

I turn back to Aurora, but she's already on her feet.

'Thank you for dinner, Hillary,' she says. 'It was delicious. But I'll be leaving now.'

'Aurora?' I stand and grab her hand, but she shakes me off and storms from the room.

I don't acknowledge anyone else. I race after her, my blood thundering in my ears, and panic clawing at my windpipe.

I'll suffocate without her.

I cannot lose her.

She's mine.

'Aurora?' I yell, chasing her down the hallway.

She's at the front door by the time I catch up with her. I reach for her hand, wrapping it in mine and bringing her to a standstill.

'Please,' I pant. 'Don't walk away from me. We need to talk about this.'

'Is it true?' She whirls to face me, rage simmering in her eyes, making the blue spark like electricity's running through it. The sight of it is like a dagger in the gut.

'I was going to tell you.'

'When?' she shrieks, yanking her hand from mine. 'After I moved in with you? After I fell in love with you?'

'Tonight, I swear. Once we got home, I . . .' I scrub a hand around my jaw. 'I wanted to get your father acquitted first, and then—'

'Then what? Hope I'd shrug it off because I'd be too distracted having him back to care?'

'No, of course not—'

'You sent him there!'

'The court sent him there!' My terror at losing her makes me fire out the words like a missile.

Her eyes widen and she takes a step back. 'Of course.' She scoffs. 'Shift the bloody blame. Maybe the court did convict him, but didn't you ever question it with all that bloody training and *expertise* you have?' she sneers.

My body vibrates with the raw need to pull her to me and hold her in my arms, but she steps back, creating more distance between us.

'I wasn't shown all of the evidence. I was asked for my opinion on whether it was feasible. Not whether it was what actually happened. And yes, it *was* feasible. Please, Aurora. I love you. Let's go home and talk about this.'

Her face falls. 'You thought he was guilty. For months you thought he'd stolen all that money. You made all those snide remarks like he disgusted you.'

Self-loathing rears its ugly head as I see my behaviour through her eyes. I'm a bastard. A rude, judgemental prick. First thing in the morning I'm calling the judge and telling him my statement was biased. That I had a financial stake in the case. I'll take whatever backlash there is from it.

My voice comes out hoarse. 'I should never have spoken about him like that. I was wrong. I know he's innocent now. And I'm so bloody sorry I didn't see it sooner. You know that.'

Aurora shakes her head, my words doing nothing to quell the onslaught of pain and disappointment in her voice.

'You don't get it, do you? I was willing to move on and leave it behind us because I believed you when you said you were sorry. That you knew my father was innocent and that you cared about the *truth*. But you wouldn't even recognise the truth if it punched you in the face. You're a liar. Everything we had was built on lies. Nothing was real.'

'No! Everything is real. I *love* you.'

She lifts her eyes to mine, and the brokenness in hers floors me.

'*This* is how you treat someone you love? This is how you make them feel?' Her voice wavers as tears fill her eyes. 'I knew we were a mistake that first time you kissed me. I should have listened to my gut.'

My lungs seize and I struggle to breathe. 'Please, Beauty, don't say that. You and I are the one thing that makes sense to me in this world. I adore you. I will do anything for you. You know that deep down. Tell me you know that.'

She looks away, her arms wrapping tightly around herself as she trembles. 'Never call me that again.'

I screw my face up, heat burning behind my eyelids. 'Aurora?' I croak, reaching for her.

She flinches, and I freeze.

'My father's a good man who was let down by a system that should have protected him. But you? You're a man who thinks that because it's a person's heart you manipulated and no money was lost you're somehow better than everyone else who's ever made a mistake. But your choices were premeditated. You've spent all these months acting like you're better than my father when, in reality, you're the crook. You've lied to me. Manipulated me.'

I swallow the growing lump in my throat. What can I say to that? She's right. I have lied to her. And in the beginning, I did manipulate her. I didn't consider her feelings for a moment. I only cared about myself. But now? Now she's all I care about. She's the one thing I've got right. Aurora Thorne isn't the sleeping beauty I call her. I was the one who was blind to all of it. Until she awoke something inside me that makes me want to be a better man. Makes me want to be who she deserves.

'I can make this right, I swear.'

The silence between us stretches for three heartbeats. Each pains me more than the last, until she parts her lips, and delivers four words that obliterate me.

'Let me go, Rafe,' she whispers.

I shake my head, a throbbing overtaking my skull. 'Let you go? I can't . . . Aurora! I love you! What the hell does "*let you go*" mean?'

She can't even meet my eyes.

A chill runs up my spine as my blood turns to ice.

'No. Don't do this,' I beg. 'I can make you happy. I know I can. I *love* you,' I say again, punctuating the words. 'I bloody love you! And you love me. You have no idea how much that means! You love me too!'

She keeps her arms coiled around herself like a shield, keeping me out. Her face crumples, but she still won't look at me.

'What's going on?'

I scowl at my sister's voice, my gaze remaining fixed on Aurora's pinched face.

'This is between us!' I snap.

'When you make my best friend cry, then it's no longer just between you!' Dove says, marching past me and stopping in front of Aurora, who's quietly wiping at her cheeks like she doesn't want me to see her tears.

My stomach plummets to my feet.

'I knew this was a bad idea. You couldn't have screwed with someone else, could you? You had to choose my best friend,' Dove says, shooting me a filthy look over her shoulder as she bundles Aurora under one arm.

'You're coming back to my place,' she says to her. 'Whilst you think about what you want.'

'What she wants?' I choke out. 'We love each other, Dove. We need to be together to figure this out. Tell her, Aurora.'

Aurora's response is so quiet I have to strain to hear it. But for one brief second, heartbroken aquamarine blue meets my gaze, stealing my last thread of composure.

'I was an idiot for ever falling in love with you.'

'W-what? No . . . don't say that.'

I claw at my chest, everything tightening and making breathing damn near impossible.

And my heart breaks again.

I swear it cracks right back down where doctors once stitched it up. Only this time surgery won't save me. My life's walking away from me, right in front of my eyes.

'Aurora! Please!' I call, staggering after her, one hand clutching my chest.

But it's too late.

Dove's already guiding her through the front door.

It closes behind them with an ominous thud.

'Brother?' Steady hands take hold of my biceps and concerned eyes scan my face.

'She's gone,' I gasp, my mouth working like a fish out of water, unable to fill my lungs as pain lances through my chest.

Gabriel's expression remains calm as he supports me.

I sag into him, my knees threatening to buckle beneath me.

'I've lost her,' I say in a haunted croak. 'I've. Lost. Her.'

Chapter 36

Aurora

Bath is such a beautiful city. The perfect place to come for a weekend away from London. To walk the streets with a lover, visit the thermal baths at dusk, then drink champagne beneath the stars.

It's not the place to lick your wounds after suffering a betrayal so huge that your entire body physically aches like every cell in it has been broken.

I sigh and take a sip of lukewarm coffee. The wooden bench beneath my legs is cold and unwelcoming, despite the clear blue sky and warm sun. It's like everything has ceased to exist in the same way. Things have lost their flavour. The sun has lost its warmth. A few days ago the world was multicoloured, a kaleidoscope of glittering possibilities. But all that stopped the moment I found out about Rafael's lies.

Hearing his confession brought memories bubbling to the surface. The hard slam of the judge's gavel, sealing my father's fate. The sag of his shoulders as they led him away without letting me hug him. The look of guilt in his eyes like it was his fault that he was leaving me. And all that time, Rafael had played a part in putting him behind bars.

All those times he kissed me, told me he loved me, did he ever feel an ounce of remorse? I guess I'll never know.

I haven't been able to bring myself to reply to his countless texts or listen to his voicemails. Blocking his number seemed like the kindest thing I could do for myself. Because if I speak to him, I don't know what I'll say. I have no words that can fully describe the extent to which he's hurt me. Because he has. He's torn me apart and left me in pieces.

And yet, I still love him with every fibre in my body. I still cry myself to sleep at night, missing him so much that my stomach churns with nausea. It's a physical torment, thinking about how safe I felt inside in his arms. But it was all a lie. I preferred when he was an arsehole with his snide comments about my father. At least that was honest, and I knew where I stood with him. Now? Now I have no idea what to believe any more.

I toss the remnants of the tasteless coffee into the bin beside the bench, then pull out my phone and bring up the email. I've opened the attachment on it more times than I can count. I can recite every single word, yet re-read it multiple times a day to torture myself.

> *Actions of an astute and calculating individual. Someone with the ability to deceive and manipulate.*

Bile lodges in my throat as I read Rafael's words. He says he was only doing his job.

His words are the farthest likeness from my father they could possibly be. But they describe another man down to a tee.

'He's describing himself. Bastard,' I mutter quietly, willing myself not to cry again.

I shove my phone back into my bag and start walking. It only takes ten minutes to get to where I need to be.

'Good morning,' the concierge greets as I pass him on my way inside the hotel.

'Good morning,' I reply, forcing a friendly smile. He seems like a nice man. He was telling me about his two grandsons yesterday, and how they love to sail remote-controlled boats on the lake near his house.

I head downstairs to the staff changing area, shoving my bag inside my locker and putting on my uniform.

Cleaning people's houses was a breeze compared to hotel rooms. I can't get over how disgusting people can be. Bedsheets covered in wet patches of God-knows-what, foul-smelling lumps in shower drains, used condoms left on the floor. The hotel is beautiful. Luxurious and expensive. But people still behave like uncivilised slobs behind its closed, ornate doors. What was it Rafael said? Loaded people have loaded secrets? Turns out some of them also have no consideration for housekeeping staff. Money can't buy manners.

Heading to the staff office to check in for my shift and get my room assignments, I pull my shoulders back, forcing myself to look on the bright side. I have a job I can do alongside my vlogging. And they're paying a decent amount, which I know is probably due to who helped me get this job in the first place. And I have a lovely furnished, one-bedroomed city-centre apartment to stay in for a few weeks whilst I decide what to do. And the train only takes two hours to go and see my father on visiting days.

I'm lucky.

My heart might be shattered, and my mind might be back in London with the man I still love, even if I'm not sure whether I ever really knew him at all. But I'm here, and I'm okay. I have more than I did when my father was first locked up and our home was taken from us.

Rafael Fairfax might have deceived me, but I won't let him take everything from me.

I've been broken once before.

And I refuse to be broken again.

Chapter 37

Rafael

The words blur as the edges of my vision close in.

'I haven't got time for this,' I grumble, shoving my thumb and forefinger into my eye sockets and giving them a harsh rub before going back to reading. But it's no use. The document still swims in front of my eyes.

Grunting, I toss it on my desk on top of the rest of the papers and swipe up my glass. The whiskey burns a trail down to my empty stomach, stripping the lining as my body fights to find sustenance in the only thing it's been fed in days.

The door to my office opens, and my sister and two brothers file in with matching stern expressions. I snort as they square their shoulders, preparing to lecture me. I expected this. In fact, I think they've done well not to interfere the past few days, but it was only a matter of time.

'You look like you're going to a bloody funeral,' I slur, spilling some of my drink down the front of my shirt.

'It'll be yours if you keep this up,' Dove says, eyeing my glass like it's the root of all evil. 'When did you last eat?'

I shrug, a belch rumbling out of my throat. I screw my nose up as the stale alcohol fumes float around me like a toxic cloud.

'Delightful,' Gabe mutters, dipping his nose into Benedict's neck and inhaling as he holds him in his arms, like the fishy breath of a cat that licks its own arsehole smells better than me. I should give it to Benedict on his eye contact, though. He's assessing me with the perfect amount of dripping disappointment that rivals the stony expressions of my siblings.

'Not cool, bro,' Angelo adds, his gaze sliding to the empty crystal decanter on my sideboard that was full this morning.

'What's the point?' I mumble. 'She's blocked my number. She's gone. *Poof.*' I explode my fingers out from my free hand, sloppily.

'You can't be here in this state. AJ said you were rude to a client this morning,' Dove says.

'Bloody snitch.' My upper lip curls before I take another swig of whiskey.

'You're a liability. Dad's coming in later,' Angelo says.

I tip my head back and let out a laugh that sounds more unhinged than amused.

'Daddy,' I slur. 'What a delight.'

But my bravado is all bullshit. I don't want my father to see me like this. Not because I care what he thinks any more.

My eyes fall to the top of my desk, covered in paperwork.

Because he'll tell me to pack it all away. To give up. That I won't get anywhere.

I can't have his voice in my head any more.

He might have been a driving force behind my feelings of inadequacy growing up and feeding my anxiety that manifested itself as a fear of heights. Aurora was right when she asked what I was more scared of – heights, or disappointing my father. Both bloody scare me. But one I can usually avoid. The other? That's the one that follows me around like a goddamn demon, whispering in my ear, making me question everything, making me feel so bloody useless.

But I won't allow him to taint this.

Not this.

'I'm getting George Thorne out of prison, even if it kills me,' I announce, casting my arm over my desk to display my efforts. But I miscalculate, and half of the paperwork is swept to the floor.

Calling the judge and informing him my initial statement was biased wasn't enough. And the solicitor Aurora hired hasn't been able to accomplish much.

It's up to me.

'If this is how you approach it, then it *is* going to kill you,' Dove snaps, striding over and pulling the glass from my grasp.

'Hey!'

'Shut up! We love you, Rafe. That's why you need this.' She stalks to my office bathroom. The sound of liquid being poured down the drain has me slumping over my elbows on my desk.

'I need to get him out,' I snarl when she reappears. 'A woman is responsible. I need to find her. She was last seen in Norway.'

'How do you know that?' Gabe asks.

'Dominic's bloody dick led me to her.'

If they want to ask more, they don't. Instead, they look at me with varying degrees of pity as I rise from my seat and lose my balance, lurching to one side. More paperwork scatters, an entire stack falling to the floor at Angelo's feet.

'Useless goddamn crap. Getting me nowhere,' I slur.

'You need to go home, brother,' Gabe says. 'Take some time. Process this. We're all here for you. But you can't be here. Not like this.'

'He's right, bro,' Angelo says, squeezing me on the shoulder.

Dove arches a brow at me.

'I'm fine. I just need to be left alone,' I mutter.

I slump back down into my chair and pull open my top drawer. A tube of crisps stares back at me. It's the one I got stuck on my arm during the meeting with Sullivan and Sterling Beaufort.

I hurl the drawer back into the desk, making the entire thing shake, then drop my head into my hands and let out a whine that sounds like a dog needing to be put down.

'I bought an engagement ring for her. I was going to ask her to marry me. Make her my wife. Get her father out and give her everything I possibly could. Now I don't even have her phone number. She's erased me from her life.'

I break into sobs.

'Rafe?' Dove says, her voice oozing concern and edged with a tinge of panic. She's never seen me like this before. None of them have. I would have even questioned if I was capable of acting so emotional before I met Aurora. I'm a man losing it in front of his siblings. And all I care about is her. How I need to hear her voice. See her face. Feel her hand holding mine.

'I have no idea where she is,' I choke. 'She could be in trouble. She could be staying anywhere. You didn't see the bloody place she was living before she moved in with me. She has nothing! She's bloody broke! And now she's alone. Because of me.'

'She's safe. She told you that,' Dove interjects.

I lift my stinging eyes to my sister in time to see a flash of guilt before she blinks it away.

'You know where she is, don't you?'

Her jaw tightens. 'I do. But she made me swear I wouldn't tell you.'

I slam my fist on the table. 'You're my sister!'

'She's my best friend! And you hurt her. You hurt her more than I ever thought you were capable of doing. If she comes back, then it has to be on her terms. She needs time, Rafe. You can't force her. I know Aurora – if you try before she's ready then you'll just push her farther away.'

'You don't understand. She has nothing. She could be staying somewhere unsafe, somewhere—'

'She's not. I rented her a place so she could have some time away to think,' Dove says.

Desperate hope blooms in my chest.

'How long for? Is she coming back? Did she tell you if she was coming back?'

'I don't know,' Dove confesses.

I choke out a strangled sound, screwing my face up. 'If she'd just speak to me, I could tell her exactly what I said to the court. She can see I never said her father was guilty. I never told them he should be convicted. I never—'

'She has seen it.'

I wrench my eyes up to Gabe's.

'What?'

He swallows, reaching up to tug on his collar with his free hand as Benedict remains curled up inside the other like a baby.

'She called and asked if I could get it for her. She knows I can . . . *access* things that are difficult through official channels.'

I stare at my brother. His IT skills have always been useful to us as a business. And even as teenagers he used to help us out of parking fines and small shit like that. But to know he's used those skills to help the woman I love see something that she would have otherwise had to get from me has my blood boiling.

'That's the one thing she might have agreed to meet me for! So I could tell her myself. Show her myself. And now what? You've gone and fucked it all up and handed it to her without me being able to goddamn explain myself! You're my brother!' I rage, flying to my feet and trying to ignore the sudden swell of dizziness making my brain feel like it's on a bloody merry-go-round.

'Don't take this out on him!' Dove steps to my desk and points a finger down at it, her eyes on fire. 'We all helped, okay? I took her to the station the morning after and set her up a place to stay. And Angelo got her a job.'

'You what?' I spit, leaning on the desk for support and still managing to deliver a glare at my youngest brother that would make most grown men wither on the spot.

'If it's meant to be, she'll come back.' Angelo looks at me, sadness brimming in his eyes.

Even my kid brother gets it. Only he's not a kid. Not any more. He knows as well as I did that I fucked up and hurt the woman I love. That this is on me.

They all love Aurora.

They're all protecting her. Under other circumstances I'd be so bloody proud to be their brother. But this is all wrong. They're protecting her from *me*. They helped her get away from *me*.

I love her. She doesn't need protecting from me. She needs to be with me. We need to talk about this. I need to make her see how sorry I am. Prove to her that I'll do anything for her. That I can't be on this godforsaken earth without her.

I look up into their solemn faces and suck in a breath, making my nostrils flare.

They all witnessed me ruin Aurora Thorne.

And now, she's ruined me too.

I grab my jacket and force my legs to carry me out of my office with a modicum of grace as my shoulder bounces off the doorframe and the floor threatens to meet my face with one wrong step.

'Where are you going?' Dove shouts, rushing out behind me with Gabe and Angelo.

'Home!' I yell. 'Like you told me to.'

'You gave Kyle the day off, we'll drive you. You're—'

'I can get a bloody cab!'

I march up to the front desk. AJ's eyes widen as he sees me.

'Mr Fairfax? I—'

'On a scale of one to ten, how big of a cunt was I to that client this morning?'

His face pales. 'Is there a number that will result in me not being fired from my job?'

'Just answer the question.'

He winces. 'Ten would be being kind.'

'Dammit,' I hiss. 'Send them a hamper. Tell them we'll cut twenty per cent off their next premium.'

'Sir?' He fumbles.

'Do it. And if they still think I'm a prick, tell them I got my arse dumped by the only woman I've ever loved. That'll make them feel better. They can have a goddamn laugh at my expense.'

He swallows, nodding furiously. 'Yes, Mr Fairfax.'

I head into the lift and punch the button for the lobby.

My siblings' worried faces shine back at me as I hold a hand up, indicating following me would be at their own peril. Behind them the window cleaners' crane lowers into position on the outside of the building.

Nausea sweeps up my windpipe, but I swallow it down. The sight of it still sickens me. But there's a new terror filling my gut now.

The thought of Aurora never coming home, and never forgiving me.

Chapter 38

Aurora

Four days later

'Thank you for the ride.' I lean down so I can smile at Joe, one of the doormen from the hotel.

'Any time. You on shift tomorrow?'

'I am.'

He gives me a cheeky grin, the dimples in his cheeks popping. 'Then it's another date.'

I shake my head as he drives away. He's cute and cocky in an endearing way. He reminds me of Angelo. Which in turn, reminds me of . . .

'Rafael?' I gasp.

He pushes off the wall of my apartment building. He's wearing one of his usual suits, but something about him is different. The fabric sits looser against his frame, like he's lost weight, and his eyes are bloodshot and ringed with dark circles. He's lacking his usual spark and confidence.

'Aurora.'

The way he says my name, so smooth and delicious, like butter sliding over hot toast, has my belly fluttering. No matter how much my brain is telling me to run, my feet are rooted to the spot.

'How did you find me?'

'Angelo admitted he helped you get a job. And I know every one of his clients. I figured that would be a good place to start. Then Dove said she took you to the station the morning after . . .' He swallows like the memory is painful. 'After dinner at my parents' house, I checked the timetable that day for all trains departing in the morning, cross-referencing their destinations with any of Angelo's clients' businesses. Then I checked Gabe's work phone for his email to you. In your reply you told him you'd just arrived and were getting off the train. I checked the time, made a list of all the places you could have travelled to, considering any delays and train cancellations on the day, and narrowed it down to three. Then I waited to see which one Dove reacted with the most anger to when I said it, and I knew I'd found you. A day spent sitting outside the hotel in my car to find out where you were staying in between shifts is all it took.'

'You did all of that?' I stare at him, impressed, and a little unnerved.

'I'd have done anything to find you. You know that.'

'Do I?' I whisper.

His eyes dull as he exhales, and I see it. His misery. His heartbreak. It's the same as mine. But he's here, when I asked him to let me go. I need time, and he's not respecting that.

'I told you I was safe. Wasn't that enough?'

'Nothing that doesn't involve you waking up in my arms every day and looking at me the way you used to will ever be enough,' he rasps. 'Please, Aurora. Can we talk?'

I search his eyes. I'm on the precipice of caving in and allowing him to sweep me into his arms again. To consume me the way he did. Whisk me off on a magical romance that made me feel like I was flying every time I looked at him.

But I can't.

Him showing up here and having me fall into bed with him again will get us nowhere. It'll only confirm to him that being calculating and ignoring my wishes gets him what he wants. Forgiving him would mean I'm enabling him to keep treating me this way. To keep calling the shots. To keep behaving like he has all of the control and power.

But that's not a relationship. That's ownership.

My words come out broken and hollow. 'You lied to me from the beginning. You lied to me every single day.'

'No. I lied to you about one thing. I kept it from you when I shouldn't have.'

I sigh. 'Raf—'

'Please, Aurora.' His eyes pinch. 'You want to know the truth? Well, the truth is that *yes*, it did start as a need for revenge, a way of finding out what I could about my money.'

I wince.

'But that was before I knew the truth, that your father had nothing to do with any of it. And it stopped being that so goddamn fast, Aurora, I swear to you. The file I had on your father changed from looking for evidence against him, to anything I could find that could help him.'

'You had a file on him?'

A muscle in his jaw clenches. 'I did.'

'What was in it?'

His lips purse. 'Not much. You can't find evidence where there's no guilt.'

'But you still looked.'

'I lost two hundred and forty million, of course I looked.'

I wrap my arms around myself, unsure what to make of that piece of information.

'You were trying to help him?'

'I was. I started before you'd even unpacked your things in my room. I don't expect you to believe me, but—'

'I do believe you.'

His eyes widen and I swallow. I can see the genuine remorse and truth in his face, clear as day. It makes my stomach twist, because it wasn't there before. There were flashes of truth, glimpses of the real Rafael Fairfax. But I think deep down I always knew he was hiding something from me.

Everything was too perfect.

He might have been the one to lie to me, but I enabled it by refusing to look deeper. Wanting to dream that what we had was real. *Because I fell in love with him.* After all the pain, I wanted to believe that something good was finally happening.

'I swear to you, Aurora. Every minute of what we had is still true. I still love you as much as I always have. You're still the only woman I've ever loved and will ever love. The only one I've ever wanted to let close. There can never be anyone else, even if you never forgive me.'

I blink up at him. How can he know what I'm thinking? How can he read me so well? How can I trust myself to think straight when he's standing in front of me, making me want to forget everything and sink back into his arms?

'I can't do this right now,' I choke, forcing myself to look away.

I lift my key to the lock for the main door to the building, my fingers trembling.

The heat from his body pours into me, melting my coiled muscles as I fight not to turn and face him. I can even smell his cologne. So rich and distinctive. Heady and addictive. Just like him.

'I'll stay here until you're ready,' he says, his breath sliding down the side of my face and neck, sending goosebumps in its wake.

'I don't know when that will be.'

'It doesn't matter. I'll be here. I'm not missing that one millisecond when you decide you'll give me another chance.'

'What if it never comes?'

I feel his pain from the shift in the air and the weight in his voice.

'It will come, Aurora. It has to. Because there isn't a version of this universe where I can exist without making this right.'

He places his hand over mine and electricity shoots up my arm like a bolt of lightning. He holds my hand steady, and slides the key into the lock for me, letting me go the moment the door swings open.

'Close it behind you,' he says gently.

My throat burns and I desperately try to hold back tears. I merely nod, then rush inside, closing the door with more force than I intend. I run up the stairs and wait until I'm safely inside my apartment before I lean back against the front door and sink to the floor.

Everything muffles as I wrap my arms around my knees and push my head into my arms.

And I sob.

One week later

'It's the same guy,' Joe says, peering through the windscreen as I unbuckle my seatbelt.

Glancing across the street at the shiny black Bugatti, and the suited, scowling hulk leaning up against it, I sigh. 'Yep.'

'You know him?' Joe asks.

'He's my . . . Yes, I know him.'

'You want me to ask him to leave?'

'What?' I whip around to face Joe. 'Why would I want you to do that?'

He stares at me like I've gone mad. 'The guy looks like he's about to murder someone, and he's been hanging around outside your place every day when I've dropped you off.'

'Rafael would never hurt me.' I flick my gaze back to his brooding form and my stomach flips at how good he looks, standing there. He's wearing a waistcoat again. He's playing dirty.

His eyes narrow on mine as he sees me watching him. Then they slide to Joe as he leans across me to open my door.

'You sure about that?' Joe arches a brow, his attention fixed on Rafael's murderous glare.

'Positive. You don't need to worry.'

'Those from him too?' Joe snorts, looking at the giant bouquet of lotus flowers blocking the doorway to my building.

My breath catches. They're beautiful. Just like the six other bunches I have in my apartment. And the handbags. And the shoes. And the jewellery. And even the tubes of crisps. The gifts haven't stopped coming since Rafael turned up here on that first day.

Climbing from the car, I turn and flash Joe a grateful smile. 'Thanks for the lift.'

His eyes flick back to Rafael. 'You want me to walk you inside?'

I shake my head. 'No, it's fine, I promise.'

Closing the door, I fish inside my bag for my keys, walking slowly towards my door. Rafael pushes off from his car and strides over to me. For the past six days he's done this. Walked to me, helped me open the door, told me I look beautiful, passed me whatever gift he's left for me, then waited for me to close the door.

He hasn't pushed for more. He's seemed content to get that small interaction from me, even if it's over within seconds.

Instead of wrapping his hand over mine to open the door like he usually does, he pauses as he reaches me.

'He wants to be your new boyfriend.'

I follow his scowl to Joe, sitting in his car and watching us like he's wondering whether to climb out and tell Rafael to piss off and leave me alone. I almost laugh at the idea. Like Joe would get anywhere, except maybe the hospital, judging from the way Rafael's teeth are grinding so hard that a muscle in his jaw is throbbing.

'Joe's just a friend.'

'Joe? That his name? I thought it was Dickhead.'

I shake my head and turn towards the door.

'He wants to get between your legs,' Rafael growls.

'How would you know?' I scoff, whirling back to face him, fire igniting in my stomach. 'Joe's been a good friend since I arrived here.'

'He ogles your arse every time you climb out of his car. Why do you think he leans across to open your door instead of getting out and doing it himself? Prick,' he mutters.

'He does not!'

'Undo another button on your blouse tomorrow, then tell me he doesn't stare at your tits.' He grimaces. 'Bloody hell. Don't do that. Don't bloody listen to me.'

Molten bronze eyes slide to meet mine and I gaze up at him, momentarily enchanted by the way they shimmer and his pupils dilate as he looks back at me. There's no mistaking the love this man has for me. It's shining down on me like the sun, warming me from the inside out, giving me life.

But it's also dangerous and deceitful. I don't know if I can ever trust it again, despite wanting to.

He bends to retrieve the bouquet, then holds it out to me.

'They're beautiful.' I bite my lower lip as I take them, and their heady scent reaches my nostrils. 'Just like the last bunch.'

Rafael's eyes shine. 'Come home.'

'I can't,' I whisper. 'Not yet.'

Determination settles in his gaze, notching up its intensity. It's the only thing that masks the pain that's lurking there, beneath the surface.

'Then I'll see you tomorrow,' he says.

'Tomorrow,' I echo.

As per our new ritual, he slides his hand over mine and helps me unlock the door. Then he waits for me to step inside.

For the first time in a week, I glance back at him, and the way his eyes flare with hope makes my stomach twist painfully. What if I'm making this harder for him? What if I can never go home with him? Forgiveness is something that seems so out of reach right now that I'm not sure I'll ever even see it on the horizon.

His eyes drop to my mouth and he takes one step backwards, like he knows if he doesn't move away, then he'll be striding inside after me and pinning me to the wall, devouring me.

Heat pulses between my legs and I force a swallow as I close the door.

I don't have any vases left, so I head to the kitchen sink in my apartment and fill it with water, placing the flowers inside, looking for the small envelope between the petals. He always leaves a handwritten card. One sentence, ranging in its wording, but always carrying one of two sentiments – either how much he loves me, or how sorry he is. Both are equally hard to read.

Today, though, the small envelope has been replaced by a larger one. I pluck it from the arrangement and tear it open, pulling out two items from inside.

My hand flies to my mouth.

The first is a photo of Freddie. He's sitting in front of a large doggy birthday cake, his black eyes glinting for the camera. I can even make out a fine string of drool as he's no doubt been told to wait before he's allowed his cake. Rafael must have asked Kate to send it to him, because Freddie's birthday is today. There's no other way he could have got it so fast.

Guilt tugs at my gut. I need to call Kate and explain. I might have taken the job initially as a way to get closer to Dominic, to see if being in his house would result in overhearing something that could help my father. But my fondness that grew for her and Freddie is genuine. And I hate the thought of her feeling deceived.

Nausea pokes at my gut as I stare at the photograph. I lied to her. To a woman I like and respect. To someone I care about.

Maybe I'm no different to Rafael.

I was lying in order to find the truth. He was lying in order to seek revenge. I'll understand if Kate can't forgive me for lying to her, but I'll still hope that she can. The same way the man I love is sitting in his car on the street outside, hoping the same.

I rub at my temple as a headache threatens, before looking at the piece of paper that accompanied the photograph inside the envelope.

I sent him a present for you. R x

His handwriting is looped across the copy of an order acknowledgement.

A laugh bubbles out of me, the sound and feeling alien after so long.

'A doggy crisp hamper. Really?' I shake my head, my eyes darting to the window.

I walk over and peer down at the black Bugatti. He parks in the same spot every day. I have no idea where he's staying, but wherever it is he's going to shower and change each day, he must do it when I'm on shift at the hotel. Because whenever I'm in my apartment, he's there. Morning, afternoon, two in the morning. *He's there.*

Waiting for me to be ready.

And a huge piece of me hopes that one day I will be.

Chapter 39

Rafael

One week later

'It's all being handled. I'm working out of the office.'

'From where?' my father splutters.

I lean back in the driver's seat, my gaze tracking up to the window of Aurora's apartment. She should have been back from work an hour ago. She's probably stayed to do overtime. She's working too hard, and I only have myself to blame for it. If I hadn't lied to her, if I hadn't driven her away . . .

'Bath,' I tell my father, grimacing at the pompous snort that erupts from him.

'You're there chasing after this girl, aren't you?'

'Aurora,' I reply coolly. 'And yes, I am.'

'You're a bloody fool.'

My jaw tightens. 'Watch your tone, Dad. That's your future daughter-in-law you're talking about.'

'I don't mean her. I like the girl. I mean *you*, son. Only a bloody fool would keep a secret like that from her in the first place.'

My brows shoot up at the unexpected fatherly lecture I can sense looming.

'Your mother and I . . . She almost didn't give me a chance. You remember I told you that story, right?'

'I recall Mum saying you sent her favourite flowers for months until she finally caved and gave you one date because she felt sorry for you.'

'One date is all it took to convince her I was the one.'

Despite the way the memory has made my lips curl up, I press on, knowing my father will have a reason for bringing it up. There's always an ulterior motive with him.

'Why are you calling? I know it's not to talk about Aurora.'

My father huffs. 'The staff were bouncing around like lunatics when I visited this morning. Anyone would think they'd had their salaries doubled. You didn't give them a bloody raise, did you, son?'

I clamp my teeth together, counting to five before I snap at him that he didn't need to be in the office this morning. That he doesn't need to check up on us all. But of course, our father has never been able to help himself when it comes to interfering.

'No, I didn't.'

'Well, something's got into them. Get your arse back in. They need you there. Not galivanting off after a woman you've already screwed it up with.'

'I love her and I'm not coming home without her!'

I lurch forward and slam my hand against the steering wheel, accidentally knocking the horn and earning myself a dirty look from an elderly man shuffling past on the pavement.

'You're being bloody ridiculous. If she hasn't forgiven you yet, she's not going to.'

'She will,' I grit.

She has to.

My father continues, spouting his demands like I'm still a kid who has to listen.

'Get yourself together or don't come home at all. Fairfax Guardian will—'

'Will be fine,' I snap. 'In fact, it's better than fine. I was informed yesterday that we've won another award.'

My father snorts. 'You got lucky.'

'Yes! I did! Because I have an entire team who worked hard to earn it!' I bark. 'And I was sure to give them a nice fat bonus to show my gratitude.'

'You're too bloody soft. This isn't how I raised you.'

'No, you raised me to be a puppet. But guess what, Dad? I'm cutting the damn strings. And I'm running the company my way because I'm the CEO now, not you.'

He falls silent and I rub at the tightness in my chest as I wait for him to say something.

'How much?' he finally asks, the fight yielding in his voice.

'Ten per cent of their annual salary,' I answer, knowing he's referring to the staff bonuses, because of course he is.

He tsks. 'I'd have got the same result out of them for five.'

'Of course you would,' I reply tightly.

'I've always known, you know?'

'Known what?' I exhale as I scan the street for a sign of that dickhead Joe's car.

'About Dominic bailing you out.'

I freeze.

'Excuse me?'

'I know he saved Fairfax Guardian after you ballsed up the Wyndham account. That he sent new clients our way. Kept the money flowing in. Stopped it all from falling apart. Why didn't you come to me, son?'

I know better than to fall for the hint of tenderness tinting his tone. The only things my father has ever truly cared about are his company, and my mother. I'm grateful he loves her the way she deserves, but it's like he ran out of love when it came to having kids, and it was too much damn work to create more.

'You're saying you would have helped?' I snort.

'I'm saying I could have come back as CEO. You weren't ready.'

I shake my head in disgust. I was more than ready. Like my father told Aurora, I was head of my field of expertise in financial fraud cases, and I understood corporate insurance just as well as my father, if not better, by the time I took over as CEO.

But I understood people better than my father. How to get the best out of them; even if some of my staff think I'm an arsehole with the standards that I set, I know what they can achieve. Fairfax Guardian have the best people in the industry. A fact that is only further evidenced by the number of awards we've won, and the scale of clients we've taken on since I took the helm.

But my father can never forget that one client.

Wyndham.

And if he wasn't so bloody blind, then he'd see that part of the reason for the way that went is him. I knew he didn't think I could close that deal and sign Montgomery Wyndham. He expected me to ask him to come along and help me. He wanted me to understand that I might be the new CEO, but that I'd never be as good as him, no one would.

But a lifetime of living underneath my father's reign, added to the scalding memory of that day on the balcony, and he was right . . . I ballsed up. Big fucking time.

And for a while, I thought losing two hundred and forty million meant I'd done it again. But it wasn't me who fucked up that time. It was Dominic. Bloody Dominic, who's now done a goddamn runner, refusing to take responsibility. The bastard could be anywhere right now.

Kate informed me she's filing for a divorce, if she can ever locate his whereabouts. I think she knew all along who Aurora was and why she was there. She said she had her own questions after discovering Dominic was having an affair six months ago. Leaving hotel statements in your suit pockets will lead to being caught out.

Kate told me Freddie misses Aurora and that he's been off his food since she left.

Same. Bloody same.

'You still there?'

I pinch the bridge of my nose. 'Yes.'

'There's one more thing,' my father says, his tone losing its usual razor-sharp edge.

'What?' I sigh.

'What you did? Putting your hand in your own pocket to save the business? I'd have done the same. I *did* do the same. And your grandfather never knew a thing about it.'

'What are you talking about?'

'Past history,' my father grumbles. 'But it's why I know you're the right person to be Fairfax Guardian's CEO. You're like me. You're my son. And I *am* proud of you, even if I don't tell you enough.'

I clear my throat, but the lump that's rapidly growing there still presses against my windpipe, making breathing difficult.

'You *never* tell me,' I choke out.

My father tuts dismissively. 'Pandering to you isn't going to help you be the great man I know you can be. Just look at what happened after your fall. I got you straight back up on that balcony. Made you face your fear. Best thing I could have done for you.'

My throat feels like it's closing over. I was a terrified boy who *pissed himself*. His tough love shaped who I am. Led me to never feel good enough. To have this ingrained urge to show my father what I can do. One that's meant I've made mistakes that have cost me everything. *Cost me Aurora.* In what fucked-up universe is that the best thing?

'But you don't think that day haunts me? I almost lost my eldest son. My boy . . .' He sighs wearily. 'If I'd taught you to be more careful you wouldn't have fallen.'

Minimising the risk. That's what I've always prided myself on.

Until Aurora.

Allowing us to grow close made me vulnerable. Made her vulnerable.

But it was a risk I'd take a million times over. *Two hundred and forty bloody million times over.*

'But I did fall, Dad,' I whisper.

'And I'll live with that for the rest of my life, son.'

I stare out of the window, blinking hard.

My father's next words carry a tenderness he's never used with me before. But they hit me like a freight train straight through the heart.

'Get yourself back to London, son. Give her up. She isn't coming back to you.'

My heart clamps painfully, like acid's being pumped through it.

'I've got to go,' I choke, ending the call.

I tug on my tie, loosening it and fumbling to undo the top button of my shirt, sweat beading on my brow.

'So damn hot,' I rasp, throwing open my car door.

But it does nothing. The fabric sticks to my back as I heave in a breath, wincing as my lungs scream out and my heart thunders between them like it's trying to break past my ribs.

I climb from the car, the cool air hitting my face as I push a hand through my hair, then run it around the back of my burning neck.

A stab of intense pain hits me in the chest, and I grab the car door to steady myself.

Reaching inside, I pull out a bottle of water, unscrewing it, and immediately downing half.

I'm fine. I just need air. I'll feel better soon.

I check my watch. She's almost an hour and a half late now.

I rub at my chest, wincing.

I'm fine.

She'll be back soon and this pain that's been coming and going since she left will ease again. It's never been this strong, but as soon as I see my Beauty's face, all will be right in the world again.

Chapter 40

Aurora

'I could have caught a cab. It's late.'

'Why? I drive this way home, it's no bother.'

'Well, thanks,' I tell Joe as we roll to a stop in his car.

We went out for one of the receptionists' leaving drinks straight after my shift, and I am more than ready for my bed.

My gaze immediately falls on Rafe's car in its usual spot. He isn't leaning against it like he usually would be. I squint at the windscreen but it's already dark outside and hard to make out if he's sitting in the driver's seat or not. But he must be. Where else would he be?

'You okay?' Joe asks.

I turn back in time to see his eyes lift from my cleavage. I changed into a dress to go for drinks, and the one I'm wearing is low-cut and figure-hugging.

'*Undo another button . . . tell me he doesn't stare at your tits.*'

I swallow at the memory of Rafael's words as Joe licks his lips.

'Did anyone ever tell you how beautiful you are?'

'My boyfriend. The guy who's here every day waiting for me,' I reply without missing a beat.

Joe's face creases into an easy smile and he throws his hands up, not an ounce of malice in his accompanying chuckle.

'Knew that guy was someone important to you. I figured he was an ex, though, or I wouldn't have . . .' He flicks his eyes to me, keeping them on my face instead of returning to my cleavage. 'You know.'

'It's okay. Thanks for the compliment.'

He leans his head back against his headrest and sighs. 'Probably a good thing, anyway. It'd have broken my heart to say goodbye to you once term starts and I have to go back to Edinburgh.'

I shake my head at his mock-wounded expression and he winks at me.

'Exactly. I couldn't have jeopardised distracting one of the country's best medical minds when he's so close to graduating.' I try to smile, but it slides from my face as I glance back at Rafael's car.

'You sure he's safe to be around? You look worried. Could he . . . be waiting for you inside?'

Joe's watching me closely as I turn back to him.

'No, I told you. Rafe would never hurt me. That's not him.'

Physically that's true, even if mentally I'm still a walking wreckage.

'Thanks again for the lift,' I tell Joe, not waiting for him to lean over and open my door before I push it open and climb out.

I stare at Rafael's empty car as Joe jumps out after me.

'The guy's always waiting for you in public. I'm not taking any chances until I know you're safely inside,' he tells me as I look at him in question.

'Fine.'

I scan the street as we pass the neighbouring building to reach mine. I spot his waistcoat first, half-unbuttoned over his wrinkled shirt, like he's torn at it in haste.

'Rafe!' I run to him and drop to the ground where he's slumped against my front door.

He looks at me with bloodshot eyes, his chest rising and falling with raspy breaths.

'You look beautiful,' he says, his eyes dragging over my face like it's an effort just to move them, let alone speak.

'What are you doing on the ground?'

'Needed to sit.'

He winces and lifts his hand. I beat him to it, placing mine over his chest, above his heart.

'Oh my God. His heart's racing! Joe!'

I turn in panic, but Joe's already crouched beside us and has taken Rafael's wrist into his hand.

'You all right there, mate? I'm just going to check your pulse.'

Rafael looks at me, his brows knitting together.

'Joe's training to be a doctor,' I explain.

I rip my eyes from Rafael's waxy face and look at Joe.

'Is he having a heart attack? He had surgery on it as a kid. Sometimes it hurts when he gets anxious.'

'I'm going to call an ambulance,' Joe says, his expression grim.

'Oh my God!' I turn back to Rafael, cupping his cheek. He blinks at me but doesn't seem able to focus on me properly.

'You're okay,' I soothe, stroking his cheek. 'You'll be okay.'

'I love you.'

My heart seizes at the gentle way he breathes the words, like he needs me to understand, even if it's the last thing he does.

'I know you do,' I croak. 'And you're going to be okay. We're going to get you checked over, and you'll be fine.'

His eyes roll and my heart flies into my throat.

'Rafe? Stay awake, okay? I love you too. I need you to stay awake.'

'You still love me?' He blinks, fighting to focus on me.

'I never stopped. Now breathe for me, okay? Big, deep breaths.'

He holds my eyes as we wait for the ambulance, breathing in time with me as I cradle his face, and Joe keeps a check on his pulse. By the time the paramedics arrive he's floating in and out of consciousness.

'Call and let me know how he is,' Joe says, watching me climb in the ambulance after Rafael as he's stretchered inside.

'I will. Thank you,' I say before the doors close.

'Let's get you fully hooked up so we can keep an eye on your heart, okay?' the young paramedic tells him.

Rafael lifts a hand clumsily to his clothes and I move in so I can unbutton his waistcoat, and then his shirt, for him.

Inches of toned, muscular skin come into view, and in the centre, the straight line of his scar. He holds my eyes as my fingers trace lightly over it, out of my control.

'Sorry,' I mumble, drawing my hand back.

He catches my wrist and holds it gently as the paramedic hooks him up to the machine.

'Don't call anyone,' he says, his thumb strolling delicate circles over my pulse point.

My breath hitches at the memory of his touch on my skin. Of the night I first touched his scar, and how he made love to me so tenderly afterwards.

My eyes sting. 'They should know, they'll be worried.'

'And if there's something for them to worry about, then you can call them, I promise. But please, Aurora, right now, I just want you here with me.'

I swallow around the thick lump in my throat and nod. 'Okay. But if we get to the hospital and something's wrong or you get worse again, then I'm calling everyone.'

His lips curl into a faint smile at the bossiness in my sniffly voice. 'Okay.'

Then his eyes roll in his head again.

'And he's going to be okay?' I ask, looking at the doctor with pleading eyes, everything resting on the next words to come out of his mouth.

'We'll keep him in for observations, but yes, he should make a full recovery.'

'Thank God.' I drop my head to my chest.

'I'll leave you both so he can get some rest and check back in a bit.'

I nod mutely as she leaves. Then I burst into tears.

The drive to the hospital is a blur. I fired questions at the paramedic the entire time, asking if Rafael would be okay. I don't know the first thing about medical treatments, but I asked him over and over if the hospital we were being taken to was the best one for treating heart-related conditions, and if they had the right equipment and specialists there.

Each time Rafael managed to open his eyes, he looked at me, and I swear it took everything in me to stay strong for him. To not show him how terrified I was. But now I know he's going to be okay the floodgates have well and truly opened.

'Aurora?' Rafael croaks.

'Don't ask if we can leave again.' I sob, giving him a stern look. 'They need to monitor you overnight first. You heard the doctor.'

He's hooked up to an ECG machine, his chest is bare. Seeing him lying here, shirtless, his scar like a beacon over his heart, brings a wave of fresh tears to me. *I could have lost him forever.*

He frowns as I cry, his forehead creasing with worry like I'm about to walk out of here.

'It was a weird episode, that's all,' he says.

I shake my head, wringing my hands in my lap. 'The doctors called it Tako . . . Tao . . .' I frown.

'Takotsubo cardiomyopathy,' he whispers.

'Yeah.' I sniff. '*Broken heart syndrome.*' Fresh tears stream from my eyes as I look at him. 'I made you ill.'

'You didn't. This is all my doing. I wasn't paying attention to what my body was telling me, that's all. I should have—'

'They said it's brought on by extreme emotional or physical stress.'

Rafe grimaces. 'I'm fine. It's reversible. I'll just be more careful.'

'You were so pale, I-I . . . We're staying until they say you can leave, okay? I'm in charge this time.'

'Okay.'

He says it so easily as his molten bronze eyes capture mine. Energy dances through my veins seeing some of the light coming back to them.

'I never want to see you like that again. It scared me,' I confess, wiping at my cheeks.

'I'm sorry.'

'You've been sleeping in your car. I've seen you through the window.'

His gaze narrows on mine for a moment, like the knowledge that I was checking on him throughout the nights brings him comfort.

'I have a hotel room nearby,' he says.

'And I bet you shower there and then come straight back.'

The muscle tensing in his jaw tells me I'm right.

'Rafe,' I whisper. 'This has to stop.'

He leans his head back against the pillows, staring up at the ceiling as he inhales slowly. I know he's gearing up for insisting he isn't leaving without me again. But the thought of going over the same thing and potentially getting him worked up when he needs to rest has concern weaving its way through my weary muscles.

'Why don't you get some sleep?' I suggest.

'Will you be here when I wake up?'

My heart sinks at the flash of fear in his eyes.

'I will. I promise.'

His shoulders relax and for a moment I think he's about to close his eyes, so I get up and turn the light in his room off, before returning to the chair. But then his voice, no more than a soft husk from his lips, drifts through the dimness towards me.

'This is my fault. I knew I shouldn't have let you get close and—'

'What do you mean?'

Even in the dark I can make out the way his face crumples and his cheeks glisten.

'I never wanted to hear anyone cry over me again. Not after hearing my mother when I . . .' He swallows thickly. 'It's why I've never let anyone to get close enough to fall in love with me. Not *truly* in love with me. I knew you hated me. I thought I was keeping you safe from all of this. My heart, it's—'

'The strongest, most beautiful one I've ever known. And you're going to get better.'

We fall silent for a moment except for the gentle humming and beeping of machines.

'I'm sorry, Aurora,' he whispers.

Something inside me curls up into a ball at the anguish in his voice.

'I know you are,' I whisper back.

'I thought—' he starts, before clearing his throat. But his voice still comes out hoarse, like it's taking a lot of effort to speak. I want to reach for his hand and hold it. Tell him he doesn't need to say anything. But for some reason I can't move or talk.

'I thought I'd broken my heart already,' he whispers into the dark room. 'But this hurts so much more. All of me is broken without you. I don't exist properly without you. I don't deserve your forgiveness, but God I want it. I've prayed for it every day since you left, and I'm not a religious man, despite my name.' He chuckles, but it's empty.

'Rafe,' I breathe.

My limbs unlock, and where a few moments ago I was frozen, now I can't stop myself from moving towards him.

I climb on to the bed, and he shuffles across to make space for me. The bed isn't big, so I have to meld myself along his side to stay on. He lifts his arm, welcoming me beneath it like it's the most natural thing in the world.

And as I lie beside him, I'm transported back to the last night we spent together like this, wrapped up in one another's embrace. Happy and in love.

He doesn't say anything. He doesn't need to.

I curl into him, my face nestled between his shoulder and neck, and just breathe him in, reminding myself of his warmth and scent again.

Soft lips brush my hair, and it takes everything in me to hold back a fresh sob threatening to break out of me.

'I've got you,' he soothes.

I swallow down a hiccup and bury my face further into his neck, determined not to cry again. Not now. Not when all that matters is him resting and being okay again.

I take a few deep breaths and wait until I'm sure my voice will come out even before I speak.

'Rafe?'

'What is it, Beaut—'

He catches himself before the whole word slips free. But I hear enough.

I screw my eyes shut.

'Is it okay if I put my head on your chest?'

Chapter 41

Rafael

'You never need to ask.'

Her body softens, like my words bring her relief. And, seconds later, blond hair brushes my chin as she rests her head on my chest and wraps her arm around my waist.

The ECG continues beeping at the same intermittent pace, despite the fact I could swear my heart stopped and started again the precise moment her cheek made contact with my bare skin.

She cried over me. Just like my mother. A sound I swore on my soul I never wanted to hear ever again.

I never wanted to be the cause of pain like that again.

I thought hearing it would break me. Deconstruct all the years I've spent fighting against feeling *weak*.

But the thought of Aurora *not* loving me back the way I love her. *Not* crying over me.

Suddenly that was worse than anything else I could imagine.

I've known for a while that I'm desperately, hopelessly, undeniably in love with Aurora Thorne. She's seen all of my scars. And loves me because of them. And hearing her cry, understanding that, makes me feel stronger than I've ever felt.

I never knew being loved could feel like a miracle and not a burden.

I gaze down at the top of her head. She feels so right in my arms. She always did. I press my lips tightly together, hoping this won't be the last time I'll ever hold her like this.

'I just need to hear your heart beating,' she whispers.

The sweet uncertainty in her voice makes my eyes burn with tears.

'I need to hear it,' she chokes, like she's holding back tears. 'You promised me you'd love me until its last broken beat, and I'm making sure you keep your promise.'

Hope flares in my chest.

'You forgive me?'

She sniffles. 'I want to.'

My heart sinks. *But she isn't there yet.* She doesn't need to say the words for me to hear them.

I tighten my arm around her, biting back a desperate beg for her not to give up. I need to let her speak.

Even if it feels like I'm dying inside.

'I want to forgive you,' she continues. 'Because I love you. And I promised you I'd never love again. Not like this. And I meant it. I'll never be able to forget you, even if I want to.'

Silent tears track down my cheeks as I lift my hand and cradle her head to my chest, sinking my fingers into her silky strands. Her words cut deeper than anything else she could have said. I'd rather she told me she hates me, that she doesn't love me any more. But to hear that I've taken her opportunity to be happy and feel love again wrecks me more than anything else she could have said.

I thought disappointing my father was the worst thing that could happen to me.

But it's not.

It's disappointing her.

It's stealing the chance of a future she deserves from her. One where she's safe to love and be loved the way she should have been when she was mine.

I've failed her.

She's the love of my life. I'd die for her. And I've been so selfish – caring about nothing more than getting her back, taking her home, thinking this was some battle to be won – that I couldn't see what I was taking from her at the same time.

I can't force Aurora back into my life. She has to come because she wants to. And no matter how hard I try to force her, ultimately it's her decision. And I need to give her the space to make it.

I sink my nose into her hair, kissing the top of her head. She wants me to rest, but if this might be the last night I hold her in my arms, then I'm going to stay awake and savour every damn second.

And then tomorrow, I'll do the hardest thing I'll ever do in my life.

'What do you fancy for breakfast? Eggs? They're full of protein. I'll make you eggs.'

Aurora's hand is soft beneath mine as I help her slide the key into the lock of her building's door, as has become our habit.

'I'm not coming inside,' I tell her gently.

'But . . . ?' She whirls to face me, her eyes wide. 'The doctors said you need to take your medicine, and then eat better today and . . .'

Her face falls as she searches my eyes.

'I'm sorry. I'll make this right. I'll be the man I should have been for you. One who would have deserved you,' I say.

'What do you mean?'

Panic tints her voice as I take a step backwards.

'Rafael?' she chokes.

She breathes out a deep sigh of relief as I take her hand inside mine and lift it back to the key that's sitting inside the lock.

'Okay, good idea. We can talk about this inside,' she says as we turn it together and the door opens.

I wait for her to step through it, and then she turns to see why I'm not following her.

It's what I've spent weeks wishing for. For her to invite me in. To talk. But I've been selfish, wanting her back because *I* love and miss her. Hearing her cry over me, *really* cry, has made everything clearer.

It's time I put her first – properly this time.

'I'm not him yet,' I say, looking into her confused eyes. 'But I will be. I promise.'

'What?' she whispers.

I pull her towards me, keeping my feet firmly on the other side of the doorway, where I belong. I screw my eyes shut as I press a weighted kiss to her forehead, allowing my lips to linger, basking in the feel of her smooth skin against them one final time.

'I promise,' I repeat gently.

'Rafael?'

I turn away before I can see the hurt in her aquamarine eyes, and I stride to where I left my car last night.

I get inside and start the engine, pulling out into the road.

I try not to look, but my eyes betray me. Tears stream down her cheeks as she watches me leave. Tears I put there. Again.

She watches until I reach the corner. Her blond hair blows around her face softly in the breeze as I look at her one last time in my rearview mirror before I turn.

I have to fix this.

If she can't love me again, then I need to find a way to set her free to love someone else.

There's no other outcome I can accept and live with.

I can't see my girl suffering because of me any longer.

Aurora Thorne won't hate that she loves me for the rest of her days.

I'll do whatever it takes.

Chapter 42

Aurora

One month later

'Why the face like a slapped arse?' Joe quips as I sit beside him in the small staff area in the garden.

'No reason.' I shrug, pretending to rub at a stain on my house-keeping uniform.

'Is it because I'm heading back to university in two days, and you're going to miss me?'

'Yeah, that's it.' I manage a small smile.

He tips his head back and exhales towards the clear blue sky. 'At least try to lie convincingly.'

'What?'

He looks at me pointedly. 'It's been a month since your scary ex went to hospital, and you've not mentioned him, except to tell me he was okay. And he hasn't been outside your place since.'

'He went back to London.'

'I thought that's what you wanted.'

'It was.' I grimace. 'I mean, I needed time but . . .'

'But you knew where you stood while the poor guy was grovelling on your doorstep.'

'Oh my God, I'm a terrible person who doesn't know what they want,' I squeak as his words hit home.

I did tell Rafael to go home, repeatedly. After I told him to let me go. But now that he's actually gone . . . I hate it. I wanted to forgive him, I really did. But I also wanted to be angry at him first. I wanted to punish him for lying to me and hurting me.

And now he's given up.

His car is never outside. He's never waiting beside it when I get home after a shift. The flowers he gave me are all dead and long gone. And the shoes, handbags, and clothes are still in their boxes and bags. I can't bring myself to wear or use any of them.

The only thing I can stomach is the photograph of Freddie that I carry around in my bag. The bittersweet gesture that he gave me, that I still didn't respond to.

I let him walk away, thinking a part of me hated him.

But I could never hate Rafael Fairfax again.

I love him more than words.

I blow out a long breath, gazing across the landscaped gardens. We're tucked out of sight from the guests here, but we can still see the rear of the hotel's expanse of perfect lawn that leads down to a small lake with swans swimming on it.

'Now he's gone, I feel even emptier than when I first left London,' I say.

'Ah.' Joe nods.

'He said he wasn't a man who deserves me, but that he would be. I thought that meant he'd be back again. But . . . he's not coming. And I need to accept it.'

'What are you going to do?' Joe asks, swirling the dregs of his coffee inside his mug and studying it.

'Any suggestions?' I smile sadly.

'Breed sausage dogs and get rich selling their puppies. Or hosting doggy parties for them.'

'What?' I can't help but laugh as Joe smirks.

'I've seen you looking at that photo you carry around, like a million times. Is that your dog? Did your ex keep him?'

'No. He belongs to a friend.' My smile falters. I'm not sure Kate would call me a friend any more, but I won't know unless I go and see her. Actually see her face to face, not just the apology note I'd posted to her without my forwarding address.

Joe snorts. 'I swear the people who stay in this hotel wipe their arse on fifty-pound notes.'

I follow his eye line above the trees as a whirring in the sky grows louder.

A helicopter comes into view in the distance.

'You think it's coming here?'

'It is. We got briefed on it when my shift started. They don't want help with their luggage. Probably travel with their own maids and butlers.' He chuckles as the helicopter flies closer.

It circles the hotel, before lining itself up over the large, flat lawn, and hovering, preparing to land.

Joe jumps to his feet. 'There's a guy hanging out of it! Do you reckon it's Tom Cruise? He does all his own stunts.'

'Why would Tom Cruise be visiting Bath?' I ask as I follow Joe to get a better look.

Management staff from the hotel line the edge of the lawn like they're waiting for royalty.

'Whoever it is, he's either brave or stupid,' I say as I stare at the suited figure who's standing in the open doorway of the rear of the helicopter, holding on to something inside as he leans partway out and scans the grounds of the hotel like he's searching for someone.

'Or just cool,' Joe says, impressed, as he grins in awe at the helicopter.

I stare at the man. At his rich wavy hair. At the way his broad body fills the open space in the side of the helicopter . . . His broad, suited body . . . complete with waistcoat.

'Where are you going?' Joe yells.

But I'm already sprinting.

I cross the lawn, getting as close as I safely can to the landing helicopter.

Rafael's eyes collide with mine from the open doorway ten metres in the air.

His mouth opens and he shouts something, but I can't hear him over the deafening roar of the blades slicing the air.

Joe catches up with me, stopping beside me as it lands.

It feels like forever as the blades stop turning and for us to be given a thumbs-up from one of the pilots inside the cockpit.

I rush over, a weird buzzing in my stomach that could be nerves or excitement. I can't tell. But the moment I'm close enough to see Rafael's face, it turns into knots.

He's white as a sheet, frozen in place like his body has seized up.

And all I want to do is fling my arms around his neck and tell him how proud I am of him.

'You don't like heights!' I cry, staring up at him from a couple of metres away. It's as if my body can't close the final distance yet, understanding that he needs a moment first.

'I still don't bloody like them. But not seeing you as soon as possible scared me more. Plus, it worked for Edward in *Pretty Woman*,' he says, shaking his head and staring at the grass like he can't believe what he just did.

I can't help it: I burst into inappropriate laughter.

He lifts his eyes to mine and I stop abruptly.

The two of us stare at one another for a beat as warmth weaves itself through me.

'It's been weeks,' I say, not caring how desperate I sound.

He's here now, and that's the main thing. He's here, and he wouldn't be here if it wasn't to see me. *Would he?*

My stomach drops when he doesn't say anything.

'Rafael?'

His gaze roams my face and his eyes soften, but then he turns, looking back over his shoulder.

'You can get out now,' he says.

Everything around me fades into a blur as someone jumps down from the helicopter.

'Dad!'

He's almost knocked to the ground as I launch myself at him, flying into his arms.

'What are you doing here?' I sob.

His arms wrap around me, the familiarity of a hug I haven't felt in far too long bringing a flurry of ugly sobs to my chest.

'I was acquitted.'

'What?'

'Got out this morning.'

'But I saw you at the weekend. You never said anything. How long have you known? How did this happen?'

'I've known, well, I've *hoped* it was coming for a while now, love.'

'I don't understand. How?'

He squeezes me tighter and I open my eyes, meeting Rafael's intent gaze over my father's shoulder.

'He did this?' I whisper.

'He did,' my father says.

'How?'

He chuckles. 'The same way I've learnt he does most things. With pig-headed arrogance, and a stubbornness that I bet gets him into trouble.'

'Why?'

'You need to ask him that.'

I hug my father tighter, reluctant to let him go, but he eases back and holds me in place with his hands curled around my upper arms.

'Talk to the man,' he says, his eyes twinkling.

I hesitate, not wanting to take my eyes from my father for a second in case this is all a dream, and he'll disappear if I'm not careful. But I drag my eyes from him to Rafael.

Butterflies erupt in my core as molten bronze shimmers at me with unconcealed adoration.

'Is this yours?' I ask, gesturing to the helicopter, unable to say what I really want to. *I love you. I missed you.*

'I borrowed it from a friend,' he says, drinking me in with his gaze in a way that makes my entire body tingle.

'Generous friend,' I reply, waiting for him to give me something – anything.

'You look beautiful,' he says.

I've been on shift since 5 a.m. and it's almost lunch time. My hair's pulled up into something resembling a nest on my head. And I'm pretty sure my uniform still carries the smell from the last room I cleaned that had a blocked toilet that almost made me puke.

I know he's wrong. But I also know he means every word.

His eyes flick past me to where I left my father, then back to me. 'And you look happier.'

I nod, emotion threatening to clog up my throat. 'I am now. How did you manage it?'

He exhales. 'It's a long story.'

'Why did you do it?' I whisper.

'Because it needed to be done.'

'Thank you,' I breathe, because there are no words great enough to describe how grateful I am to him in this moment.

He gifts me with one of his rare smiles and it's like feeling the sun on my face for the first time in nearly two months.

'You're welcome, Aurora,' he says simply.

I wait for him to climb down from the helicopter. But instead, he ducks inside and says something to the pilots. They put their headsets back on and start flicking switches.

'Wait! You're leaving?'

He looks at me, and for a fraction of a second I see the raw pain in his eyes, hidden beneath a smile that's purely for my benefit.

'This isn't about us right now. It's about you and your father.'

I shake my head, not wanting to believe what he's saying.

'You're just going to leave again? I haven't seen you in a month, and now you're going already?'

The way he looks at me, like he wishes he could pull me into his arms, but won't, wrenches a sob from my chest.

So much has happened, I can't blame him. The months apart have felt like walking through hell. I know it was the same for him. Some things change you for good, and there's no coming back from them.

'Rafael?' I breathe. 'You're done, aren't you? With you and me?'

He jumps out of the helicopter, his eyes on fire.

'No! I'm not done!'

He pulls me into his arms the exact moment my first tear breaks free.

'I'll love you more and more every day. Can't you see that? I'll never stop. This will never be done. *We* will never be done. I love you, Aurora. That could never be done.'

He cups my face in his hands, and I fist the front of his shirt.

'But I haven't seen you in weeks and you're going again. I don't understand.'

'It needs to be this way. You need time with your father.'

'I need you too!'

He tucks a loose strand of hair behind my ear.

'I hope you listen better than I did.'

'Wha—'

'Let me go, Aurora,' he says softly.

'No!' I weep.

He brings his lips to mine in a tender goodbye kiss that makes my heart feel like it's breaking all over again. I grip on tight, holding him to me so he can't move away. And I kiss him the way I've missed doing since that night I walked away from him.

It's a kiss that tells him I missed him.

It's a kiss that tells him I love him.

But most of all . . .

It's a kiss that tells him I forgive him.

His eyes are misty as it ends. He rests his forehead against mine.

'*I'll love you until the last beat of my broken heart, Beauty*,' he whispers.

'And I'll love you until the final beat of mine,' I whisper.

He uncurls my fingers from his shirt with aching gentleness. Then he kisses me one final time and climbs back into the helicopter.

My father comes to stand beside me and we watch it fly away until it's no longer even a speck on the horizon.

He wraps his arms around my shoulders.

And I cry the entire time.

Chapter 43

Rafael

Two months later

The French armoire glistens in the late-afternoon European sun, taunting me. But no matter how hard it is to watch, not watching would be even harder.

'They have a wedge heel, and this really pretty detailing on the strap,' she says, her smile bright as she holds up the brand-new shoes she's unboxed so the camera can pick them up. 'My dad and I are going to the local market later, so I'm going to wear them with this dress.' She gestures to the white broderie sundress she has on. Her blond hair is flowing around her shoulders and she's a vision in white.

She looks like a goddamn angel.

That day in the hospital, and the day I left her in the helicopter . . . She *cried* for me.

She loves me.

I've spent my entire life since my accident avoiding it. Then when I finally got it, allowed myself to want it, I screwed up royally.

I lost the best thing that ever happened to me.

'Jesus.' I scrub a hand around my jaw, my eyes burning.

I've done this every day, watched her vlogs, the same as I always did. Only now instead of my dick throbbing, it's my goddamn heart.

She's been gone two months, and I've died a little more each day without her.

But I knew letting her stay would have killed her eventually.

She wouldn't have known it to start with, but if I'd let her come with me that day I returned her father to her in the helicopter, then she wouldn't have had what she needed: time.

Time to reconnect with him without anyone else placing demands on her attention. Time to heal together after what they've been through, if healing is even possible. And time to decide for definite if I'm worthy of her. If she still loves me enough to truly forgive me deep in her heart. Because if there's even a shred of doubt left, then I could never live with myself if I let her ignore it, or gloss over it, thinking that's the best she's going to get.

Aurora deserves a man who loves and adores her. But she also deserves to be one hundred per cent free to love in her own way in return. I can't look into her eyes for the rest of my life knowing I've stolen the purest form of love from her if she's only ninety-nine per cent. She needs to be completely sure. She needs to choose me, all by herself.

I pause the video. Her beautiful smile freezes on the screen, suspended in time. Her and her father are staying in a chateau in the south of France. Walking, swimming, cooking together. Dancing in the kitchen at night after bottles of wine from the vineyard the chateau sits on. George has given me those little snippets when he's messaged me, and I've clung to each one like a lifeline. She's getting what she needs. My girl's happy again. She has her father back, just like she dreamt of. I'd be a greedy arsehole to ask for more.

She hasn't messaged me. I don't know whether she's even tried. I asked George to delete my number from her phone. She needed to do this without me and our relationship hanging over her like a cloud.

I just didn't realise how hard it would be to see her so clearly thriving without me when I'm barely functioning without her.

I'm rubbing at my temples with my head in my hands when there's a knock at my office door.

'Ready for the meeting?' Dove asks, barging in, giving me no choice, not that I would have said no anyway. It's our tradition. With one small tweak . . .

'Sure am. I don't need to say, "Make yourselves at home".'

Despite the constant dull ache in my chest, I smile as my sister and two brothers spill into my office – our new location. Dove flings herself on to one of the couches and Gabe deposits Benedict into one of the cat beds he somehow managed to sneak into my office. And for some unfathomable reason, I haven't drop-kicked it back out the door like I would have once. The big ginger furball is actually a good listener when he chooses to hang around in my office, which he's taken to doing. Not that I'll tell my therapist that; he might think his bi-weekly sessions are in jeopardy. Or more likely, he'll tell me I'm making progress again and give me one of his looks of pride like I'm a star student. I chuckle to myself. I hate the guy because I need him. But each time I walk out of his office I also feel lighter.

I rise from my desk as Angelo flicks on the coffee machine and starts fixing one for everyone.

'Beautiful day,' Dove comments, gazing out of the floor-to-ceiling windows beside the seating area.

'It is,' I agree, strolling over to the window and sliding my hands into my pockets as I look out at the clear blue sky, and then across the city skyline.

The others continue getting things set up, understanding me enough that they don't interfere. I might look calm, standing less than a metre from my office windows, but they know better than anyone that my hands are inside my pockets to hide the white knuckles as I curl my fingers so tightly into my palm that I'll leave nail marks.

But I'm standing. Not falling.

And each time I move a little closer, or push myself a little harder, the swirl of anxiety in my gut lessens, and my heart pounds just that tiny bit slower.

I'm making progress. One day at a time.

'Let's start with the Dellainy case. How's that going?' I ask, turning away from the view and taking a seat beside Dove.

'Walk in the park,' Angelo replies with a cocky grin.

I raise a brow. 'A simple "signed", or "still in progress" will do.'

He chuckles, lifting his palms up, either side of the armchair he's sunk into. 'Signed. And I got a referral from them for a friend of theirs who has a collection of private art they want to insure.'

'Good. Keep us updated. How about Ketteridge?' I direct at Dove.

The client has gone quiet since the party at their house months ago, but I expected that to be the case. The business has been going through some big restructures.

'We've got the contracts ready. I'm meeting with Phillip on Wednesday to go over them. He sounded keen to sign when I spoke with him yesterday.'

'Where are you meeting him?' Gabe asks, looking up over the top of his laptop where he's taking notes.

'He's coming here,' Dove says.

'Phillip Ketteridge is coming here?'

'Yep.'

My brother's gaze fixes on Dove's for a moment before he clears his throat and looks back at his screen. 'I have a meeting with the building's security firm to go over some upgrades on Wednesday. Benedict and I will be out all day.'

'Don't they usually come here?' Angelo pipes up.

Gabriel's lips thin, but his fingers don't slow from flying over the keys. 'Not this time.'

Dove narrows her eyes in his direction, her lips twisted in thought for a moment, before the meeting continues.

We go over everything that's coming up for the week, then Angelo and Gabe head out, taking Benedict with them.

Dove stays seated. 'Have you heard from Dom?'

She doesn't try to sugarcoat it, getting straight to the point.

I suck in a sharp breath.

'Of course I haven't! The bastard's disappeared off the face of the earth. You think I'd keep it from the police if he'd contacted me?'

Dove winces. 'I'm sorry. It's just . . . such a bloody mess. Where do you think he would have gone?'

I purse my lips. 'Dom might be a liar and a cheat, but this Ella woman had his baby. I still know him well enough to understand that'll be eating him up, not knowing whether he has a son or daughter, or what their name is and if they're doing okay. I think he's gone after her.'

'Yeah, well, actions have consequences,' Dove mutters. 'And he'll have to face them when the police find him.'

'Yeah, he will,' I agree.

Dominic was dropped from the board immediately after they found out he tampered with internal records. And he could be facing a prison sentence himself for his role in everything. But he was already long gone by the time the police went to his house to question him. Despite our history, I can't bring myself to feel an ounce of sympathy for him.

'How are you doing?' I ask Dove carefully as she looks away, unable to meet my eyes.

'Fine.'

'Fine,' I repeat, not believing a word. I know my sister. And the extra weight she's been carrying around on her shoulders recently isn't only from her best friend being absent.

'I know what you're thinking,' she huffs.

'Do you?'

'Yes. And I'm fine. Seeing him again was a shock. But I'm good now.'

'Still, the sooner Vance Falcon disappears back to Singapore, the better for everyone, hm?'

I study the pinch at the corners of her eyes as she shrugs. 'I haven't thought about it.'

My challenge to that statement is cut off by her phone ringing.

'It's Aurora,' she says, glancing at me with a mix of guilt and sympathy in her eyes.

'Answer it,' I say as calmly as I can muster, despite the fact my pulse rate just trebled.

I did the right thing asking George to delete my number, but it still feels like my chest is torn wide open every time I hear her name. But this time together is theirs. I have no reason to be a part of it. Not when I'm a contributing factor to why they lost so much in the first place. If I'd only dug deeper, not been so fast to accept that he was guilty, then I could have . . . Bloody hell, I don't know what I could have done. But I could have done something.

'Hi,' Dove answers. She smiles, nodding along as she listens.

I can't hear what Aurora's saying, even though I wish I could. Just to have that sliver of *her*. To hear her voice and know what she's thinking at this exact moment.

'Yeah, he's here.'

My heart pounds as Dove looks at me, listening intently to whatever it is Aurora's telling her.

Maybe she's ready to talk to me. Sourness swirls over my tongue. Or perhaps she has something to tell me. *What if she's met someone new? What if she's in love with them? What if she's calling to tell Dove she's marrying some French arsehole who's never hurt her like I have?*

'I'll tell him,' Dove says. 'Okay. Bye.'

I stare at her as she ends the call.

'Aurora says thank you for the video of Freddie.'

'Freddie?'

She nods.

I exhale, my body sagging. Of course that's all she said. I've been sending videos Kate's shared with me to George's phone so he can show her.

'Thanks.' I nod at Dove. 'I'll catch up with you later.' I stand and return to my desk, busying myself with sifting through a stack of papers on top of it.

'Loving someone isn't just the highs, you know?' she says, eyeing me with concern.

'Excuse me?'

Her eyes shine with a rare vulnerability she never usually lets anyone see.

'It isn't just the highs,' she repeats. 'It's sitting beside that person when their parents die. It's holding their hand when they bring your children into the world. It's bathing you if you get sick, feeding you when you're hurting too much to eat. If Aurora comes back to you, then she's choosing all of that. She's telling you that she'll be there for you in grief, chaos, uncertainty. The beautiful and the ugly.'

She rises from the sofa and looks me dead in the eye.

'You did the right thing, Rafe. I'm proud of you. You gave her time to heal. And space to decide if you're meant to be all of that for one another. It's a big decision. And her taking her time to make it isn't a bad thing. It means that if she comes back, then you can be sure it'll all work out, no matter what else life throws at you.'

My throat thickens and I nod.

She walks to the door, but before she can leave, I call out, 'What if she decides I can't be all those things to her?'

She looks at me sadly. 'Then you have my deepest sympathies.'

She turns and leaves, closing the door behind her.

I fall back into my desk chair, the air punched from my lungs. Aurora might never come back to me. And seeing the understanding in my sister's eyes as she spoke told me something else.

Vance Falcon didn't just break her heart once like we all thought he did.

He broke *her*.

And it's only because I know exactly what that feels like now that I recognise it in Dove.

If I ever see the bastard again, I'll not just want to deck him like Angelo did, I'll want to kill him.

My phone chimes with an alert, and I wipe my clammy palms on my trousers. I only have that sound set up for one thing.

Aurora has posted a new video.

Despite knowing it'll only hurt to watch it, I pull my phone out and press 'play'.

Her smile hits me first. It isn't as bright, almost as if she's worried, or cautious about something. Or . . . nervous.

But maybe she just looks different because the sun isn't streaming into the room like usual. In fact, it's not even the same room she's been filming in these past two months. An empty rail fills the screen behind her, flanked by a set of open shelving on either side. Both are empty.

Like me without her.

I lean forwards in my seat, squinting at the screen as she holds up a purse, showing off the little compartments in it.

A flash of fabric comes into the periphery of the shot as she repositions the camera.

My mouth goes dry.

She's in my dressing room. She must have filmed this months ago, then only chosen today to upload it for some reason.

But her skin is bronzed, kissed in the same way the southern French sun has done to her in her newer videos. And her hair is longer, the same length as in her most recent videos.

I look closer, raking my eyes over her face, absorbing every detail.

I know her. I know every little piece of magic that makes her *her*. I've studied them all. Kissed each one. *Loved them.*

She puts the purse down and looks directly at the camera, her eyes glassy.

'Sorry it's a little bare in here. I have some unpacking to do.'

My heart skips a beat . . .

And I know.

She isn't talking to her followers.

She's saying those words for one person.

Me.

I jump out of my seat, sending it crashing to the floor. Blood rushes in my ears as my vision tunnels for the door. For my exit out of here.

My route to her.

The door crashes against the wall as I throw it open.

I sprint out of my office like my life depends on it.

I'm coming, Beauty. Bloody hell, I'm coming.

Chapter 44

Aurora

I peer inside the cupboard and pick up a crisp tube, expecting it to carry more weight, but it's like a feather in my hand. I give it a little shake and the sound of leftover shards rattle inside the tube like a sad maraca.

'I eat them when I'm missing you so badly that I feel like I might pass out.'

I whirl at the sound of his deep voice and the tube clatters to the floor.

Molten bronze irises are waiting to anchor me to them. The sight of them again is enough to make tears rush to my eyes.

Rafael remains rooted to the spot in his kitchen doorway. I don't know how long he's been there, watching me. But I doubt it's been long, because even from across the room my body recognises his presence. It's like a wave flowing through me, starting at my toes and working its way to my head.

He runs his tongue over his lower lip, his confession delivered with a quiet huskiness that warms my skin.

'And then I wish I had passed out. Because maybe I wouldn't wake up.'

'Don't ever say that. Please don't ever say that,' I choke out in a strained whisper.

He holds my eyes. 'Those first fractions of a second when I wake are the worst. Because my brain's a bloody sadist. It lets me forget that I won't turn and see you there, lying beside me. It lets me have a moment of denial. One where I didn't lose the best thing that's ever happened to me.'

My mouth goes dry, wishing he would move. Step closer. Reduce this gap between us that feels like a chasm. Because even though I want to go to him, my body's frozen, unable to do anything other than soak in the sensation of breathing the same air as him once again.

Two months.

It's been an amazing time with my father. But there wasn't a second that went by that I didn't think of Rafael and wonder what he was doing and how he was. How he *really* was.

I allow myself a slow sweep of him, taking in his pristine suit – a grey one with a fine white pinstripe – complete with matching waistcoat, and his starched white shirt beneath it. The faint lines he gets around his eyes when he's tired are deeper, more defined. And they're framing what I can only describe as windows to a soul that's been shattered, but is determined to keep going, for there's still a glimmer of hope, alongside the bronze flecks.

His attention drops to the gold sequin top I'm wearing, and he fixates on it as his Adam's apple bobs in his throat like he's barely holding himself together.

'Your chateau is beautiful.'

That gets his attention, and I can't help but feel relieved when he meets my eyes again.

I smile softly.

'I know you, Rafe. And there are only so many people it could have belonged to. Plus my father would change the subject every time I asked him.'

He clears his throat. 'I rarely visit. I don't keep anything personal there, I didn't think you'd notice. I hope . . .' He winces. 'I hope it being mine didn't—'

'It was perfect. Thank you for letting us stay there.'

He nods curtly.

'Where is your father?'

Joy that the answer is no longer 'in prison' makes my chest lift.

'Looking at properties. He's been talking to a solicitor. He's going to be compensated for being wrongly convicted. He should get enough to buy somewhere for himself.'

'For himself?'

'Yes.'

Rafael stares at me, his expression unreadable, and it hits me . . . He isn't going to come to me. He's waiting for me. He's handing the control over to me.

I take a deep breath.

'I'm moving back into my old place,' I announce.

He still doesn't move.

'Raf—?'

'Tell me you don't mean that hovel where Mike is your neighbour,' he growls.

I bite back a shocked laugh. So much has changed, but not everything. Rafael Fairfax is still a dreadful snob.

And I love him.

'I mean the one where my roommate likes to imprison me inside his arms as he sleeps,' I say.

'It's the only thing that keeps his nightmares away,' he replies without missing a beat.

My throat aches and I slowly move towards him.

'No secrets this time. No lies. Complete honesty,' I whisper.

He still doesn't move. It's like he can't bring himself to in case I change my mind.

'I swear on Freddie's life.' He lowers his voice. 'I swear on *my* life.'

I stop directly in front of him. Holding his eyes, I lift my hand and place it over his chest where the scar sits beneath the fabric.

He sucks in a sharp breath, his pupils blowing wide.

It's the first contact we've had in two months. And the deep thrum of his heart pushes against my palm like it's trying to jump into it. Trying to sacrifice itself to me.

He screws his face up like he's in pain.

'Every beat is yours, Aurora,' he breathes. 'You know that.'

'I know.'

We stare at one another in silence as his heartbeat against my skin speaks for us.

'I've watched every one of your videos. *Every single one you've ever made*,' he says in a hoarse confession.

My breath hitches. 'What do you mean, *every* one?'

His gaze roams over my face. 'I've watched them since the first time Dove started talking about you. Telling us all about this brilliant new friend she'd made. I thought my reaction to you was a passing attraction. Something I'd never act on because you were my sister's friend.'

'You never told me you watched them all before . . . I thought . . .' I stare at him, struggling to process what he's telling me. 'I thought you always hated me.'

'I wanted you first. I wanted you so damn much, even though I knew I shouldn't. Until the day I lost two hundred and forty million pounds. And suddenly watching your videos became a *compulsion* that I couldn't feed enough, no matter how hard I tried. I was obsessed, trying to figure out how I'd been deceived. I thought you must have known about your father – how could you not? I questioned whether I'd been blinded by lust, fooled by this attraction. I don't get fooled,

Aurora. I calculate for every risk, every possibility. I didn't understand how there could be one I missed right under my nose.

'And I was angry at myself. So goddamn angry. I kept hearing my father's words circling in my head. Telling me I was a disappointment, a failure. Like the Wyndham case all over again. So, I continued watching you, telling myself it was a way of seeking revenge. But all it did was root you deeper inside me until I couldn't imagine existing in a world that didn't have you in it. I found my reason for everything instead. *You.*'

I nod, hot tears streaming down my face at how raw and honest we're being.

This is what we need.

This is our new start.

'I thought I hated you every time you made a comment about my father. But, really, I hated myself for not being able to get him out of there. Except when you actually were an arsehole, and then I think I actually did hate you.' I sniff through a small laugh. 'At least, as much as I could, knowing the way Dove talks about you. I knew you weren't as awful as you were being. I knew there was a good man underneath it all. I just didn't know why you wouldn't let me see him.'

I step closer and Rafael breathes in slowly, watching me.

'Letting you close to me meant having a harsh look at myself. And I wasn't ready, not in the beginning,' he rasps.

I nod again, a sob breaking free.

Rafael reaches up and gently wipes my tears away with his thumb. I lean into his palm, savouring every millimetre of where our skin connects.

'I cried for two days straight after you flew away in that helicopter. Some were tears of sadness that you'd gone; some were happiness that I had my father back. You gave him back to me. You thought you weren't the man I deserved, but you always were. I just needed to process the hurt first. I hated that you lied to me, but I never blamed you for what you did. It was a job, like your father said. It's probably one of the only things I'll ever agree with him on. But I didn't really blame you. I just wanted to hurt you, because you'd hurt me.'

'You're the only woman, other than my mother, whose tears have ever meant anything to me. And the one who I hope I never cause to shed them ever again. I'm so sorry. Lying to you was the biggest regret of my life. I'm not—'

'Don't tell me you aren't a good man.' I sniff. 'Dad told me how hard you campaigned to get him out. That you visited him every week and took it public. And he showed me this.' I pull the newspaper clipping from the back pocket of my jeans.

I unfold it, but he doesn't need to see it to know what's on it.

It's him. Looking determined, dressed in an impeccable navy suit and matching waistcoat as he strides out of number ten Downing Street.

'Only you could get a bloody meeting with the prime minister about my father's case,' I snort.

He doesn't even acknowledge the paper in my hand. His eyes are trained on mine like he never wants to look away.

'I wish I'd done it months ago.'

'Sometimes the right things still happen. Even if they're delayed.'

His brow creases, notching the intensity in his gaze up to blistering as he searches my eyes. 'What are you saying?'

'I'm saying I forgive you. I forgave you a long time ago. And I still love you. I always will.'

I place my hand back over his chest and it's there, beneath my palm, a stutter in the rhythm of his heart as he processes my words. As he *understands* them.

'You love me, Beau—' He catches himself, wincing like he's in physical pain.

'Say it,' I urge. 'I've missed you saying it.'

His pupils flarc.

'You love me . . . *Beauty*?' he whispers, all deep, and gravelly, and delicious, as he finally slides a hand around my lower back and pulls me into him.

'I do. More than anything.'

'And you forgive me?'

'Yes,' I sob.

The relief runs through his body like a flowing river gathering speed on its race to the sea. It softens the lines around his eyes and dissolves the dark pain between the molten bronze flecks. But most of all, it travels to his chest, and it softens the harsh edges of each beat of his broken heart, until they're a smooth, rich melody playing inside him instead.

'Beauty?'

'Rafe?' I whisper, running my fingers in gentle sweeps up and down his chest.

'Please tell me I can bloody kiss you.'

I break into a smile. 'Y—'

His lips crash to mine, stealing the word straight from them. The newspaper clipping flutters to the floor as I wrap my other hand around the nape of his neck and pull him close.

I kiss him back as fiercely as he kisses me. As desperately. Our faces screw up, cheeks wet with a mix of salty tears.

'You won't regret it. I'll never let you regret it for a moment. I'm going to spend every day loving you so much that you'll feel it, I swear,' he says, kissing me again.

I whimper into his kiss, clutching on to him and holding him as close as I possibly can. Our bodies meld together, the need to feel the heat of him against me outweighing everything else.

He slides his tongue inside my mouth, sending a shot of pure heat straight to my clit.

I squash my breasts to his chest, starving for more than just his kisses. Starving for his touch. I *need* him. I need to know this will all be okay. That no matter what happens, we're going to be okay.

'Rafael,' I pant. 'I want you.' I tug his shirt from the waistband of his trousers, then reach to loosen his tie.

His rock-hard dick presses between us like a giant beacon.

He groans like it's taking everything in him to exercise restraint as he takes my hands in his and stops me from unbuttoning his shirt.

'We can't.'

'What? Why?'

'I haven't been able to . . . Since you left I haven't even touched myself,' he confesses. 'I'll hurt you.'

'You won't.'

'Aurora, it'll be like a pressure washer aimed at a flower. Complete destruction.'

I snort at the dry tone of his voice. 'I don't believe you.'

But looking at his anguished expression, I can tell he isn't trying to be funny. He really believes he could hurt me.

Wetness gathers in my panties at the raw need darkening his eyes and I lick my lips. Sex with Rafael has always been amazing. But feral Rafael? The one looking at me right now like he could come with a single touch from me has a fire burning through my veins. I'm in control, and one word from me is all it will take to stop this. Or to . . .

I curl my hand around the raging erection in his trousers and look him directly in the eye.

'I want everything. Every drop. It's mine. And now I'm back, I'm taking it.'

He sucks in a sharp hiss, his heavy dick swelling inside my grip. 'Bloody hell.'

We crash back together. Rafael's hands drop to my jeans, and he unfastens them within seconds, pushing them and my panties down over my hips. I break the kiss to push them down my legs and pull them off.

He unzips his trousers and pulls his weeping cock out. It's both as perfect and as intimidating as I remember.

Hoisting me up in his arms, he slams me against the wall. My legs wrap around his waist on instinct, and the broad head of his dick slides through my wetness, seeking my entrance.

'Wait!' I pant.

His chest rises and falls with rough breaths as I pull his tie off and undo more of his shirt buttons until what I'm looking for comes into view.

I press my fingertips to his scar, and he shudders.

'Now you can,' I whisper.

'You sure?'

I nod. 'One hundred per cent.'

Something softens in his eyes, and he locks gazes with me, pushing inside me slowly, taking his time to fill me, inch by thick inch.

Our mouths fall open, gentle, combined gasps mixing in the small gap between us as we meld into each another, neither one of us wanting to look away.

He stops once he's nestled deep inside me. And we just stay, unmoving, looking at one another, frozen in a moment.

'I love you,' he groans, the tendons in his neck tightening, like being inside me without moving is torture.

'I love you too.'

I clench around him.

'You can't do that,' he grinds out through gritted teeth.

'Why not?' I pant, arching my chest towards him so my hard nipples drag against him through the gold sequins.

'Because it'll make me come. I haven't come since the last time I was inside you, and . . . Fuck . . .' He tenses as I squeeze him again.

I bring my lips to his ear. 'It's okay.'

'It's. Not. Okay. Aurora,' he hisses. 'I'm not going to blow like a teenager when I've just got you back. You deserve better.'

I kiss his neck, leaving my lips lingering there. 'We can do it again, straight after.'

His breathing stalls, and I kiss the hammering pulse in his neck.

'You don't even have to pull out. Just stay inside me all night, Rafe. I need you to. I need to be us again. *Please.*'

'Are you begging me to make love to you all night, Beauty?'

'I want you to fuck me too. Gentle, rough, slow, hard. I want everything. I *need* everything. Please.'

I clench around him again, knowing I'm playing dirty, but I don't care. I need him to understand that this is what I want. It's what we both need.

'Jesus!'

He slams his mouth back on to mine and growls as he kisses me. He pulls his hips back, and then drives forward, impaling me.

'Yes!' I cry out.

'Like this?' he growls, moving like a man possessed. 'This what you wanted, Beauty? You wanted to be fucked like I adore you? Fucked like I can't get enough of you? Fucked so hard and deep because you're everything to me? You want me to lose control?'

'God, yes! That's what I want, Rafe. I want you!'

'You've got me. You've always had me.'

He fucks me savagely against the wall until I'm crying his name into his mouth.

'Rafe!'

He slams one palm against the wall beside my head and drives back inside me with a rich grunt.

And the sound of it makes me fall apart.

'I'm coming!' I pant. 'Oh my God.'

My mouth falls open, and he moves back enough to be able to drink me in as I shatter and come hard. My body convulses around his and I cry out with every ripple around his thick cock inside me.

'I can't . . . it's too much, it's too . . .'

'Good girl. Let it go,' he croons as a second orgasm crests and has me dissolving into a whimpering mess as I lose all ability to control my body.

'Beauty,' Rafael growls. 'Oh fuuuuccckkkk.'

He comes inside me with force, just like he warned he would. The heat of him fills me, spreading through me like a wildfire, until it's running down my thighs with each thrust.

'Jesus Christ,' he grunts, shaking with the effort of his release, every muscle in his body rigid.

Our bodies make obscene wet sounds as he wedges himself back inside me without showing any signs of slowing.

'I feel so full,' I whine, my lower stomach cramping.

'It's okay,' he soothes.

He holds my eyes and pulls all of the way out. The unmistakable sound of a rush of liquid hitting the floor echoes around the room.

'Better?'

'Uh-huh,' I whimper, missing the feel of him inside me already. 'Don't stop. Do it again.'

He pushes straight back inside me, his dick still solid as steel.

He thrusts a few more times, his jaw clenching.

'Fuck . . . I'm going to come again,' he grunts.

'Do it,' I beg.

He groans, and my God, if it isn't the sexiest thing I've ever heard. He's literally coming just seconds after being back inside me and feeling my body hug his.

'Aurora,' he groans.

He comes again, and my stomach cramps in the same spot.

'Rafe.' I squeeze his shoulder, biting my lower lip, because despite the discomfort, I'm ridiculously turned on, seeing how his body is taking over and giving him what it needs.

'So damn beautiful,' he groans, leaning back and spitting down between our bodies.

It hits my pussy, running down over my clit, where he chases it with his thumb, rubbing it over me in circles.

'Rafe!' I cry, coming without warning.

He pulls out as my body is clenching, and the movement of my muscles sends more hot liquid racing down my thighs towards the floor.

He pushes back inside me again and reignites my orgasm, making it fall into a whole new succession of desperate clenches around him.

'Just like that. Good girl. Fuuccckkk.'

He thrusts harder, then growls, his cock swelling inside me again.

'Are you . . . ?'

'I told you. I haven't come since I was last inside you. I have so much for you. You need to take it. You've broken the bloody seal. There's no going back.'

I can't help it. I burst into laughter.

'Fuck, don't.' His lips curl into the hint of a smirk, but it's ripped from his face as my laughter makes my core tighten and my body vibrate in his arms.

'Beauty,' he warns.

But it's too late.

He groans, low and rough, as another orgasm is dragged out of him, making his whole body shudder.

'Jesus.' He rests his forehead against mine, sweat beading his brow. 'I'm taking you to bed. It's going to be a long night.'

I bite my lip through my smile and blink up at him.

'You okay?' He frowns, concerned.

‘Yes.’

He slides his hand to cup my neck, pinning me in place so I can’t look away. ‘Is it too much?’

‘No. I’m perfect. I want you to keep going.’

‘Jesus.’ He exhales, a disbelieving smile painting itself over his handsome face.

‘And I love you,’ I breathe.

I stroke my fingers over his scar, loving the way his eyes soften. He swallows, and I feel the weight of his words, wrapping around my soul, creating an embrace around it that can never be undone.

‘I love you too, Aurora.’ He slants his lips back over mine. ‘I love you too. So damn much.’

Epilogue

Rafael

Two months later

Gold sequins cast a honeyed glow over her skin as I gaze up at her from between her thighs.

'That's it, dirty girl. Come on your fiancé's face. Soak me in it.'

'Rafe!' Aurora squeals, her fingers scrunching in my hair.

The hard edge of her diamond ring presses into my scalp, and I hiss, my throbbing cock leaking in my underwear.

The sound of her vlog plays in the background. It's *that* one. The one I can't stop watching on repeat. The one I filmed of her, then *assisted* her in, but that she never actually posted, because we would probably have both been arrested.

Vlog Aurora squeals on the screen as I kneel behind her on the floor of our dressing room at home, pounding her pussy with rough grunts as I grip her hips and bring her back on to my cock over and over.

She squirms on my desk, her eyes flicking from the phone screen to my face, then back again.

'You look so good when you're being fucked,' I groan, sinking my face back between her thighs and sliding my tongue over her.

She shudders, her breath coming in needy little pants as her body tightens around my pen like it's desperate for it to be replaced by my cock.

'That's it,' I groan, sliding the soaked black length from inside her pussy and replacing it with my tongue.

'I'm going to come,' Aurora moans. 'Oh God, Rafe. I'm going to come.'

'Do it,' I urge, sealing my lips around her swollen little clit and sucking.

She practically leaps off my desk, and I pin her back down, letting out a guttural groan as her pussy quivers and sends a spray of cum out into my waiting mouth.

'That's what I'm talking about, Beauty. More,' I grunt, drinking it up greedily, as some runs over my chin.

She whimpers and writhes, but I keep her locked in place until her pussy falls into another set of rhythmic spasms against my tongue. I let her ride them out, gently circling her clit to drag her pleasure out as long as possible.

'No more,' she begs. 'It's too sensitive.'

I ease off my assault on her pussy, grinning smugly as I press a final kiss to it, then relax back in my desk chair.

'I was only meant to bring you lunch,' Aurora pants, gazing at me, her cheeks flushed.

I bring my pen to my mouth, sucking her taste from the end of it.

'You did. And I enjoyed eating it at my desk very much.'

'Fiend,' she murmurs, her lips twisting into a smile.

'Devoted fiancé,' I counter.

She laughs, and the sound is like goddamn music to my ears.

I can't believe I get to marry this woman and call her my wife soon. It was only a matter of weeks after she came back to me that I got down on one knee and asked her. The ring on her finger was burning a hole in my pocket from the moment I received it. Now I understand why my friend, Sullivan Beaufort, turned from grumpy arsehole to a man who looks like he's winning in life every time I call him. The right woman changed him. The same way Aurora changed me.

And the moment she becomes Mrs Aurora Fairfax cannot come soon enough.

She adjusts the drenched lace back over her glistening pussy lips, then smooths her skirt down and hops off my desk.

'I'll go and clean up.'

I catch her wrist in my hand before she can head inside my office bathroom. 'Not so fast.'

She rolls her eyes as I pull her into my lap, but I know she secretly loves that I can't ever let her go without her kissing me first. I've become one of those romantic saps I used to question the sanity of.

And I love every bloody second.

'I love you wearing this,' I murmur against her lips as I slide my hand around her ribs and over the gold sequined fabric.

'You love me in everything.' Aurora shakes her head softly as she runs her fingers along my jaw and kisses me back tenderly.

'The common denominator in both of those statements is *you*. I love *you*.'

'Charmer,' she hums, kissing me again. 'But I can't stay any longer. I have a client meeting this afternoon. Then we have dinner with my father tonight, remember?'

'Of course I remember. He and I talked about it earlier.'

'Earlier?'

'We had coffee. He wanted to go over interview techniques before Friday.'

'You helped him prepare for his interview?'

I shrug. 'He asked me for my input, so I gave it.'

'Over coffee?' Aurora bites her lower lip, her eyes twinkling.

Her father's interviewing for the board job that Dominic held. It's a weird twist of fate, and I asked George if he was sure that's what he wanted. But he insisted that if he's going to prevent things like what happened to him happening to other people, then he needs to be at the top, where he can make changes.

I might have thought I hated the man once, but now I can't deny the amount of respect I have for him. What he and Aurora have been through has only made him stronger and more determined. Just like his daughter.

'And biscuits, if we're going to be specific.'

Aurora grins. 'Oh? Biscuits. Mm-hm, I see.' She presses a lingering kiss to my lips. 'Should I find it weird how well you and my father get along?'

'We have lots in common,' I muse, curling my fingers around the back of her neck and pulling her to me for another kiss.

'Like what?' she breathes against my lips.

'Loving you,' I murmur.

She giggles. 'You're so smooth. How did I never notice it?'

'Because I was an arsehole before,' I reply, claiming her lips again.

'True.' She smiles against my kiss. 'But now you're my arsehole. And you're going to make me late.'

'I'll drive you.'

She moves back. 'I'll get the Tube.'

I fix her with a look that has her rolling her eyes.

'Fine, you can drive me. But I need to leave in the next ten minutes.'

She hops up from my lap and I drink her in hungrily as she crosses the room to my wardrobe, where she now keeps her own sets of spare clothes. And panties. Lots and lots of spare panties to replace the ones I'm in the delightful habit of ruining whenever she comes and visits me at work.

'This lady's another friend of your mother's,' she calls as she slides open the drawer containing her lingerie.

'She has good taste,' I comment as Aurora holds my eyes and wiggles a pair of white lace panties up her legs.

Aurora's now following *her* dream of blending fashion with helping people, by starting up her own personal styling business alongside her vlogging. I know it took a lot for her to give up on the idea of the internship she'd worked so hard towards before her father went to prison and accept the fact she was never going to work in the wardrobe department for TV or film. But it's like she confessed to me one night: that was her mother's dream, not hers. And she can still honour her mother's memory and keep her legacy alive by doing what's right for her. By being a daughter her mother would be proud of. One who's making her own destiny and is happy and thriving as a result.

The white lace slides over her perfect pink pussy, making me frown as it's covered from view. I rise from my seat, stalking towards her, but she holds a palm up, laughing.

'No, you don't. We don't have time.'

'I always have time for *that* with you,' I purr.

I reach for her, but she sidesteps me, moving into the bathroom and grabbing her hairbrush.

'Rafael Francis Fairfax.' She lowers her voice. 'I already came on that big, beautiful dick of yours before you went down on me on your desk.'

'I recall.' I smile wide at the memory, making her blush.

'So now I have to get back to work.'

I lean against the doorframe, watching her straighten herself out and touch up her lipstick.

'You're so beautiful,' I breathe. 'And so goddamn talented,' I add.

She looks at me in the mirror above the sink, and the way she smiles makes my heart swell. She doesn't just make me feel good. She makes me feel like I'm goddamn flying.

She's already got a waiting list to work with her after my mother helped introduce her to some of her friends who were eager for help, alongside some clients Kate sent her way.

That's the other thing . . .

The sound of barking from the hallway outside my office is swiftly followed by Gabriel marching into my office, a disgruntled, hissing Benedict hooked beneath one arm.

'Freddie tried humping him again. He was not impressed,' my brother says.

A small, sausage-shaped tornado whips past my ankles, making a beeline for Aurora.

'Thank you so much for watching him for me while we ate. I feel sorry for him. Kate said he's on a diet,' she says to Gabe, bending to fuss the little menace.

Her making up with Kate was what she needed. And I was so happy for her when she told me the two of them had talked everything through.

But I didn't factor in their re-blossoming friendship having the downside of Aurora dog-sitting whenever Kate travels. Making Freddie our problem – I mean, *responsibility* – for the next few days that he's staying with us.

'No problem.' Gabe pushes his glasses up his nose. 'They'll get used to one another.'

Benedict makes a growly sound that resembles more demon than cat, and fidgets in my brother's arms, wanting to be let loose on Freddie.

'This is where you all are,' Angelo announces, striding into my office.

I need to start insisting that Aurora locks the goddamn door. She thinks if she doesn't that it'll stop me from making her late by fucking her on my desk. But she should know me well enough by now to understand that when it comes to her, *nothing* will ever stop me.

'Aren't we popular?' I mumble, but one look at my brother's grim face and my heart rate picks up. 'What is it?'

Angelo walks over and thrusts his phone out. Gabe steps closer so we can both read the article.

'Son of a bitch,' I murmur.

'I'm on it. I'll see what I can find out,' Gabe says, exiting my office swiftly.

'I'll help.' Angelo's hot on his heels.

'I'll call Dove,' I growl.

Aurora comes out of the bathroom. 'What's going on?'

'Vance Falcon,' I spit.

She frowns. 'Dove's ex?'

'He was never her ex. He was just a mistake,' I grit, unable to hide the rage simmering in my tone.

'What's he done?' she asks.

I grab my phone and search for the news article that Angelo just showed me.

'This.' I hold it out to Aurora.

Her eyes widen. 'He's relocating his company to London?'

'Looks that way. Research labs. Trial centres. The lot.'

'But Dove . . .' Her brow wrinkles as she reads the article. 'He says his future is here and it's time to reclaim it.'

She lifts her eyes to mine as I clench my jaw.

That means one thing.

The bastard who broke my sister isn't just back for good.

He's here for Dove.

And he thinks he's getting her.

'Rafe?' She turns my face towards her.

My shoulders soften as I gaze into her aquamarine eyes. She's the only person in the world who can calm the storm that rages in my chest when something as unnerving as my sister's goddamn past comes back to claim her.

'I love you so much,' I say, brushing some errant blond strands back from her face.

'You've got that look,' she says, searching my eyes.

'What look?'

'Revenge,' she whispers.

I pull her into my arms. My sister's strong enough to deal with him. But it doesn't mean I don't want a piece of him.

'Revenge?' I hitch a brow.

'I'd recognise it anywhere,' Aurora says.

I exhale, my gaze roaming over her face softly.

'I'm sorry you ever saw it in the first place.' My gut twists, the same way it always does whenever I think about how I hurt her.

'Don't, Rafe. Don't do this to yourself,' she breathes. 'We wouldn't be here now if things hadn't happened the way that they did.'

I search her eyes. So pure and forgiving. She gets it from her father. Because George Thorne gave me his blessing to marry his daughter, despite how things began between us.

'I just wish you'd got your money back,' she adds.

The incessant rage no longer burns inside me like it used to, thinking about the two hundred and forty million I lost. Dominic's mistress is still missing and so is all the money she took. The irony isn't lost on me, that if I'd insured the investment myself rather than trusting Dominic, I would never have been in this situation. I'm never going to see a penny of that insurance payout unless he's found. I took a risk, handing over the funds to him in blind faith, because the deal was too good to pass up and I trusted him.

The first big risk I've ever taken that hasn't paid off. Not financially, anyway.

'It led me to you, Aurora. And there's no amount of money I wouldn't lose to have you brought into my life.'

Her nose wrinkles and an adorable snort slips free. 'You romantic. What did you do with the grumpy arsehole I fell in love with?'

I tilt my head. 'Threw him off a balcony.'

'Stop.' She laughs, her eyes bright as she swats my chest lightly.

'You and me. Revenge turned to love,' I say.

She bites her lower lip, her eyes glittering as I gaze at her adoringly. 'You know we're using that in our wedding vows? In love and revenge.'

I take her hand in mine, pressing it to my chest so she feels the beats that exist purely for her.

Her breath hitches in wonder, the way it always does, proving to me that as much as I love her, she loves me right back.

'Just love, Beauty.'

'Always?' she whispers, stroking the centre of my chest with tenderness.

I smile and pull her closer.

'Until the last beat of my broken bloody heart.'

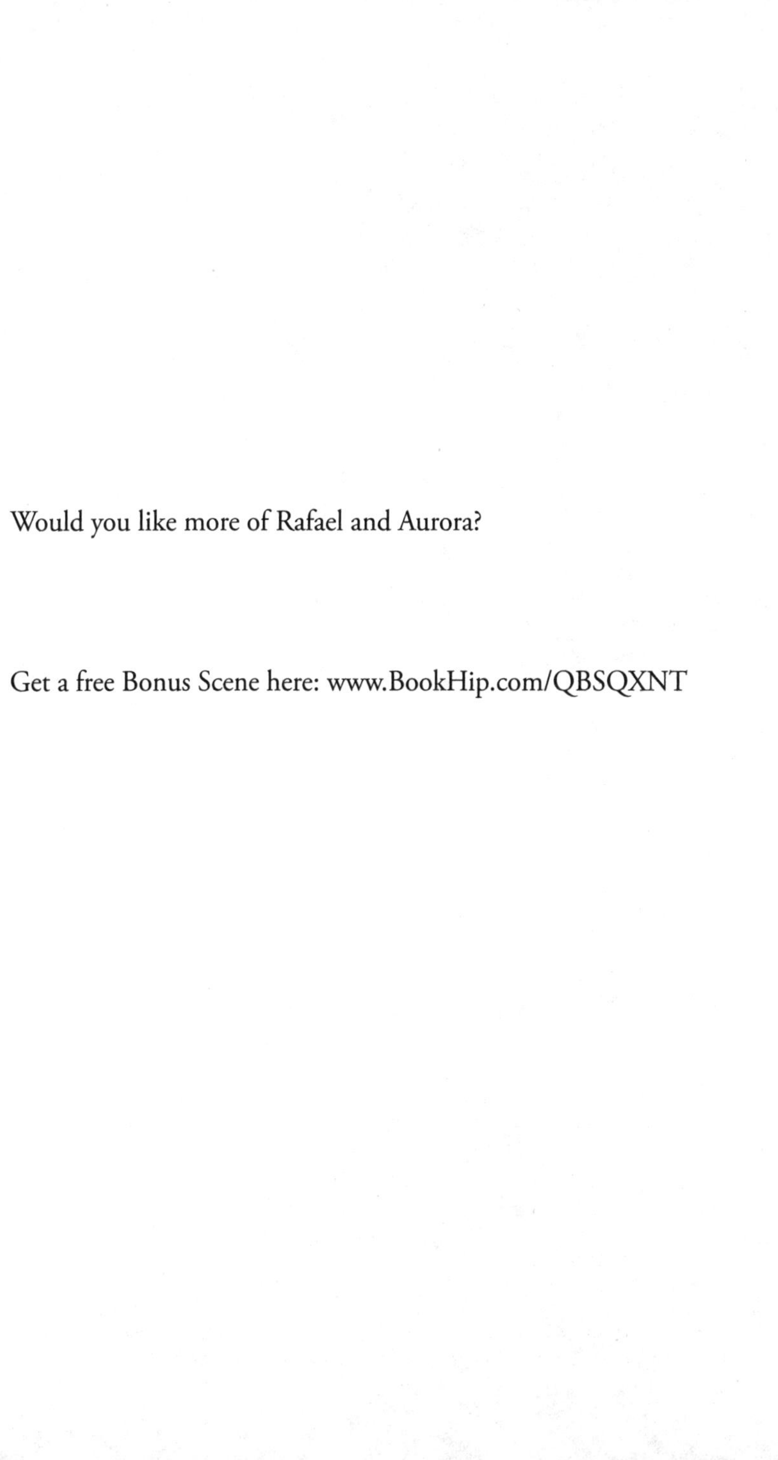

Would you like more of Rafael and Aurora?

Get a free Bonus Scene here: www.BookHip.com/QBSQXNT

Read on for a chapter from *The Matchmaker* in the Beaufort Billionaires series by Elle Nicoll.

Chapter 1

Halliday

Present day

"It's a shame I won't be here for long. I could get used to living in New York." Excitement bubbles in my stomach as I walk through JFK airport alongside the other passengers who landed on the flight from London.

"You think he's going to be easy to match?" my friend Sophie asks.

I readjust the bag on my shoulder and pull my suitcase, keeping the phone glued to my ear with my other hand.

"Totally. I've already been through his social media. He knows a lot of women. I might even find a good energy match with someone who's already in his life." I smile at a lady holding up a homemade 'Welcome Back' sign as I walk past. "I'm telling you, one month and I'll have found someone with a vibration that complements his. In fact, make it three weeks. I'll be home before you know it."

"You're—"

"Gifted?"

Sophie chuckles. "Sure. Gifted. Because whatever magic it is you possess, you know how to make people fall madly in love with one another. I'm sure Sterling Beaufort will be no different."

My fingertips tingle with energy. "He won't. Love's coming his way, I can feel it."

Sophie hums her agreement. We've been friends for years and couldn't be more different. She's a lawyer for the Crown Prosecution Service in London and deals with facts and evidence all day long. And I've built a successful business matching people on their vibrations and energies, finding them their spiritually aligned partners with whom love can flourish. I have a waiting list to work with me, and I love my job.

Adore it.

"I guess being a billionaire makes dating harder. Maybe he only meets women who are after his money."

I snort. "If you're a successful man, women line up to date you. If you're a successful woman—"

"Men are intimidated," Sophie finishes.

"Exactly," I huff.

I'm a shining contradiction of my recently exploding success. I find people love. Yet I've been single for years. And it's gotten worse as my business has grown. On the measly dates I have been on, the men's unease over my success vibrates off them with more buzz than a fully charged sex toy. I've given up waiting for that burst of energy when I meet someone. That bolt of divine intervention from the universe, telling me there's something there. Something special. *Something magical.*

Voices echo on the other end of the line as someone speaks to Sophie.

"I'm sorry, I've got to go. My meeting's about to start. Will you call me when you get to your apartment?"

"Sure will," I promise before ending our call.

I toss my phone into my purse and walk outside.

"Hello, New York," I sing happily.

Autumnal coolness greets me as I scan the line of vehicles. Sterling's daughter, Sinclair Beaufort, whom I've been liaising with, said she'd arrange a car to collect me, but I have no idea what to look for.

I study the line of waiting traffic before a horn honks, a hand extending from a car window in a wave. I head in its direction, pulling my suitcase along.

The door of the sparkly white sports car flies open, and a blond woman jumps out in sky-high heels and white jeans hugging her long legs. Sinclair Beaufort, twenty-three-year-old supermodel daughter of Sterling. Face of the family empire, Beaufort Diamonds, and model for numerous luxury brands.

The woman who hired me to find her father love.

She sees me staring at her car and giggles.

"They're Swarovski crystals. Dad joked they should be diamonds because of the business. I told him that would be impractical. I mean, can you imagine?"

I step closer to the gleaming vehicle. It's covered in tiny crystals. I run a hand lovingly over it, caressing the texture the crystals create. Personally, I'd go for rose quartz, if I had to choose. The crystal for love. Although, for a vehicle, maybe black tourmaline would be a better choice due to its protective properties.

"People would try to prise diamonds off to steal, though," I muse.

"Exactly!" Sinclair bobs her head enthusiastically. "Plus, every time I scrape it and lose some, the repair bill would be insane." She flicks a hand in the air before holding it out to me in a flourish. "Anyway." She flashes a mega-watt smile. "I know we've spoken on the phone, but it's great to finally meet you in person, Halliday. I've been counting down the days."

I take her hand, and she pulls me into a hug, my face landing in her long hair.

"It's good to meet you too, Sinclair . . . You smell incredible."

She laughs as I let her go. "A brand sent it to me as a gift. I forget the name. Hang on." She turns and grabs a nude Birkin bag from the front seat of the car. She rummages around inside and then pulls out a frosted perfume bottle shaped like a moon. "Here." She reaches forward and pulls open the top of my purse, depositing it inside. "It's yours now. First new thing you've got in New York."

I gush out a surprised thanks, and she waves a hand at me. "Don't mention it. You ready to go?" She pops the trunk and then lifts my giant suitcase into it with surprising ease for someone who can't weigh more than 120lbs.

"Sure."

I climb into the passenger seat, and she sinks into the driver's side.

"Is the temperature okay? I can adjust it. What about the radio? What music do you like?" She looks at me eagerly, toying with her necklace with one hand.

"Put on anything you like."

"Okay." She chews her bottom lip and then her brows shoot up. "Ooh, how about this one? I set the station when I knew you were coming. It's got relaxing music on it. I thought you might like it. It sounded meditation-y."

Guilt niggles inside my gut that I dubbed Sinclair 'Park Avenue Princess' when I was telling Sophie about her. The press makes out she's a bratty party girl. But meeting her face-to-face, I can tell she's really sweet and just excited that I'm finally here after all of our chats.

A yip from the back seat makes me jump.

"Monty!" Sinclair tuts. "Sorry if he scared you." She reaches into the back, sitting forward with a bundle of grey and white in her arms. Two shiny black eyes blink and a tiny nose sniffs the air in my direction.

"Oh my goodness, he's so cute."

I've always fancied having my own dog, but work takes me all over the place. It wouldn't be fair to have a pet that I'd keep leaving behind.

"He really is." Sinclair kisses him on the nose. "You want to hold him?"

"Yes, please." I hold my arms out.

She deposits him into them, where he wags a tufted tail and sniffs happily at my face.

"He's a Chinese Crested. You're such a handsome boy, aren't you?" she coos.

Monty pants happily from his position in my lap as I stroke the white hair on his ears.

"I like your sweater," I tell him, earning myself a flurry of licks over my hand.

"Oh, Prada sent him that one. He gets cold being mostly hairless. We need to post a picture of you wearing it, don't we, Monty? We can't forget." Sinclair winks at him. "He has his own following online," she explains.

I continue fussing him. "That's great. Well done, Monty."

Sinclair's lips twist into a thoughtful smile, watching him lap up my attention. "You know, he isn't normally good with new people. But he loves you. I think dogs are the best judges of characters. They can sense things. You've passed the Monty test."

I smile. "Maybe I could employ him as my assistant. He can help with the matchmaking."

"Oh my God. I cannot wait to see you in action." Sinclair revs the engine and then swerves out into the traffic, earning an angry blare of a horn. She blows a kiss and an apologetic wave in her wingmirror to the car behind.

"Why don't you get me started?" I reach past Monty to grab my notebook and pen from my purse. I always start with handwritten notes. They resonate more and stay in my memory better than typed ones.

"Put him in the backseat if he's in your way."

"No, he's good." I straighten up and open my notebook as Monty settles in my lap, curling himself up so he can fit without falling off.

I've learned to go with the flow in my job as a divine power facilitator. Some people would call me a matchmaker or dating coach, but my title is more accurate. I truly believe the divine power of the universe sends love our way. I help people to recognize the signs, that's all. And signs are around us all the time. Like Monty accepting me. He's reinforcing Sinclair's belief in me. A belief that will help create positive energy around us as I work. And the more positivity, the faster love manifests.

Forget three weeks, I should have told Sophie to expect me home in two.

"So, Mr. Beaufort. He's been single for almost two years?"

"Yep, since my mother died."

"I'm sorry," I say, recognizing the lines caused by grief pinching the corners of her eyes. "What made him decide he was ready to open himself up to love again?"

I'll ask Sterling these same questions when I meet him, but getting a picture from loved ones first can be immensely helpful.

"He's ready," Sinclair says decidedly. "He's been dating a little, but it never develops into anything meaningful. He's lonely and he doesn't deserve to be."

"He's told you he feels lonely?"

"He doesn't have to." She sighs. "It's in his eyes. You'll see. He'll realize you're exactly what he needs."

I place the cap on my pen and close my notebook, careful not to disturb Monty.

"You have told your father that you hired me, right?"

She waves a hand in the air with a dismissive hum. "It's what he needs. He'll see that the minute he meets you."

I take a deep breath, looking out of the window at Manhattan's skyline looming on the horizon. I suspected this could be the case when Sinclair avoided questions surrounding Sterling's knowledge on our calls, and I've never actually spoken to him directly.

"Did I do something wrong? You can help him, can't you?"

I turn and the pure anguish in her eyes makes my heart sink. She cares a lot about her father's happiness, but it's important I'm honest with her.

"Your love for him radiates from you like warm waves. It's beautiful." I smile reassuringly. "And no, you didn't do anything wrong. I'm often hired by loved ones rather than the client themselves. But they are made aware of it before I arrive. You should understand, if the person isn't open to love, the chances are—"

"You've never failed though, right? You find everyone happiness."

I press my lips together before I speak, careful not to snuff out the hope glimmering in her eyes. "Y-yes, but it's not always straightforward. When I was asked to match the Prince of—"

"Oh, please." Sinclair wrinkles her nose. "I follow him online. Complete arrogant jerk. If you managed to find him love, then you'll have no problem finding it for my father. You're going to adore him. Everyone does. He puts everyone else before himself. He's a gentleman."

She turns toward me with renewed energy, causing another outraged horn to blare next to us as our car drifts out of the lane. The other driver shakes his head, but as he looks into the car and sees Sinclair blow him an apologetic kiss, his mouth curls into a smile.

I get it, Buddy. She's gorgeous. I want to stare at her too.

She sighs and refocuses on the road. "Trust me, finding love for my father will be easy. I have complete faith in you. We'll go to the apartment I set up for your stay, then I'll take you to meet him. Sound good?"

"Sounds great."

Excitement thrums in my veins. I don't need to worry. I can feel in my gut that I'm supposed to be here. Sinclair has faith in me. I have faith in myself. My instincts have always served me well. I've made love matches for even the most difficult clients. Including those who had completely given up on love.

This time will be no different than any other client I've been hired to work with.

I'll find the woman who will steal Sterling Beaufort's heart.

I have no doubt.

ACKNOWLEDGEMENTS

There are so many people to thank, all of whom played a part in Rafael and Aurora's story coming into existence. And I must begin with T L Swan, who is one of the most generous and inspiring women I have met. If it weren't for her amazing support, then I don't know if I would have had the courage to pursue my dream of writing a book, let alone it actually turning into something that I get to do every day. I will be forever grateful!

To Hannah, for believing in me. And to Victoria for your wonderful insight, and for loving Rafe. And to all of the team at Montlake, I'm still pinching myself that we get to do this together, so thank you!

To Nat and Heather, for your amazing eyes for graphics and reels, and your endless patience!

To my author friends who amaze and inspire and lift one another every day, you ladies are incredible!

To my family who have helped decorate my writing nest with pictures and words of encouragement, and who have forgiven me for many TV shows being talked over when I need to sound out plot ideas.

And finally, to you, dear reader. Thank you for giving up your precious time to step into these worlds with me, and for allowing these characters into your hearts. And for everyone who has shared their excitement for this book online and with their friends, thank you so much!

May reading continue to bring you bucketfuls of joy.

If you enjoyed *In Love and Revenge* then please leave a review on Amazon and share it with your book besties, it really means the world to an author.

Thank you, and until the next book . . .

Elle x

ABOUT THE AUTHOR

Elle Nicoll is a British author, and ex long-haul flight attendant, who was born in Sheffield and now resides near the south coast.

She writes steamy and angsty contemporary romance novels, all based around love, and is known for her BookTok-favourite novel, *Pleasing Mr. Parker*.

Elle loves putting her characters through challenges that make them grow from the beginning of the story, until they get their HEA. They have to fight hard for it . . . but when they get there, it's so worth it.

All of Elle's characters are different. Whether they are a brooding CEO, the best friend who always held the heroine in his heart, a Hollywood heartthrob, or a silver fox with gentlemanly manners and a deliciously filthy tongue, they are all unique and infuriating in their own way.

Because no one is perfect.

When Elle isn't writing she is either on her spinning bike (where many ideas come to her), adding to her crystal collection, or sipping lattes at the beach.

It means the world to Elle that you're reading her stories, and she loves to hear from readers.

Follow the Author on Amazon

If you enjoyed this book, follow Elle Nicoll on Amazon to be notified when the author releases a new book!

To do this, please follow these instructions:

Desktop:

1) Search for the author's name on Amazon or in the Amazon App.
2) Click on the author's name to arrive on their Amazon page.
3) Click the 'Follow' button.

Mobile and Tablet:

1) Search for the author's name on Amazon or in the Amazon App.
2) Click on one of the author's books.
3) Click on the author's name to arrive on their Amazon page.
4) Click the 'Follow' button.

Kindle eReader and Kindle App:

If you enjoyed this book on a Kindle eReader or in the Kindle App, you will find the author 'Follow' button after the last page.